RICHARD H

RADIOACTIVE
EVOLUTION

HUMMEL
BOOKS

Author: Richard Hummel
Cover Artist: Dusan Markovic
Typography: Bonnie L. Price
Formatting & Interior Design: Caitlin Greer

ISBN-13: 978-1-7323374-1-1 (Paperback)
ISBN-13: 978-1-7323374-2-8 (Hardback)
ISBN-13: 978-1-7323374-0-4 (Digital)

To my beautiful wife and girls.

01 EVOLUTION UNLOCKED

Jared stood at the precipice of almost certain danger, the yawning black chasm simultaneously beckoning and repelling him. The last six months of exploration led him to this moment, and now he hesitated to follow through. For months he'd searched for evidence of others.

In a city this size he expected to find something. Remnants of a battle, bones picked clean by the many carnivorous creatures that roamed the area, or anything worth scavenging. However, the only evidence he'd found was a series of *tags* painted on the walls around the perimeter of New York City. Only one set of markings, distinct in their pattern, delved further into the streets of the once great city. It was these patterns he found himself following, stupidly assuming he'd find treasure at the end of the veritable rainbow. Except there was no leprechaun or pot of gold, only a staircase descending into utter darkness. A faded sign announced it as "Metro Tr…"

Tram? Train?

Jared shrugged. He didn't know for certain, but he'd read

about old means of transportation before the nuclear wars obliterated most of the planet.

Taut as a bowstring, his eyes and ears strained, Jared looked for any sign of predators. In a city this large, he was at the bottom of the food chain, and his only protection was his father's Colt Peacemaker, a .45 caliber revolver. In the two years since he'd left his home colony, it'd saved his life on more occasions than he could count. Absentmindedly, he reached down to finger the weapon in its holster, contemplating if he dared risk the underbelly of the city.

Six rounds…

Agonizing over the decision, Jared flicked his gaze to the corner of his vision. A holographic outline of his body floated, where a countdown timer showing a little more than two months remaining. It represented how many nanites he had left before he needed to use an injector and replenish his stores. These microscopic machines were the only thing preventing humans from dying excruciating, radioactive deaths. He hoped the trail leading down would end at the body of whomever left all the tags, and that they had some of the life-giving injectors on them. On the other hand, it was a gamble and he had no way to know for sure without making the trip.

What should I do…

Jared sighed and ran his hand through his hair. It was a two-month journey back home, and he wasn't sure he'd survive the trip before his body deteriorated from radiation poisoning, or some creature overpowered him when his body began to weaken.

His mind screamed at him to run the other way, but Jared ignored it and walked back to the staircase leading down. He couldn't discern the bottom even with his ability to see in the dark. Slowly, he crept down the stairs, gun at the ready. It felt like an eternity until he reached the bottom. Time became irrelevant as every minute stretched into what felt like hours. He jumped at every creak and sifting of pebbles. At the bottom, the markings pointed off into the darkness. An absolute darkness that pressed in on him. The shadows writhed at the corners of his vision. The hair on the back of his neck stood on end as cold shivers raced down his spine. The natural sunlight failed to penetrate the inky black and Jared's eyes transitioned to night vision, a by-product of nanite enhancements. It seemed that when pushed into extreme circumstances, or survival depended on something, the nanites adapted and allowed him to obtain special abilities, like night vision and the ability to survive extreme temperatures.

Just as he started relaxing, Jared heard a soft scrape and a nearly imperceptible pressure as something brushed past his head.

He flicked the safety off the Colt .45 as he threw himself to the floor. His eyes widened at the creature. A grotesque, mutated lizard clung to the ceiling, its legs coiled to spring at him. Thick, discolored saliva dripped from fangs as long as his arm, dozens of golden spider-like eyes following his movements. With no hesitation, Jared squeezed the trigger. The creature's head exploded in a shower of black ichor and bits of gray brain matter. It plummeted towards him. He shoved away from it, barely avoiding being crushed by its shiny silver body as it slammed into the concrete floor. The quick evasion did nothing to prevent the shower of blood and gore. Spluttering and spitting, he tried to eliminate the metallic tasting remnants that made it into his mouth.

Jared shook his head, the gunshot ringing in his ears. He needed to move, and fast. The gunshot might've been a homing beacon for more of these things. Desperate to put distance between himself and the disgusting creature, Jared sprinted up the tunnel following the other explorer's path. While he ran, he kept his eyes peeled, careful to watch the ceiling for more of the lizards.

Jared no longer cared about stealth or caution. He needed to find the body, recover the supplies, and get out of the city. He rounded the next corner following the markings and almost fell headlong into a large crater. He caught himself on the edge and wind-milled his arms to regain balance. His tiptoes teetered on the edge of the crater and he felt his balance shift back and forth. Finally, after a several moments of sheer terror, his balance returned, and he managed to step back from the ledge.

He'd almost fallen into a pit that looked like the site of a bomb detonation. A closer examination revealed piles of bones, refuse, and a collection of random equipment.

Tilting his head to the side and moving further from the corner, Jared tried to determine what he'd found.

It looks like— His mouth dropped open in astonishment. *It's a nest.*

The blood drained from his face, and he shrank against the wall, cursing himself for making this journey. Paralyzed in fear, it took him several minutes before he was calm enough to peek around the corner. The last marking he'd followed ended a couple pillars back, and he didn't see a new one. Fear coursed through him as he realized this might be the farthest his guide had made it. As if fate were playing a cruel joke on him, it was then he spotted a pair of black boots at the bottom of the nest. Jared slid to the ground and buried his face in his hands.

The explorer. I've come too far to abandon this farce now. With shaky legs, he rose and skirted the massive nest.

Psyching himself up, Jared repeated a mantra in his mind. *It's just a crater, it's just a crater…*

If he dwelled on the nest and what might live in it, he'd succumb to cowardice and flee.

Delicately, he picked his way through the pile of refuse,

periodically stopping to extricate large bones that blocked his path. It was eerily quiet, the only sound his ragged breathing as he tried to push past the overpowering scent of rot. With each passing moment, his anxiety grew.

This is taking too long, and I don't want to be here when this thing returns!

Finally reaching the pair of worn leather boots, he started extracting bone after bone, looking for any other equipment. Several minutes later, he uncovered a tattered backpack hooked over a human ribcage. An audible gulp escaped his throat as he looked into the empty eye sockets of the skull that used to sit atop the skeleton. Holding his breath, Jared bent closer and breathed through his mouth. The smell of death and decay intensified and raised bile to the back of his throat.

Careful not to disturb the rest of the pile, Jared unhooked the straps from a cracked shoulder blade and what was left of the rib cage. He'd successfully extracted the pack and turned to leave when a strange object partially hidden by yellowing skeleton limbs caught his attention. Already in over his head, Jared looked closer, eager to find anything of value. He reached out and felt heat emanating from what looked like a large rock.

Strange, he thought.

As his fingers brushed the strange object, a jolt of electricity shot through his hand.

"Ow!" Jared grunted and snatched his hand away. "What is this thing?"

Curiosity piqued, he reached out again. When his fingers neared the object, the hair on the back of his hand stood on end. Jared snatched his hand back again and decided that he needed to bring whatever this was with him. This was by far the most unique object he'd ever come across. If it generated some kind of electricity, it could be invaluable to him during his travels. As quickly and quietly as possible, Jared slid his pack off his back, stuffed the other explorer's gear inside, and grabbed a spare shirt to wrap up the strange object. The electrified rock secured, Jared began the painful process of picking his way back across the crater to climb back up to the platform.

His trip up proved much easier, and he breathed a sigh of relief after he'd made it to the platform. No sooner had he reached it than he felt a reverberation through the ground. Thinking it was his nerves and imagination, he ignored it until he distinctly felt the vibration and with it a distant thump.

What the— Panic flooded through him. *What could make the earth shake?*

No way was he waiting to find out. Jared sprinted back the way he'd come. Just as he passed the decapitated corpse of the lizard, an ear-splitting roar shook his body to the core. A violent thrashing and growling erupted behind him as the unknown creature unleashed mayhem in the tunnel he'd just vacated. A moment later, a wave of intense agony assaulted his mind, causing him to stumble into the wall.

Jared glanced over his shoulder at his bag and contemplated dropping whatever it was he stole, but instead he bolted up the stairs, taking them four at a time as he sprinted up the shaft of daylight in the distance. Before he reached the halfway point, he caught sight of something lunging at him from his periphery. Ducking, another lizard-like creature soared over his head, crashing into the wall. He didn't pause, but raced up the stairs, the creature fast on his heels. Jared dove through the opening, the sun's golden rays bathing him in warmth. The split-second of euphoria didn't last as the lizard launched through the opening, landing right on top of him.

Dangit! Stupid. Idiotic.

He violently reprimanded himself for thinking these creatures confined to the underground tunnel. The lizard pinned his arm before he managed to free his Colt. The overgrown reptile snapped at his face, its shiny metallic head filled with razor-sharp teeth and fangs. Gooey, hot saliva bathed his head and obscured his vision.

Straining his muscles, Jared tried to force the creature off, but failed. It was strong, and if he didn't find some way to turn the tables, it would rip into his face.

In a desperate move, Jared slammed his feet down and thrust his pelvis upward, throwing the lizard back just enough to extricate his Colt. He angled the revolver into the body of the creature and squeezed the trigger three times before the lizard stopped moving.

Soaked to the bone in gore from both scuffles, Jared recovered quickly, picked up his pack from where it'd fallen, and sprinted for the city's edge.

The gigantic creature raged beneath the city, judging from the echoing of rock crumbling behind him. He thanked his good fortune no other creatures barred his path, and whatever he'd angered hadn't surfaced to track him yet.

His panicked flight led to his safe haven, a small room in the remnants of the Statue of Liberty. Breathing heavily, Jared dove into his hideaway beneath the melted hunk of rusting statue. When he'd first come to New York, he'd cleared out the entry and made his own barrier he could bar from the within.

Safe in his bunker, he sat back against the wall in exhaustion. He didn't know how much time passed, but from the slant of the sun's orange rays peeking in through the cracks, it neared dusk. He didn't need the light to see, but trepidations about what the night would bring made him wish for the day to last longer.

"I almost died in there," Jared muttered to himself. "This

backpack better be worth the risk. There's no freaking way I'm going back into that city."

Even hours after the harrowing experience, he shook with adrenaline and fear. He could do nothing but sit there in abject terror waiting for his body to give him a moment's reprieve. Eventually, it gave way to exhaustion and pushed him into a fitful slumber.

When he woke several hours later, he could still hear distant shrieking and buildings collapsing. Thankfully, it didn't sound like it was any closer.

Rested and ready to see what treasures he'd found, Jared pulled out the explorer's pack from his own. The mysterious electrical object discarded to one side, he opened the flap on the other pack.

"Whoa," breathed Jared.

Inside lay five injectors. More than he'd even seen in one place, let alone in the possession of one person.

"I guess this explains why I didn't find anything around the city," Jared rambled to himself, his voice tinged with excitement.

Feverishly, Jared examined the rest of the contents. He found half a dozen munitions credits, a form of currency for any explorer. He could get several boxes of ammo for one credit. Up until a couple years ago, he'd reloaded his own bullets using a press his family owned. As much as he'd wanted to bring it with him, it was much too bulky to carry around in his new life.

Sometimes colonies exchanged the credits for weapons, but most often it was only ammo, as pistols and rifles became too rare to trade. The credit could also buy phase batteries, but he'd need a phase pistol for that to be useful. There was very little chance someone like him would ever hold one of the coveted weapons. A single phase pistol was more valuable than an entire armory, and very few people ever laid their eyes on one, much less claimed ownership of one.

No sense dwelling on what I'll never have, thought Jared as he pushed thoughts of phase weapons from his mind.

Besides the injectors and credits, he found a notebook with a bunch of scrawling in it and a small black ballistics case. The pages of the notebook sported dog-eared corners and stains, making many of them illegible. The scribblings made little sense to him, but he suspected it was a journal documenting the places this person had visited. One of the pages held a crude map outlining a zig zagging path through NYC. It showed which paths they'd taken, confirming Jared's suspicion that it was the same path he'd traversed.

Setting the notebook aside, he opened the black ballistics case.

"What? How?" Jared asked incredulously. There, in all its glory, was a phase pistol with two full battery packs. "Why in the world didn't this person use the weapon while they explored the city?"

His question went unanswered, but a disturbing thought crept in.

Did they have a second phase pistol? Why else would this one still be in its case? Did I leave it behind in that nest?

A pang of sadness and loss made him curse his cowardice. If he'd just spent a few more seconds, he might have two of them now.

Jared's shoulders sagged. *Nothing I can do about it now.*

The sadness was fleeting as he quickly switched his Colt to the other side and strapped the phase pistol to his right thigh. He didn't insert the power pack just yet. He needed to learn how to use it first. Having only seen pictures of one before, he knew little about their functionality. His future was looking up. The phase pistol alone could set him up for a life of comfort, or what approximated comfort in this destroyed world, if he chose to sell it.

For a fleeting moment, Jared thought about gaining access to the cities above, but quickly dismissed the idea. Before the war, wealthy billionaires pooled their resources to create floating islands in the oceans and skies that allowed only the elite of society to survive the nuclear fallout. The remainder of the population they considered an acceptable loss. Not everyone outside the islands died, but many of them wished they had as technological advancements became obsolete and a new dark age began. Clearly, those in power in the cities had no desire to help the rest of the world, and Jared wanted nothing to do with them.

Turning his thoughts back to the epic find, he forgot all about the strange object an arm's length away. His thoughts revolved around the countdown on his status screen and spurred him to pick up one of the nanite injectors. In his haste to extend his nanite supply, his hand brushed the side of the strange electrical rock he'd stolen, sending another jolt up his arm.

"Ah!"

The unexpected shock made him drop the syringe he held. Careful not to touch the sphere again, he slowly picked up the injector and moved it a few inches, but then stopped. When he'd moved it, the weird rock shifted. Cautious not to touch *it*, he moved the injector over the top of the object, and it shuddered back and forth.

The unexpected movement made him jump. "Whoa...ouch!" he hissed, rubbing the back of his head where he'd hit the ceiling.

His heart raced as he removed the shirt he'd used to wrap it. Slowly, Jared moved the injector over the object and watched as the nanites inside became agitated.

Jared's eyes widened in surprise. "What is this thing?"

There was definitely a physical attraction between them, but it looked like a rock and he couldn't figure out why it showed a reaction at all.

Does it have nanites? The nanites are machines; perhaps this thing has something to do with them?

Thoughts cascaded through his mind. Realizing he had no answers to any of them, Jared didn't know what to do. Every time he touched it, it shocked him.

I wonder...

Jared slowly lowered his hand to touch it. As before, the shock made him wince, but prepared for it this time, it didn't make him withdraw his hand. Now that the shock passed, it actually felt pliable to his touch. It was still extremely hard, like pewter or clay, but definitely not rock. Once again, Jared brought the nanites closer while touching the object, only this time he felt movement within when he did so.

Jared grunted in surprise, wondering what would happen if he used the nanite injector on the object. Then again, they were very valuable, and he couldn't bring himself to waste an entire injector on the thing.

Maybe a tiny bit? he thought.

First things first, Jared needed to take care of his immediate problems and then he could decide what to do with it. Sticking the tip of the syringe to his arm, he pressed the plunger, but released it before they'd all entered his arm. There was only a tenth of the dose left, and looking at the countdown timer on his status screen, it showed almost two years.

Shrugging, Jared decided he could spare a little of the nanites since he now had enough for twelve more years, plus the two he'd just gained from the partial injection. More than enough time to find more or move to a new colony. The closer the nanites were to the surface, the more they vibrated. He watched in fascination as its surface smoothed. It now felt resilient under the injector. Before he changed his mind, Jared jabbed the plunger home.

Jared screamed.

Intense, excruciating pain pierced his mind. His body felt like it was on fire, burning him from the inside out. Rocking back and forth, he wished for the tormenting anguish to end. His vision darkened, but just before his vision faded to black, the round sphere before him cracked in half, and a tiny, scaled head looked at him with slitted eyes.

CONGRATULATIONS EVOLUTION UNLOCKED!

Attention: this message is hard-coded into all hybrid nanotechnology and is intended for anyone that evolves.

My name is Igor Jonovich.

I was wrong.

In my haste to create nanotechnology, I didn't consider the cost and resources required to produce it. When my city rulers learned of this, they hoarded the technology.

My original creation confiscated, I soon realized the truth of the situation the cities engineered. To make up for my lack of foresight, I started development on a new form of nanotechnology that integrates into human cells and uses human biology to self-replicate, reducing the cost of production exponentially.

Initial experiments and test subjects were promising, showing improved abilities and controlled mutations. Not wanting to delay and cause further deaths, I used my personal drop ships to disperse these bio-nanites into the jet stream, where they spread across the globe.

A year later the biological components of the nanites mutated because of corruption in the coding, giving rise to a techno-virus. The efficacy of my creations increased tenfold, resulting in destabilization of cellular processes in its human hosts. Combined with the high levels of background radiation, even in the safe zones, it induced mutations in its victims.

The cities' leadership discovered what I had done and demanded a cure. I quickly discovered a cure impossible. However, a booster shot could hold back the mutation. The survivors on Earth were sold a lie that these shots contained nanites that needed to be replenished every few years. Predictably, the local governments would do anything to save their populace, providing an unending stream of materials, all in exchange for a handful of cheap booster shots.

When I realized their desire to horde the nanotechnology and how they intended to use the rest of mankind as nothing more than cheap labor, I began working on a way to fight back.

My research culminated with the discovery that the bio-nanites could instantiate a bond between a human host and non-human creature. Each booster contains a unique set of nanites that when shared between host and creature, irreversibly connect the two together.

I sincerely hope this message hasn't reached you too late, and that you are able to use it for the betterment of mankind.

Absent the human DNA element, these creatures absorb nanites and gradually increase in strength over time, with none of the virulent side effects caused within humans. My initial experiments allowed me to artificially enhance and mutate these creatures, but absent a human to control the mutations, the nanites largely remain dormant, only increasing the strength of their host, or developing abilities over prolonged periods of time.

What you have just experienced is the first stage of this evolutionary process.

Take care of each other. Grow in strength by defeating other infected creatures and assimilating traits mapped by their own bio-nanites. Only then will you have the strength to expose the lies that I unwittingly helped create.

COMPANION UNLOCKED - DRAGON

"What the—" Darkness descended on Jared.

02 A LUCID DREAM

"**J**ared, wake up!"

Dad? Hello?

"Jared, you better get out of bed before I finish breakfast. We have a lot to do today and you need to earn your place at this table."

Wh—Why do I hear my dad's voice?

His dad was dead. He died three years ago. Jared struggled against the throbbing pain that beat against his eyelids. The last thing he remembered was a strange message before the pain rampaging in his body made him pass out. As much as he tried to open his eyes, it was as though cement glued them together. They refused to obey him, until he heard—

"Leave him alone, John, he's only five. He's not even of official age to work."

Mom!

Jared's eyes snapped open. A suffocating, all-encompassing blackness enveloped him.

Where am I?

Jared turned in circles, searching for a way out. No matter where he looked, nothingness greeted him.

Finally, a pinprick of light stabbed a hole in the black canvas before him. He tried to walk forward, but his body betrayed him. As the light grew brighter, he looked down to see why he couldn't move.

What the...Where is my body? What is happening?

The thought echoed in his mind. Trapped in this nightmare, he fought for control. Every attempt to change his situation resulted in failure. After a prolonged bout of rage and incomprehensible phrases, Jared gave up, his willpower evaporating. It was only then the tiny hole in the fabric of his reality grew brighter, and Jared watched the scene unfold. A room, familiar to Jared, brought him back to his childhood home.

How can this be?

At the table stood Katie and John, his mom and dad.

Mom? Dad?

The two words reverberated in his mind, but he couldn't speak to them any more than they could see him. The unfolding events felt surreal.

Why is this happening now? I...Why does it feel so real?

Looking at his parents—alive and well—made his heart break all over again. He thought he'd never see them again. His dad died when a pack of bears raided their colony three year earlier and his mom died five years ago from radiation pois—

Wait.

Noooooo! Jared screamed in his mind, wishing he could vent his anger in some way. In this incorporeal state he could only watch, his thoughts the only outlet for the frustration, anger, and hurt.

He knew the truth now. *The rulers of the cities lied to us. They lied to everyone!*

The scene before him froze, his rage built to a crescendo until he couldn't take it anymore, and he slipped into unconsciousness again. When he woke the second time, the same frozen scene greeted him. It wasn't until the five-year-old version of himself joined his parents at the table that he snapped out of the stupor. Any rage remaining dissipated as he gazed upon the excited, youthful face eager to greet the day.

Jared smiled as he recalled the day. It was the first time he left the boundaries of the colony. His dad planned to show him the farms he managed and teach him how to harvest resources. The jubilation in little Jared burst outward as he bounced on his toes. Watching from the sidelines, and many years under his belt, he looked at both his parents' faces. The love they held for him was as plain as the clothes they wore. He also witnessed a small trace of fear in his mother's gaze. When his father noticed that same look on her face, he reached up to squeeze her hand with a knowing look.

"Let's go, Dad!" Jared's miniature version all but shouted, and the looks exchanged between his parents morphed into broad smiles as his excitement infected them.

Just before they left the small room, Jared heard a light, female voice whisper, **ADVENTURE. CURIOSITY.**

Jared strained his ears, listening for the voice and wondered if he imagined it while the scene faded to black.

No! Stop!

He tried clawing his way back into the room, but his efforts proved futile as it slowly faded into the distance. Once again, the oppressive darkness surrounded him.

Am I dead?

Where is this place?

What happened to my body?

Is this some kind of hell?

What did I do to deserve this nightmare!

Maybe the bonding—or whatever it was—killed me?

Maybe I'm losing my mind and stuck in my own head?

He shouted, cursed, screamed. Nothing worked. Jared lingered in the formless void. Resigned to his fate, he gave up and let his frustration go. The moment he relaxed, a brilliant light blinded him, and he squeezed his eyes shut against the pain.

"Stay down, you loser!" said a voice filled with disdain.

"Nobody wants you here, you little pipsqueak."

Voices all around cajoled and mocked. Jared forced his eyes open and saw himself at ten. He lay on the ground with a bloody lip and shiner on his left eye. Three larger boys loomed over him spitting hateful words and phlegm. He could've cried or called for help, but instead the little ten-year-old Jared struggled to his feet. The larger of the three boys, nicknamed "Tiny," pushed him back to the ground and the name calling resumed.

Get up! Jared tried yelling at himself.

As if he'd heard himself, ten-year-old Jared rose to his feet and squared off with the leader of the trio. He stood, ready to take anything they dished out. They tried to goad him into attacking, but he refused to take the bait. Frustrated, Tiny launched his fist into Jared's other eye and knocked him back to the ground.

He lay on the ground stunned. It looked like the fight was over until they heard a groan, and Jared tried to stand. He stood on shaky legs, both eyes swollen. Tiny roared in rage and embarrassment at this little pest and his tenacity. He cocked his arm back to strike again when a voice boomed from across the field.

"Stop!"

Everyone scampered away as Jared's dad sprinted to him. He picked him up and carried him across the field to their home. Just before they crossed the threshold, little Jared smiled through his split lip and with pride in his voice said, "I stood up to him."

Perseverance, Courage, Determination, Toughness, Pride.

This time he knew it wasn't his imagination. There was someone else here.

Who are you? Jared asked into the emptiness. When no one responded, he shouted, *Answer me! What do you want?*

Silence reigned, and Jared's mind started to spiral out of control. Frustration threatened to overwhelm him until he remembered the last scene occurred only after he stopped trying to force the situation. Eyes closed—not that it mattered in total darkness and no physical body—he tried to clear his mind. A moment later, another memory flitted into view. He opened his eyes to see himself at age nineteen working the fields near the tree line. His dad worked a few paces away from him, testing the soil.

No. Anything but this memory! Please, stop! I can't see this again, Jared wailed, effortless to stop the memory from replaying in his mind.

This was the second worst day of Jared's life.

Horrified, he watched a trio of giant, mutated bears charge from the trees. Each of the bears stood eight feet tall on all fours, their sickly yellow claws slicing through the ground as they gained on Jared. His dad yelled at the same moment Jared heard their tiny fence shatter. Their thundering footfalls sent vibrations through the ground. He watched his dad sprint toward his younger self. Carefully lining up his shots, John downed two of the bears with headshots, his Colt pulverizing their skulls. The headless bears rampaged in circles, their bodies unaware they were already dead. The third and largest bear bore down on Jared.

"Get down!" John yelled.

The bear swung its massive paw, easily twice the size as his head. His dad lunged forward, knocking Jared out of the way. Firing a round point-blank into the bear's massive head, his dad intercepted the paw meant for him. The claws, at least six inches long, sliced through his father's body, decapitating him with one swipe. His lifeless corpse fell to the ground, half buried under the giant thrashing bear.

"NO!" Jared heard himself cry out at the same time as his younger self.

He cradled his dad's body, hot blood pooling over his hands and dripping into the dirt. The lifeless bear stared up at him with a snarling rictus plastered on its partially-ruined head. Jared remembered sitting there for hours as his friends tried to pry him away. He'd refused to move. His dad was all he had left after his mom passed. A part of him refused to believe what happened and prayed he would wake from the nightmare. Only it hadn't been a nightmare. His dad really did die, and he'd just relived the most horrific thing he'd ever endured with vivid clarity.

Sobbing, or at least trying to in this ghostly form, Jared wanted the pain to end.

Why is this happening? Please, just let it stop.

His parents' deaths ultimately led him to strike out on his own as an explorer. Perhaps it was destiny, perhaps fate. Either way, it all led to this moment. He didn't know whether he lived, was in a coma, or had died and now suffered through some form of personal hell. No matter the scenario, he felt like dying then and there, and he wished it'd all go away for good.

LOVING, FAMILY.

The voice echoed in his mind again, but he no longer cared. He felt despondent, empty. The years he'd spent coming to grips with his parents' death, all for naught. Conflicted and uncertain, he let go of his awareness and the sweet escape of sleep claimed his consciousness.

Jared didn't know how much time passed while he slept, but when he woke, he was refreshed, and the memories distant. As with many dreams, only fragments remained. He remembered seeing his mother and father. He recollected Tiny, but everything else slipped through his grasp.

"There was...something else in the dream," muttered Jared. He shook his head to clear his thoughts and tried to recall what he'd heard. "What was it?"

Hard as he tried, it eluded him, and he couldn't recall any more of the dreams he'd experienced. His head wasn't the only thing wrong with him. His body burned, like he had dipped himself in a vat of boiling water and all his nerve endings screamed in protest. Any slight movement made him groan, his sore muscles protesting.

"What happened to me?"

Hello, Jared.

"Ah, what the—who—what?" Jared yelled as he stumbled back into the wall. He fumbled for his Colt when the voice spoke again.

My name is Scarlet.

"You—are...What are you? You can talk?" He kept his weapon drawn as he eyes focused on the small scaly reptile peering up at him with its head cocked to the side.

I am a dragon. The voice sounded amused, whimsical.

"Dragon? Dragons aren't real!" Jared protested vehemently.

I assure you, we are very real.

The voice sounded silky to his ears. Feminine without a doubt, but mature, with an edge of curiosity to it.

How can dragons exist? This is insane. I must be dreaming still.

Jared squeezed his eyes shut hoping the aberration would go away. *Dragons are not real. They can't be real—right?* He tried reasoning with himself, convinced it was impossible.

Slowly, Jared opened on eye and peered in the direction of the dragon, but all he saw was a cracked sphere, the same one that made him blackout. Breathing a sigh of relief Jared opened both eyes, realizing it was just his imagination.

"Dang, that was quite the hallucination," Jared said as he turned toward the door of his little home. "What—What are?" Jared fell back on his butt. The small, vibrant red lizard stood poised in front of the barricaded doorway.

You are not hallucinating. Anymore.

"The voice—the one from my dreams. Th-tha-that was you?" Jared asked, and the tiny blood red creature bobbed its head up and down. "Why did you—how? How are you talking?" The questions poured out of his mouth so fast it sounded like incoherent spluttering.

Do not fear. I will not harm you, and I will try to answer any questions you may have.

Jared squeezed his eyes shut hoping it would all just go away. The voice suffused his mind and made his skin crawl. Realizing he wasn't dreaming, Jared took a steadying breath, trying to calm his fluttering nerves.

"All right, okay. First, can you please tell me how you're talking into my mind? It's—I—it feels strange."

Telepathy.

"Telepathy? You can't mean--"

I'm speaking to you with my mind.

Is this some kind of trick? Jared wondered. *Some machination of those above? Telepathy and dragons?* It seemed too fantastical to be real. While he sorted through the jumble of thoughts that was his mind, Jared moved against the far wall, keeping his Colt held at the ready in case it attacked. It took him several minutes to compose himself sufficiently before he was ready to continue his conversation with this otherworldly being.

Tentatively at first, but with increasing speed Jared asked about dragons, their existence, the nanites he'd used, the *bond* he'd seen in some weird message, and finally about the *Companion Unlocked* message. The questions tumbled out of his mouth in rapid succession, barely giving him time to breathe.

Scarlet's laughter tinkled in his head. I'LL ANSWER THE EASY QUESTIONS FIRST. I HATCHED NOW BECAUSE IT WAS TIME, AND THE INJECTION OF NANITES EXPEDITED THE PROCESS. AS FOR THE HISTORY OF DRAGONS, WE'LL GET TO THAT EVENTUALLY, BUT IT IS A LONG STORY AND TOLD BETTER BY MY MOTHER.

The tiny lizard paced in a small circle before finding a place to lie down and curling into a ball, its head resting on the coiled body to look at him.

DO YOU REMEMBER THE MESSAGE YOU READ BEFORE YOU BLACKED OUT?

"I think I remember most of it," Jared said, trying to recall the whole message. The message flared into view causing him to flinch back. "Whoa! Did you?"

YES.

Irritated at the invasion into his mind, Jared expressed that irritation with Scarlet. "Please let me know before you do something like that. This is already a bit overwhelming. Your— telepathy, the images from the dream, and now this. It feels..." Jared paused.

What did it feel like?

It felt like cool tendrils, the silky voice sending shivers down his spine and calming his nerves.

VERY WELL.

Shaking the remnants of confusion away, Jared re-read the message. Some of the dreams came flooding back as he read about the techno-virus, and rage flooded into him.

What now? Jared thought. There were no instructions, nothing about dragons.

His voice shaky, Jared asked, "I see Igor's note about bonding, but what do we do now?"

I... Scarlet paused, lifted her tiny angular head and said, I MUST SEE MY MOTHER.

"Let me guess, she was the one destroying the city after I stole your egg?"

CORRECT, SHE WAS VERY ANGRY. IF NOT FOR OUR BOND, I HAVE NO DOUBT SHE WOULD FLAY YOUR MIND OPEN AND DESTROY YOU.

Jared blinked and turned an ashen color. A hollow pit opened in his stomach and he suddenly had zero desire to see another dragon in his lifetime.

DO NOT WORRY. SHE WILL NOT HARM YOU ANY LONGER. THE BOND PREVENTS HER FROM KILLING YOU, BECAUSE IT COULD KILL OR SEVERELY HARM ME.

"How do you know all of this?" Jared asked, sounding incredulous. "You were just born—er, hatched!"

JARED, I INCUBATED FOR FIVE HUNDRED YEARS.

"Wait a sec. You incubated for half a millennium?"

CORRECT, BUT IT WASN'T UNTIL A FEW YEARS AGO THAT MY MOTHER LEFT THE DEN SHE'D MADE BENEATH THE EARTH'S SURFACE.

to exist? What is a *domain*?"

IT IS HARD TO EXPLAIN, BUT OUR GENDER IS DETERMINED BY OUR POSITION, RATHER THAN PHYSICAL TRAITS. WHEN THE LAST FEMALE DRAGON DIES, THE ELDEST MALE BECOMES THE MATRIARCH, ABLE TO PASS ON THE LINEAGE.

Jared blinked in confusion, taken aback at the idea. "Then any dragon can...lay eggs?"

NOT EXACTLY. AGAIN, ONLY ONE FEMALE EXISTS AT A TIME, BUT WHEN THERE ARE NO FEMALES LEFT, THE ELDEST MALE BECOMES THE FEMALE, THE MATRIARCH, AND IS CAPABLE OF LAYING AN EGG TO PRODUCE AN HEIR.

"I'm not going to lie—that's extremely confusing to me."

IF IT HELPS, YOU MAY CONSIDER US GENDERLESS, SINCE PHYSICALLY THERE IS NO DIFFERENCE BETWEEN US SAVE FOR OUR VOICES.

"I'm sorry you have to lose your mother, Scarlet. I know how hard that can be." Jared shuddered at the memories he'd relived the previous night.

I KNOW HOW MUCH YOU LOVED YOUR PARENTS. THAT LOVE YOU HAD FOR YOUR PARENTS AND THE REVERENCE YOU HOLD FOR LIFE IS THE ONLY REASON YOU'RE STILL ALIVE. THE DREAM YOU EXPERIENCED WAS PART OF THE BONDING PROCESS AS I SIFTED THROUGH YOUR CORE MEMORIES. I ASSESSED YOUR CHARACTER TO DETERMINE IF I SHOULD LET THE BOND CONTINUE. IT RESONATED WITH THAT OF DRAGONS, AND I DEEMED OUR COMPANIONSHIP COMPLEMENTARY TO ONE ANOTHER. I BELIEVE WE CAN HELP EACH OTHER IN THE DAYS AHEAD.

"Incredible," responded Jared. "Were you aware while in th
egg? Is that how you know so much?"

I WAS CONSCIOUS FOR HUNDREDS OF YEARS, AND I SHARED
MENTAL CONNECTION WITH MY MOTHER THAT ALLOWED US T
SHARE OUR THOUGHTS.

"Scarlet, your mother. I'm sorry for stealing you away. I didn
know," whispered Jared. He truly meant the words. If he coul
have just a few more hours with his own mother, nothing woul
stand in his way.

SHE HAS COME TO PEACE WITH IT.

Alarmed, Jared asked, "Wait, how does she know?"

WE COMMUNICATED WHILE OUR BOND COMPLETED. SHE IS
UNHAPPY BUT WILL NOT HARM YOU.

"If you could talk to her this far away, why didn't she find us
when I carried your egg? She could've easily caught up to me."

PRIOR TO HATCHING, I WAS ONLY ABLE TO COMMUNICATE
THROUGH PHYSICAL CONTACT. NOW THAT I AM OUT, I CAN
SPEAK WITH HER FROM ANY DISTANCE.

"Still, what's to stop her from coming here and whisking you
away, bond notwithstanding?"

FOR STARTERS, MY MOTHER DOES NOT HAVE MUCH TIME
LEFT BEFORE SHE LEAVES THIS WORLD. DRAGONS LIVE FOR
THOUSANDS OF YEARS, BUT A MATRIARCH DIES AFTER BIRTHING
ANOTHER FEMALE DRAGON. THERE IS ONLY ONE FEMALE
DRAGON OF EACH DOMAIN ALIVE AT ONE TIME, SAVE FOR THE
FEW DAYS TO HAND OFF THEIR LINEAGE TO THE NEXT IN LINE
SHE WILL PASS A PART OF HERSELF TO ME BEFORE SHE DIES
I'LL NEED TO BE BY HER SIDE WHEN THAT HAPPENS.

"So, what happens if all of the females die? Dragons just ceas

"You really could've stopped the bond?"

I WOULD HAVE KILLED YOU BEFORE THE NANITES ASSIMILATED.

Jared glared daggers at the little lizard. "You what?"

I AM SORRY IF THAT OFFENDS YOU, BUT I AM THE FUTURE OF MY KIND. I DO NOT VALUE ONE LIFE MORE THAN THE REMAINDER OF MY BROTHERS.

The answer made him re-evaluate this bond. He was already reeling from the influx of information. Now he was irreversibly bonded to a dragon that held the fate of her kind over his own life. They stared at each other across the room, a frown creasing his brow.

I CAN SEE YOU ARE UPSET. I...DID NOT MEAN TO UPSET YOU, BUT YOU MUST ALSO KNOW THAT I HAVE A DUTY TO MY KIND. THOUGH, I BELIEVE WE CAN AID EACH OTHER. I WILL HELP YOU WITH YOUR VOW TO SEEK VENGEANCE, AND YOU CAN HELP ME PROTECT AND RE-INTRODUCE DRAGONS INTO THE WORLD.

"You know how all of this works?"

THE PROFESSOR EXPLAINED IT IN HIS NOTE. WE KILL OTHER CREATURES AND ABSORB THEIR NANITES TO GROW IN STRENGTH.

"Wait, I can increase my strength or other physical attributes too?" Jared asked excitedly.

YES. THOUGH I HAVE HAD A DECADE TO STUDY THESE TINY MACHINES, MY MOTHER AND I WERE UNABLE TO INSTRUCT THEM. SEEING THIS MESSAGE, IT IS CLEAR TO ME NOW WHY.

Curious, Jared looked to the corner of his vision where the status screen lived. The display changed little from what he could see, but it was also hard to tell with it just barely in his periphery. It showed a simple outline of his body, basic descriptors of the nanites in his body and a percentage of viability that ticked down towards his next injection. As Jared's eyes relaxed, he flicked his gaze over to the screen, and it expanded to cover his entire view.

"Whoa..."

There was much more information than he'd noticed on the minimized version. He also found an outline of Scarlet he could toggle between. The descriptive text around the outline of his character showed percentages, all zeroed out, but a notification showing *100% available* floated on top. The areas he could modify included *Mind* and *Body*, but there were dozens of sub-aspects for each.

Body included *Physical Augmentation* and *Physical Enhancement*. Augmentation included things like *Muscle Mass*, *Physical Defense*, and *Body Manipulation*. Within the defense category, he could harden his skin, increase *Toughness*, and obtain *Natural Armor*. The manipulation category was a bit more cryptic, and he didn't immediately understand categories such as *Regeneration*, *Density*, and *Remodeling*.

The *Physical Enhancements* category was much easier to understand and allowed him to increase *Strength*, *Reflex*, *Senses*, *Speed*, *Stamina*, and *Endurance*.

"I understand most of these *Body* augmentations and enhancements, but I'm not sure about *Regeneration*, *Remodeling*, *Natural Armor*, and *Density*."

I CREATED THE DESCRIPTORS TO HELP YOU UNDERSTAND WHAT THE NANITES CAN DO. REGENERATION LETS YOU HEAL YOUR BODY FASTER, REMODELING ALLOWS YOU TO CHANGE AND SHAPE YOUR BODY, NATURAL ARMOR CREATES A NANITE BARRIER NEXT TO YOUR SKIN FOR PROTECTION, AND DENSITY

INCREASES THE DENSITY OF YOUR BONES AND MUSCLES. THE LAST SHOULDN'T BE CONFUSED WITH STRENGTH. IT DOESN'T MAKE YOU STRONGER, BUT IT ENABLES YOU TO GET STRONGER BY MAKING BONES AND MUSCLE MORE DURABLE.

"You created these categories?"

YES AND NO. THE ACTUAL NAMES OF THEM WERE ALREADY PRE-PROGRAMMED, BUT I PUT THEM INTO A DECISION TREE TO HELP YOU MAKE SELECTIONS. I DO NOT KNOW IF THE PROFESSOR EVER THOUGHT ABOUT HOW THIS WOULD LOOK TO A HUMAN HOST, SINCE THERE WAS NO INTERFACE.

"Is it possible for you to put descriptive text by each one? Like, if I focus on one of them, I can get an explanation from you on how it works?"

Scarlet tilted her head back, before answering.

DONE.

"That's it? How..." Jared cut off his question and just pulled up one of the *Mind* abilities.

TELEPATHY

Telepathy is a form of non-verbal communication. Dedicating nanites to the development of this area will allow near instantaneous communication between sentient beings at the speed of thought.

"Wow, this is intense! I feel like I'm in a video game."

WHAT IS A VIDEO GAME?

"Oh, uh...do you know what electricity is?"

Scarlet blinked at him and narrowed her eyes. I MAY NOT KNOW YOUR CULTURE, BUT I AM NOT AN IDIOT.

"Hey now, I didn't mean to offend you! It was a serious question. I've no idea how much you know about current technology, but we can do a brain dump on current state of the world later. Let's get through the rest of these options first."

Listed under *Mind*, one main category, *Brain Augmentation*, branched out into several individual areas including: *Hyper-Cognition*, *Telepathy*, *Memory Recall*, *Enhanced Senses*, *Intelligence Enhancement*, and *Perception*.

"Most of these I understand, but what is *Hyper-Cognition?*"

HYPER-COGNITION ALLOWS YOU TO ACCELERATE YOUR SPEED OF THOUGHT SIGNIFICANTLY. YOU WILL THINK IN AN ACCELERATED STATE AND THE WORLD WILL SLOW TO A CRAWL, ALTHOUGH YOUR PHYSICAL BODY REMAINS AT NORMAL SPEED.

Jared marveled at the information before him. *Telepathy* was something he didn't know existed, and now he could augment his brain to use the ability.

"I have zero percent in all categories and one-hundred percent to allocate. If I've nothing in *Telepathy* how are you talking in my head right now?"

YOU DO NOT NEED IT TO HEAR A DRAGON'S VOICE, BUT WE ARE BONDED, AND YOU WOULD BE ABLE TO USE IT WITH ANY BONDED CREATURE.

"So, I can talk to you using *Telepathy* right now?"

Testing...Um, can you hear me? Am I doing this right?

A soft snort escaped Scarlet's mouth. YES, I CAN HEAR YOU, BUT YOU DO NOT NEED TO SHOUT.

Oh, sorry.

YOU WILL GET USED TO IT IN TIME. ONCE YOU INCREASE YOUR TELEPATHY SUFFICIENTLY, YOU MAY GAIN THE ABILITY

TO SPEAK WITH OTHER HUMANS. DRAGONS HAVE MUCH MORE COMPLEX METHODS OF COMMUNICATION, WHICH YOU MAY LEARN IN TIME.

"Well, I'm going to keep talking out loud for now. It's still a little weird having a voice in my head and even more weird speaking with my thoughts."

ALL OF THESE ABILITIES WILL REQUIRE ADAPTATION. THEY ARE NOT LIKE YOUR NIGHT VISION AND TEMPERATURE REGULATING. THOSE TWO ABILITIES WERE A NATURAL PROGRESSION OF THE NANITES. THE REST OF THESE WILL FORCE BIG CHANGES.

"It's a lot to wrap my head around." Jared was grateful he had someone to help him understand all of this. He shuddered to think what would've happened if he bonded with something lacking intelligence.

A dragon, thought Jared. *Surely there's nothing stronger and more intelligent in this world, right?* The mere existence of dragons amazed him. But if one legend proved accurate, what was to stop others from also being true? The idea that all the creatures of myths and legends existed made his heart flutter. There were a lot of fantastical beings in the stories told to him as a child. If they were all real, his view of the world needed some major tweaking.

Pushing those thoughts to the side, Jared focused on the nanite descriptions and assignments. He had one hundred percent to assign after all.

"I think I should increase my physical attributes first," Jared muttered. He thought back to the recent encounters with the lizards in the subway. He was much too weak and had no defenses outside his current set of clothes and weapons, which were still caked in layers of gore.

PHYSICAL UPGRADES WOULD BE GOOD. Scarlet looked him up and down as she said this, and a hint of condescension entered her tone.

"Hey now, just cause I'm not like some of the barbarians you might have in your memories, doesn't mean I can't hold my own in a fight." Although he had ample muscle, he was leaner, with an athletic build more so than a fighter.

"Okay, so physical enhancements for most of the nanites I currently have, and a little into enhancing my senses. I could've used the boost to them in that tunnel. I might've noticed the lizard clinging to the ceiling before it nearly pounced on my head."

His choices primarily focused on *Physical Enhancements*.

JARED – NANITES AVAILABLE: 100%

BODY

Physical Enhancement

Strength - 30%
Reflex - 20%
Muscle Mass - 20%
Speed - 10%

MIND

Brain Augmentation

Enhanced Senses - 10%
Perception - 10%

Maybe I should increase speed and endurance some, mused Jared.

In the end, he decided that he'd survived the last two years without any enhancements and left them alone. The little boost he'd get from these changes should suffice for now. He moved the sliders around to match his choices and tensed, waiting for the changes to occur.

"Um, Scarlet? Why is nothing happening? I feel no changes,

and nothing happened when I moved the sliders."

ALTHOUGH THE MESSAGE FROM IGOR DID NOT SAY IT, THE CHANGES ONLY TAKE PLACE WHEN YOU ARE UNCONSCIOUS. YOUR MIND COULD BREAK UNDER THE STRAIN ON YOUR BODY DURING THE CHANGE. DO YOU RECALL THE PAIN YOU FELT WHEN WE BONDED?

"Yes," Jared responded tentatively. "How could I forget that? It was the worst pain I've ever felt," Jared added, cringing at the memory. He still felt the twinges of pain, and his body ached like he'd spent the day doing intense weight training.

THE PROCESS THE NANITES USED TO CHANGE YOUR BODY AND MIND ARE THE SAME, AND YOU WOULD FEEL THE SAME AGONY ONCE AGAIN. WAITING UNTIL A SLEEP CYCLE, THE NANITES RENDER YOU UNCONSCIOUS, SHIELDING YOUR MIND FROM THE PAIN.

"What about you? Did the changes hurt you?"

I ALSO WENT THROUGH SOME OF THE CHANGES WHEN THE NANITES CONVERTED TO YOUR DNA STRUCTURE, BUT I CAN SEPARATE MY MIND FROM THE PAIN, SO IT WILL NOT INCAPACITATE ME.

Jared stared at the little dragon in wonder. If a newly-hatched dragon was this smart and could do so much, he wondered what her mother was capable of. A part of him was still in denial about the existence of dragons even though he sat across from one. Deciding he could come to grips with his new reality later, he minimized his status screen and focused on Scarlet's.

Standing at just over a foot tall and three feet long, Scarlet resembled a lizard or snake with legs more than a dragon and could do with a little physical augmentation. She didn't have wings yet, and the scales on her body appeared more akin to patterned skin than individual scales. Her body matched the color of blood, save for tiny claws and nubs on her head, which were black as ebony. Scarlet was definitely a fitting name for her, but Jared was curious if that was her given name. It seemed too human.

"Scarlet? Is that your full name?"

IT IS THE NAME OF THE EXPLORER WHOSE GEAR YOU FOUND. IT... RESONATED WITH ME. HOWEVER, MY GIVEN NAME IS SILDRAINEN MAILDREL. IT IS A DRAGON NAME AND NOT MEANT FOR HUMAN LIPS. IT SEEMED MORE APPROPRIATE TO USE SCARLET, BEING BONDED TO A HUMAN. DRAGONS ARE SELECTIVE ABOUT SHARING THEIR TRUE NAMES, AND WE ONLY DO SO TO TRUE FRIENDS OF OUR KIND.

"Sildrainen Maildrel." Jared attempted to pronounce the name and failed miserably, making Scarlet chuckle at his ineptitude. "What does it mean?"

IT IS DIFFICULT TO EXPLAIN IN WORDS, BUT IT MEANS FIRST OF THE FIRE DRAGONS, FIRSTBORN OF THE FIERCE AND POWERFUL DRAGON QUEEN. IT IS MEANT TO BE MORE OF AN IMPRESSION, RATHER THAN A TITLE, THAT OTHER DRAGONS UNDERSTAND. THE NAME REPRESENTS MY HERITAGE AND THE NATURE OF MY MOTHER.

"Wait, you aren't the first, though. Also, your mother is a queen? So that makes you what, a princess?"

BECAUSE EACH MATRIARCH PASSES THEIR ESSENCE TO THEIR SUCCESSOR, WE ARE COLLECTIVELY REFERRED TO AS THE FIRST.

Jared's mind spun as he tried to wrap his thoughts around what Scarlet told him. She snorted upon seeing his confused look and he thought she might be annoyed by his endless tirade of questions.

I URGE YOU TO WAIT FOR MY MOTHER TO EXPLAIN IN MORE DETAIL.

"So not only did I steal a dragon from her nest, I stole a soon-to-be queen from a dying mother!" Jared's voice squeaked, panic obvious in his demeanor. "So, when did you say we need to meet your mother, exactly?"

As SOON AS POSSIBLE. SHE IS ALREADY DYING, AND I MUST BE BY HER SIDE.

Jared felt shame and guilt wash through him for keeping Scarlet from her mother. No matter his fears, they needed to get moving.

Without further delay, Jared pulled up the status screen for Scarlet. Carefully reading through the options, he realized she only had one extra category, *Physical Defense/Attack*. She also didn't have the *Natural Armor*, option under *Body Manipulation*.

That'll make these selections easier, thought Jared. He'd already read all the descriptions for each of the enhancements, so he focused on the four new areas in *Physical Defense/Attack*, which included *Skin Hardening, Scale Hardening, Bone Hardening*, and *Fire Breathing*.

"It looks like our enhancement areas are pretty similar. Well, aside from the whole *Fire Breathing* bit."

THAT WAS INTENTIONAL TO MAKE THIS EASIER. THOUGH I HAVE A LITTLE MORE CONTROL OVER THE NANITES ASSIGNED TO ANY PHYSICAL AUGMENTATIONS. ONCE YOU MAKE THE SELECTIONS, I CAN INFLUENCE THEM TO ACT A PARTICULAR WAY. FOR INSTANCE, IF YOU ASSIGNED SOME TO REMODELING, I CAN DICTATE WHAT THEY REMODEL AND WHERE. IN TIME, YOU WILL GAIN THAT ABILITY FOR YOURSELF.

"I'll leave these selections up to you, but I do think most of them should go into *Body*. No offense, but you're a bit on the scrawny side at the moment."

I CAN GIVE YOU A LITTLE TELEPATHIC SLAP TO THE HEAD IF YOU NEED HELP REMEMBERING THAT I JUST HATCHED A FEW HOURS AGO.

Jared held up his hands in apology. "I meant no offense! I just pointed out the obvious. There's a lot of creatures out there, and a rat could probably take you on physically at this point."

NOTED, Scarlet said icily. I WILL RECEIVE A SIGNIFICANT BOOST TO MY PHYSICAL STATURE AND AVAILABLE NANITES ONCE MY MOTHER TRANSFERS HER ESSENCE TO ME. RIGHT NOW, THE AMOUNT IS NEGLIGIBLE, BUT PHYSICAL ENHANCEMENTS WILL PROVIDE THE MOST IMMEDIATE BENEFIT.

"What is… essence?" Jared said, but Scarlet cut him off.

WE WILL DISCUSS IT LATER.

Geez, I just got verbally shut down by a foot-tall sassy dragon. This companionship is going to get interesting, he thought. *Perhaps I made a huge mistake injecting those nanites into her.* Doing his best to let the stern dismissal slide off him, Jared listened attentively as Scarlet walked him through her status screen.

SCARLET – NANITES AVAILABLE: 100%

BODY

> Physical Augmentation
>> Muscle Mass - 25%
>
> Body Manipulation
>> Regeneration - 15%
>>
>> Remodeling - 10%
>
> Physical Defense/Attack

Skin Hardening - 10%

Scale Hardening - 15%

Bone Hardening - 10%

Fire Breathing - 15%

"Okay, I allocated everything into *Physical Augmentation*. Can you actually breathe fire right now?"

I CAN ONLY MAKE A TINY SPARK, AS IT TAKES TIME FOR MY FIRE GLANDS TO MATURE. WITH THE AMOUNT OF NANITES YOU DESIGNATED, I SHOULD BE ABLE TO BREATHE A SMALL TRICKLE OF FLAME, NOT MUCH USE IN AN ATTACK UNTIL IT GETS STRONGER AND I GROW IN SIZE.

Jared finished going over both of their status screens. Before he closed them out, he asked, "Scarlet, didn't the professor's message say something about assimilating traits?"

THE TRAITS HE MENTIONS ARE ABILITIES. WHEN CREATURES ABSORB NANITES THEY CAN DEVELOP SPECIAL ABILITIES. IF YOU KILL THE CREATURE, THERE'S A HIGH PROBABILITY THAT YOU ALSO ACQUIRE THE SPECIAL ABILITY DUE TO THE NANITES RETAINING THE NATURALLY EVOLVED CODING.

"So you're saying I can become a superhero?" The excitement made his voice crack like a prepubescent teenager.

SUPERHERO?

"Demigod? Fallen angel?"

SUPERNATURAL POWERS. YES, I SUPPOSE GIVEN ENOUGH TIME YOU MAY DEVELOP INTO A BEING OF GREAT POWER.

His excitement only grew as he thought of the possibilities. He wouldn't need to worry about chance encounters with bears or wild dogs. He'd strive to become impervious to the predators that normally hunted him. *Bottom of the food chain? Not anymore!*

"Woohoo!" Jared fist-pumped, unable to contain the torrent of emotions running through him. *Igor, you mad genius, I hope one day I get to meet you and thank you for this opportunity.*

Elated, Jared felt like he could take on the world. "All right, Scarlet let's go see your mother."

Jared removed the barricade from his temporary shelter and stepped outside to stretch when he felt something breathe down his neck. He froze.

Stay inside! Jared thought to Scarlet, but she shrugged off his command and slithered out of the room, scampered around Jared, and made a mewling noise.

Dang, Jared thought, *Scarlet's mother.*

03 A DRAGON'S LEGACY

I'm going to die, I'm going to die...

Slowly, arms stretched out to show he meant no harm, Jared turned around. He expected to see an angry maw filled with razor-sharp death descending toward him, regardless of what Scarlet said. Instead, all he saw were massive tree-trunk legs covered in blood-red scales.

Jared swallowed hard and craned his neck up. *Whoa.*

Unprepared for the visage before him, Jared stood in muted shock, and a cold sweat broke out on his forehead.

How could such a creature exist? Why hasn't anyone seen her before? Can the cities really be that ignorant of a creature so massive?

Scarlet's mother stood at least two hundred feet tall and had a wingspan that required Jared to crane his head as far left and right as possible. Her scales, the color of fresh spilt blood, covered every inch of her body. Massive legs tipped with razor sharp claws showcased her lethality, easily slicing into the concrete and metal as if made of butter.

Jared shuddered as his gaze swept upward where her arms gave way to the enormous scaled wings. Massive spiked protrusions jutted from her wings, ready to impale any creature that dared attack.

A snort and gout of superheated breath snapped Jared out of his stupor. The great behemoth dropped to all fours, and the ground shook with the force causing rocks and debris to cascade down the slope. On all fours, the dragon stood at least one hundred feet tall and was no less imposing a figure.

How in the world did this creature fit into the subway tunnels?

The magnificent dragon lowered her head, and Jared saw curved horns that swept back toward her tail, where a row of spikes that started from the crown of her head tracked down her back all the way to a barb-tipped tail, similar to Scarlet's own. Each horn looked like deadly katanas, and they could impale a man with room to spare.

This creature from myth and legend lowered her head, folded her wings against her body, and stared at the puny human. Jared looked into her eye and felt his innermost thoughts laid bare for this sentient being. Cold tendrils of pressure invaded his mind and sent shivers racing to his very soul. Nothing remained hidden. Her slitted irises burned with an inner light and reflected flame like molten pools of magma. Jared felt naked in front of her gaze and dared not move an inch lest she forgo her promise to Scarlet and end his very existence.

The dragon's lips pulled back into a feral grin as he had these thoughts, and he heard a great huffing noise like a steam-powered engine wheezing to life. When her lips pulled back, Jared smelled the fetid scent of death and decay from the many creatures whose life ended in her jaws. He could see pieces of flesh and bone between her sharp teeth , causing him to shudder in fear and disgust.

Unable to move his body even an inch, he couldn't form a single coherent word or thought. While he stood immobile, Scarlet slithered around her mother's legs and came to rest near her head. With a monumental effort of will, he shifted his eyes to Scarlet to see her relaxed and curled up next to her mother. He felt some of the tension ease.

When Jared thought he could take the scrutiny no more, a deep, rumbling voice thundered in his mind.

JARED CARTWRIGHT, I FIND YOU WORTHY.

Jared screamed. He dropped to his knees, cradling his head in his hands. It felt like his skull split in two and the pressure of a mountain crushed it flat. Liquid trickled down his face. Instinctively, he reached up to wipe it away and his fingers came away stained with blood.

She doesn't even have to eat me, she can just talk me to death, Jared thought wryly, the pounding in his head making it difficult to think.

MOTHER, Jared heard Scarlet say. HIS MIND IS WEAK. YOU MUST SPEAK TO HIM AS A HATCHLING.

Scarlet turned to look at him and said, JARED, PLEASE COME CLOSER AND PLACE YOUR HAND ON MY MOTHER.

"You—you want me to," Jared stammered. "I don't—I—"

YES, YOU WILL COMMUNICATE THROUGH TOUCH. MY MOTHER'S PSIONIC ABILITY IS TOO POWERFUL FOR YOU TO BEAR. UNTIL YOU INCREASE YOUR MIND ABILITY, THIS IS THE ONLY WAY YOU CAN SPEAK WITH A MATURE DRAGON.

"Move," Jared whispered under his breath. Shaking in fear, his body refused to obey him. Summoning the last of his willpower, Jared raised his eyes to gaze into the fiery eye once more. Just before his hand made contact he hesitated and glanced at Scarlet. She nodded her head, and he placed his palm down.

Jared's vision faded to black. *Not again...*

A dragon's ferocious roar ripped through the last vestiges of Jared's foggy mind. The roar sent vibrations through his body.

Blinking in confusion, Jared asked, *Where am I? Wait. How? I'm using telepathy. Why can't I speak?*

Completely ignoring his questions, a deep, melodic voice that sounded otherworldly and ancient invaded his thoughts. F<small>ROM</small> <small>THE VERY BEGINNING, OR EVER THE</small> E<small>ARTH WAS, WE EXISTED.</small> W<small>HEN DRAGONS FREELY ROAMED THE EARTH, THEY RULED THE</small> <small>LAND, THE AIR, THE WATER, AND FIRE.</small> The emphasis on *fire* did not escape his notice, and it was clear which she belonged to. The scene before him played out as he watched dragons, similar in color and size to Scarlet's mother, darting in and out of volcanoes.

W<small>E HAVE ALWAYS HAD ONE QUEEN FOR EACH DOMINION.</small>

Jared's vision blurred and re-focused, showing Scarlet's mother in all her majestic glory diving into an active volcano. She reveled in the searing heat of the liquid magma against her scales. Jared didn't know how, but the heat and comfort of its caress washed over him, and he felt...*home*.

M<small>Y CHILDREN...</small> Love and anguish exploded into his mind.

Conflict warred within him while he gazed at her progeny.

What happened to them? asked Jared.

The scene fast-forwarded in time, pausing to show humankind bent on eradicating dragons from the Earth. Jared watched primitive men with crudely-made weapons wage war against hibernating dragons, slaughtering them as they slept. Every time a spear or sword pierced the flesh of a dragon, a pang of sorrow stabbed at his heart. The visions flew by so fast, but somehow, he understood them all. Mankind multiplied, creating weapons of war to trap and imprison them. The imprisoned dragons became sport and entertainment in colosseums.

Amongst the chaos and brutal nature of mankind, he also witnessed those that worshiped and cared for the dragons. In return for their friendship, these humans became exiles, and many died alongside the dragons as outcasts to society. Thousands of years passed, and the persecution continued. Mankind wanted to reign supreme, lords of the earth. Over time, *heroes* arose in the human kingdoms, and statues were erected to showcase their accomplishments. It was these *heroes* that waged war against dragon kind.

The flashback slowed to a crawl and focused on the last remaining fire dragons, flying around a massive volcano spewing steam and smoke. Forlornly, Scarlet's mother looked around her before she arced into the air and dove straight down the mouth of the volcano, never to resurface. The moment the dragon, whose perspective and feeling he shared, dove into the volcano, a tidal wave of emotions surged into him. Sadness and loss of other dragons. Anger and hatred against mankind. A desire to fight overruled by duty and obligation to protect the last of the dragons.

He didn't know if it was his own emotions or the lingering effects of the dragons, but his heart broke. He felt compassion for them and anger at what others of his kind did to them. *Prideful and arrogant fools. All of them!*

WE BURROWED UNDERGROUND THREE THOUSAND YEARS AGO, ENDING OUR REIGN ON EARTH.

Still floating in the void, an image of Scarlet appeared in front of him. At the sight, love blossomed inside him, and he had no doubt everything he'd seen and witnessed was from Scarlet's mother's perspective. The love she held for all her kind paled in comparison to the tiny lizard curled at her feet.

A TIME OF DRAGONS HAS BEGUN ANEW. EVEN NOW MY FAMILY STIRS AND WILL ONCE AGAIN TAKE TO THE SKIES.

Alarmed, Jared blurted, *Humankind has only grown more hostile over the years. Are you sure you want your family to re-emerge into the world?*

FROM YOUR MEMORIES AND AS FAR AS I CAN SENSE, HUMANS NO LONGER POPULATE MUCH OF THE EARTH. IT WILL BE MANY YEARS YET BEFORE THE REST OF MY FAMILY RE-EMERGES. SCARLET WILL WORK TO CARVE OUT A HOME FOR DRAGONS HERE ON THE SURFACE.

The moment ended, and Jared knew her decision was final. Nothing he said would change her mind. A resolute desire to see her family grow and flourish drove her motivations, regardless of the peril. Somehow, he knew that thousands of years in hibernation was no existence at all, and dragon kind wanted to live again.

The finality of the moment abruptly shifted, and a new landscape faded into view. The temperature dipped precipitously, and an involuntary shudder wracked his body. Glaciers and blinding white snow-capped peaks surrounded him.

A moment later a brilliant white shape darted in front of him.

White dragon?

THESE ARE THE LAST OF THE ICE DRAGONS WHO HELD DOMINION OVER THE AIR.

Jared's perspective zoomed in to the largest dragon where they flew over a glacier with a massive gash rent in the earth. Instinctively, Jared knew this particular rend in the earth descended miles below the surface. Just before the largest dragon descended into the depths, a psionic wave of energy rolled across the earth, announcing their departure from the affairs of the world.

I... Jared's vision swam yet again, making him lose his train of thought. When it cleared, he floated above the ocean, untouched by the ravages of the war that later destroyed most of the earth.

It's beautiful, Jared said breathlessly. His eyes roamed the vast emptiness stretching before him and he longed to see an ocean like this someday. *I've seen nothing like it before!*

The vastness of the open space overwhelmed him, making him realize how insignificant he was in comparison. The ocean's surface, marred only by the gentle lapping of waves, made him relax. It soothed him like nothing he'd ever experienced before. The sound was peaceful and tranquil-

A low, deep moan vibrated through his body, and deep sadness pervaded his thoughts. Such a contrast to the feelings he'd just experienced, it angered him that anything could feel such loss when gazing upon the splendor before him. In the distance, several shapes drew near. His vision blurred and zoomed forward into the midst of titanic blue dragons. These majestic creatures dwarfed Scarlet's mother and differed in so many ways. Where the ice and fire dragons had razor-sharp claws and a single row of spikes down their back, these midnight blue dragons sported webbed appendages, and their entire bodies looked smooth as glass. He saw individual scales, but rather than overlapping, they merged to create sleek bodies. Their tails ended in a deadly looking trident instead of the barbed tail on Scarlet and her mother. Only one word could describe what he felt at that moment: awe.

Words eluded him, and all he could do was stare in incomprehension while these dragons flew through the skies.

WATER DRAGONS ARE THE LARGEST OF OUR KIND. THEY LIVE LONGER AND HAVE PROFOUND WISDOM EXCEEDING ALL

OTHERS. THEY ALSO GOVERN ALL THE OTHER DRAGONS, THOUGH THEY DO NOT DICTATE OUR ACTIONS.

One by one they disappeared beneath the surface. He followed the path the dragons took, descending miles beneath the water. If not for a faint glow emanating from the dragons, the darkness would've swallowed them from sight. Once the dragons reached the bottom of the trench, they settled in to rest and closed their eyes.

UNLIKE MOST OF THE DRAGONS, WATER DRAGONS WERE NOT FORCED TO ABANDON THEIR HOMES AND BURROW INTO THE EARTH. THIS IS THEIR HOME, AND THEY STILL ROAM THE DEPTHS. SINCE WE REMOVED OURSELVES FROM THE WORLD, THEY HAVE REMAINED BENEATH THE WATER, HIDDEN FROM MANKIND.

Will they surface now that dragons are returning to the world?

THEY WILL REMAIN IN THE OCEAN UNTIL THEY ARE CERTAIN MAN WILL NOT HUNT THEM AGAIN. ALTHOUGH THE LARGEST OF OUR KIND, THEY ARE THE MOST KIND AND GENTLE, PREFERRING PEACE AND ISOLATION TO THE VIOLENCE SHOWN BY MAN. CONTRARY TO HOW HUMANITY PORTRAYED OUR KIND, WE DO NOT WAGE WAR ON THEM, NOR DO WE RULE OVER THEM. WE PREFER TO LIVE PEACEABLY, CO-EXISTING, BUT THEY ONLY SAW US AS A THREAT TO THEIR SOVEREIGNTY.

Jared's resolve hardened, he'd do everything he could to help bring that vision to pass.

THE LAST OF OUR KIND, THE EARTH DRAGONS HAVE HIDDEN DEEP UNDER THE MOUNTAINS.

The scene shifted once more, and Jared stood atop a plateau, a dry heat blasted him in the face as he stood on the edge of a desert butted up against a huge mountain range. He looked down to see a dozen dragons trudging toward the mountains. The slow, lumbering steps of these behemoths sent vibrations up his legs. These dragons didn't have wings, and their backs looked covered in many layers of scale and bone. Jared recalled pictures of prehistoric dinosaurs and marveled at the similarities.

I wonder if the history books got it wrong, and they uncovered fossilized remains of dragons.

DINOSAURS WERE CLOSE RELATIVES TO THE DRAGONS, BUT ONLY IN PHYSIOLOGICAL SIMILARITIES. HOWEVER, IT IS LIKELY MANY OF YOUR ANCESTORS UNEARTHED SLAIN DRAGONS AND MISTOOK THEM FOR DINOSAURS. IN FACT, BEFORE WE LEFT THE WORLD TO ITS OWN MACHINATIONS, THE WORD DINOSAUR DIDN'T EXIST. HUMANS REFERRED TO THEM AND US AS DRAGONS COLLECTIVELY AND ONLY DIFFERENTIATED BASED ON SUPPOSED SPECIES. SOME HUMANS KNEW THE TRUTH, BUT MANY DID NOT CARE TO LEARN ABOUT OUR KIND.

Um, thanks. Jared hadn't meant to say those thoughts aloud. *Did I say it out loud?*

Scarlet's voice echoed through his thoughts. YOU SPOKE THEM IN YOUR MIND, BUT WITH INTENT. I CAN HEAR YOUR THOUGHTS MOST OF THE TIME. AT LEAST UNTIL YOU LEARN TO CLOSE THEM OFF FROM ME. MY MOTHER CAN HEAR THE THOUGHTS YOU FORCEFULLY PROJECT WHILE TOUCHING HER.

Thanks, Scarlet. So the main difference between dragons and dinosaurs is sentience or self-realization? Physically, it is difficult to place you into an entirely different kind, but mentally you're even more advanced than humankind.

At a high level you are correct, but there are many physical differences as well. No doubt you'll learn of these in due course.

Jared stood atop the plateau and watched the land dragons make their way into a large cave within the mountain. Once the last dragon entered, the mountain sealed itself off with a thundering boom. The looming mountain faded into obscurity as the darkness once again closed in on Jared, but quickly the destroyed skyline of New York City came into view.

Thank you, that was beautiful. He enjoyed the experience and visions. Experiencing all of the views and emotions firsthand was an experience he'd never forget. *Perhaps one day, we can share visions such as this again. I'd love to see and experience a world free of destruction.*

One day, Scarlet whispered. The time has come for you to make a choice, Jared.

Right after Scarlet finished speaking, her mother's voice reached his ears. It had a clear note of authority.

I charge you, Jared Cartwright, to guard, protect, and strengthen my daughter. Seek to right the wrongs committed against dragon kind and usher in a new age where dragons and man thrive side by side.

DRAGON'S LEGACY

Alestrialia Maildrel, Queen of the Fire Dragons, charges you to become the guardian for her only daughter and right the wrongs committed by mankind thousands of years ago. Alestrialia will grant you a boon if you vow to honor her request and never stray from the task assigned.

What is this? A quest! This is so cool!

JARED, PLEASE DO NOT BE FLIPPANT ABOUT THIS REQUEST. I GENERATED THE MESSAGE FOR YOU. THIS IS THE LAST WISH OF A QUEEN. IF YOU AGREE TO THE REQUEST, MY MOTHER WILL ALTER YOUR NANITES AND MIND, INFUSING THE VOW. IF YOU SHOULD GO AGAINST YOUR VOW, IT WILL KILL YOU. IF YOU CHOOSE TO SAY THE VOW, YOU WILL ALSO GET A BOON IN THE FORM OF NANITES WHEN MY MOTHER TRANSFERS HER ESSENCE. SHE WILL SHARE THEM EQUALLY BETWEEN US. THE ONLY REASON I GENERATED THE MESSAGE IS THAT YOU MUST MAKE AN ACTIVE CHOICE TO ACCEPT THIS VOW AND ALLOW MY MOTHER TO ALTER YOUR NANITES.

Jared felt the weight of the words, a mountain pressing down on him. His shoulders slumped under the burden. Tiredly, Jared cradled his head in his hands, thinking through the request. He found no reason to reject the offer since he wanted nothing more than to exact vengeance on the people responsible for killing his mother. Coincidentally, they were also the people that would try to enslave or eradicate dragons once again. Their purposes aligned, Jared placed his hand on Alestrialia's head once again.

"I vow to protect Scarlet and seek to right the wrongs done to dragon kind."

Jared grunted as pain erupted in his head. He dropped to his knees in agony, severing his connection to this ancient queen. The moment his knees hit the ground, the pain abruptly vanished.

LET THIS PAIN BE A REMINDER OF YOUR VOW.

"I...I can hear you without touching you? How?"

SCARLET AND I SHARE THE SAME GENETIC CODE. I'VE JUST FUSED A PORTION OF OUR NANITES TOGETHER, IN A SIMILAR

FASHION AS THE BONDING YOU SHARE WITH SCARLET. HOWEVER, I'VE ISOLATED THE REMAINDER USING A PSIONIC BARRIER SO THAT WHEN THE TIME IS RIGHT, YOU BOTH MAY ABSORB ANY NANITES I HOLD.

"You—how can you do that? I thought only humans could control the nanites?"

I AM MERELY BLOCKING YOUR ACCESS, NOT CONTROLLING THEM.

"Wait a second. So, you're telling me that if you share the same DNA, I can bond with more than one creature?"

THE SHORT ANSWER IS NO. SCARLET AND I ARE NEARLY IDENTICAL IN GENETIC MAKEUP, AND THUS THE BOND WILL WORK WITH BOTH OF US.

"I think I understand, but I want to know more when the time is right. I—"

Interrupting his thoughts, Alestrialia said, SILDRAINEN, MY TIME GROWS SHORT. WE MUST COMPLETE THE TRANSFERENCE SOON, BUT FIRST WE MUST GO BACK TO THE NEST BENEATH THE CITY. NO CREATURES WILL ENTER MY DOMAIN, AND I WILL SET UP A PSIONIC BARRIER TO PREVENT ANYTHING FROM INTERRUPTING.

Curious, Jared interrupted Scarlet's response, and asked, "Psionic barrier?"

IT IS A FORM OF A PSIONIC ATTACK BUT PROJECTED OUTWARD FOR A TIME. IT WILL ATTACK ANYTHING WITHIN RANGE AND RENDER THEM INCAPACITATED UNTIL DEACTIVATED. SCARLET SLITHERED UP TO HER MOTHER'S BACK WHILE SHE EXPLAINED THE ABILITY. I WILL ACCOMPANY MY MOTHER BACK

TO OUR DEN AND PREPARE FOR THE TRANSFERENCE. PLEASE ARRIVE AS SOON AS YOU ARE ABLE.

Alestrialia rose to her feet and leapt from the island, crashing to the dried ocean floor below. Jared blinked in shock. That drop was insane, and she'd made the leap without hesitation. Then again, it was a short hop for her.

Jared grabbed his backpack, stuffed all the boosters inside, and checked to ensure both the phase pistol and Colt remained secure in their holsters. The closer he got to the city, the more apparent Alestrialia's destructive and frantic search became apparent. When he reached the area near the subway entrance he'd used previously, he saw every building in a two-block radius lay toppled, smashed to pieces from Alestrialia's rampage.

Scarlet? Can you hear me?

I CAN HEAR YOU.

How exactly will I get down to the nest? The staircase doesn't really exist anymore.

CIRCLE AROUND THE RUINED BUILDINGS TO THE SOUTH. THERE IS ANOTHER STAIRCASE LEFT MOSTLY INTACT.

Jared circled around the destruction and found the staircase next to a massive crater, easily explaining how Alestrialia entered the sub-level.

All right, I'm in the tunnel. Which way do I need to go?

HEAD TO THE RIGHT. WHEN YOU GET TO A SECTION OF THE TUNNEL THAT COLLAPSED, CLIMB OVER. THE NEST IS JUST ON THE OTHER SIDE. MY MOTHER WILL ACTIVATE THE PSIONIC BARRIER AS SOON AS YOU ARE WITHIN RANGE AND INSIDE THE RADIUS.

Jared picked up his pace, found the pile of rubble, and climbed over. Sure enough, Scarlet and her mother were in the center of the nest. Jared sat on the edge of the crater until Scarlet turned to look at him.

IT IS TIME. PLEASE COME CLOSE AND PLACE YOUR HAND ON HER HEAD.

Jared followed Scarlet's instructions, once again picking his way through the hundreds of bones and bits of debris that made up the nest. After he'd made it to a clear space next to Scarlet and her mother, he sat down and placed his hand on her head. A prick of static shocked his hand and he pulled it away in surprise.

Scarlet, what—

His thoughts interrupted, Scarlet said, PLEASE GET COMFORTABLE. THIS WILL BE ANOTHER PAINFUL PROCESS, AND THERE IS NOTHING I CAN DO TO SHIELD YOU FROM THE PAIN.

Crap.

He'd already endured so much pain in the past twenty-four hours, his nerves were already screaming in protest. Drawing in a deep breath, he placed his hand against Alestrialia's head. The jolt shot up his arm once again, but he forced himself to remain in place.

ARE YOU READY, MY CHILDREN?

I AM READY, MOTHER. Sadness laced Scarlet's thoughts, but threaded through the sadness was a reassurance that her mother would live within her.

A pregnant pause lingered before Jared said, "I am ready."

He really didn't want to go through another round of torturous pain, but in the end, his desire to grow stronger prevailed.

I, ALESTRIALIA MAILDREL, QUEEN OF FIRE DRAGONS, HEREBY RELINQUISH MY SOVEREIGNTY TO SILDRAINEN MAILDREL AND HER GUARDIAN JARED CARTWRIGHT. HENCEFORTH, SILDRAINEN SHALL CARRY HER BIRTHRIGHT AND

RULE AS QUEEN. JARED AS HER FAITHFUL GUARDIAN WILL PROTECT HER AND REMAIN TRUE TO HIS VOW ON PAIN OF DEATH.

To Scarlet, she whispered, GOODBYE MY LOVE.

To Jared, she whispered, PROTECT MY CHILD.

With the last utterance of these words, many lifetimes of memories and emotions flowed through him. Time was nonexistent in this moment as the memories flitted by faster than he could focus. Fast though it was, understanding blossomed into his mind and he knew. He knew Alestrialia as if he had lived every moment of her life. Every momentous occasion, every battle, all the heartache and loss—he experienced it all until brightness transcended all else. This moment eclipsed all the memories in the thousands of years Alestrialia lived. It was the moment of Scarlet's birth.

Jared felt guilt and pain at denying Alestrialia the opportunity to be physically present for her birth. In that moment, he would've moved heaven and earth to turn back time and let her experience the most joyous occasion. Sadly, he could not. He should've felt animosity and anger from her, but all he felt was love and acceptance.

He'd passed her examination, and she had accepted him into their family. Tears trickled down his face as he thought about his mother and father. He missed them so much, and he never expected feeling whole again, of feeling that sense of belonging that only family could give.

Yet here he was, accepted by Scarlet. Accepted by Alestrialia. Given the opportunity to experience their entire lives in so intimate a fashion. Joy and happiness bolstered him, and he knew then, no matter what obstacles stood in front of him, he would lay down his life for Scarlet. Their fates sealed, Jared reveled in the emotions and memories that swirled through him.

The moments stretched into minutes, and then hours. Abruptly, the vortex of memories ceased, and his skin started crawling.

Pain.

Agony.

Gut-wrenching, torturous pain ripped through his body as if a torrent of fire shot from Alestrialia, searing the flesh from his bones.

"It. Hurts. So. Much," Jared said through gritted teeth. He lasted only a few seconds longer before blackness enveloped him, and unconsciousness rescued him from the pain.

Jared awoke in darkness. As his mind cleared, he looked around and found himself curled up next to—

"Scarlet!" Jared exclaimed.

HELLO, JARED, Scarlet said in a smug tone.

"Wow! You look…"

Scarlet no longer resembled the small red lizard with nubs for wings. She stood as tall as Jared on all fours, and a beautiful pair of scarlet wings protruded from her back. Her eyes reflected Alestrialia, and Jared knew that she lived on within Scarlet. Where her mother had radiated deadliness, Scarlet personified majesty and grace. Her scales shone with a soft inner glow, highlighting the pattern that adorned her entire body.

"You're beautiful!" breathed Jared.

THANK YOU!

Pride shot through their bond and Scarlet reveled in the compliment. He couldn't wait to see her in the sunlight and observe her soaring through the sky. She was an amazing sight to behold.

Jared realized he'd stared for a long time and awkwardly

cleared his throat before asking, "How long was I unconscious?"

You were asleep for three days.

"Three days! Why was I asleep for so long?"

The transference taxed your body significantly, and you needed the rest. I also rested for two days. Do you need more time?

"No, I...I'm fine. In fact—" Jared examined his body and realized he did feel great. "I feel amazing, and my body no longer hurts from the bonding or the nanites your mother..." Jared's voice trailed off. He didn't want to upset Scarlet with the memory, but she only smiled in response.

She lives within us. We absorbed her essence and nanites while her physical form dissolved.

"Can all dragons do that? Transfer themselves like that?"

No, the process only occurs between a matriarch and a female progeny.

Jared nodded his head. He thought he understood it now, but time for questions could come later. Now that they had an influx of nanites and *essence*, he had more pressing questions.

"Now that the process completed, how do we—I don't know, use this essence?"

The essence is for me alone, but the nanites should be available on your status screen.

Flicking his eyes over to the outline of his body, it expanded into view. "Whoa! According to this screen, I've only assigned twelve percent of the available nanites! I thought I assigned a hundred percent of them from our bonding process?"

You assigned only the nanites granted to you from the booster and any nanites you already had within

YOUR BODY. THOSE NANITES HAVE ALREADY TAKEN EFFECT. WE CAN ASSIGN THE REMAINING NANITES NOW AND LET THEM TAKE EFFECT BEFORE THE PSIONIC BARRIER LAPSES.

"Already taken effect? I don't feel any changes." Jared looked down at his body and froze.

What the—

04 AMBUSH

Jared launched to his feet, peeling off his blood-caked shirt. Bones scattered around him in his excitement to see the massive physical changes wrought on his body.

Previously, he'd stood around six feet tall and had a lean, athletic build. No longer was that the case. He stood several inches over six feet, and bulging muscles adorned his entire body. Rippling abdominal muscles replaced a normally flat stomach. He probed and prodded himself, enjoying the improvements. Before he finished his self-examination, a huffing, wheezing noise interrupted him.

Jared whipped his head around to see Scarlet staring right at him as he admired his body, her mouth pulled back into a grin. His face burned with embarrassment, and he quickly pulled a fresh shirt from his pack, discarding the other one permanently.

Turning away from her, Jared cleared his throat and said, "Scarlet, this is—it's incredible! This seems like a pretty radical enhancement. How did the nanites alter my body so much? I was expecting incremental changes, not a metamorphosis. Especially not in three days. And why am I not hungry after all that? It seems like I'd use a lot of energy up."

Scarlet snorted and laughed derisively. IF YOU LIVED DURING MY MOTHER'S REIGN, YOU WOULD REALIZE MEN WERE...LET US JUST SAY THEIR STATURE WAS MUCH MORE IMPRESSIVE EVEN AFTER YOUR NEW CHANGES.

Jared narrowed his eyes at her, about to utter a snarky comment for deflating his ego, but she spoke right over his objections.

YOU HAD A LOT OF DORMANT NANITES. ONLY THOSE USED FOR YOUR NIGHT VISION AND TEMPERATURE REGULATION WERE USED. AS FOR ENERGY, I CAN ONLY SPECULATE THAT THERE IS SO MUCH RADIATION AND NUCLEAR WASTE IN THIS AREA THAT YOUR BODY DIDN'T NEED ADDITIONAL SUSTENANCE.

"I didn't think about that, but I suppose it makes sense. Is there a—I don't know—physical limit to these augments? I don't particularly want to be ten feet tall, and I definitely don't want so much muscle it hinders my movement. Speed is sometimes the only thing that's kept me alive."

THERE ARE NO LIMITS NECESSARILY, BUT IF YOU GAIN TOO MUCH MUSCLE THAT YOUR MOVEMENT, DEXTERITY, AND SPEED DECREASE, YOU COULD THEN INCREASE YOUR HEIGHT TO EVEN IT OUT.

"Wow! No limits? But, surely there's only so many nanites I can fit into my body."

YES, BUT IT COULD TAKE DECADES TO GATHER THAN MANY NANITES. EVEN WITH THE NANITES GRANTED FROM MY MOTHER AND WHAT YOU ALREADY HAD, IT IS BARELY A FRACTION OF WHAT YOU WOULD NEED TO REACH THAT STAGE. THOUGH, IF

YOU DID REACH THAT STAGE, YOU WOULD EFFECTIVELY BE A NANITE CONSTRUCT MORE THAN HUMAN.

Jared shuddered at the idea of converting to a machine and decided to shelve that conversation for a later date. "Is there a way to specify how tall or how much muscle I want? The percentage thing makes it hard to guess."

ONCE YOU UNDERSTAND THE NANITES YOURSELF, YOU CAN INFLUENCE THEM TO A GREATER DEGREE, BUT YOU MUST INCREASE YOUR MIND ATTRIBUTES FIRST. SPECIFICALLY, YOUR INTELLIGENCE.

"So, you're saying I'm too dumb to understand and control them?"

PRECISELY.

Jared blinked in response to Scarlet's brutally honest answer. "You know there's a word called tact?"

YES.

Jared's mouth resembled a fish, opening and closing. He had no response to her comments, and though she was absolutely right, it stung a little to be reprimanded by a creature that was barely taller than his ankle just a few days prior. Overcoming his shock, Jared chose to ignore the snarky attitude...for now.

"I think I'll get used to this new body before making any more changes. It feels a little strange being taller." Jared busied himself getting ready and ensuring he had all of his gear on him before saying, "We need to get moving and find a safer place to camp. I'm guessing I'll be out for several days again if I assign the nanites from your mother, and we can't afford that down in these tunnels. At least, not in this wide-open area."

Before heading out, Jared searched through some of the bone piles, hoping to find something worth salvaging when he remembered the other explorer, the other Scarlet, might have had another phase pistol with her. It took a few minutes to find the boots and the rest of her body. Nothing was where it'd been before. No doubt, more evidence of Alestrialia's rampage after he'd stolen her egg.

"Aha!" Jared exclaimed, his search unearthing a beat-up, mostly depleted phase pistol.

Two phase pistols. Who was this explorer that she'd have two? Was she even an explorer? Was she from the cities, perhaps?

It made sense until he remembered her journals and the tags she'd left around the city. Cleary, she lived in the area for some time based on the number of places she'd visited, so he ruled out the possibility of her being from one of the floating cities.

"Scarlet? Do you have any of the memories from her?" Jared pointed to the resting place of Scarlet.

I HAVE IMPRESSIONS AND FEELINGS, BUT NO FULL MEMORIES TO RECONSTRUCT HER LIFE. FOR INSTANCE, THE WEAPON YOU JUST FOUND, I FELT THAT IT BELONGED TO HER, BUT NOTHING MORE.

Perhaps if they retraced the explorer's steps, they'd find out where she came from. For now, Jared shoved these thoughts to the back of his mind and put the second phase pistol into his pack. He preferred to use the newer one that had a fresh battery pack.

"All right, let's go. I don't know about you, but I'm ready to hunt for more nanites! I feel incredible, and with these phase pistols we should be able to take on any creatures down here."

I THINK WE SHOULD BE CAREFUL. THERE ARE SOME VERY NASTY CREATURES MY MOTHER KILLED, AND EVEN MORE THAT REFUSED TO COME NEAR WHILE SHE WAS HERE. WITH HER DEPARTED, WE MIGHT BECOME THE PREY.

"Hopefully it takes a while for the smarter creatures to learn of her departure. Between the changes we've both gone through, I think we can handle quite a bit. Though we should assign the rest of our nanites soon. The faster we grow in strength, the safer we'll be."

Jared climbed to the top of the crater and looked down the tunnel. Aside from the added destruction caused by Alestrialia, it was the same path he'd taken when first entering the sub-level.

"Keep an eye on the ceiling. Last time I came through this area I killed some kind of lizard clinging to the roof."

They walked nearly a mile when the scene of his last battle revealed only a skeleton of the creature he killed.

Picked clean in just a few days.

Jared increased his vigilance in case more of the creatures lurked nearby. Several paces from the bones, a half-buried door led to another section of the tunnel. He'd missed it before in his haste to get away.

Holstering his pistols, Jared bent down and braced his feet against the wall to move a large block of concrete. He expected it would take a significant effort to move the large slab, but it shifted out of the way abruptly launching him headfirst into the wall.

"Son of a..." Jared groaned and grabbed his head. He gingerly pressed his fingers to the wound, inspecting for blood. His hand came away clean, but he heard Scarlet make the weird huffing, wheezing noise again. Jared whipped his head around to glare.

"Ugh," he groaned. "That was a mistake." The movement sent a spike of pain through him and his vision clouded with stars. "I think it'll take time for me to get used to this new strength."

His temples throbbed in time to his heart and he sat against the wall to collect himself.

"I...need a minute. Please keep watch. That was a lot of noise, and it might've attracted attention to us."

Thankfully, it didn't attract any notice, and several minutes later Jared resumed excavating the buried door. Only this time, he was careful not to underestimate his strength. His head still ached, but it was at least manageable, for now. The debris cleared, Jared yanked open the door to an ear-piercing screech as the rusted hinges protested the movement.

"Dangit," hissed Jared.

He froze, straining his ears for any signs they'd been made. Just as he thought they were in the clear, he heard skittering and shrieks emanate down the hallway. He slammed the door shut and put his back to it as a thump shook the door.

Jared jumped when a deafening roar split the air. He whipped his head around to see Scarlet face off against three mutant lizards.

"Scarlet, watch out!"

A fourth creature prepared to leap onto her back, but rather than jump back, Scarlet lunged at the nearest lizard and clamped her jaws on its throat. Jared whipped out his phase pistol and fired at the creature dropping from the ceiling. It was the first time he'd used a weapon like this, and he wasn't sure what to expect. Surprisingly, there was no recoil and his over-compensation made him score only a glancing hit, sending the overgrown lizard cartwheeling away from them. It also served to attract the rest of the lizards his way, giving Scarlet time to defend herself.

The banging against the door sent reverberations through his back. The scratching and angry chittering coming from behind him made him shiver. Whatever existed beyond desperately wanted out. Bracing his feet against a pile of debris, he kept his back to the door and pulled out his Colt to fend off the remaining lizards.

After Scarlet downed her first attacker, she focused on the injured enemy Jared had shot. He tried to quickly eliminate a third, but it dodged out of the way. Pulling his arm back, he rocketed a fist into the creature's face as it descended toward him. Its head snapped back with a sickening crunch, its head imploding. The lizard's forward momentum arrested, the creature's corpse somersaulted backward.

Unfortunately for Jared, bits of brain matter obeyed the laws of physics and splattered across his body. The hot remnants of flesh reeked of decay, and blood oozed down his face, temporarily blinding him. Furiously wiping his face, Jared had no time to assess the damage or if he'd killed the creature when the remaining lizard clamped its jaws around his extended forearm.

Jared sucked in a sharp breath as a line of fire ignited along the length of his forearm. His arm spasmed, but he forced the pain away and focused on surviving the next few seconds. He twisted his phase pistol around and unloaded three energy beams point-blank into the lizard's head. It exploded in a gout of blood and brains. Thankfully it wasn't as gory as his first encounter with these lizards. He'd used his Colt then, and the ballistic round made the head pop like an over-ripe melon. In contrast, the phase round cauterized the wounds. Although, enough blood and gore shot outward to raise bile in the back of his throat.

The immediate threat gone, he searched for the one he'd punched to see it twitching where it had crashed into a column. Before he finished the creature off, Scarlet's tail pierced the creature through the neck spraying blood against the wall.

"Scarlet, please help me hold this shut! I need to get a bandage on my arm. It's bleeding too much, and I'm starting to feel woozy."

Scarlet rushed over, a violent crash against the door making him scoot back several inches. It sounded like a horde of creatures chittering on the other side.

"I don't think these are lizards."

Scarlet took his place, and Jared propped some loose rubble

against the door to keep the creatures from getting out. Then he grabbed a medical kit from his pack and wrapped his arm as quickly as he could. Thanks to the nanites coursing through his body, he'd didn't worry about infections, but the loss of blood could make him pass out. Two deep puncture wounds spurted blood everywhere, thanks to the lizard's fangs. He'd need to change the bandage again after their fight, but he hoped his nanites would stem the blood loss quickly.

"Okay, Scarlet. I'm ready. The rubble should hold it closed for a little while if you stand back. I'll try and take them out through the crack in the—"

The upper part of the door shattered on impact, angry rat muzzles sniffing the air.

"On second thought…"

To buy them some time, Jared walked closer, placed the muzzle of his phase pistol to the crack and squeezed the trigger a few times. Muffled screeches and cries of rage assaulted his ears. The creatures' rampage intensified, and Jared had to help Scarlet hold them back.

"Can you breathe fire yet? I mean, now that you're bigger? It'll probably help more than phase rounds and that way I can save some ammo."

I...I WILL TRY.

Scarlet hesitated and took a tentative step forward. This was the first time she'd attempted to breathe fire, and Jared understood the trepidation. Standing a few paces away from the crack in the door, they observed grotesque muzzles, dripping blood and saliva, from what looked like rats peeking through the crack.

Scarlet took a deep breath that sounded like a high-pitched whine. The sound cut off suddenly as Scarlet's roar split the air once again, echoing down the tunnel. Her roar transitioned into a whoosh of air, an orange gout of fire streaming from her maw.

A terrible cacophony of cries and shrieks filled the air as the rodents roasted alive. Scraping claws and thrashing bodies painted a ghastly picture in Jared's mind. It took fifteen minutes for the last of the moans and whimpers to stop, but once all the creatures died, everything returned to silence save for the sizzling flesh on the other side.

Jared looked at Scarlet in awe and watched steam and smoke coiling around her head. She stepped back, winded from the endeavor, and sat on her haunches.

"That was amazing!"

I NEED TO REST. THAT HURT, A LOT. I—IT HURT MUCH MORE THAN I EXPECTED.

Jared creased his brow. "Are you sure you're okay?" Jared asked, concerned. "We can retreat and leave this area if you need rest."

I JUST NEED A FEW MINUTES.

"Take all the time you need. I'll finish off any creatures still alive."

Jared walked to their makeshift barricade and shoved the huge slab of concrete away once again, marveling at his new strength. The debris cleared, he opened the door to survey the damage.

Carnage. Absolute carnage. Everywhere.

"Whoa."

Jared stumbled back and retched. His stomach clenched as if an invisible fist squeezed it tight. Bile burned the back of his throat, adding to the discomfort. The mutilated creatures looked like rats the size of dogs. Half a dozen lay in smoldering pools of liquified fat, all hair singed from their bodies. The shriveling rat fur created an acrid smell that burned his eyes. What remained of their maws showed a row of serrated yellow teeth that secreted viscous green fluid.

Their feet ended in claws several inches long. The corridor bore witness to their passing as claw marks covered every inch of the floor and lower walls. Along with the creatures they killed, piles of bones resembling rats littered the space.

His breathing came in ragged gasps as he fought for control of his gag reflex. This was the single most disgusting scene he'd ever seen by a long shot. Jared carefully picked his way through the small entrance, doing his best to avoid the pools of steaming liquid. After he passed the smoking corpses, Jared looked further down the corridor and froze. A pair of beady red eyes glared at him. A lone rat, untouched by the fire, crouched at the far end of the tunnel. Jared's hackles rose as he stared at the eerily quiet sentry. He glanced around the corridor nervously and imagined another horde of rats clawing their way from the shadows.

"Scarlet, I hope you're feeling better since we might have more company soon."

I DO NOT THINK I CAN BREATHE FIRE FOR A WHILE YET, BUT I CAN FIGHT.

The creepy rat remained poised at the far end of the tunnel, its eyes drilling holes into him.

Distractedly, Jared said, "Before we go, we should figure out how to absorb the nanites from these things. Actually—should we absorb them? You said we might gain abilities from some creatures, and I don't particularly want to gain an ability from either of these creatures."

He looked from the congealed puddles of fat to the lizards' mutilated bodies and cringed.

TOUCH THEM TO ABSORB THE NANITES. I HAVE ALREADY ABSORBED SOME FROM THE LIZARDS SINCE I KILLED THEM WITH MY TEETH, BUT I WON'T KNOW IF I'VE GAINED AN

ABILITY UNTIL I HAVE TIME TO ANALYZE THEIR NANITES.

Without preamble, Jared walked over to the lizards he killed and placed his hand against their rough, slimy skin. A soft glow swirled out of the bodies and into his hand, similar to what he'd experienced when Alestrialia transferred her essence over. The volume of nanites from these lizards was negligible in comparison. The brief swirl of color felt like an illusion, as it was over the moment it began. Just like that, he leeched the last vestiges of life from them.

After he finished absorbing the nanites, he walked back to the corridor and steeled himself for what came next. Keeping his eyes trained on the living statue down the hall, Jared placed a tentative finger into the still smoldering heaps of rats. His finger sank into the gooey flesh and Jared had to fight back convulsions. As quickly as possible, he finished absorbing the nanites and moved on.

The lone rat sat motionless in its vigil as Jared stalked forward, raising his phase pistol. Right before he squeezed the trigger, the rat let out a shrill cry, the phase round silencing its howl. He paused to listen, and a low droning buzz reached his ears. An avalanche of skittering and scraping claws on concrete announced the arrival of a massive horde of carnivorous rats. The noise escalated as dozens of rats rounded the corner at a full gallop.

Oh sh...

"Scarlet, run!" Jared screamed at the top of his lungs.

Even as he yelled, Jared extricated his second phase pistol from his pack and unloaded dual streams of phase rounds into the mass of rats. The initial volley slowed their rampage, but he knew it wouldn't last long. Backpedaling to the entrance, he kept up a steady barrage of fire at the incoming horde. Forcing himself to remain calm, Jared made sure each round found its mark. With so many rodents crowding the corridor, it wasn't a difficult task.

Scarlet, get ready to slam the door as soon as I make it through. Jared switched to Telepathy because the noise from the massive pack of rats had reached a deafening level, and it took every ounce of willpower he could muster to keep up the volley and not turn tail and run.

Wait!

The rats earned every inch with their blood as the phase pistols sent rays of death streaking at them. Several seconds later, the older phase pistol clicked empty.

NOW!

Scarlet slammed the door just as half a dozen of the creatures jumped at the opening, knocking the door off one of its hinges.

"Crap. We've got to move. This won't hold them. Brace it while I reload."

Another violent crash on the other side made the door bend outward, shaking debris loose around its frame.

"Dang, never mind. We need to buy some time to get away."

Hurriedly, Jared shoved every piece of refuse and concrete he could find in front of the destroyed sheet of metal, turned on his heel, and sprinted down the tunnel. His target was the staircase he'd used on his first trek into the sub-level. With the high ground, the rats shouldn't pose as big a threat.

Before they rounded the corner, the door flew off its hinges, and the horde of rats surged forth. His jaw dropped at the sight. It looked like a demon legion of rats clawing their way to freedom. Committed to his plan, there was nothing else he could do but hope and pray he'd not made a fatal error.

If those creatures catch us... The hair on the back of his neck stood on end. *I don't want to find out!*

"Hurry!" Jared shouted.

Head down, he didn't dare look behind him as he focused on

each step, fleeing down the tunnel. Spotting the stairs, he took them four at a time with Scarlet close on his heels.

"When we get to the top, I need to reload my phase pistols. If any of them get too close, knock them back until I'm ready."

As he climbed the stairs, Jared slid his pack off his back and fished for the black ballistic case holding the fresh battery packs. Jamming them into place, he thanked whatever fate smiled upon them that the dead explorer had these weapons. Without them, they'd be dead already.

The rats slowed just enough at the base of the stairs and allowed him to reload. Feeling a moment of jubilation at their narrow escape, Jared whooped and yelled, "Target practice!"

He got to work, picking them off one at a time, aiming as quickly and carefully as he dared. As he killed the creatures, several of them reverted to cannibalism and ripped into their dead allies with abandon. The sounds of tearing flesh and the squelching of blood from the rats feasting made him queasy, but it provided a needed distraction and allowed him to shower them with deadly phase rounds. The bodies piled up, yet more and more of the rats rounded the corner.

There must be hundreds of these things.

Finally, the endless stream of rats ended, and Jared adjusted fire to target rats further down the stairs. It served as a great diversionary tactic, since the rats didn't care whose body they gorged on.

"Scarlet, is there anything you can throw at them?"

Instead of answering him, a human-sized chunk of concrete spiraled into the midst of the feral rats.

"Yes! Keep going!"

No sooner had he whooped in delight when he felt a trickle of rocks pelt him in the head and glanced up.

"Whoa! Whoa, wait! This whole area will collapse!"

Suddenly, his phase pistol's hissed and stopped firing. Confused, Jared looked at the batteries and saw he had half a charge left in each of them.

Why is it—

It was then he noticed a red light flashing on the side of the gun. With no time to figure out why they'd stopped, Jared holstered the weapons and drew his Colt. He fired the six shots in rapid succession tearing holes through the creatures and making them pause in their mad dash up the stairs. All his guns rendered useless, Jared readied himself to face the rats with the only weapon he had left, his body.

With just a few seconds to catch his breath before the critters reached him, Jared centered his mind and prepared to fight for his life.

The first rat lunged at him, and he booted it into the ceiling. It dropped into the crowd below, its previous allies ripping it to shreds.

Legs and arms flashing forward, Jared realized his efforts wouldn't be enough. Right before a rat would've landed on his head, Scarlet's tail flashed by, punching holes through the creature. The body dropped to his feet, creating the start of a barrier in front of him. The pile of bodies in front of him quickly grew and restricted his movements. At this point, his kicks and punches only served to push the rats back down the stairs a few paces.

"Scarlet, I'm out of options here."

Switch places with me.

Launching a couple more punches to give him space, he jumped back, and Scarlet surged into his spot. She wasted no time and became a whirlwind of death and destruction, head and tail darting back and forth wreaking havoc on the rats. She tore throats out, gouged eye sockets, and skewered the rats like kabobs. Transfixed by Scarlet's deadly dance, Jared watched in awe as the rats failed miserably in the pursuit of their next meal.

Focus Jared! I cannot do this forever.

Snapping out of his stupor, he quickly reloaded his Colt. His phase pistols were still blinking the angry red, so the revolver would have to do. Leaning to the side and waiting for an opening, Jared fired into the attacking rats. At the same time, he glimpsed a view below and realized they'd almost vanquished all the rats.

"We're almost there, Scarlet! There's only about a dozen left."

He aimed carefully, making sure he didn't hit Scarlet, and squeezed the trigger. Again, he reloaded and fired into the last few rats. Just to be safe, he reloaded a third time and waited for any last-minute heroes to emerge. A few moments of tense silence announced the end of their desperate battle. Jared exhaled in relief and slumped to the ground. Scarlet plopped down next to him, her sides heaving as she caught her breath. Recovering from the ordeal, Jared stood up to survey the butchery.

Ratmageddon.

That's what it looked like to Jared. Heaps of dead rodents, blood flowing freely down the stairs, and the entire area looking like a blood bomb exploded. He and Scarlet looked like walking nightmares, covered head to toe in bits of flesh.

"I hate rats!" declared Jared. "Filthy, disgusting creatures. Mindless walking infections. Do you know rats wiped out entire populations before? They carry all kinds of diseases. Well, at least they used to before these nanites invaded everything."

Jared prattled on about his extreme dislike of rates, while kicking out at the pile of bodies surrounding them, sending half a dozen carcasses tumbling.

Scarlet stood and interrupted his hate-filled speech. We need

TO MOVE. ALL THIS BLOOD WILL ATTRACT WORSE CREATURES THAN RATS.

"Ugh," Jared groaned. "We need to find someplace to rest soon. I don't know how much more I can take."

ABSORB THE NANITES FROM AS MANY OF THESE AS YOU CAN, AND WE NEED TO LEAVE THE AREA.

Jared looked at the creatures in disgust as he tried finding a clean place on his disgusting pants to wipe his hands. Removing yet another destroyed shirt, he used it to wipe his face and hands of gore.

"I'm ready. Let's head back to the same corridor where these things came from. I'm willing to bet we killed the entire den, and we might find some respite there."

Besides the single rat he'd killed at the bend in the corridor, he saw no other rats and heard nothing to indicate there were more. Just to be safe, he checked his phase pistols, only to see the red light still shining. Frowning and hoping he hadn't broken them, he double-checked his Colt to see he had a full chamber.

"It looks like we killed the last of them, but keep your guard up just in case."

Prepared for an encounter, they rounded the corner. An awful, fetid scent blasted him full in the face, curling his nose hairs.

The corridor opened into a massive room where rat remains, bones, garbage, and every conceivable kind of waste littered the space. Mounds of bones served as impromptu dens and molted rat fur covered every inch.

"I don't care how tired I am. There is no way we're resting in here," Jared said with a nasally voice. He'd pinched his nostrils together to help with the smell, but unfortunately, he could also taste the noxious fumes.

LOOK FOR ANOTHER EXIT TO THIS PLACE.

"Let's start on the left and work our way around. Stay together, who knows what might live in here."

Picking their way around the room, they navigated to the back corner and saw nothing that suggested another way out, aside from small holes with claw marks punctuating the sides of the room.

"I'm guessing that's how the rats got in and out of here," Jared said, pointing to the small holes. "I don't see another way out--"

An ear-splitting screech smashed into Jared's mind, dropping him to his knees. He grabbed his head while Scarlet whined and squeezed her eyes shut. The thunderous shriek pierced his skull and left his ears ringing. Shaking his head to clear it, he looked towards the only entrance, or exit, to the room and found a huge wall of fur blocking the passage.

It stood on its hind legs and screeched again. The shrill noise stabbed into his brain and he groaned against the pain. Standing at ten feet tall on its hind legs, a massive, black rat screamed in impotent rage at these two intruders. No doubt they smelled of its smaller brethren, further inciting the rage of the behemoth. Its red eyes burned holes into them. Its jaw, filled with massive canine-like teeth, radiated a cloud of green fumes.

Screaming in rage, the truck-sized rodent mutation rushed them.

The blood drained from Jared's face, and an empty feeling formed in his gut.

What have we done?

05 BOSS FIGHT

"**S**carlet, move!" Jared screamed, diving to the side. He barely evaded the overgrown mountain of fur. Glancing behind him in mid-flight, he saw Scarlet narrowly avoid the rat.

He hit the ground with a crunch of bone. Thankfully, not his bones, but a pile of bones and flesh in various stages of decomposition. He felt a sharp jab into his shoulder as a shard of bone broke off and embedded itself into his flesh.

Jared rotated his arm, and the bone caught between his shoulder blade and rotator cuff. Rather than delay the inevitable, he reached behind him and ripped out the bone before he second-guessed himself.

The edges of his vision blurred from the pain. Scalding blood trickle down his back, soaking through his shirt. Ignoring the pain, Jared moved his arm, the bone no longer constricting his movement. Mobility and staying alive was worth the added pain.

Scarlet, we need to avoid this thing while I shoot from a distance. I don't think either of us will survive in a physical confrontation with it.

Scarlet acknowledged his mental communications and darted

away. Meanwhile, Jared freed his Colt and fired six rounds in rapid succession. The bullets definitely hit the thing, but he couldn't tell where. They seemed to disappear inside the layer of fur. The only reason he knew he hadn't missed was it whirling about to chase him down.

Fishing a few rounds from his pocket, he reloaded on the run, careful to avoid more piles of bones. If he slipped and fell, he was dead. The ground bounced as the rat pursued him around the room. Three rounds loaded, Jared risked a glance behind him and fired a round into the creature's face. Two of the rounds missed, but the third punched through one of its eyes.

The giant rat screamed again, piercing his mind and leaving a throbbing headache in its wake. He didn't know how much more he could take before passing out from the mental assault. The only saving grace to the headache was the sight of this massive rat stopping dead in its tracks as it pawed furiously at the injured eye. Taking advantage of the situation, Jared quickly reloaded his weapon.

Before he could fire more rounds into the creature's face, it looked at him with its good eye, burning an even brighter shade of red.

It charged like a bull.

Again, Jared dove to the side, but this time he wasn't as lucky, and the thing scored a gash along the length of his leg spilling blood everywhere.

The rat's momentum carried it several yards past him before it skidded to a stop. The furious scrape of its claws echoed around the room as it scrambled for purchase to charge him again. Jared tried standing, but collapsed, his leg unwilling to support him. Worse, he felt a searing pain rip through his back and leg. Looking down, he saw maggots as thick as his fingers, with sharp teeth ripping into his flesh where blood flowed freely.

Unable to stop himself, Jared dry-heaved wishing he had something in his stomach as his body tried to vomit his intestines.

Scarlet, help!

I'M COMING, HANG ON!

Scarlet bounded over from across the room and made short work of the filthy maggots feasting on his flesh. At that point, the rat finished its turn and sped toward them.

BOOM, BOOM, BOOM. Six shots, fired in rapid succession, drilled a hole into the creature's remaining eye. Blinded and dazed, the rat plunged forward at maximum speed intent on destroying everything in its wake.

GRAB MY TAIL!

Jared did as he was told without question, and Scarlet leapt out of the way, carrying Jared with her. It wasn't enough. Jared's lower half was still in the path of the rat, and he felt bones shatter as the creature barreled over him.

Intense agony and numbness caused Jared's vision to dim as the pain threatened to send him into oblivion.

Not yet. Not yet.

Through sheer force of will, Jared kept himself conscious, but only just.

The blinded rat continued its rampage across the room, destroying anything in its path until it ran full speed into the wall. A sickening splat and crunch of bone sounded through the room, and the creature came to an abrupt stop.

"We...need...to...leave," Jared wheezed as he looked across the room and saw hundreds—if not thousands—of maggots writhing across the floor towards the downed rat.

YOU NEED TO ABSORB ITS NANITES FIRST. Scarlet walked toward the creature, but Jared called out after her.

"Scarlet, I can't walk." Jared looked down at his mangled legs. Blood poured freely from several deep gashes, and bones protruded at random intervals. "My legs..."

His mind nearly shut down from pain as exhaustion and shock set in.

CLIMB ON MY BACK.

Jared didn't respond.

JARED!

The shout, accompanied by a telepathic slap to the face, jolted Jared out of his dazed state.

"Wha...?"

CLIMB. ON. MY. BACK. Scarlet commanded.

Jared numbly obeyed and inched his way onto Scarlet's back. The pain threatened to overwhelm him, but it was distant. He felt distant. *Numb.*

Jared knew something was wrong, but he couldn't bring himself to care. He dragged himself onto Scarlet's back only because he couldn't disobey the demanding voice. His legs dangled uselessly behind him and Jared heard, more than he felt, bones rattling and scraping with every step that Scarlet took.

He also heard squelching noises as they walked across the room. Looking down despondently, he watched nonplussed as the maggots popped like zits, pus and green goo shooting out of their bodies. His mind screamed at him to react, but it refused to take hold, and all he could do was cling desperately to Scarlet's back. Even that effort of will felt pointless.

When she drew alongside the rat, Scarlet told Jared to reach out and touch it. Not understanding why, he obeyed, and a curious iridescent glow roiled around his body.

As soon as the process finished, Scarlet set off through the tunnel. They passed the ruined corpses of the rats Scarlet had deep-fried, and she dashed through the sub-level looking for someplace to rest and recover. Throughout the process, Jared faded in and out of awareness. He noted the occasional hallway, lights peeking through from above, and even the distant noise of creatures battling. However, everything rolled off his mind.

HANG ON JARED! Scarlet pleaded, her voice the only tether Jared had to the present; the only thing that kept him anchored to her back as she urged him to hold tight.

Sometime later, Jared felt Scarlet lower herself to the ground.

YOU CAN LET GO.

"Finally," Jared breathed, releasing his death grip on her shoulders, and sliding to the ground. Before he hit the ground, darkness enveloped him.

JARED. JARED.

"Who is it?" grumbled Jared, irritated at being woken.

JARED, WAKE UP!

His mind groggy, Jared opened his eyes and saw Scarlet's face peering at him from mere inches away.

Flinching, Jared answered, "I'm awake—"

He screamed. His entire body throbbed. It burned. He couldn't move or think.

His memories came back in a rush, and he looked down to see his crushed legs. The bleeding had stopped, but the damage to his legs was extensive.

YOU NEED TO ASSIGN YOUR NANITES NOW.

"Where—where are we?"

Jared looked around what looked like a small closet with barely enough room for the two of them. The door opened inward, and

Scarlet's body rested against it, acting as a barrier from any would-be assailants.

IT IS SAFE, AND THAT IS ALL YOU NEED TO KNOW. NOW ASSIGN YOUR NANITES BEFORE IT IS TOO LATE!

"Okay, okay!" Jared said, clearly still irritated and groggy from sleep.

He opened his status screen and quickly made some adjustments.

"Thank you for saving me, Scarlet," Jared said as he moved the sliders around. "I don't remember much after the rat shattered my legs."

YOU WERE IN SHOCK FROM BLOOD LOSS AND PAIN. I WAS— YOU ALMOST DIDN'T MAKE IT.

Jared felt fear and sadness pulse through their bond and knew she was scared to lose him. It warmed him, and he returned the feeling as best he could, the bond still a curious thing to him.

"I'm sorry, Scarlet. I'm supposed to be the one protecting you from danger," Jared said angrily with a note of shame. "How can I protect you if I can't even survive a fight with a stupid rodent?"

YOU PROTECTED ME. IF NOT FOR YOU, WE BOTH WOULD HAVE DIED IN THERE. JARED, PLEASE FINISH ASSIGNING THE NANITES. IF YOU WAIT MUCH LONGER, YOU MAY NEVER WALK AGAIN.

Never walk again.

The thought scared him into action and he put everything else from his mind to focus on his status screen.

"It looks like we didn't get a lot of nanites from all those rats and lizards we killed. Even the big rat only gave us a small amount."

AS YOU POINTED OUT, THEY WERE STUPID RODENTS,

POSSIBLY THE LEAST DANGEROUS PREDATOR IN THE CITY.

Jared went back to studying the status screen and all the options he had available. He understood the urgency of the situation, but he also wanted to ensure he chose strategically. Many of these changes would be irreversible.

In the end, Jared chose to increase mostly physical attributes, with fifteen percent of what he had available into *Enhanced Senses* and *Perception*.

Jared finished making his choices and shared with Scarlet.

JARED — NANITES AVAILABLE: 90%

BODY

<u>Physical Augmentation</u>

Physical Defense

Skin Hardening - 10%

Natural Armor - 10%

Body Manipulation

Regeneration - 25%

Density - 20%

<u>Physical Enhancement</u>

Reflex - 5%

Speed - 5%

MIND

<u>Brain Augmentation</u>

Enhanced Senses - 5%

Perception - 10

DID YOU CONFIRM THE SELECTIONS?

"Yes, I..."

SLEEP.

Immediately, Jared's vision faded, and sleep welcomed him in its embrace. Consciousness fading in and out, Jared lost track of time. After what seemed an eternity, Jared finally awoke.

"Scarlet?" She raised her head to look at him. "How long was I out?"

FIVE DAYS.

"Holy crap, why so long?"

Scarlet dipped her head and Jared swore he saw chagrin on her face. I KEPT YOU ASLEEP UNTIL THE NANITES FINISHED HEALING YOUR LEGS.

"My legs." Jared looked down and pulled his tattered pant legs up. They looked whole again. He found no cuts, obtrusions, or even bruising. "Wow. That's awesome!"

Jared traced a finger along a line of pink flesh where the rat had sliced it open. Feeling the length of his legs, he found them completely healed and...*harder?*

They still very much felt like flesh, but tougher, less tactile. Pressing his thumb down, he watched as the skin flexed, but felt only a pressure when he dug in his nail.

Curious about the differences between *Skin Hardening*, *Natural Armor*, and *Density*, Jared pulled up their description.

SKIN HARDENING

Increases the resiliency and durability of flesh, making it harder to penetrate

NATURAL ARMOR

Creates a nanite barrier, protecting against any foreign invasion

DENSITY

Increases the molecular density of muscle and bone, resulting in harder and stronger skeletal and muscular framework

"I really love all this enhancement stuff! We're going to be invincible." Jared exclaimed.

Be careful Jared. I need not remind you, you felt the same way just a few days ago, yet you nearly died from a rat. A rat!

Jared pursed his lips and glanced at Scarlet with narrowed eyes.

I was just stating a fact, you—

Jared held up a hand to cut her off. "I get it. I'm not invincible, and there are much stronger creatures in the world. Still, you have to admit that all this nanite stuff is pretty awesome. I mean look at me! My legs were crushed, and now I'm whole and well. Not even the best doctors back home could've done something like that, let alone in five days."

Yes. I have never seen anything like it. Even dragons cannot heal that quickly, though we do heal at a faster rate than humans.

"Okay, I'm all set and feel like I could take on the world. How about we assign your nanites and let you rest? I'll keep watch while you change."

We need to move to a larger space first. I barely fit through the door as it is. Another transformation and I cannot leave the room.

Jared smacked his forehead. "Good point, I didn't even think about that."

He was about to leave the room when something on the other side caught his attention. Skirting around Scarlet, he prodded the rubble with his foot and found a lockbox that looked intact. The letters on the side were indistinguishable, but he'd seen similar designs throughout this sub-level. He tried to open the lid, but it wouldn't budge. Jared grabbed a jagged scrap of metal nearby and jammed it into the crease of the box.

The lid refused to budge until he started bashing it with a chunk of concrete. With a hiss, the lid popped open.

Jared peered inside and saw several sealed packages, including a pair of utilitarian black pants and several black shirts.

A uniform? wondered Jared.

It didn't matter what they looked like at this point. Anything was better than the nasty rags he wore, and he'd already discarded his last shirt before the previous fight. At the same time, he didn't want to put clean clothes on his filthy body. Stripping off his pants, Jared flipped them inside out and furiously scrubbed his dirty body.

It wasn't the best way to clean off, but without any water or sand, it was the best option at the moment and he didn't want to walk around shirtless. His body as clean as he could get it, he threw them into a corner and donned the new outfit. The shirt was a little baggy, while the pants too snug, but it was better than nothing and he didn't complain.

Who cares? Jared shrugged. *I'm just happy to have clothes that'll protect me.*

"Okay, let's get out of here."

Jared paused at the threshold, a thought tickling the back of his mind. *Did my increased perception help me see that box?*

Shrugging, he stepped into the hallway, his Colt held in front of him as he surveyed the area. He looked around and noticed a layer of dust coating the floor. The only footprints were Scarlet's.

"Which way to the stairs?"

Follow me.

Jared followed Scarlet a short distance back the way they'd come. He sprinted up the stairs, shielding his eyes from the bright sunlight as he neared the top. Upon reaching the top, he stood in the warmth of the sun for several minutes, basking in its embrace and the freedom of the open air.

WE NEED TO MOVE; SOMETHING IS STALKING US.

Where? Jared asked in his mind, immediately going on the defensive but careful not to give away that he was aware or make any sudden movements.

I DO NOT KNOW FOR CERTAIN, BUT AS SOON AS WE EXITED I HEARD SHUFFLING, AND THE NOISE MOVED TO SEVERAL DIFFERENT POSITIONS THE PAST FEW MINUTES.

Let's head out of the city and see if it follows us. We can deal with it when there aren't so many places to hide.

Jared jogged back down the street towards his makeshift home. He stayed alert, listening for signs of something, or someone, following them. Sure enough, he could hear the slight shifts of rubble Scarlet described.

Scarlet, we'll skirt the city before heading away from it. I don't want to lead whatever is following us to where I've been sleeping.

They reached the outskirts of the city and headed north, following the perimeter. After they'd traveled about a mile, Jared walked towards a fallen bridge and started down its length. Reaching an exceptionally steep area, he turned around to descend, using the opportunity to scan behind him. What he saw made him pause.

A lithe figure darted behind a fallen piece of the road.

It's another explorer!

Jared hadn't seen another human being in over a year. He hadn't realized it before, but he ached to speak with another person. Acting as though nothing was amiss, he continued his descent.

Scarlet, there is another explorer following us, but they're probably afraid to approach with you nearby. Let's cross over to my shelter. I don't anticipate we'll stay there any longer after today anyway. In fact, it's probably best we get as far from this city as possible. The destruction caused by your mother might attract the cities' attention, and I don't want them to find out about you.

Two hours later, Jared entered his small shelter beneath the Statue of Liberty. Scarlet barely fit inside but managed to squeeze herself through the opening.

"I'll see if they want to confront me without you around," Jared said as he walked outside and sat on a boulder.

He waited for an hour before he heard a slight rustle and looked up to see a figure crouched on the roof of the structure.

"Hello, my name is Jared," he said, giving a friendly wave.

Jared winced at hearing his own voice. He bumbled like an idiot, his words coming out choppy. He was definitely lacking in social interaction these days, and for whatever reason, he felt more comfortable talking with Scarlet, a dragon, than his own kind.

"Hello?" Jared asked again. "Do you speak English?"

Crouched as they were and wearing a balaclava, he couldn't tell if it was a skinny man, woman, or child. Several minutes passed, but they refused to speak. This small, unassuming person didn't appear a threat to him or Scarlet, but Jared remained wary just in case.

Scarlet, there might be more than one person, but I can't be certain. Please keep your senses on guard for anyone else approaching. For all I know, this small person could kick my butt, but for some reason, it strikes me as odd to see someone so small out solo.

"All right, suit yourself. I'm going inside before it gets dark," Jared said, walking back into the room. Half an hour later, the tiny person crept through the opening. As soon as the stranger passed the threshold and saw Scarlet, they drew their weapon on her.

"No!" Jared dove in front of Scarlet to protect her from the intruder. "Do not harm her!" Jared roared as he leveled his Colt at the intruder.

"B-b-but—it's a—"

"I know what she is. If you harm her, I *will* kill you." Jared warned, pulling the hammer back on his Colt. For emphasis.

The strange woman placed her weapon back in its holster and held up her hands. "I mean no harm. I—I've never seen a d-dragon before. It's a dragon, right?"

She. Yes, I am a dragon!

Scarlet rose from the corner and bared her wickedly sharp teeth at the newcomer.

The tiny woman grabbed her head and stumbled back in surprise. Her eyes darted between Scarlet and Jared in shock, unbelieving that she'd just heard a voice in her head.

All right, you've had your fun Scarlet, Jared said, a hint of amusement in his words.

Scarlet lay back down and closed her eyes, feigning disinterest, but Jared knew her senses were on high alert as she listened for other people nearby.

"That was Scarlet's way of saying she'll eat you if you try anything."

If Scarlet could smile, she would've had a malicious, ear-to-ear grin plastered on her face. She positively radiated smug satisfaction. Jared shook his head, a smile tugging at the corner of his lips.

The small woman stammered in fear, saying, "M-m-my name is Iliana."

She had a faint accent, but Jared couldn't quite place it and asked, "Where are you from?"

"I traveled from a survivor colony down south, near the Florida panhandle, at least what was left of it. Most of the coast along the gulf no longer exists. Earthquakes and erratic weather patterns are eroding the coast. I wouldn't be surprised if Florida eventually breaks off from the rest of the continent," explained Iliana.

"I've never traveled that far south. I think the furthest I've been is North Carolina," Jared stated. "What are you doing this far north?"

"I came in search of nanite injections. I'm almost out." The despair in her voice reminded Jared of his own desperate search just a short time ago, and although he wanted to help her out, he thought better of it. He didn't know this person or her intentions. Part of him wanted to tell her about the real reason they had to take a shot every few years, but caution prevailed, and he left it unspoken.

*What if...*an idea formed in the back of his mind, and Jared mentally nudged Scarlet to ask about it.

Scarlet, if she touched you, would you be able to project images to her like your mother did with me, or find out what her intentions are?

I CAN.

I think we need to find out why she's really here, and it might be the fastest way to make sure she's not a threat.

"Iliana, what are your plans? Will you stay here?"

"Well, based on the looks of this place and your gear, you've already been here for quite some time." She pointed to the phase pistol strapped to his side.

Jared berated himself for leaving it out to see.

"I imagine anything worth finding, you've already found. So, we—I—I'll move on, but I could use a place to rest tonight?" she said hopefully.

Jared feigned ignorance at her slip of pronouns confirming she wasn't alone. Pretending as if he hadn't notice, Jared sent Scarlet a mental confirmation of his suspicions.

"I have a request before I let you stay with us. Scarlet has a...unique way of communicating. She can project thoughts using telepathy. You already experienced one aspect of it. I'd like for you to speak with her to confirm your story."

"I have to touch her?"

Iliana sounded skeptical, but Jared reassured her and even shuffled over to sit next to Scarlet.

Slowly, Iliana inched her way closer and tentatively reached out to touch Scarlet. As soon as her hand made contact, Scarlet dove into her mind.

"Whoa!" Iliana broke contact and fell back on her butt.

"It's okay. It scared me at first too. I probably should've warned you to sit before you touched her."

With more confidence, she reached out her hand again and touched Scarlet on the tip of her snout. Scarlet dove into her thoughts again.

JARED, SHE IS AFRAID OF SOMETHING. IT IS HARD TO SEE, BUT SHE DOES NOT WANT US TO FIND OUT.

"Iliana, are you here by yourself?"

"Yes."

SHE IS NOT TELLING THE WHOLE TRUTH.

Jared amended his question and asked, "Did you come to this city by yourself?"

"Um, uh," stammered Iliana.

SHE'S NOT ALONE, JARED.

Alarm shot through Jared, and he drew his Colt. He'd not heard or seen anyone else, but it was possible Iliana kept them occupied long enough for them to sneak up on them.

Scarlet, can you hear or sense anyone else close by?

NO, BUT MY SENSES ARE STILL DEVELOPING, AND THIS

CONCRETE ROOM PREVENTS ME FROM SENSING VERY FAR.

"Where are your friends?" demanded Jared.

"I don't know."

Jared looked to Scarlet.

Truth.

"Won't they come looking for you?" Jared interrogated her, brandishing his Colt in front of her.

"Yes, b-but I d-didn't tell anyone where I was going. If they didn't see me leave the city, they—"

"Quiet!" Jared held up a hand to cut her off.

Did you hear that?

Yes, there is movement outside.

Jared wracked his brain for a way out of this predicament. They had no idea what these people wanted yet and if they had more firepower than Iliana, he and Scarlet might be in trouble.

"Iliana, why did you come to this city? The truth. You cannot lie to Scarlet." Jared pointed his Colt at her while she tried to hedge away from Scarlet. "Don't even think about it. Also, if any of your friends walk in here, I'll shoot first and ask questions later. Tell them to stay out."

Iliana pressed her lips into a thin line and narrowed her eyes. Jared cocked the hammer on his weapon once more.

"Now!"

"Loch..."

No one responded to her call.

"Call him again," Jared demanded.

"Loch!" A few seconds passed before a deep accented voice punctuated the silence.

"Iliana? Are you okay?"

"I am."

Jared shook his head at her and narrowed his eyes.

"I am fine for now. Stay out there. There's a man and a—"

Jared pressed the revolver against her head and whispered, "Say nothing about Scarlet."

"There's a man here named Jared. He wants you to stay out there until he finds out what we're doing here." Jared nodded his head at Iliana and lowered his weapon.

"Jared? My name is Loch. I'm in charge of our group here. We are explorers on a scavenging mission to find weapons and injectors."

"Why did you follow me here then? I'm not giving you any of my gear, and there's no other reason for you to sneak up on me unless you have ill intent."

Scarlet? Can you get a read on any of them, or Iliana here?

I can hear them talking outside. It is jumbled, but it sounds like they are discussing ways to get in here.

"Iliana, why did you follow me here?" asked Jared quietly, his voice promising violence if he didn't like the answer.

"I...I wanted to find out what she was," Iliana said, pointing to Scarlet.

Partial truth.

"Why else?"

Iliana looked nervous, her eyes darting back and forth between himself and the doorway.

Jared could see the calculation in her eyes, debating if she could make it through before he pulled the trigger.

"Don't even think about escaping. I promise you won't make it a single step before I shoot you or Scarlet bites you in half."

Jared watched her eyes widen in fear, and he heard an audible gulp as her shoulders dropped in defeat.

"We—we would've taken your gear from you," she said, deflated.

Jared's brain went into overdrive. He needed to find a way out of here, preferably without killing anyone. He had no qualms about killing mutated creatures, but he wouldn't kill another human being if he could help it.

Scarlet, I think we need to go on the offensive before they come up with a plan to storm this room.

Before she could answer, a deep bass voice called from outside.

"We've got you surrounded. Send Iliana out and no one needs to get hurt."

Time's up.

Jared needed to act before it was too late.

06 THE DAGGERS

What are we going to do, Scarlet?

Kɪʟʟ ᴛʜᴇᴍ.

Scarlet's response frightened Jared. Although, given the history of dragons with humans, it shouldn't. Still, it wasn't something he'd considered at all. He'd never killed another person, nor did he plan to unless forced into a situation where he had to defend himself or Scarlet.

We aren't killing them, Jared said with a note of finality. *I know you don't trust humanity yet, but if you haven't figured it out by now, I'm not a murderer.*

Aѕ ʏᴏᴜ ᴡɪѕʜ.

Jared knew she didn't approve, but thankfully would follow his lead.

Scarlet, can you stun them using telepathy? Like what your mom did when she spoke to me that first time?

I ᴄᴀɴ ᴛʀʏ, ʙᴜᴛ ᴍʏ ᴛᴇʟᴇᴘᴀᴛʜʏ ɪѕ ᴍᴜᴄʜ ᴡᴇᴀᴋᴇʀ. Aᴛ ᴛʜᴇ ᴠᴇʀʏ ʟᴇᴀѕᴛ ɪᴛ ѕʜᴏᴜʟᴅ ᴄᴏɴꜰᴜѕᴇ ᴛʜᴇᴍ.

"Wait!" Jared yelled to the people outside. "Iliana. How many companions do you have out there?"

She hesitated, clearly not wanting to answer the question. She flicked her eyes to the revolver in his hand and reluctantly answered.

"Four."

Can you put Iliana to sleep like you did with me?

Iliana slumped unceremoniously to the floor, and Scarlet stepped over her unconscious form.

We take them on the count of three. Don't use lethal force unless absolutely necessary.

Jared held up his fingers and slowly ticked them down. On one, he crouched and lunged for the door accompanied by a wave of psionic pressure he felt at the back of his mind. Thankfully, his bond with Scarlet shielded him from the mental assault, otherwise he'd be disoriented like their assailants.

Jared blurred into motion, his new strength and speed easily pushing beyond normal human limits. One blow was all it took to render each person unconscious. The closest assailant to the door was a tall six-foot, six-inch brute dual-wielding pistols. Even with his massive size, one punch to the temple was all it took to bring him toppling down. Looking around for the fourth, and final target, Jared found him crouched on top of the room he'd just left. The man recovered from Scarlet's mental assault and fired at him. Jared dove behind a rock as the bullet sent shards of rock flying on impact.

He heard the person scramble for a better position, but before they could fire another round, a wet slap and thump announced the arrival of Scarlet. Peeking from behind his cover, Jared saw Scarlet standing over the last member of the party.

"Scarlet, is he—"

HE IS ALIVE, Scarlet said tersely.

Jared could do nothing to appease Scarlet at the moment, nor was it a good time to address their disagreement. Jared gathered all of their weapons and gear into a pile, just inside his shelter. Their packs he set off to the side for inspection. One by one, he dragged their bodies into the room and tied their legs together using belts and straps from their own gear. The party of five seemed an unlikely group. However, a tattoo on each of their necks spoke of their involvement. It portrayed a dagger dipped in blood, surrounded by a tribal pattern with a nuclear hazard symbol encompassing the whole design.

Maybe it's a symbol for the group they belong to, thought Jared.

He'd ask about it once they woke up. In the meantime, he went through their packs and discovered a dozen boosters and dozens of boxes of ammunition. Jared thought back to Iliana's sob story about being low on nanites and reprimanded his naivety. She'd acted genuine, but from now on, Scarlet would fact check anyone's story.

"Looks like she lied to us Scarlet," Jared said, holding up the boosters for her to see. "I should've been more cautious from the start."

I KNOW YOU HAD GOOD INTENTIONS, WHETHER I AGREED WITH THEM OR NOT.

"Thank you, Scarlet. That means a lot to me. I've never encountered hostile explorers before and I...well, I didn't think something like this would happen."

Jared resumed his search through their gear and found a half-depleted battery pack for his phase pistol. Since none of them had phase weapons, they'd either stolen or found the battery during their escapades.

After searching through their gear, he leaned against the wall, letting the coolness of the stone seep into his back. The crowded room quickly becoming stuffy, and he wished there were some windows to generate a cross-breeze. Another thirty minutes passed before anyone stirred. The three Jared knocked unconscious were the first to recover, followed by Iliana. Jared worried that Scarlet underestimated her strength and permanently injured the last member of the party since he was still unconscious, but aside from a dislocated jaw, he looked fine.

The tied-up intruders quickly realized their predicament and started squirming to free themselves.

"Don't move, try nothing, and you make it out of this alive," Jared warned. "Iliana claims you came to explore the city for supplies, yet the moment you saw me, you abandoned that plan and followed me. Now, Iliana was already kind enough to spill the beans that you'd rob me and leave me defenseless, but I want to know why."

The three explorers glared at Iliana, promising retribution for giving away their plans, and she tried to defend herself. "I-I-It w-wasn't m-my f-f-fault. She read my mind."

Jared saw doubt and skepticism in their eyes as they darted a glance at Scarlet. Though none of their gazes lingered on her, and Jared didn't blame them. Scarlet stood on all fours, her horns and the spikes brushing the ceiling. A menacing expression cowed them into cooperation.

"Answer me!" Jared cocked the hammer back on his Colt. "You'd better start talking. From my perspective, you're just a group of thieves stealing from those who can't defend themselves. Worse, it's five against one."

Jared felt sick to his stomach. He hated acting like this and that he was holding humans hostage. His parents taught him to value life above all else, no matter who that person was. It's the same reason he'd never fought back against Tiny when he was a kid. If these *thieves* knew the turmoil in his mind, they'd try to attack and subdue him. Breathing deeply to calm his nerves, Jared repeated his question, clipping each word to make sure they got the point.

"Why. Are. You. Here?"

"We were just exploring the city!" Iliana exclaimed. "I wasn't lying when I told you that. We've been exploring every city from Florida up the East Coast."

"Following me is not exploring the city, and it doesn't explain why you wanted to steal from me," countered Jared.

"I already told you! I was just curious. I saw you walking around with—with that thing. I've seen nothing like her before and I thought—" Iliana stopped speaking.

"Thought what?" Jared pressed, letting his rage bubble to the surface. "Thought you'd waltz in here and pull your weapon on her? Kill her? Steal all my gear? Take the only things keeping me alive out here?" Jared narrowed his eyes and clenched his fist in anger.

"With that creature by your side, I thought maybe you were from the city."

"Do I look like I'm from the city?" Jared retorted. "Look at me! I'm hardly a display of good fortune. My gear is falling apart, and the only reason I have clean clothes is that I found some in a sealed container beneath the city just this morning."

"But your phase—"

"Which I also found," interrupted Jared. "Yes, I found it. Me!"

A muffled voice gurgled across the room and Jared turned to look at the speaker.

"Loch!" Iliana exclaimed and tried to move to his side.

"Stop!" Jared yelled. "No one moves. Got it?"

Loch tried boring holes through Jared with his gaze. Jared humored him, stared right back, and raised his revolver. He had to give the guy credit, Loch didn't flinch in the slightest with a weapon pointed at his head. Either he'd been in situations like this before or he was a superb actor. Based on Iliana's performance earlier, perhaps it was the latter. Finally, Loch consented and motioned for Iliana to speak.

Iliana narrowed her eyes at him, clearly outraged at not being able to tend to her comrade. To appease her somewhat, Jared said, "If none of you try to escape and you answer my questions, you will walk away from this alive. That is a promise whether you believe me or not. My quarrel is not with other explorers."

"Let me look at his jaw," said Iliana.

"Not yet. You'll answer my questions first. He's not bleeding. He'll survive."

Frustrated, Iliana returned to her seated position and began telling their story.

"We are—"

"Wait." Jared held up his hand.

"What are you—"

"I said wait!" Jared repeated.

Scarlet, I want you to tell me if she's lying.

SHE MUST TOUCH ME AGAIN.

"Iliana, please come next to Scarlet and place your hand on her," Jared commanded. "And no, I won't untie your feet. You can squirm your way over."

Iliana grunted and growled in frustration.

"Look, you should've thought twice about crossing me, especially after you found out I have a *dragon*." Jared enunciated the word to emphasize his point. He couldn't believe she'd wanted to confront a dragon given their intentions to steal from him.

They must be desperate, thought Jared. *Scarlet, when Iliana told us about only having one and a half months left for her injection, was she telling us the truth?*

Scarlet hesitated. SHE WAS. I DON'T—

I don't understand either. They clearly had enough in their packs, so I'm not sure why she didn't use one. We need to figure out what's going on here.

While Jared and Scarlet held their silent conversation, Iliana wormed her way across the floor and hesitantly placed her hand on Scarlet.

"Remember Iliana. You cannot lie to her. I want to know your whole story, starting with your names." Iliana looked at Loch again, but Jared raised the revolver, demanding that she continue.

"Don't look at him, look at me."

"All right, call down!" Iliana said, holding her bound hands up in a placating gesture. "My name is Iliana Harle, the man your *dragon* hit is Loch, my brother." She mimed air quotes at the mention of dragon, and Jared smirked at her denial. If they pissed Scarlet off enough, they'd learn a hard lesson.

"The big guy there is Jon Davis, the silent one is Lee Sakumota, and then you have Rob O'Neille." Iliana pointed out each person as she introduced them. "We've been exploring cities all the way from Florida up the East Coast."

"You said that already. Tell me why and what you want with my injectors when you already have more than enough for the five of you." Iliana darted her eyes at Loch once again.

Jared sighed in irritation. "No, don't look at Loch. If you try to lie, Scarlet will detect it, and Loch gets a round through the head. Do we understand each other?" Jared raised the gun again and Iliana nodded her head.

"We've been looking for my nanite injections, weapons, and ammunition for our fraternity," explained Iliana.

"That symbol on your neck? That's for your fraternity?"

"Yes, we call ourselves the Daggers."

"How many of you are there?" Jared grew concerned thinking there might be more of them in the area. "Better yet, how many of you are here right now? In this city."

"There are forty-three of us, but only the five of us came north. Another party went west, but the bulk of our people are back at the camp in the northern part of Florida."

"Camp? You don't live in a colony?"

"Many of us are exiles of the colonies," she replied.

Jared grew alarmed, and it must've shown in his face because Iliana was quick to add.

"Whoa, Whoa, calm down. It's not what you think! The leaders at our colony think everyone should work for the greater good of the colony and that means helping with resource harvesting to keep a steady supply of needed items and injectors coming from the cities. When we refused to help and instead set out to explore, they told us to never come back, and they would no longer give us anything, injectors included. That's how most of us ended up exiled, because we wanted adventure."

"So, what? You plan to use the weapons and ammo to go after your colony?" Jared's voice turned menacing as he thought about these people taking the lives of other humans. Jared exhaled, calming himself, and motioned for Iliana to continue.

"We want to take the fight above."

Scarlet, is she telling the truth?

YES, SHE TOLD THE TRUTH, BUT I CAN TELL SHE IS HOLDING INFORMATION BACK.

"You want to attack the free cities? How? No one's ever even been to one. They'd shoot you before you got close. Plus, how do you plan to get up there?" Jared was incredulous. These people thought they could attack a city floating in the middle of nowhere.

"I can't tell you."

Jared held up a hand. "I'd think very hard about the next words out of your mouth."

Nervously, she turned to Loch who considered Jared. After a long, pregnant pause, he motioned for Iliana to continue.

Looking flustered, Iliana said, "We know when the drop ships will be at our colony and plan to ambush them."

It was Jared's turn to look shocked. "You want to take out a drop ship?"

"Not take one out. Capture it, so we can use it to get to the city."

"And you don't think they'll notice a captured ship? They'll blast it out of the sky!" Jared said, incredulity laced in every word.

"We'll force the pilot to—"

"What if these *pilots* can interact with the ship using nanites? What if they send a warning you don't know about, and a boarding party is ready to shoot you as soon as you land?"

"We have no other options!" The desperation in her voice was all Jared needed to hear to know she told the truth. For good measure, he asked Scarlet and she confirmed. He just shook his head at the audacity of these people. They thought they could commandeer a ship, and then make it back to a free city. It was insane.

"Well, that is not an option unless you want to commit suicide, but you know what? I don't even care. I thought we could help each other out, but I can see that's not likely to happen. Move back over to the others." Jared pointed to the other side of the room.

After she'd taken her place, he tossed all of their gear and weapons outside the room.

"What are you doing?" They all shouted and wriggled on the ground. Jared reminded them of their predicament, pulled his phase pistol, and fired a warning round into the ground next to their feet. Chips of concrete chips sprayed the tied-up explorers hard enough to inflict pain.

Oops.

Jared hadn't meant to harm them. He only wanted to show them that he wasn't messing around and that he'd do what was necessary. Secretly, his mind railed at him in opposition to his current actions.

"If you need another reminder, the next shot takes out someone's leg. We'll see how far you get when you need to carry that brute over there." Jared pointed at Jon, eliciting an angry growl from the meathead.

"Listen up. I'm only going to say this once, and then I hope to never see you all again. Your gear, weapons, and ammo are going outside. I'll only take what I can use and leave the rest. The boosters? I've no need of them, so you get to keep those. Don't mistake my generosity for kindness. I'm just not in the habit of preying on my own kind." Jared bit out the words, showing his displeasure at their immoral behavior. "I'll then barricade you in here and release you when I'm ready. If anyone tries to escape before then, I'll shoot without hesitation."

Jared paused to make sure they understood the situation and his instructions.

"Got it?"

Everyone nodded their heads in agreement, and Jared left the room. He grabbed the biggest piece of concrete he could find and propped it against the entryway. He also took a couple of smaller pieces and stacked them on top to make it harder for them to get out.

I CAN SENSE THEIR FEAR.

Jared looked at Scarlet to see her staring at the room. "You can sense them from here?"

YES. THEY MAY NOT SHOW IT, BUT ONCE YOU PUT THAT BARRICADE IN FRONT OF THE DOOR I FELT A SHARP STAB OF FEAR FROM THEM.

Jared felt a little bad, but then thought about their willingness to harm Scarlet, and those feelings evaporated.

"They deserve to suffer a little after what they put us through."

FOR WHAT IT'S WORTH, I DID NOT SENSE HOSTILITY FROM ALL OF THEM. LOCH AND ILIANA APPEARED...RELUCTANT. I THINK THEY HAD NO CHOICE.

Jared paused. "We didn't find out why they can't use the injectors they already have." Jared contemplated going back in to ask the question but thought better of it. It didn't change anything anyway. The two of them needed to get far from this place, and these Daggers.

Jared upended the packs, took any ammo he could use for his Colt, and a couple first aid kits.

"I think we've done all we can here, Scarlet. Let's get moving."

WHAT ABOUT THEM?

"Eventually they'll tire of waiting and push their way out. I want to be far enough away by then they won't find us."

WE MAY WANT TO FIND OUT MORE ABOUT THEIR FRATERNITY. IF THEY REALLY PLAN TO GO AGAINST THE CITIES, WE COULD USE THEIR HELP.

"At what cost, though? I won't go up against anyone in the colonies. If they attempt to capture a drop ship, innocents will die. The leaders of a colony will want to protect that ship at all costs, because it's their livelihood. Without regular supplies from the cities, the colony dies."

JARED, Scarlet's voice sounded cold, harsh. YOU MUST GET

PAST YOUR REFUSAL TO HARM ANOTHER HUMAN. AT THE VERY LEAST, WE WILL FACE OFF AGAINST THEM IN THE CITIES, BUT IF WE RUN INTO MORE PEOPLE LIKE THESE MERCENARIES HERE, YOU WILL NEED TO GET YOUR HANDS DIRTY.

"When the time comes, I'll do what I must, but I won't condone killing innocent people to exact our vengeance. We'd be no better than the cities."

ARE THEY INNOCENT? YOU HEARD WHAT ILIANA SAID. THEY EXILED THEM AND DENIED THEM INJECTORS. THEY PREY ON THOSE WEAKER THAN THEMSELVES, AS EVIDENCED HERE.

"Did they steal though? Or, would they have done so purely because I had these phase pistols? As for their exile, maybe it was just that simple and they only wanted to explore?"

YOU JUST MADE MY POINT. WE MUST LEARN MORE ABOUT THIS FRATERNITY.

"We could follow them to their camp and verify their story? After we find their camp, we can head south to the colony they came from and ask questions. Maybe they'll allow me to enter if I'm not there for nanites."

WE WILL NEED ALLIES IN THE FIGHT TO COME, AND THESE PEOPLE, THOUGH UNSAVORY, MIGHT BE WILLING TO HELP.

"All right, I get it. We'll follow them, but if I find out they're willing to hurt—or kill—people in the colonies for no other reason than to achieve a desired end, I won't work with them. In fact, I'll label them as an enemy."

AGREED.

"So how do you propose we follow them? They have at least one rifle with a scope on it here. I could bring it with, but it's bulky, and my pack is already nearing capacity."

I WILL FLY!

Scarlet's voice held an edge of excitement and Jared knew she couldn't wait to soar through the sky.

"Let's move away from here first. Once you can fly, circle back and keep an eye on the group. I'm guessing they will abandon their plans to search this city and instead head back to their camp."

Jared and Scarlet walked for at least two hours before he felt certain they were far enough away. The area Jared chose was flat, open, and lifeless. It seemed like the perfect place for Scarlet to try flying.

"You're up!"

Scarlet eagerly opened her beautiful wings. They shone with ruby brilliance as the sun beat upon them. Scarlet spent several minutes flapping her wings and stretching them to their limits. Then, without warning, she bunched her legs and thrust into the air with a massive beat of her wings. The dust swirled around him, creating small cyclones. At first, she hovered in place bobbing up and down. Then, the speed of her wings increased, and she rose into the air.

YES! Scarlet cried out in joy.

Jared imagined the exhilaration. The feeling of the wind whipping around her. He couldn't wait until she could bear the weight of them both. She rose higher into the sky before she tucked in her wings, straightened her tail and thrust forward. She shot through the air for hundreds of yards and then flared her wings to stop in midair where she resumed the steady flapping. It sounded like a rhythmic thump, even from this distance.

Scarlet, can you hear me?

I CAN.

See how high you can go before we lose mental connection. Hopefully, you can fly high enough they won't be able to hear you above them.

I CAN SEE THE RUINED STATUE AND CITY FROM HERE. I
BELIEVE THEY ARE STILL INSIDE.

Scarlet flew higher into the sky until he could barely make out
her form. If he hadn't watched her ascent, there's no way he'd see
her up there.

*Can you find some place for me to wait? Maybe someplace that has
some shade?*

THERE IS AN OUTCROPPING A MILE TO THE EAST. I WILL
KEEP WATCH, THOUGH I DO NOT KNOW HOW LONG I CAN
MAINTAIN FLIGHT AT THE MOMENT. WHEN I TIRE, I WILL LET
YOU KNOW.

Jared walked to the outcropping Scarlet had observed, a barren
and dusty area, but at least he'd have a reprieve from the sun while
they waited. Hopefully, the party was impatient and would leave
the room soon. It wasn't a good idea to remain out in the open like
this at night, even if they could see in the dark.

Speaking of…

*Hey, Scarlet? I know you can see in the dark, but will you be able to
tell if they make a move during the night?*

YES. I CAN ALSO GET CLOSER IN THE NIGHT. EVEN IF THEY
HEAR ME, THEY WILL NOT SEE ME.

It was only late morning and Jared assumed they wouldn't wait
long before attempting to leave. After spending six months in that
little room, he knew with certainty there was only one way out, and
it could get extremely hot during the day.

With nothing but time on his hands, Jared rummaged through
the gear taken from the Daggers. He'd picked up three boxes of
ammo for his Colt, along with two first aid kits.

At this rate, I'll need to get a bigger pack soon.

The box for the phase pistol took up a lot of space, so he

ditched it. It wasn't like he needed to protect the weapons, and he only had the half-spent power pack in addition to those already loaded in the pistols.

JARED, I SEE MOVEMENT. IT LOOKS LIKE THEY ARE TRYING TO GET OUT ALREADY.

Already? I thought they'd at least wait a another few hours, Jared grunted. Apparently he hadn't been scary enough to deter them further. *Keep watching and let me know when they move out.*

Whatever could be said of this group, they were brave, accustomed to battle, and had a much larger force backing them. If Jared persuaded them to do things without endangering the lives of innocent bystanders, they could be a real asset to him, and to the dragons.

Jared didn't particularly hate these explorers. They were humans struggling for survival and stuck in the same predicament he was. Except they still believed in the lie. Thanks to Igor, he knew the truth, but as far as Jared knew, he was the only one. He hoped their story panned out and he could count on them as allies, but it was too early to tell, and they could yet end up on opposing sides.

JARED, THEY ARE MOVING.

07 STALKING THE PREY

On my way!

Jared set out toward the other explorers.

Let me know when I get within two miles. I don't want to be any closer than that especially when we are walking across these wide-open areas.

IT LOOKS LIKE YOU WERE RIGHT. THEY ARE BYPASSING THE CITY AND HEADING SOUTH.

They followed the group for several hours before he heard Scarlet's flapping as she came in for a landing.

I MUST REST. THEY HAVE A LARGE, OPEN AREA TO TRAVERSE NEXT AND I SHOULD HAVE NO DIFFICULTY PICKING UP THEIR TRAIL AGAIN.

"Thanks Scarlet. So...flying?" Jared asked, a knowing smile playing across his lips. "Judging by your emotions across our bond, it seems pretty amazing, right?"

IT...I. SCARLET PAUSED TO COLLECT HER THOUGHTS. IT IS HARD TO PUT INTO WORDS, BUT IT FEELS LIKE FREEDOM? Scarlet tested the word, before confirming. YES, FREEDOM.

"How long do you think it will be before you can carry me?" Jared asked excitedly. "Wait, can you carry me? I guess I just assumed you'd be able to after you got stronger."

I COULD CARRY YOU NOW, BUT ONLY FOR A SHORT TIME. PERHAPS AFTER WE ASSIGN THE NANITES I HAVE AVAILABLE.

"Oh, right! Sorry, Scarlet." Jared admonished himself. "I got so caught up in all the activity I totally forgot you needed rest after our ordeal in the subway. You're probably exhausted after everything we've been through. We can forget about these Daggers and go our own way if you need to sleep."

I WILL BE FINE UNTIL THEY STOP FOR THE NIGHT. ALSO, I WOULD LIKE FOR YOU TO ADJUST MY NANITE ASSIGNMENTS.

"What're you thinking?"

I MUST FORTIFY MY DEFENSES, GROW IN SIZE, AND INCREASE THE ONLY RANGED ATTACK I HAVE AVAILABLE, FIRE BREATHING, Scarlet explained, craning her head to look at him. TOUCH MY SIDE.

Jared obliged, and an image of her selections expanded into his view. He saw no issues with her choices and was in no place to question a several-hundred-year-old dragon.

"I'm guessing by the number of available nanites, you barely had any the last time we did this."

COMPARED TO WHAT MY MOTHER TRANSFERRED? YES, IT WAS A TINY AMOUNT.

Jared couldn't wait to see what these enhancements did for her. She'd grown so much last time, but he didn't know if that was the result of her mother's essence or the nanites themselves.

He pulled up her actual status window and made the selections requested.

SCARLET — NANITES AVAILABLE: 99%

BODY

Physical Augmentation

Muscle Mass - 20%

Body Manipulation

Regeneration - 10%

Remodeling - 10%

Physical Defense/Attack

Skin Hardening - 10%

Scale Hardening - 10%

Bone Hardening - 10%

Fire Breathing - 20%

MIND

Brain Enhancement

Senses - 10%

Curious about one of her choices, Jared asked, "What do you plan to use *Remodeling* for?"

BECAUSE I AM INCREASING MY MUSCLE MASS SIGNIFICANTLY, I NEED TO ENSURE THAT MY SKELETAL FRAME CAN SUPPORT THE CHANGE.

"How do you choose what to remodel?"

IT REQUIRES A DEEP UNDERSTANDING OF THE NANITES AND THEIR CODING. ONCE YOU HAVE THAT, YOU CAN MANIPULATE INDIVIDUAL CHANGES INSTEAD OF THE CATEGORIES I CREATED FOR YOU.

"Maybe I should assign all the nanites I get from now on into *Mind*. It seems like there are a lot of things I'm missing out on because I'm not *smart* enough," Jared said wryly.

YOUR PHYSICAL BODY MAY BE STRONG, BUT YOU COULD

ALWAYS USE MORE DEFENSE. HOWEVER, I DO BELIEVE IT WISE TO INCREASE YOUR MENTAL PROWESS NEXT.

Jared made up his mind and declared, "Any more nanites I get will go into *Mind* and defenses. Tell me more about the changes you can make with *Remodeling*. It seems a bit impractical for a human, but maybe I just don't know enough about it yet."

ANY PHYSICAL CHANGE YOU DESIRE.

"Any?" Jared's mind spun with the idea. He didn't know enough about his own anatomy to effect the changes, but if he learned, the possibilities were endless.

YOUR NIGHT VISION IS A GOOD EXAMPLE. THE MUSCLES BEHIND YOUR EYE CONTRACT ALLOWING YOUR PUPIL TO EXPAND BEYOND NORMAL HUMAN LIMITS. THE NANITES ALSO BUILT ADDITIONAL RODS IN YOUR EYES FOR MUCH GREATER VISIBILITY AT NIGHT.

"Wow, I had no idea." He was eager to learn more about himself and truly understand the tiny machines inside him.

A BENEFIT OF INCREASING YOUR MIND, IT WILL ALLOW YOU TO UNDERSTAND THE NANITES AT THE MOLECULAR LEVEL. FROM THERE, IT IS JUST A MATTER OF TIME BEFORE YOU UNDERSTAND YOUR BODY THOROUGHLY.

"I'll take your word for it. I imagine I'm quite far from reaching that point. It sounds cool, but also impossible at the moment."

YOU WILL LEARN IN TIME. IN THE MEANTIME, I MUST FIND SOMETHING TO EAT.

"Eat?" The concept startled him. "Why do you need to eat? Besides, what could you even eat around here?"

Ever since nanites first entered the picture, he barely needed to eat any food. The little bio-machines lived off the nuclear waste saturating the air.

I NEED TO EAT BEFORE I ADD SO MUCH MASS TO MY BODY. THE NANITES CAN SUSTAIN ME FOR NOW, BUT THEY CANNOT BREAK DOWN THE NUCLEAR WASTE FAST ENOUGH FOR RAPID SIZE INCREASES.

"What about my changes? I didn't eat before."

YOU INCREASED MUSCLE MASS, BUT IT DID NOT ALTER YOUR PHYSICAL DIMENSIONS SIGNIFICANTLY. THE CHANGES I'LL UNDERGO WILL BE MUCH GREATER AND WILL EXPEND A LOT MORE ENERGY.

"All right, I'll keep heading south while you go find something to eat. Just keep an eye on me and the other group and make sure I don't get too close."

VERY WELL.

With that, Scarlet launched herself into the air, showing much more grace than her first attempt. Jared admired Scarlet's form as she flew, the sun reflecting off her body making her look like a giant phoenix clothed in fire. He watched until she disappeared from view, and then resumed his trek.

Jared couldn't wait to experience the same freedom Scarlet spoke of. It was something he'd never really felt in his entire life. He had everything a kid could want growing up, but confined to their small colony, it wasn't freedom. After his parents died, the cage closed in around him, stifling him until he could take it no longer. He'd left without a backward glance, hoping to find that freedom elsewhere. Unfortunately, it wasn't freedom either. There were no physical walls, but the desolate world was a prison all on its own.

What would it be like to experience true freedom? The wind whipping through my hair—

JARED! Scarlet yelled, interrupting his thoughts.

What is it? Are you okay? Where are you?

THE EXPLORERS—THEY ARE BEING ATTACKED! THERE IS A PACK OF...UM, I DON'T KNOW WHAT THEY ARE, BUT THERE ARE A LOT OF THEM. THEY ARE HOPPING STRANGELY, HAVE ENORMOUS, FLOPPY EARS, AND COVERED IN WHITE FUR.

Jared guffawed, trying to relay his thoughts to Scarlet through bouts of laughter.

Scarlet, those are just rabbits; they should be able to handle them. We took out an entire horde of rats by ourselves, and those are much more dangerous. You can swoop in and grab some of them to eat. It helps them out and gets you what you need.

Jared waited for a response, but after a full minute with no reply he grew concerned.

Scarlet? What's going on? Scarlet? Again, no answer. *Come on Scarlet, I didn't mean to tease. It sounded silly—*

"Whoa! What...Hey!" A large blob of fur collided with Jared's face, knocking him to the ground. He also heard a thud as Scarlet landed a few yards away.

Batting the ball of fur away, Jared jumped to his feet and backed away. The huge, white cotton ball launched itself fifteen feet into the air to land on his head again.

"Get off!"

Jared dove to the side and pulled his phase pistol. He shot at the creature, but it reacted too fast and jumped at him again.

"Fine, have it your way," growled Jared.

Jared cocked his arm back, and as the creature's momentum carried it toward him, he punched right through it.

"Ugh."

His arm plunged straight through its body, but its bloody corpse continued its forward momentum directly into his face.

Not again.

Hot blood and bits of fur shot into his mouth causing him to retch. He flung the creature off his arm and used his clean arm to wipe bits of the rabbit from his eyes and mouth.

Scarlet stamped her foot and laughed at him with that strange huffing noise.

"What the heck, Scarlet?"

JUST RABBITS? Scarlet teased, mirth flitting across the bond as Scarlet radiated extreme satisfaction at his predicament.

"That was disgusting."

A new round of huffing ensued, and Jared glared at Scarlet while blood dripped from his hair and brow.

"If that was payback for teasing you, I think it was a little overkill."

Although he tried to sound stern, a small tick at the corner of his mouth betrayed his amusement at her antics. Jared busied himself cleaning the blood off and then examined the eviscerated rabbit.

You are an ugly little bugger.

The rabbit was about two feet by two feet and resembled a rabbit only from the fur and ears. Its face looked more like a pug, squashed flat and sporting oversized incisors. Its legs were long and well-muscled, which explained its fifteen-foot leap at him. Other than its teeth, it had no other attack ability.

"I bet these things only survive because of their agility. They are...squishy," Jared said as he examined the hole he'd punched clean through it. "I don't think those explorers will need help killing THEM."

I WOULD NOT BE SO SURE. THERE WERE AT LEAST FIFTY OF THEM, AND THEY WERE GAINING GROUND.

"Show me."

Jared moved over to Scarlet and placed his hand on her side.

Jared's vision grew fuzzy before it materialized into an aerial view. He looked on as the horde of rabbits bounced and surged at the five explorers. They looked like a wave of fluffy popcorn bounding toward the group. Jared nearly laughed at the absurdity of the scene but held himself in check.

"Please go check on them." Jared sighed and started walking in their direction in case he needed to intervene.

A few moments later, Scarlet reported in. You were right. They killed over half of them, and the rest are retreating.

Are they all okay?

It looks like there are superficial wounds, but they are otherwise whole.

"Too bad," Jared muttered. Would serve them right for how they treated him.

You should pursue the rabbits and eat your fill. This will probably be one of the easiest and tastiest meals you can find.

Scarlet flew off after the retreating rabbits. Several minutes passed when Jared heard a roar in the distance.

Scarlet? Is everything okay?

Just cooking my meal before consuming.

Why would you cook them first? Can't you eat them whole?

Why would I want to eat all that fur?

"Oh, um." Jared had imagined she'd just grab them up in her mouth and chomp them down wholesale.

Shaking his head, Jared thought back to just a few weeks ago. If someone told him he'd be sitting next to a rabbit he punched a hole through while his dragon companion roasted them for a midday snack, he'd have questioned their sanity.

After she'd eaten her fill, Scarlet tracked and followed the group until she observed them come upon a burned-out building. Based on Scarlet's description, it looked like they'd stayed there before, and judging by the sun's position, they'd use it as a camp once again.

THEY ARE MOVING THROUGH THE BUILDING NOW. IT LOOKS LIKE THEY ARE MAKING SURE IT IS EMPTY.

See if you can find someplace for us to sleep. Preferably something with walls, Jared added. He'd had enough close calls and wildlife encounters for a while and just wanted a peaceful night.

THERE IS A LONG METAL BOX WITH LOTS OF LITTLE OPENINGS ALONG THE SIDE, A HALF-DESTROYED BUILDING, AND A CRATER WITH SOME RUINS ON ONE SIDE.

Let's head for the partially downed building. It'll be easier to defend if something decides to attack us. It's too bad you can't set up a psionic barrier like your mother. That would be extremely useful in situations like this.

KEEP IN MIND MY MOTHER WAS THOUSANDS OF YEARS OLD. IT MAY YET BE YEARS BEFORE I DEVELOP A SIMILAR ABILITY. ONCE I DO, IT WILL BE MUCH WEAKER, ALLOWING CREATURES WITH MENTAL RESISTANCE TO SHRUG IT OFF.

I guess I shouldn't assume or take anything for granted. We'll make do with what we've got, and defeat anything that comes our way.

Jared followed Scarlet's instructions to the building and found it exactly as described. The ruined wall allowed Scarlet to fit inside, and hopefully to get back out once she'd gone through her changes.

"All right, it's your turn to sleep while I keep watch. Did you see any indications of creatures in the area when you flew in?"

NO, THE AREA LOOKS ABANDONED.

"Thank you, Scarlet. Rest. I'll keep you safe." Jared stepped outside the small building as Scarlet found a mostly clear section of floor and settled in to sleep. The moment her head touched the ground, her breathing deepened, sleep instantly taking hold.

I wonder if I can learn how she does it? Near instantaneous sleep on command would be pretty nice.

Jared sat for several hours thinking about the possibilities open to them. There were so many ways in which he could enhance himself and grow stronger, including absorbing abilities from other creatures. His future looked brighter than ever and —

Jared's musing cut off abruptly when he heard the scraping of rocks, like something being dragged. He jumped to his feet and whipped out his phase pistol. Looking around for some other threat, but he saw nothing. He heard it again and looked behind him.

"Whoa," Jared whispered and quietly approached Scarlet.

A translucent wave of energy pulsed from within her as she increased in size. At the same time the scales on her body thickened, overlapping each other to create an impenetrable barrier. The vibrant red of her skin and scales darkened, growing thicker.

Jared stood dumbstruck, entranced by her beauty. He felt small and inadequate next to her and couldn't believe she was his companion. He lost track of time, lulled into a state of catatonia as he watched the dancing lights pulsate over her body. It wasn't until he felt something nudge his foot he snapped out of his reverie. Looking down, he realized she'd grown several more feet in just a few hours. He took a step back and noticed for the first time the row of spikes developing along her back.

Jared squinted and looked closer at the nape of her neck. Instead of the spikes continuing along her neck and to the crown of her head like Alestrialia's, it ended as a bony indentation formed. At first, it looked like a small flat disk, but gradually curved, the back getting taller.

"It's a seat!" Jared said excitedly. The back of the seat was just high enough to protect him from the spikes down her spine, but not so large that it'd restrict her movements.

How in the world is she growing so fast? It took me days! Jared needed to find out how she managed to accelerate the process so much. *Maybe it's because she can control them and understands them more?* Shrugging, Jared resolved to ask her later. Walking over to a broken portion of wall, Jared sat down facing Scarlet.

A noise outside the building startled him. Ducking below the partition, he peeked around the corner looking for the source of the noise.

There was nothing directly in front of him, but he heard it again and knew something lurked in the shadows. Rounding the corner Jared ran directly into a rabbit.

Dang, not again. What is it with these things?

He'd only just finished cleaning his clothes and gear from the last gruesome encounter.

Maybe I can scare it off.

Jared tried shooing the fur ball away by throwing rocks, but it just sat there staring at him. He didn't want to fire any weapons and wake Scarlet, so he prepared to grapple with the irritating fur ball. As soon as he approached, it hopped away. He turned to follow and stopped in his tracks.

Oh crap!

It looked like the rest of the rabbit horde that attacked the Daggers. Though, they all looked alike, so it was hard to tell. If this was the same group, more than twenty of the puff balls had survived their earlier battle and Scarlet's appetite.

He fingered his pistol, debating if he should risk waking Scarlet. Glancing over his shoulder, he saw the light glow indicating she was still going through the transformation process.

No time like the present to test my new abilities.

Jared rushed them.

As if controlled by a hive mind, they all faced him at the same time and leapt.

"Two can play that game!"

Jared jumped to meet them, grabbing one in midair and launching a fist into another's face with a sickening crunch. He was a whirlwind of destruction, and these creatures never stood a chance. At this point he didn't care if he got blood and fur on him. He was already coated in the gore and needed a good scrub anyway. Rabbit after rabbit fell at his feet dead. In the heat of battle Jared didn't know how long he fought, but it seemed like only an instant before there was nothing left to punch or kick.

Fist-pumping in victory, he turned back to the building.

Jared grunted as something heavy booted him in the back, lifting him off his feet.

He landed ten feet away, only his increased agility allowing him to get his feet under him before landing. "What was that?"

On instinct, Jared rolled to the right and a pair of feet the size of his torso touched down like a whisper. Jared's eyes widened in shock and he sprang away, running twenty yards in the opposite direction. He spun around, ready to face off against whatever hit him, but when he turned around, he saw nothing.

"What was that?"

Glancing up, he saw a giant cloud of fur about to land on top of him. Jumping back in the nick of time, it landed right in front of him, soft as a feather, only a slight disturbance of the wind evidence of its passing. He came face to face with a rabbit that stood as tall as him, and just as big around.

"Not another boss," Jared groaned. "What's up with all these things having ridiculously oversized leaders? This isn't a game! It's real life!" He tried to rationalize the scene before him, but the situation was just too absurd, and it was everything he could do just to avoid the giant rabbit.

This thing was much faster and stronger than its smaller counterparts.

No wonder they waited when I charged them, thought Jared. *These things are more intelligent than I gave them credit for.*

He could end the fight right now with a well-placed phase round but decided to test himself instead. The little guys were a piece of cake to dispatch, but this guy would be tough.

"All right, you long-haired, buck-toothed, floppy-eared hairball, let's go!" The taunt worked, and it leapt into the air at him. It jumped thirty feet into the air, intent on dropping directly onto his head. In a move that surprised even himself, Jared contorted his body to deliver a spinning side kick squarely into the thing's side. However, the agile rabbit flipped in the air, landing nimbly on its feet only to launch at him yet again.

How am I supposed to hurt this thing with all that fur? wondered Jared. The kick didn't even phase it. The only portions not covered in several feet of fur were its legs and face. Both of those represented the only dangerous parts of the rabbit and he didn't like the idea of trying to kick a face sporting foot-long incisors.

While he thought up a plan, Jared barely dodged the rabbit's lightning fast attacks. Exasperated, he almost pulled his pistol and ended the fight. Then he caught sight of a piece of rebar ending in a chunk of concrete, and an evil smile touched his lips . His defensive maneuvers took on a purpose. Each roll and somersault brought him closer to his desired weapon until he was able to grasp the cold iron bar. Before his strength increases, there's no way he could've used the rubble as a weapon. The end attached to concrete weighed at least fifty pounds.

Perfect! Jared though, hefting the makeshift weapon onto his shoulder. He poured on a burst of speed to put some distance between the two of them. Finding a solid spot to make a stand, he whirled and stepped into a batter's stance. The evil smile he wore now covered his entire face as Jared prepared to smash a home run.

He didn't have to wait long, as the creature leapt. If not for the very real fact that this rabbit was trying to eat him, the scene would've been comical. A six-foot-tall-and-wide cotton ball flew through the air at him, its beady little eyes reflecting the moon, and its mouth opened in preparation to plunge its teeth into him. It was like the ultimate nightmare for a kid as they envisioned their favorite fluffy stuffed animal coming to life and attacking them, only here it was ten times the size.

Jared wound up and swung the rebar with all his strength. A whistling sound was the only warning the rabbit had before fifty pounds of rock and metal rocketed into its fat face.

"Oh no," Jared whispered, a split second before impact.

His movement already committed, there was nothing he could do but watch as the chunk of concrete smashed into the large blood sack about to burst open. A wave of blood gushed over him as the concrete pulverized the rabbit in a puff of exploding fur. If the blood wasn't enough, the rabbit's fur coated his body, sticking to everything. His eyes shut to prevent blood and fur entering them, Jared didn't see the brief flash of light as he absorbed the nanites from his most recent kill.

"Yuck!" yelled Jared. He pawed at his face, sputtering and spitting the blood and bits of fur from his mouth.

While pawing at this face, Jared heard a rumbling from the building behind him and whirled around to face it. Jared looked up just in time to see the wall nearest him bulge and crash to the ground, a ten-foot tall dragon standing in its place.

"Scarlet?"

Shocked, Jared wondered, *How long did that fight last? Surely not too long. How is Scarlet already done?*

Hearing his voice, Scarlet turned to look at him and guffawed at his appearance.

And to think I was about to compliment her, Jared thought wryly.

JARED? she asked, confused. WHAT HAPPENED TO YOU?

Jared just shrugged in embarrassment and said, "The rabbits. They came back."

Louder than he'd heard it before, Scarlet wheezed and huffed, collapsing back to the ground as her head bobbed up and down, an uncontrollable bout of laughter wracking her body.

Jared just stared at her with slitted eyes. He said nothing, but he did push his annoyance along their bond to let her know he was not amused and promised revenge for her teasing.

JUST RABBITS, HUH?

08 CAPTURED

Jared looked at Scarlet and shook his head, causing gobs of rabbit fur and guts to splatter on the ground.

"All right, all right, you win! I won't tease you about the dang rabbits anymore." Jared held up his hands and found a rock to sit on.

Stripping off his nasty clothes, he scrubbed them using the sand. Water was a scarce commodity, so he often resorted to scrubbing his skin and clothes with sand. It sucked, and he always felt chaffed after, but it was better than walking around with blood and guts all over.

It rarely rained anymore and when it did, there was a fifty-fifty chance it was acidic. He'd learned that lesson the hard way since the first couple times he'd been without shelter, the rain was fine, drinkable even. However, the next rain brought with it some acidic residue. His eyes and skin burned, turning a bright shade of red.

I could use a good rain about now, mused Jared. It would've made this cleanup go much smoother and help him get the last remnants from his gear as well. He hated using sand, since it really diminished the life of everything he wore. He was really only concerned about his weapons and pack though. Everything else was disposable. The pack he wore was a gift from his mother. She'd hand-stitched it for his eighteenth birthday but hadn't been able to give it to him before she got sick. He fingered a ragged seam toward the bottom. It was his attempt to finish the work his mother started. Crude in comparison to her masterful handiwork, but it was the last possession he had from her, and he tried his best to take care of it.

Shaking his head, Jared calmed himself, the melancholy receding back into the depths of his mind.

It took him an hour of scrubbing to rid his body and gear of the sticky substance. His skin felt raw to the touch, this being the second time he'd done this today. Thankfully, the nanites would help with the abrasions and take care of any leftover particles he had missed. That was a definite benefit to the technology, their ability to consume waste and convert it into energy. Especially since there was no place for him to bathe regularly.

Finished wiping his embarrassment away, Jared walked over to Scarlet, admiring her new form.

"Scarlet, you're huge." Jared choked out the last word, failing to stop himself from saying it. "Err, uh, in a good way. What I meant to say was, you've grown a lot!" Jared amended, feeling chagrinned at his lack of tact. To Scarlet's credit, she wasn't offended by the remark, and in fact it didn't seem to bother her at all.

I GREW MORE THAN EXPECTED. THE ESSENCE GRANTED BY MY MOTHER HAS YET TO RUN ITS FULL COURSE.

"Does that mean you'll grown even more later? Is that how you grew so fast?"

I BELIEVE THAT IS PART OF IT, BUT ALSO BECAUSE I CAN DIRECT THE NANITES. IT IS DIFFICULT TO EXPLAIN IT NOW,

BUT ONCE YOU UNDERSTAND YOURSELF AND THE NANITES BETTER, YOU WILL LEARN TO PARTITION YOUR MIND. ONCE YOU DO, YOU WILL BE ABLE TO CONSCIOUSLY CONTROL THE NANITES EVEN WHILE YOUR MIND SLEEPS.

"So that's why it takes me days to do what you just did in hours?"

IT IS.

"Yet another reason for me to sink the rest of my nanites into *Mind*," Jared said, a bit annoyed at himself for sinking everything into physical changes. "Well, regardless of how you did it, it's impressive, Scarlet. You are—you look incredible," Jared said, and meant every word. She truly did look amazing, and at ten feet tall they were quickly becoming a serious force.

THANK YOU, JARED.

"May I?" Jared asked, his hand paused a few inches from her scales.

Scarlet nodded, and Jared ran his fingers along her scales.

"Wow. They've hardened a lot, and it looks like they overlap a bit more. Also, the color changed. Is that normal, or something you did?"

THE COLOR OF MY NATURAL SKIN WILL NOT CHANGE, BUT AS THE SCALES GROW STRONGER, THEY WILL DARKEN. I BELIEVE THEY ARE HARD ENOUGH TO WITHSTAND SHARP OBJECTS LIKE CLAWS AND TEETH AT THIS POINT.

Scarlet radiated pride and satisfaction at his praise while he ran his hands along her side.

THANK YOU, FOR EVERYTHING. MY JOURNEY HAS BEEN MUCH EASIER THAN IF YOU HADN'T COME ALONG.

You are family now! Jared said through their bond, pushing all of his feelings at Scarlet so she understood how he felt about her, and how thankful he was for her companionship.

Scarlet expressed gratefulness and said, IF NOT FOR YOU, I WOULD BE ALONE, WITHOUT PROTECTION, AND WITHOUT THE ABILITY TO USE THESE NANITES. ALL MY FAMILY IS IN HIBERNATION, AND GIVEN THE WAY CREATURES MUTATED IN RECENT YEARS, IT IS POSSIBLE I COULD HAVE DIED. THANKS TO YOU, I NOT ONLY SURVIVED, BUT AM STRONGER AND BIGGER THAN I EVER THOUGHT POSSIBLE IN SO SHORT A TIME.

"We will find your family Scarlet," Jared promised.

DRAGONS REVERE FAMILY ABOVE ALL ELSE, AND EVERY DRAGON TAKES ON THE RESPONSIBILITY TO RAISE A NEW HATCHLING. FOR A VERY LONG TIME MY MOTHER FEARED WHAT WOULD HAPPEN TO ME AFTER SHE WAS GONE. YOU MIGHT THINK SHE WAS MAD ABOUT OUR BONDING, BUT IN THE END, IT GAVE HER REASSURANCE THAT I HAD SOMEONE TO HELP AND PROTECT ME. FOR THAT I WILL EVER BE THANKFUL.

Jared felt the sincerity of her words.

For the next several hours, they simply sat next to each other, enjoying one another's company. The stayed that way until the sun crested the horizon and Jared rose to his feet.

"Well? Shall we get a move on? I'd guess the other explorers, will set out shortly to make the most of the daylight. You want to do the same thing we did yesterday? You fly overhead, and I'll hang back a couple miles."

OR YOU COULD FLY WITH ME.

"Seriously?" Jared tempered his excitement to make sure it wasn't premature. "Will it tire you out too quickly?"

Scarlet flared her wings, an impressive twenty-five-foot

wingspan, and said, I CAN MANAGE IT FOR QUITE SOME TIME NOW.

"Then, yes! A hundred times yes!"

Jared couldn't contain his excitement. When he was a little boy, he'd sit at the drop site in his colony all day waiting for shipments to arrive from the cities. He used to love watching the ships rocket through the sky, wishing that someday he'd get to experience it. Today was that day, and it was all he could do to restrain himself from jumping up and down like that little boy so many years ago.

BEFORE WE GO, YOU SHOULD KNOW WE GAINED TWO ABILITIES FROM THE LIZARD CREATURES WE KILLED. ALTHOUGH, I SUSPECT IT IS JUST ONE ABILITY WITH MULTIPLE APPLICATIONS.

"Wait, what? Why didn't I get this ability?"

YOU ALSO HAVE THE ABILITIES, BUT I WAS UNAWARE UNTIL YOU TOUCHED ME A MOMENT AGO AND I EXPLORED YOUR NANITES. THE TWO ABILITIES ARE HEAT SIGHT AND MAGNIFIED VISION.

Jared cocked his head to the side, thinking about the abilities, and distractedly said, "How do I activate...whoa."

The moment Jared thought about *Heat Sight*, his vision blurred, and a blinding bright inferno seared into his retinas. Shutting his eyes against the intensity, Jared looked down and slowly opened one eye. Turning away from the sun, he looked to the darkened landscape and saw small flashes of heat in the distance, small creatures darting about. Careful not to look at the sun again, Jared turned to Scarlet and his mouth dropped open in surprise.

"Scarlet, you—"

Fire roiled within her body. Her very being radiated heat. At the center of her chest a ball of light spun in circles. It writhed and undulated like a living organism. Jared had no words to describe what he witnessed, but he would never forget it as long as he lived. Unable to stop himself, he placed a hand on the spot directly over the flame in her chest and felt the heat through her skin.

"Scarlet, is this where your *Fire Breathing* originates?"

YES.

"It's beautiful! I can see the glowing flames."

Reluctantly, Jared turned away and asked, "Scarlet, how do I turn...ah, got it."

Again, the moment Jared thought about turning it off, his eyes switched back to their normal vision.

SIMILAR TO MY OWN VISION, THE HEAT SIGHT ENABLES YOU TO SEE THERMAL WAVELENGTHS. I CAN GO INTO TECHNICAL DETAILS IF YOU WISH, BUT THE NANITES CREATED YET MORE CONES IN YOUR EYES, AND DEVELOPED A MUSCLE CALLED THE TRIGEMINAL NERVE TO HELP INTERPRET THE HEAT SPECTRUM YOU JUST WITNESSED.

"How do you know all of this? I understand a little of what you just said, but you lost me at *trigemini* something."

THE NANITES ALTERED YOUR EYE STRUCTURE SO THAT THEY CAN RELAY THERMAL WAVELENGTHS TO THEM AND ALLOW YOU TO SEE HEAT SIGNATURES. I KNOW QUITE A BIT ABOUT HUMAN ANATOMY. MY MOTHER LIVED WITH HUMANS FOR THOUSANDS OF YEARS AND PASSED THAT KNOWLEDGE TO ME. ALSO, THE NANITE CODING IS VERY SPECIFIC, AND I CAN READ THEIR INSTRUCTIONS TO FIGURE OUT HOW THEY WORK.

"I don't know what I'd do without you to explain all this to me." Jared shook his head ruefully. "I hope we can return the favor to others in the future."

When we wake my brothers, they will assist.

"Where are they?"

Far beneath the earth's surface. I am not yet strong enough to attempt the journey, but when the time is right, you will know.

"What about the others? The air, water, and earth dragons? Do you know where they are?"

I...Scarlet paused as she delved into her mind. A moment later, she said, I know the general locations, but not like my own family. It would take quite some time to find them.

"Well, you've got my word that I'll do everything in my power to help you do it."

First, we must strengthen ourselves.

"Speaking of, let's try out this magnification. Wow!" He'd picked a jumble of rocks in the distance to focus on, and after the vision activated, it looked as though he stood right in front of them. It had to be at least two miles away.

"This is awesome!"

He toggled the vision back and forth, taking the opportunity to examine his surroundings. It was an incredible ability.

"How does this one work?"

The nanites fuse the lens of your eye with the ciliary muscle. Both control the curvature of the lens over your eyes. When you focus on magnifying your vision, the lens squeezes together which allows you to see further.

"Can I upgrade them further?"

No, these abilities only have a single purpose, and

ASSIGNING NANITES TO THEM WOULD BE POINTLESS.

"Gotcha. What if I wanted to make my own abilities?"

YOU COULD, BUT YOU MUST UNDERSTAND YOUR BIOLOGICAL FUNCTIONS INTIMATELY. IT IS ALSO LIKELY TO CONSUME AN EXORBITANT AMOUNT OF NANITES, RENDERING IT INEFFECTIVE TO USE SO MANY FREE NANITES ON IT.

Scarlet paused, making sure Jared understood her explanation. He understood everything she'd said, and although a part of him wanted to create a new ability, it made sense to focus his efforts elsewhere.

THINK ABOUT IT THIS WAY. DID YOU KNOW THAT SQUEEZING THE LENS OF YOUR EYE TOGETHER COULD MAGNIFY YOUR VISION? DID YOU KNOW THAT INSTALLING CONES AND RODS IN YOUR EYES AND THEN INSTRUCTING NANITES TO SEND THERMAL WAVELENGTHS THROUGH THEM ALLOWED YOU TO SEE THE HEAT SPECTRUM?

"Point taken. Though I don't think I'd attempt anything like it for a long time. Still, it's an interesting idea, especially if there was a particular ability that could make my life easier."

EVENTUALLY YOU WILL HAVE THE UNDERSTANDING TO MANIPULATE THE NANITES TO A GREATER DEGREE, AND RAPIDLY, LIKE THE CHANGES I JUST WENT THROUGH. FIRST, YOU NEED TO ENHANCE YOUR MIND AND INTELLECT QUITE A BIT TO ACHIEVE A FEAT LIKE THAT.

"Man. I feel bad about it, but now I want to go find some other vermin to eradicate. Well, as long as it's not rabbits and rats." Jared shivered. He'd had enough of them to last a lifetime.

That reminds me. Jared pulled up his available nanites. "Wow, I got a decent number of nanites from that rabbit boss. Not too bad for an easy..."

Scarlet grunted, cutting him off.

"Okay, maybe it wasn't exactly easy, but it wasn't nearly as dangerous as the rats and lizards we killed. In fact, I only got hit once when it kicked me in the back, and that's only because it moved silently, and I thought I'd killed them all."

Excuses.

"Oh, all right, miss all-powerful dragon. You get the next batch while I get to be lazy and take a nap." Jared smirked. "Go ahead, keep on teasing. I'll find some way to repay you!"

Scarlet just shook her head in amusement and flared her wings, the sun's rays reaching their position.

"Sun's up, let's move!"

Scarlet knelt down as Jared clambered aboard. He double-checked his gear, tightened the strap on his pack, and settled into the surprisingly comfortable seat Scarlet had made for him. Even though he had a seat, there was nothing securing him to her back, and he was a bit nervous about falling off.

"Where am I supposed to hold —"

Scarlet launched herself into the air with no provocation or warning, and Jared promptly fell off her back, smashing his shoulder into the ground.

His arm went numb, and a throbbing ache shot through his shoulder. Rotating it in an arc, he massaged his elbow, trying to return feeling to it.

"Maybe warn me next time so I can brace myself? There's not exactly a harness up here, and not much to hold on to."

Oops. Scarlet said, chagrined and little amused.

Jared ignored her slightly vindictive response. "Let's try this again." Settled back into the seat, he pressed his knees to her side and wrapped his arms around her neck. "Okay, I'm ready!"

Scarlet tensed her legs and lunged upward. His stomach plummeted to his toes and his insides performed somersaults. The force of the acceleration pinned him to Scarlet's neck. Her wings unfurled, and the powerful thrusts carried them higher. The bobbing motion while Scarlet gained altitude caused Jared's equilibrium to rebound like a yo-yo. Breathing deeply to calm the churning in his gut, he closed his eyes until the jerking movement leveled out. When at last they had smoothed out, Jared opened his eyes.

"Wow," Jared whispered, expelling the breath he'd held. "It's—I—"

I TOLD YOU, WORDS CANNOT DESCRIBE IT.

The sun stepped off the earth on its perpetual race across the sky, while early morning reds and oranges cast a shimmering veil over the landscape. From his vantage, the land almost looked beautiful. On one side, the sun shimmered and painted a picturesque landscape. On the other, a dark foreboding disquiet overshadowed a ruined and twisted, scorched earth. The two halves stood in stark contrast. One side promising a future free of desolation, while the other the harsh reality of devastation and hardship.

"Perhaps one day," sighed Jared. Maybe it was never meant to be, but Jared would try his best to see that future come to fruition.

JARED?

"Sorry Scarlet. Just lost in my own head for a moment. This...it's overwhelming. I feel—" No matter how he tried, Jared couldn't form words for the conflicted emotions running through him. Instead, he projected those feelings and thoughts to Scarlet over their bond, hoping he'd convey some of the conflict warring within him.

A short time later, Scarlet replied, I UNDERSTAND. IT IS

PARTLY WHY I COULD NOT DESCRIBE MY FIRST EXPERIENCE. ON THE ONE HAND I FELT JOY AND AWE, BUT ON THE OTHER SIDE WAS PAIN AND HEARTACHE AT WHAT USED TO BE OR COULD HAVE BEEN.

"I wish there was more we could do now, but we are in no position to exact change on a scale of such magnitude. Perhaps in the future, when we are strong enough, we can lay claim to some of the land and rebuild."

THAT WILL BE MUCH EASIER TO DO WHEN MY FAMILY RETURNS. MY FIRE DRAGONS, AND THE REST OF DRAGON KIND.

"I think we could go back and forth about our desires all day, but right now we need to focus on gaining strength and allies. Let's make a pass to see if the Daggers broke camp yet. We've got to start somewhere, and this is as good a place as any."

Scarlet banked and headed toward the last known location for the explorers. They arrived overhead right as the group finished packing up their camp and began their trek south, using the dried ocean floor of Upper and Lower Bay to avoid having to detour around the bay itself.

Scarlet was far enough from the group to avoid detection, both from sight and sound. It was easy to track them since there was not much of anything for dozens of miles in the direction they travelled, and Jared assumed they'd follow the same path until they reached Philadelphia or follow the coast all the way down to the Carolinas. Either way, it'd be easy to pick up their trail again using his enhanced vision and their ability to fly.

"Let's fly ahead and see what lies in their path. When we get closer to Florida, we can try and locate their camp ahead of them as well. It might be good for us to see how the rest of the fraternity reacts upon hearing about their encounter. A dragon isn't something you see every day, and it could be telling how they respond." Jared knew that Scarlet was a bit irritated about letting these people go, but he shrugged it off. He'd made the decision, and they'd live with the consequences.

IT IS INEVITABLE THAT SOME PEOPLE WILL COME TO HARM IF WE CONTINUE DOWN THIS PATH.

"I know," Jared said solemnly. "When the time comes, I'll do what must be done. Until then, I'll do everything in my power to protect innocent lives."

Grudgingly, Scarlet yielded to this desires.

One small step at a time.

Jared knew they'd need to build an army if they ever hoped to have an impact against the cities' totalitarian control over the world. If the Daggers proved a bust, they'd head further inland, west, or northwest, and seek other like-minded people and colonies.

They'd flown for half an hour before Jared spotted an island and some fortified installation. "Scarlet, let's head toward those buildings." Jared pointed in the distance, at the same time activating *Magnified Vision.* "It looks like some sort of abandoned military installation. If he remembered his geography lessons, they were about to fly over an island just off the coast of New Jersey called Sandy Hook. It looked like half the island was gone, the result of a direct nuclear strike, or tremors, following the shockwave.

"Let's make a couple passes of the island before we land. I don't want to disturb another den of rabid beasts. This close to a nuclear strike, we'll probably find some extreme mutations."

NEW YORK WAS MUCH THE SAME, ONLY MY MOTHER DROVE MOST OF THEM AWAY.

"Well, let's make the rounds just to be sure. It's a good chance for me to get familiar with my new abilities, and hopefully prevent us from getting into trouble."

Scarlet circled the island while Jared used *Heat Vision* to scan for any creatures. They found several life forms of average size, one bigger than the rest, but by itself and unmoving.

"Scarlet, how far underground do you think we can see using *Heat Sight*?"

Likely not far. The ground acts as a natural barrier

"Okay, let's circle one more time and I'll zoom in on some of the areas I saw heat signatures. Maybe I can see what we're up against."

They spent the next hour flying circles around the island to make sure they'd be safe landing to explore. Jared paid close attention to a large cluster of buildings off the north western coast. A mile off the shoreline, several large boats sat on the dried ocean floor, arranged in a semi-circle and perhaps previously docked near the pier.

"Let's head over to the cluster of buildings there," Jared said, pointing to the location.

Scarlet landed in a wide-open space before a large, domed structure. He jumped off her back and headed toward what appeared to be a hangar. The interior was dim, and shadows permeated the room, making it impossible to peer into the corners. Activating *Heat Sight*, Jared looked around for any signs of life. Thankfully, he saw nothing to pose an immediate threat save for a couple *normal* sized rats. Ignoring them, Jared thoroughly explored the large hangar. The ceiling was at least forty or fifty feet tall in the center, and a lattice of supports held up the dome-shaped roof. The space was empty save for some destroyed boxes and rusting equipment in the corners of the rooms. There were no rooms along the perimeter, but a doorway set into the back led down to a lower level.

Jared recalled the view from above and found it curious that these stairs led under a small hill butting up to the large hangar. After the subway tunnels in New York, this staircase seemed much less ominous, and he barely had any reservations going down them.

"Scarlet, I'm heading down. Let me know if you need me."

Cracking the door, slowly this time, Jared made sure he didn't cause the door to scream like last time. He had no desire to disturb another horde of rats. The hinges resisted at first, but with a sharp tug and a whispered grinding, they gave way and the door swung open.

He paused at the top of the stairs to make sure nothing charged up at him. After ensuring he was alone, Jared started down the staircase, which descended several stories into the ground. Thankfully, he saw no signs of instability in the structure. Even so, he kept a constant rotation of normal, heat, and night vision looking for any hostiles or evidence of unstable areas. His first pass of all the rooms in the basement he used *Night Vision* looking for anything of value to scavenge. Finding none, his second pass was with *Heat Sight*.

Moving room to room, Jared ensured that no creatures lurked in the recesses of the rooms. *Night Vision* wasn't always reliable, especially since there was no ambient light in the area, but it showed the most detail and was his go-to for exploring dark areas. A final pass with *Heat Sight,* and he nearly missed a dim glow from one of the side rooms. Cautiously, he crept to the room and drew his phase pistol. Standing to the side of the door, Jared leaned around the doorjamb, but as before, the room was empty, the glow from a moment earlier nowhere to be found.

Furrowing his brow, Jared moved into the room, studying his surroundings. Toggling back to *Night Vision,* he moved from wall to wall, examining every inch.

Maybe I'm seeing things.

To pacify his curiosity, he flipped through his abilities again and back to *Heat Sight* one last time. The moment he did, the muted glow flashed into existence and abruptly winked out. Quickly, Jared swapped back to *Night Vision* only to see the back wall, empty.

I wonder. Maybe there's a hidden compartment or door to the other side.

Jared checked the rooms on either side but saw no way to get beyond. He moved back into the center room and scrutinized the back wall.

Stumped, with nothing to lose and no apparent creatures in sight, Jared grabbed a metal pipe leaning against the wall and started probing for weak spots or a seam to indicate it opened to a room beyond. First, he tapped where the light originated, but it sounded and felt as solid as everything else. Working out in a circular pattern, he reached the sides of the room and still found no entrance or evidence of something beyond.

Scarlet, there's something on the other side of a wall down here, and I can't find a way around or through it. I'm going to see if I can break the wall down. The noise might attract attention, so stay vigilant. I didn't see any creatures down here at least, but there could be something nearby.

I will watch and listen.

Testing the pipe he'd been using, Jared slammed it into the center of the wall.

"Ouch!"

The pipe bent in half, the impact sending sharp vibrations rampaging through his hands and arms. They instantly went numb, and he dropped the pipe to the ground with a sharp metallic clang. Jared massaged his hands as the ache receded.

"That was stupid, you moron," Jared berated himself.

Wait. Where's the light?

The heat signature hadn't appeared after he hit the wall. The sudden absence of the pulsating light sent a spike of alarm through him. Jared slowly backed away from the wall brandishing his pistol.

Why would it stop after I hit the wall? Unless...

Immediately after Jared had the thought, the light behind the wall returned and intensified. Just as swiftly, it blinked out of existence.

What the—

It flared again, even brighter this time accompanied by a tremor that knocked debris loose from the walls. The light winked out again and silence filled the room.

Maybe I scared it away.

The floor bucked and sent him sprawling back.

Scarlet! There's something down here. I think I made it mad.

SO THAT WASN'T YOUR INCREDIBLE STRENGTH SHAKING THE GROUND?

Good guess, Jared said sarcastically. He sprinted up the stairs but didn't make it before the ground bucked again, sending him careening into the ceiling.

"Dangit," Jared cursed, spots appearing in his vision.

Gathering his wits, he stumbled up the stairs and found Scarlet waiting for him at the top.

"I don't know what's down there, and I don't want to find out. Let's get out of here!"

Jared and Scarlet neared the hangar doors when a massive cylindrical *thing* shot out of a hole in the floor and barred their passage. He'd dismissed the holes before, thinking age and battle caused them. He was dead wrong.

A giant worm blocked their only exit from the building. Jared pivoted to run around the creature, but a second tentacle blocked their path.

Jared jumped back as the heavily-muscled cylinder swiped at him, sending drops of a slimy substance raining down on him. Whatever it was had a musty, earthy smell.

The tentacles writhed before them, randomly swiping the air. Jared didn't see any eyes on the creature and wondered how it sensed them.

Sound? Or Heat? Jared's eyes lit with an idea, and he called out to Scarlet.

"Use your fire!"

Scarlet sucked in her breath and let loose.

The roar deafened Jared and was much stronger than it'd been the first time he'd heard it. A jet of blue-tinged fire burst from Scarlet's mouth.

Blue? It was orange last time.

Jared pushed the thought to the back of his mind. Now was not the time to ask questions. They desperately needed to find a way out of this situation.

The bright blue flame assaulted the first part of the creature to appear. It did not like the heat and violently thrashed around the room before receding a short distance back into the hole. Jared used the opportunity to sprint forward with Scarlet and out of the hangar. He vaulted onto Scarlet's back and she leapt into the air. They'd made it thirty feet off the ground when, unbelievably, the *thing* slapped them from the sky. Jared watched its gray flesh accelerate toward them and was powerless to do anything about it.

"No—"

Darkness claimed his consciousness as they fell over the edge of the cliff.

A sharp stab of pain in his side, caused Jared to open his eyes.

At least, he tried to open his eyes, but a splitting headache and the blinding sun made him squeeze them shut. Jared coughed, spitting blood onto the ground. He tried to wipe his mouth but found he couldn't move his hand. Confused, disoriented, and his body throbbing in pain, Jared tried to sit up and take stock of his surroundings.

His mind screamed in protest, and he couldn't formulate a coherent thought for several minutes. When he finally managed to see clearly, he found himself bound hand and foot. The grogginess vanished in an instant, and he wriggled against the bindings, trying to free himself. Unable to gain any leverage, he rolled back to his side and saw Scarlet several paces away, also bound and hurt.

"Scarlet!" Jared yelled. Or tried to yell. It came out as a croak. Swallowing to wet his throat, he tried again. "Scarlet!"

JARED, I...I COULD NOT STOP THEM.

Stop who?

Jared looked around for the source of their imprisonment. Standing just behind him was Loch, and sitting not fifty feet away at the base of the cliff they'd fallen over, Iliana.

Loch turned to look at someone on the other side of Jared, causing him to whip his head around. The last thing he saw was a menacing sneer on Jon's face before he slammed Jared's own Colt into his face.

09 STABLES TURNED

Jared came to several hours later, his brain addled from the fall and the blow to the head. He had enough mental fortitude to remain still as his consciousness returned. He wanted to assess his situation without the gang knowing.

Scarlet, can you hear me? Jared's tone had a manic edge to it, his concern for Scarlet negating anything else.

JARED! ARE YOU OKAY?

I'm fine. Don't move. I don't want them to know I'm awake.

As much as he wanted to rip free of his bonds and teach these people to leave him alone, he forced himself to remain calm and motionless.

Can you sense them or see where they are?

Scarlet responded by sharing her impressions through their bond. He wasn't in physical contact with her, so she couldn't share any images, but she sensed all five of the gang several yards away, conversing in hushed tones.

What they are saying?

I CAUGHT SMALL PHRASES AND OUR NAMES MENTIONED

MULTIPLE TIMES. THEY ARE DEBATING WHAT TO DO WITH US. THE BIG ONE, JON, SUGGESTED KILLING ME, DRAGGING YOU BACK TO THEIR CAMP, AND TORTURING INFORMATION OUT OF YOU. THEY DO NOT BELIEVE YOU ARE AN EXPLORER. THEY THINK YOU CAME FROM THE CITIES BECAUSE OF THE PHASE WEAPONS, ALL THE BOOSTERS YOU CARRY, AND BECAUSE OF ME. THEY THINK I AM SOME SORT OF CREATION FROM THE CITIES AND THAT YOU CONTROL ME.

What? Jared's anger peaked. *Kill you? Torture me?* The idea sent waves of white-hot rage him, and he desperately wanted to vent his anger on them.

I won't let them harm you, Scarlet. You have my word. If I have to, I'll kill every one of them if it means protecting you.

Jared tested his bonds. He had no wiggle room but believed he could snap the rope with his increased strength. It wasn't the time to do so with the group so far away, since they'd pull their weapons and shoot him before he made it across the distance. He'd also tipped his hand when he'd first attacked them by the Statue of Liberty, and they knew how fast he was. His strength and the ability to break his bonds were the only advantages he had.

Are you in a position to help if I attack them?

THEY HAVE MY MOUTH TIED SHUT, MY WINGS BOUND, AND MY LEGS TIED TOGETHER WITH MY TAIL. MY WING IS ALSO BROKEN, AND I CAN'T HEAL THE WAY THEY TIED ME UP.

Jared took a deep, calming breath and forced himself to remain calm. They'd hurt his companion and were talking of killing her. A fire lit in his belly, a wild burning rage, that threatened to take over any rational thought.

Jared's rage reached the boiling point, and he shouted, "I'm going kill you! All of you! First, I will break your limbs, tie them together like you did to Scarlet, and then I'll blow your brains out with your own weapons."

"Tough talk for someone hogtied," said Jon, his voice a rumbling bass.

"You think all that muscle will protect you? Seems to me you're overcompensating for something," sneered Jared.

Jon took a few steps toward Jared before Loch intervened.

"We need to keep him alive."

"He doesn't have to be in one piece," spat Jon through clenched teeth.

"Let's go, meathead. How about you untie me, and I show you how pathetic you really are?"

Jon blew past Loch and launched a fist at Jared. He maneuvered his body to take the hit on his shoulder and an explosion of pain ignited through his arm. It wasn't enough to render it useless, but it definitely hurt.

Jared didn't relent as he continued to berate them.

"How about you, you little Irish prick? You think you got the stones to stand toe to toe? You'd probably crap yourself before you took the first swing." Rob started toward Jared as his cheeks flushed red.

Insult his heritage and masculinity, check. Jared grinned an evil smile at them, hoping it conveyed his malicious intent.

"What's the matter? Your mama too soft on you? Did She wean you until you grew that splotchy little stubble on your face? I bet she's got a bigger beard than you."

Jared grinned in triumph as Rob drew his pistol and advanced on him.

"I say we kill 'em right here an' now." Rob's voice promised pain and violence.

"Enough!"

Loch stepped in to referee. It was exactly what Jared wanted.

Get ready, Scarlet. I don't think the mental blast will work the same as before, but try your best to confuse them.

Jared centered himself as best he could, twisted his body and flexed. The ropes on his hands and feet snapped, earning him burns across his wrists and ankles. Ignoring the pain, Jared shot to his feet and dove at Rob, who was the only one with his weapon free.

He hit Rob with a football tackle and wrested his pistol from him. Jared heard joints pop and guessed he'd snapped Rob's fingers. His guess proved correct when Rob snatched his hand back with a cry of pain.

As soon as Jared hit the ground, he rolled, placing Rob between him and the others. Using Rob as a body shield, Jared fired around him at the others.

Aim left, Scarlet instructed.

Jared followed Scarlet's instructions and heard a cry of pain, rewarding his efforts.

Everyone but Jon dove for cover, drawing their own weapons.

Jon stood in the same place, staring at Jared, blood dripping from his fingers. A crimson stain spread across Jon's shirt, and he toppled face first into the ground.

In normal circumstances Jared would've panicked or froze, but all he felt was a sense of urgency with Scarlet bound and unprotected. He'd have time to reflect on his actions later, but right now all that mattered was getting out of this situation and keeping Scarlet safe.

Rob struggled to free himself, but Jared proved too strong. Before letting go, Jared pressed the pistol to Rob's chest and squeezed the trigger. His body went limp, and Jared rolled away from him, coming up in a crouch.

Loch, Iliana, and Lee sprinted in the opposite direction, looking for shelter. Lee was the only one close enough to cover, so Jared focused on chasing him down first. Plus, he had the only rifle of the group, making him the more dangerous adversary.

Neither Iliana or Loch showed an interest in harming or killing them, but he also didn't want to risk testing that theory. If they surrendered without a fight, then perhaps he'd have mercy on them.

Lee darted for an outcropping, while Iliana and Loch sprinted for the cliff face where they could hide amongst the natural caves and crevices.

Jared smirked. They didn't know he had *Heat Sight*, and that he could find them easily amongst the shadows. A feral smile crept up his face just as Lee glanced behind him. His eyes widened, no doubt seeing the manic look on Jared's face, and he put on a burst of speed, diving behind the rock.

Right before he reached Lee's position, the small Asian man leaned from cover, the rifle pressed to his shoulder. Jared launched himself into the air as the shot sailed beneath him. He fired the pistol in a desperate maneuver, hitting the rock and causing shrapnel to assault Lee's face. A sharp sliver of rock embedded itself in Lee's cheek and he screamed in agony.

A testament to his fortitude and battle prowess, the experienced sharpshooter held onto his rifle and fired in Jared's direction. Moving erratically, Jared managed to avoid the shots, if only barely. If the shrapnel hadn't impeded his vision, Jared didn't think he would've been able to avoid getting hit. This guy was good. Pouring on a burst of speed, Jared dove through the air, sailing over Lee's crouched form. In a feat of acrobatic flair, he finished the dive by spinning in the air and firing into Lee's exposed back. He'd tried to shoot twice, but the chamber clicked empty.

The single shot hit true, and Lee slumped forward, his rifle falling from his lifeless hands. Jared landed hard, his twist in the air not allowing him to cushion his fall. He slid across the hard-packed dirt and rocks. Pain erupted along his back, where he hit the ground. Jared ignored it and bounded over to Lee's corpse.

Keeping a watch on the cliff face and a mental link with Scarlet, Jared quickly rummaged through Lee's pack and found several boxes of ammunition for the rifle. He didn't know what kind it was, but he was at least familiar enough to reload and chamber a round.

Three down, two to go.

Scarlet, I've got them cornered in some caves over here. I think I know a way I can get there without leaving myself exposed. Will you be okay over there until I finish this? Or, should I come back and untie you first?

I AM FINE. DO WHAT YOU MUST.

Do you think we're safe here? Jared flicked his eyes to the top of the cliff, making sure the worm couldn't see or sense them. *If that thing made it down here, I'm not sure we'd survive another encounter with it.*

I DO NOT KNOW, BUT IF IT COULD, IT WOULD HAVE ALREADY DONE SO AFTER IT KNOCKED US FROM THE AIR.

We'll worry about it later then. If you sense it getting any closer, please let me know.

Jared truly didn't want to hurt Loch and Iliana, but if they'd left him no choice, he'd end them just like their comrades. His and Scarlet's safety was paramount to his goals, and he had a vow to keep to Alestrialia.

Jared skirted a series of jagged boulders when an idea formed in the back of his mind. He raised the rifle to his shoulder, using the scope to study the cliff face. He didn't think looking at the cliff from this distance with *Heat Sight* would allow him to find the pair, but if he activated *Magnified Vision* while looking through the scope, it's possible the two abilities could work in concert to help him find them.

Scanning the cliff face one more time, Jared located the pair in a shallow depression covered in shadows. A grim smile crept up Jared's face as he peered down the scope, his *Magnified Vision* and *Heat Sight* still active. He centered the crosshairs of the scope on Loch's head and moved his finger to the trigger. Willing himself to end their troubles and be done with these people, Jared couldn't bring himself to pull the trigger. He drew in a deep breath, exhaled slowly, and tried again, and again, he couldn't pull the trigger.

Sighing in exasperation, Jared tried a different tactic. He aimed the rifle just to the left of the pair and fired into the rock wall. Debris exploded outward, making Loch and Iliana jump.

"Stop! Don't shoot!" yelled Loch. They threw their weapons and packs on the ground and walked out with arms raised. "We don't want to harm either of you."

Jared knew it would be safer to kill them and walk away, but he didn't know if he'd be able to live with himself after killing someone that'd surrendered and hadn't intended or done harm to him. It was one thing to kill the other three in defense, to protect Scarlet. However, he couldn't bring himself to murder these two in cold blood, especially when they'd been in favor of keeping him and Scarlet alive.

"Stop!" Jared instructed, as they neared within fifty yards. "Get down on your knees and keep your hands where I can see them. I won't hesitate to shoot if I think you're reaching for a weapon."

Jared kept a healthy distance from the pair as he circled around, retrieved the packs, and picked up their weapon. His weapons. Of course, they'd choose the best weapons after stripping his gear from him. A small knot of anger coiled in his stomach and he nearly changed his mind about keeping them alive.

Re-attaching the holster, Jared checked the battery packs to ensure they hadn't wasted their charge. He slung the rifle over his shoulder and leveled the phase pistol in their direction.

"Lie on your stomach."

They did as instructed and Jared patted them down to ensure they had no hidden weapons.

"Get up. Walk back to Scarlet."

When they reached Scarlet, Jared made them sit off to the side and used the remnants of the rope from his bonds to tie their feet.

"If either of you try escaping or fighting, you'll end up like your friend's over there." Jared gestured to the lifeless form of Rob, a pool of blood soaking into the dirt beneath him.

His prisoners secured, Jared turned his attention to Scarlet, examining her wing.

Scarlet, I need to straighten your wing and bind it to your side. How serious is the break? He made sure to communicate with Scarlet mentally. He had no desire to let Loch overhear their discussion about Scarlet's injuries and her regenerative abilities.

IT SHOULD TAKE NO MORE THAN A DAY. I ALSO HAVE YET TO EXPEND THE LAST OF MY MOTHER'S ESSENCE, SO I SHOULD BE WHOLE AND MUCH STRONGER AFTER RESTING FOR A NIGHT.

Wow, again? You've already grown so much in such a short time! I can't wait to see what happens next. Okay, I'll leave your wing bound after adjusting it and loosen the rope when you sleep. No need to show them just how fast you can heal.

Grimacing at what he had to do, Jared asked, *Ready?*

I AM READY.

Gingerly he probed her injured wing.

Spasms of pain made Scarlet flinch.

Saying a silent apology, Jared grabbed the thick part of her wing, just before the joint that allowed her to fold them against her body and yanked them back into place.

Scarlet growled low in her throat and steam rose from the sides of her mouth.

Sorry, Scarlet, Jared apologized. *Are you okay?*

I. **WILL. BE. FINE,** replied Scarlet, pain evident in her tone.

As gently as he could, he guided her wing to her body, threw a rope over her back, and carefully tied the ends together.

I'll tighten it to make sure it's immobile, but let me know if It gets too tight.

Every movement of the rope sent a stab of pain rippling across their bond. It took every ounce of willpower he possessed to prevent him from walking over to Loch and breaking his arm. As it was, he shot disgusted glances their way and at one point found Iliana staring.

She blanched and looked away after seeing the anger etched into this face.

Scarlet taken care of as best he could, Jared raised his voice so that everyone could hear. "We need to get away from here. Whatever it was that knocked us out of the air is still awake up there and I don't want to tempt fate staying here in case it decides it hasn't had enough to eat."

Jared walked over to Rob's lifeless body. Looking at the corpse, he didn't experience the revulsion he thought he should. Examining his own feelings, he barely felt any guilt at killing them given their desires for him and Scarlet. Though it could have been the adrenaline coursing through his body. He would need to dedicate some self-reflection later to what he'd done here and come to grips with it, but for now they needed to move, and he didn't want to leave all their gear behind.

Jared looted Rob and Jon's corpses, taking Jon's boots as well. They happened to wear the same size, and his desperately needed replacing.

His dad's Colt was also on Jon's body, and he angrily ripped the belt from his waist. He'd give it a thorough inspection and cleaning later to make sure the idiot hadn't ruined it.

Once he'd finished gathering the gear and weapons, he slung everything he could over his shoulders, stuffed all he could into his pack, and left a random assortment of junk in another satchel, which he slung over Loch's shoulder.

"All right let's move. You two will walk in front of us, and no dawdling. We need to find shelter before nightfall."

Jared reflected over the last couple days while they walked southwest, toward Virginia. If the remainder of the Daggers fraternity held the same views as those he'd killed, there was no point in them continuing their journey south. If, on the other hand, the leaders were more like Loch, they had a shot at finding ready allies. After a long internal struggle, Jared realized it wasn't worth the risk and shared his decision with Scarlet.

Scarlet, I think we should head away from the coast after you heal up. We have a long way to go before we're even remotely ready to fight, and I want to put some distance between us, the Daggers, and the cities out this way. Who knows, maybe we can find other settlements that will help us, but I don't think it's a good idea for us to follow Loch and Iliana to their camp. We're not likely to get a warm welcome after what I just did to their people.

They do not have to find out.

Scarlet, we've been over this. I won't kill them. Besides, can you honestly say you wouldn't have done the same thing in their shoes? I mean, they see a lone traveler with phase weapons and a dragon poking around a very dangerous location. It raises all kinds of red flags. I wouldn't try to rob or kill anyone, but I wouldn't rule out detaining someone for questioning.

I agree, but my concern still stands. For now, we

WILL HEAD AWAY FROM THE COAST AND FOCUS ON GAINING
STRENGTH.

Speaking of growing stronger. Jared glanced over his shoulder at
Sandy Hook island. *What do you think about trying to kill that...worm?
Was it a worm? A snake? Whatever it was, we know it's there, where it
lives, and how fast it is. If we can kill it, it's bound to have a ton of nanites.
I mean, how else could it get that big?*

IF WE LURE IT OUT, WE MIGHT STAND A CHANCE.

Jared spent most of the trek to the coast working out a way to
kill the creature. If only they had explosives, they'd make short
work of it, but they only had phase and ballistic rounds, along with
Scarlet's fire.

Not knowing what species didn't help, but if it was a worm,
then it stood to reason they could kill it by taking out its brain. Jared
knew from school that one side of a worm has a darker, wider
segment that signified where its brain lived. If they could bait the
worm out and find that portion of its body, they'd barrage it with
Scarlet's fire and his weapons.

*You have a photographic memory, right? I mean, your mother seemed
to, so I assume you do as well.*

I DO.

*Can you recall images of the creature that batted us away and show
me?*

YES, YOU WILL NEED TO TOUCH ME. PERHAPS CLIMB ON MY
BACK SO WE CAN KEEP WALKING.

Scarlet paused just long enough for Jared to mount. After he
found a comfortable position and had a clear line of sight to his two
prisoners, she showed him the hangar just before the creature
appeared. Then, as if in slow motion, the body shot out of the two
holes in the ground. Studying its physical appearance, everything

pointed to it being a massive worm. There were no scales on it to indicate a snake, no suction cups announcing it as some sort of land octopus, only a thick, slimy membrane-like texture. Its gray, ashen color resembled a rotting corpse.

"Fast forward until its body reaches out for us in the air."

The scene flashed and paused on an image mere millisecond before he'd blacked out. Scarlet's vantage allowed her to see both sides of the creature, one of which emerged more than thirty feet from the hole. Immediately, Jared spotted was he was looking for.

There, you see that dark, brownish black band around it? That's where its brain exists. If we take out that segment, we can probably kill this thing. I know my lessons had more to say about worms, but for the life of me, I can't remember them right now. Maybe you can do that memory sifting thing and look deeper?

Now that he knew what it felt like, it was obvious when Scarlet rooted around inside his mind. It was an odd sensation; Not painful or intrusive, but alien. It felt like cool tendrils of force massaging his mind.

Scarlet remained silent for a time before she said, THE BRAIN OCCUPIES THE THIRD SEGMENT, BUT IF WE DESTROY THE BRAIN, THE REST OF THE WORM MAY GO INTO UNCONTROLLABLE CONVULSIONS. WITH THE SIZE OF THAT THING, WE DO NOT WANT TO BE ANYWHERE NEAR WHEN THAT HAPPENS.

I think we can lure it out, but we need to find bait.

We have bait, Scarlet teased, motioning her head toward their prisoners.

Ignoring Scarlet's comment, Jared suggested, "After you've healed, you can hunt down a few wild animals. Maybe a couple dogs or rats. There's plenty of them around to snatch up."

Although this worm had easily dispatched them before, Jared looked forward to a rematch.

The few miles to the coast passed quickly, and by the time they'd come up with a viable plan, Jared saw a number of buildings along the shoreline. There were way too many places for creatures to hide, the buildings so close together. They walked south, following the coast until they came upon a destroyed marina, hundreds of destroyed boats lay in heaps next to partially collapsed docks. Just off the north western side of the harbor was a trio of buildings split out from those around it. Jared jumped off Scarlet's back and trotted ahead of everyone, intent on checking the buildings for danger.

"Scarlet, please keep an eye on them while I check out these buildings."

A quick search of the three buildings revealed no cause for concern, and Jared ushered everyone into the largest building to give Scarlet some room for her transformation. Jared double-checked the bonds on Loch and Iliana and asked Scarlet to keep an eye on them once again so he could scout their immediate surroundings.

Jogging around the area, he looked for a way to get on top of the building for a better vantage. There were some handholds and even a ladder, but the bottom half rusted away and stood fifteen feet off the ground. If he could reach a ledge about eight feet off the ground, he might be able to pull himself up and jump for the ladder from there. Dropping his gear into a pile on the floor, Jared secured his weapons and snapped the straps closed on his holsters. Crouching a few times to flex and limber himself up, Jared crouched low and leapt.

"Whoa!"

Jared's shout echoed between the buildings as he launched twenty feet into the air, right to the edge of the roof. Surprised by the insane jump, he almost failed to grab the edge before he fell back to the ground. Scrambling for purchase, Jared climbed over the ledge and collapsed onto his back, adrenaline surging through him after the incredible feat.

How the heck did I jump so high?

There's no way he'd jumped this high using just his strength. Granted, it was all new to him, but it seemed impossible even given the massive enhancements he'd gone through.

Scarlet, I think I gained a new ability!

I DID NOT THINK TO CHECK EARLIER. AFTER YOUR RABBIT... ADVENTURES.

Jared sighed. He'd never live this one down.

"Let me quickly check the area, and I'll head back in for you to check it out". Jared jumped to his feet and scanned the area three times using all his sights and senses. Seeing nothing to pose a threat, he carefully climbed down the building. Jumping up had been one thing, but standing on the edge, he just couldn't make the leap of faith to jump off. Especially not knowing more about this ability, or if it was an ability. After grabbing his gear, he hurried over to Scarlet and sat next to her, placing a hand against her side.

IT LOOKS LIKE THE NANITES FROM THE RABBITS GAVE YOU AN ABILITY TO TAP YOUR STRENGTH RESERVES IN SHORT BURSTS. IT LOOKS LIKE THE NANITES RAPIDLY FORCE ADRENALINE AND BLOOD FLOW THROUGH YOUR MUSCLES, GIVING YOUR BODY MAXIMUM STRENGTH AND SPEED FOR A SHORT DURATION. THE DRAWBACK FOR THE ABILITY INCLUDES INCREASED STRAIN ON YOUR BODY AND COULD CAUSE INJURY.

What if I increased bone and muscle density? Jared asked, finally starting to get a handle on how all of this worked.

THAT WOULD HELP, THOUGH THERE WOULD ALWAYS BE A RISK OF PUSHING YOURSELF TOO HARD. HOWEVER, YOU SHOULD

BE ABLE TO USE THE ABILITY PERIODICALLY WITH NO NOTABLE SIDE EFFECTS.

Thanks, Scarlet. If ever I want to increase any more physical aspects, just smack me in the head until I choose Mind. I'm glad that I've got you to help me out here, but I want to understand all of this myself.

Very well, said Scarlet, her words playful.

Jared smiled. He enjoyed Scarlet's teasing nature.

How much bigger do you think you'll get tonight? Do we need to move those two? Jared nodded his head at Loch and Iliana.

THEY SHOULD BE FINE OVER THERE. ALSO, REMEMBER THAT I WILL BURN THROUGH THE LAST OF MY MOTHER'S ESSENCE, AND MY GROWTH MAY BE UNPREDICTABLE.

This whole essence thing seems like a hugely unfair advantage, teased Jared.

AS A MATRIARCH, I CARRY THE CONTINUED EXISTENCE OF OUR FAMILY SOLELY ON MY SHOULDERS. IT IS A BURDEN, NOT AN ADVANTAGE.

Ah, fair point. All right, I've got things on lock here. Feel free to sleep when you're ready.

Jared settled in to wait and busied himself by going through all the gear and weapons from the other explorers. He grabbed all the boosters and the ammunition for the rifle and Colt. At first, he placed all the other pistols in a separate pack, intending to leave them for Loch and Iliana, but he changed his mind and left them only one pistol each. He also put one booster for each of them in the pack in the event they really were low on time like Iliana said. Jared looked at Iliana in his peripheral and found her watching him rummage through their belongings.

We could've been friends in another life, thought Jared. *Maybe that chance still exists in some future scenario.*

For now, Jared intended to go it alone with Scarlet until he found people willing to help without compromising his moral center, if such people even existed.

Jared saw Iliana flinch, and her eyes widened in surprise. Glancing over his shoulder, he found Scarlet the source of her enthrallment. The transformation had started but wasn't quite the same as the pulsating flow from nanite enhancements. Rather, she shimmered, a wispy haze covering her body for a split second. With each shimmer, her form changed. It looked like a mirage, and it made him blink a few times to make sure he actually witnessed the phenomenon.

"She's beautiful, isn't she?" whispered Jared.

Iliana looked over to find Jared's gaze focused on her. She lowered her eyes and replied, "She's incredible."

Turning back to Scarlet, Jared became mesmerized with the shimmering veil of light, his thoughts churning in time to the movement. Jared was so lost in thought, thinking about Iliana and the choices that might've led her to this situation that he hadn't realized everyone but himself was asleep.

Jared felt pity for the two explorers. They'd fallen in with the wrong crowd. Perhaps that wasn't who they were, and absent the fraternity, maybe they were good people. It wasn't too late for it to happen, but not today or any time in the near future. If he ran into them again in the future and they altered their ways, then perhaps he'd consider working with them.

The night passed quickly as Jared stripped all his weapons down and cleaned them, spending extra time on his Colt and its holster. Jon's blood caked half the weapon and belt, and it took several hours to rid the contamination from his beloved revolver. Several hours later, Scarlet was the first of the three to rouse, and she mentally nudged him.

I am awake.

Jared turned to see the much-improved Scarlet. Even though he'd watched some of the changes take place, he hadn't paid attention to how much she'd actually grown.

Whoa. I thought you said there was only a little of the essence left?

I was mistaken. Though I think the last time, it changed other aspects of my body. This time, only my physical size changed.

Wow, Scarlet. These changes are impressive. I can't believe you were an egg barely more than a week ago, you've got to be almost twenty feet tall now!

Although she still had a long way to go before she reached her mother's stature, she was well on her way.

I need to eat soon. I feel weak and need to replenish my strength. The Regeneration and physical changes drew on my vitality, and I need to replenish it before we do anything else.

Jared assured her they'd find something for her to eat before hunting the giant worm.

We'll leave these two here. Jared motioned to the still forms of Loch and Iliana. *I'll make sure they're tied up, toss this survival pack either into another building or up on the roof, and we can head out for the island. Once we get far enough away from here, you can take to the sky. I just don't want them to find out how fast we can heal.*

Scarlet grudgingly accepted the plan, but that was fine by him. It wouldn't be the first time they disagreed on something, and they both needed to learn to accept each other, quirks and all.

Jared grabbed the extra pack and left the room. He looked through each of the buildings for a hiding place, but they were empty, a couple loose rocks here and there. He found nowhere to stash the gear.

Walking back outside, Jared circled each building, assessing which was the easiest to scale. The smallest of the three had a brick exterior and enough of the bricks missing to provide ample handholds up the side. Jared tossed the pack onto the roof and returned to Scarlet.

"Good, you're awake," said Jared, seeing the two blinking the sleep from their eyes. "We're leaving, and I'm leaving both of you here. I'll leave you tied up, and I've also left a pack with two injectors and a couple pistols. I put the pack on top of one of the buildings, but you'll have to figure out which one on your own."

"You can't—" Iliana started to say, but Jared cut her off with a sharp tug on the rope as he finished tying them together.

"I can, and I will. The only reason I'm leaving you alive is that you didn't want to harm Scarlet and me directly. If you'd tried, both of you would've experienced the same fate as your friends. This is not a negotiation, and I won't change my mind. Free yourselves, find the pack, and head back to your camp down south. We have other plans, and they don't involve babysitting the two of you or looking over our shoulders to make sure you aren't following us."

Iliana looked terrified, while Loch looked resolute and accepted the situation with a firm nod.

Jared suspected he knew they'd barely escaped with their lives and this was a favorable outcome compared to their demise. Jared motioned for Scarlet to exit the building and secured all his gear. Taking one last glance over his shoulder, he felt a small stab of guilt at what he'd done and was about to do. Iliana must've seen the conflict in his eyes as her frightened look morphed into one of desperate hope.

That hope evaporated as Jared narrowed his eyes and promptly left the building. He felt a slight tug of guilt but quickly dismissed the feeling. They deserved much worse than the mercy he was granting them. He could deal with his unresolved conflict at a later time.

Jared mounted Scarlet and said, *Let's move!*

10 GODZILLA WORM

Once he was certain they'd moved far enough from the buildings, Jared hopped off Scarlet and untied her wing.

"Go hunt."

Scarlet needed no further prodding as she bunched her legs and launched herself into the sky.

"Oh, let me know if you see Loch or Iliana. In the meantime, I'll keep heading toward the island," Jared called after her.

Every step he took brought him a step closer to the worm that almost ended their lives.

It was payback time, and although they faced a creature that might've rivaled Scarlet's mother in size, in its own habitat for that matter, Jared believed they had a strong chance of success. He also wanted to exact some vengeance for hurting his companion.

Instead of waiting for Scarlet to finish the hunt and pick him up, he decided to stretch his legs and run toward the island. He could get things set up while he waited for her. She also needed to get some bait for the worm. Flexing his muscles, Jared poured on the speed. He ran at a fast clip for five miles before tiring. At that point, he'd nearly reached the island and slowed his pace to a walk.

How's the hunt coming along? Jared asked, unsure if she'd be able to hear him at this distance.

I FOUND A PACK OF WILD DOGS. I AM CHASING THEM DOWN, BUT THEY ARE AGILE, AND IT IS PROVING BOTHERSOME.

We're not in a rush. I'll get started here. By the way, how far away are you? From the island that is?

NEARLY SEVEN MILES.

Oh wow! I'm almost at the island. Your range must have increased after all your changes. It will definitely help when we need to coordinate things like this.

Jared busied himself getting ready for their fight, scaling the cliff he'd fallen over just the day before. It was a simple enough plan: lure the worm out, attack with ranged weapons, Scarlet dive-bombing with fire attacks, and retreat. If they needed to repeat the scenario multiple times, then so be it. The worm itself probably didn't fear anything. It was the apex predator on this island, and anything else on it was just a nuisance to kill.

Halfway up the cliff, he almost decided to wait for Scarlet to carry him up, but decided it was just laziness. Pushing his body, Jared forced himself to finish the precarious climb.

Upon reaching the top, he held in place for a long time, ensuring he hadn't disturbed the worm. They didn't know how far the underground tunnels networked across the island, or if it could sense their presence.

Slowly, he walked toward the hangar, looking for a place to anchor his rope. He'd tie off one end up here, and the other around his waist. If the worm got too close or started its death throes, he could sprint off the edge of the cliff and get away from it. The other option was to have Scarlet fly below the ledge and he'd leap off onto her back, but he wanted that as a last resort on account of her recent injury.

His rope attached to a concrete and metal pillar, Jared shimmied over the edge and found a crevice ten feet down to stuff all his gear in. He then climbed back up, sitting on a natural outcropping to wait for Scarlet and their bait. Occasionally he felt tremors rock the island, but they felt far enough away that it didn't warrant concern.

I'm all set, Scarlet. See if you can carry two of the dogs as bait. This thing is definitely still awake and moving around. I felt the ground shake just a moment ago.

I HAVE TWO OF THEM AND WILL DROP THEM DOWN ONCE YOU ARE READY.

Jared put some weight on the rope and gave it a few sharp tugs to make sure it would hold his weight. Satisfied, Jared told Scarlet he was ready, come what may.

There were a lot of variables here, but it was the safest plan they could come up with. Still, it would be a tricky battle, and anything could change the outcome. Once the creature revealed itself, Jared would climb over the edge of the cliff and pepper it with phase rounds. His attack was more of a distraction, with Scarlet providing the real firepower. The plan was for her to remain in the air where she could avoid the creature's attacks, and hopefully its death throes.

With her increased size, she might even have a chance at physically fighting the worm, provided its entire body wasn't involved. The two halves of its body he'd already seen had to be thirty feet long, and that was just the ends of it. They had no idea how much of it remained beneath the earth.

Jared hesitated as he thought about the actual size of the thing.

Scarlet, I'm having second thoughts about this. I was just doing calculations about the size of this thing, and I'm not sure if it's a good idea for us to go head-to-head.

Let us give the plan a chance. I think it is safe enough, and if we run into trouble, I will fly away, and you can jump over the edge. It will be worth the effort if we are able to kill it.

Hearing the rhythmic beat of Scarlet's wings, Jared looked out from his perch and found Scarlet flying overhead with two squirming dogs in her claws. They looked like rabid, flea-infested monstrosities. Unlike the rest of their kind, they didn't have any fur, but a thick black hide that served as their skin. Scars and claw marks indicated they'd seen a lot of fighting, perhaps amongst themselves for dominance. The dogs' eyes were black, and sunken into their heads, giving them a deadly, ferocious visage. Massive canines dripping spittle completed the terrifying look and Jared immediately hoped he never met a pack of these things in the wild.

Those dogs look disgusting Scarlet. You really ate them?

There are few options in the area, and I needed to gain my strength back as soon as possible.

Jared shook his head. The things Scarlet put into her mouth amazed him, but she was right. There weren't a whole lot of food options around. One of these days they'd find something that actually tasted good. If not for Scarlet's sake, then for his. Rats, lizards, and now wild dogs looked nasty, and no doubt tasted disgusting as well. About the only decent thing she'd eaten since being hatched was the rabbits. Jared shrugged. If it helped her regain strength, then who was he to judge? Scarlet's cuisine choices were hardly something to dwell on at the moment.

Taking a deep breath to calm his wild nerves, Jared said, *All right Scarlet, dogs away.*

He glanced above and watched Scarlet bank toward the structure. She swooped low and threw both dogs past the broken doors into the hangar.

They yipped and growled, scrambling across the floor. Shortly after they landed, he heard them growling and barking at each other as a dog fight ensued.

If the crazed dogs didn't lure this creature out, then they'd call it quits and leave the worm alone. He wasn't about to risk himself or Scarlet as bait, and the racket the dogs were making could be heard a mile away.

Jared waited for several tense moments as the dogs continued their ferocious duel. A tremor rocked the ground, but it didn't feel any stronger than the previous one, and he wondered if the creature was too far away. A moment later another tremor vibrated the ground, increasing in tempo and intensity. Jared panicked, and a wave of doubt rolled through him.

WE WILL BE FINE, said Scarlet, picking up on his emotions.

There was no use second-guessing himself now. They'd set things in motion and he intended to see it through. Jared grabbed both of his phase pistols and waited.

The sounds from the hangar abruptly cut off with one of the dogs issuing a mournful whimper. The victor from the duel limped out of the hangar, looking severely injured from the fight. The dog sniffed the air, turned around, and trotted back into the hangar. After a short pause, Jared heard a sharp squelching crunch echo from the hangar. Bile rose in the back of his throat, imagining the dog ripping into its companion. He did his best to block out the noise, but it still sent a shiver down his spine.

"That's disgust—" Jared started, when the ground shook violently, cutting off his words.

Scarlet, get ready!

Jared heard the dog stop eating and start to whimper.

As suddenly as it began, the ground stopped moving and everything went silent for one long moment.

Then a deafening crack split the air as slabs of concrete exploded upward in a shower of debris.

Although Jared couldn't see the dog, he heard a yelp and its claws scrambling across the floor as it tried to escape. Bracing himself for the worm's appearance, Jared leveled his phase pistols in the direction of the hangar.

The dog bolted from the building, tail between its legs, and right on its heels, the worm.

A giant—*massive*—Godzilla-sized worm.

Now that he had a chance to observe it when not running for his life, he realized just how big it actually was, and he feared he'd made a mistake trying to take this thing on.

Jared had to give the dog credit. Even injured it was fast, but it quickly realized it had no place to go except to jump from the cliff. As the form barreled after its runaway meal, Jared grew concerned. At twenty feet he still didn't see the third segment.

Scarlet, I don't—aha, there it is! Go, go, go!

Just as in Scarlet's vision, the first two segments of its body were thirty feet in length, the brown band marking their target immediately after.

Jared steeled his nerves, took aim, and rapidly squeezed the triggers on his phase pistols. He was careful with each shot, making them count. One after the other, the phase rounds sizzled into the worm's side, tiny burn marks marring its thick flesh. Surprisingly, the phase rounds did little damage to its skin, but it definitely served its intended purpose to distract the worm and lure it further out of the hangar.

It paused in its pursuit of the dog and hesitated, torn between the two targets. Eventually, it chose Jared for whatever reason. Perhaps he was a larger meal, or an easier target. Regardless, Jared needed it to exit the hangar just a few more feet to give Scarlet a perfect opportunity.

Jared sprinted toward the edge of the cliff and stopped right on the edge. The worm paused again, as if re-evaluating its chosen morsel.

I've got get this thing to commit.

He redoubled the pace of his shots on the worm, hoping to enrage it. At first it seemed to no avail, and then it lunged.

Scarlet, attack!

The worm moved a few more feet out of the tunnel, fully exposing the segment that housed its brain. Scarlet dove through the air, sucked in a breath of air and attacked.

Blue flames erupted from her mouth, sizzling into the side of the worm.

It recoiled from the fire with an ear-piercing screech. The ground trembling while its body thrashed about in the tunnels below.

It was impossible for him to get off a clean shot at the creature while he stumbled about, but it looked like he might not need to do much more as the hangar collapsed on top of the writhing body.

A large steel beam disconnected from the joist, swung toward the ground, and fell straight down, puncturing the body of the worm and pinning it in place.

Scarlet, hit it again! It's pinned!

Scarlet whipped her head around, making an impossible flip in midair. The move cost her a bit of momentum and she dropped below the lip of the plateau before she regained the altitude and roared in for another pass.

Hurry Scarlet! I don't think this will hold much longer.

As if on cue, the steel beam started to wobble.

Scarlet's next assault served to enrage the creature beyond any rational thought. All self-preservation fled, as the worm ripped itself free, nearly cutting its own body in half.

Surprisingly, both sides appeared fully functional as it continued the mad rampage to reach Scarlet.

She was much too fast in the air and managed to fly well beyond its reach.

After Scarlet's attack, it completely forgot about Jared and allowed him to retrieve his rifle. He hoped the ballistic rounds would pierce its hide and allow Scarlet to spew flames into the open wound.

Carefully lining up his shots to make them count, Jared rapidly pulled the trigger until the small clip clicked empty.

Where the phase rounds only aggravated the worm, the rifle punched holes straight into its side.

Shrieking in rage, it whirled around to face him, and Jared prepared to leap over the ledge if it attacked. Instead of lunging at him directly, the other side of it emerged from the ground not ten feet away, spraying him with dirt and rocks. Squeezing his eyes shut, he blindly leapt from the edge, bracing himself for the impact against the wall. Only he didn't hit the wall, and the rope pulled taut as soon as he reached the lip of the cliff, pinning him against the ledge.

Glancing behind him, Jared realized the second half of the worm's body lay across his anchor rope and wouldn't budge no matter how hard he pulled.

"No!" Jared shouted, as the worm reared up to slam on top of him.

Just then, Scarlet dove back for a second attack and breathed flames directly into the wounds his rifled had drilled into the worm's side.

The creature convulsed, freeing the rope enough to let him drop over the edge.

Get out of there, Scarlet!

I THINK THAT LAST ATTACK DID IT.

Scarlet's statement rang true when Jared heard a loud pop followed by a forceful sucking.

The next instant a stream of translucent goo and chunks of slimy ashen flesh sailed over the cliff's edge.

Thankfully, he was close enough to the wall to avoid it. Immediately following the explosion of gore, he heard two loud thumps accompanied by a tremor that reverberated through the ground and caused him to jostle against the cliff wall. He quickly grabbed the ledge in case the rope came loose. Jared was about to peek over the edge when Scarlet shouted at him.

GRAB THE WALL!

Jared felt the rope give way, and relief flooded through him that he'd had the foresight to secure a handhold. Without Scarlet nearby to catch him, the fall would be an instant death.

The only sound he heard was the pop and sizzle of the worm's slimy skin, and Jared wondered if the whole death throes thing was just a myth.

Scarlet, I—

STAY THERE, she interrupted him.

He'd been about to send her a rebuttal when the ground vibrated beneath his hands. Just to be safe, he climbed down another fifteen feet and wedged himself into an alcove. The rumbling grew louder as the quaking intensified.

The convulsing worm must have been demolishing anything in its path.

He heard buildings crumbling to the ground, great crashing

noises from the earth ripping apart, and sickly wet slapping as the body of the worm flailed about.

Several minutes later everything went silent. Jared's fingers ached from the strain of holding himself in place while the earth bounced up and down.

Is it safe to come up?

YES, THE CREATURE APPEARS DEAD.

Jared climbed back up the cliff and opened his mouth in surprise at the sight.

Flat.

The single word popped into his head and was the only descriptor that fit the current reality of the area. Not a single building remained standing, mini craters bore evidence of the creature's underground passages, and the little hill behind what used to be the hangar looked like a bomb had blasted it apart, a great chasm splitting the middle. From his vantage, the chasm descended deep into the earth, the worm's body weaving in out and out of large holes.

His first thought was that they'd been idiots to go up against this creature. It rivaled Scarlet's mother in size. That size alone made this thing deadly.

Next time I get a hare-brained idea like this, please try and talk me out of it. Frankly, I'm very surprised we survived, let alone killed it. I mean, look at that thing! How the heck are we supposed to absorb the nanites from it anyway? It's like a mile long! Okay, that's a slight exaggeration, but seriously, how are we supposed to absorb them? Do you think we can just touch any part of it?

THE HOLES ARE BIG ENOUGH FOR YOU TO ENTER.

You can't seriously mean — Jared cut off his next words as Scarlet thumped down next to him. He wasn't claustrophobic, but walking into the lair of a mile-long worm was insanity.

While he deliberated his next move, Scarlet walked over to the upper part of the worm cloven from the rest of its body and sunk her teeth into its flesh.

Jared looked at her aghast. "Ugh. Really, Scarlet? That's just...I can't," Jared said, fighting back gags as he walked several paces away from her. "How can you possibly eat that thing?"

I NEED TO REGAIN MY STRENGTH. THE DOGS I ATE EARLIER HELPED, BUT IT WAS NOT SUFFICIENT. I WILL EAT MY FILL AND ABSORB NANITES AT THE SAME TIME. YOU SHOULD GET MOVING; WE DO NOT KNOW HOW LONG THE NANITES ARE VIABLE ONCE THE HOST IS DEAD.

Sighing, Jared walked over to the other side of the worm. A terrible, pungent smell curled his nose hairs, sending waves of nausea rolling through him. He doubled over, holding his sides. With his nose plugged, Jared breathed in huge gulps of air to keep from retching.

Before dropping into the hole, he wanted to try absorbing the nanites from here. If there was a way to do it without going underground, he'd take that option, even if he missed a small portion of them. The other side of the creature was still visible over by the cliff's edge where he'd jumped off, so they could at least absorb from both ends.

Tentatively, Jared reached his hand out to touch the worm. Squeezing his eyes shut, he pressed his bare hand into the slimy flesh, his insides recoiling from the sensation. It was cold, wet, and gooey. He snatched his hand away in disgust, shaking the thick mucus from his fingers. He glanced over his shoulder at Scarlet only to see her chomping away, a large chunk of the worm missing.

The sight was enough to push him over the edge. An uncontrollable urge to vomit made him heave. His stomach tried squeezing out of his mouth, but all that came up was stomach acid, further increasing his disgust. Jared's breathing came in shallow gasps. Forcing air through his diaphragm helped the turmoil in his stomach and warded off the urge to expel his insides.

"I don't know how you're eating this thing," Jared forced out through clinched death. His every word tasted bitter from the bile. "It's horrendous."

I ALREADY TOLD YOU MY REASONING. BESIDES, IT REALLY HAS NO TASTE. AS LONG AS YOU CAN OVERCOME THE TEXTURE, IT IS NOT UNPLEASANT.

Baring her teeth at him, Jared saw bits of its flesh in her mouth, and he quickly turned away. Shuddering, Jared tried to rid the images from his head.

Recovered, he pressed his hand to the worm's flesh again. At first nothing happened, and then he saw the familiar glow and swirl of the nanites leaving the worm and entering his body. Only, this time, it wasn't just a small flash of light like with the rabbit.

The glow grew rapidly, becoming a raging torrent of multi-colored lights shooting into his body. His skin crawled from the sensation, and in no time at all, it began to get uncomfortably hot.

"Scarlet," Jared said, concerned. When she didn't answer, Jared shouted into her mind, *Scarlet!*

The nanites rushed into his body unbelievably fast, and no matter how hard he tried, he couldn't remove his hand from the worm's body. The heat intensified, sending his body into spasms. The fire consumed him, making his vision go dark around the edges. His mind tried protecting him from the pain by sending his consciousness into oblivion.

A sharp blow to his side sent him flying ten feet away, abruptly cutting off the flow of molten lava into his body.

He lay there panting as Scarlet walked over to him and nudged him with her snout, a snout dripping with nasty slime and worm fragments.

"Ah, come on, Scarlet, seriously? Ew, just...ugh."

Jared rolled away from Scarlet, his freshly battered body protesting. He levered himself onto all fours and looked at the worm.

"Thanks for getting me out of there. I don't know how much more I could've taken. If feels like I was just burned alive. Is that why I was unconscious during your mother's transition? I remember it being painful, but it only lasted a few seconds before I blacked out."

I AM UNSURE. AT THE TIME, I WAS QUITE PREOCCUPIED. THOUGH, IF I HAD TO GUESS, THEN I BELIEVE YOU ARE RIGHT.

His breathing returning to normal, Jared stood painfully to his feet. It was then he noticed small flashes of iridescent lights cascading across his skin as the nanites integrated into his body.

"Maybe you should absorb the rest. I don't think I can handle any more right now." Jared held up his hand and watched the shimmering veil of nanites until it stopped.

"I'm guessing we don't have to touch multiple parts of this thing to absorb the nanites. They all just came rushing through its body into mine."

Scarlet walked over to the dead worm and was about to chomp down when Jared interjected. "Wait. I don't think I'll be able to knock you out of the way like that if it becomes too much for you."

THERE IS NO CHOICE HERE. WE NEED TO GET STRONGER AND IF ENDURING PAIN ACCELERATES OUR GOALS, THEN I WILL ENDURE THE PAIN.

With that, Scarlet bit into the exposed flesh, the glow of nanites resuming its flow into the dragon.

Jared watched in fascination as the nanites rushed into her. The scintillating light intensified and rippled across Scarlet's body, seeping into her flesh and scales.

"Are you okay?"

Yes, the pain is bearable. If I were to absorb all of them, including the ones you already did, it would have hurt me in much the same way. Though I can disconnect my mind from the pain, so it is difficult to know for sure.

"Based on the number of times I've blacked out or nearly blacked out, in the last week, I think I'll need to learn how to do that sooner rather than later."

Once you enhance your mind sufficiently, you will have a greater control over abilities like that. This worm should be a good start down that path.

The glow of nanites dimmed as the torrent came to an end. Scarlet bowed her head in silence and collapsed right next to the bisected worm to collect herself.

Jared, look at your status screen.

Jared hesitated. *Did something bad happen?* He focused, willing the screen to appear before him.

"Holy crap! Scarlet, how is this possible? How does one creature have so many nanites?" Jared read the available nanites again, shook his head and read it a third time. "I have ninety-five percent to assign!"

Scarlet's status showed she had sixty percent, but given her rapid growth already, that was still a massive amount of enhancements. "How did this thing have so many more nanites than your mother?"

Jared assumed this thing had more on account of all the nanites he'd already absorbed only being five percent of what coursed through his body.

I BELIEVE THEY WERE ROUGHLY EQUAL, ONLY MY MOTHER PASSED MOST OF HERS TO ME INSTEAD OF YOU. AS FOR HOW THIS CREATURE ACQUIRED SO MANY, MY FIRST THOUGHT IS THAT THERE MIGHT BE SUBTERRANEAN BIOLOGICAL LIFE IT CONSUMED. THESE TUNNELS COULD EXTEND MILES BELOW THE SURFACE.

"Well, dang. This was a huge risk but was well worth the effort. We'd have to kill hundreds, if not thousands of rats to get an equivalent amount."

IT LOOKS LIKE WE GAINED ABILITIES FROM THIS WORM TOO. I NEED MORE TIME TO STUDY THEM, BEFORE I UNDERSTAND HOW THEY WORK. ONE OF THEM ALLOWS YOU TO CONTROL YOUR BODY TEMPERATURE, AND THE OTHER IS SOME KIND OF HIBERNATION CAPABILITY, THAT ALLOWS YOU TO SLOW DOWN YOUR HEART RATE.

Jared stared at his status screen for a few more minutes, contemplating his next moves. As planned, he was definitely going to be sinking most of these nanites into *Mind*. It was his biggest detriment to getting stronger at the moment. Although he knew which areas to upgrade, he closed the screen without making any selections. Deciding in haste was stupid, and they'd have plenty of time to take care of it later.

Jared turned to Scarlet and asked, "Are you strong enough to carry me now? I think it's time we head away from the coast."

YES.

Jared fetched his gear and leapt onto Scarlet's back.

"Let's fly!"

Scarlet bounded into the air and banked to the west. The sun had just crested its zenith, and they had half a day to fly as far inland as possible, putting as much distance between the Daggers and any of the coastal cities as possible.

It's time for us to disappear and work on getting stronger.

11 ABANDONED CITY

Jared and Scarlet lazily soared through the sky enjoying the freedom of the open sky. Closing his eyes, he enjoyed the wind whipping through his hair, the smell of fresh, crisp air, free of death and decay.

Travelling on foot became monotonous while crossing a barren wasteland, but up in the sky, with no fears and worries, and the sun's warmth a pleasant companion, Jared's burdens disappeared for a time. They needed no words to communicate, their emotions easily apparent across their bond while physically touching. Scarlet enjoyed the freedom and sensations just as much. If they could fly forever…

Maybe this is why the cities remain isolated? thought Jared. *It's infinitely more peaceful up here. They don't have to fear mutations, and there's much less radiation to contend with.*

While understanding started to take hold, it also irritated him that those in power could be so selfish and keep the rest of the world from experiencing the same.

Someday that will change.

Jared returned his thoughts to their current situation to watch the landscape pass below.

Occasionally they witnessed small creatures darting about, but nothing they cared to confront. The small gains they'd get from these creatures wouldn't propel them forward and Scarlet didn't need to eat yet.

Plus, Jared didn't want to stop flying. It was exhilarating. The moment they were on the ground again, it was like entering a prison. At least up here, they were completely and utterly free.

They flew for hours, headed northwest toward upstate New York. Most of the earth was scorched from the war, the radiation, or the acidic rains that followed. The only plant life they saw was near larger bodies of water, which he tried to avoid. Some nasty creatures lurked in the depths. The one time he'd wandered out to the ocean helped him learn he never wanted to venture there again. At least, not until he was much stronger and could face the terrors beneath the surface.

After five or six hours, Jared spotted a long body of water surrounded by more green than he'd ever seen, and it piqued his interest.

"Let's take a closer look at these lakes," suggested Jared.

Scarlet banked and they dropped closer to the ground. From up high they resembled massive blue claw marks in the earth. When they drew near, Jared's eyes widened at the view before him. Thick green vines and creeping plants pushed outward from the lake in every direction.

"Wow, look at that." Jared's intrigue grew, and anticipation ran through his body. This was the first time he'd seen anything like it. Excited, he said, "We've got to stop here for a while. Just don't land too close to the water. We have no idea what lives in there."

Jared switched to *Heat Sight* and looked back to the water

where an even more incredible view greeted him.

"Wow, those lakes are teeming with creatures."

Jared watched all sizes and shapes of aquatic creatures darting about the lake. Although it was difficult to make out individual creatures, he saw long, angular bodies that looked like crocodiles. There were schools of small fish darting about. One area in particular showed a massive ball of writhing bodies, but he couldn't pick out individual creatures. Further north, Jared caught glimpses of some truly massive creatures as big as Scarlet. At first, he wondered if they were sharks, or just really big fish that'd mutated over the years, but then recalled fish were cold-blooded and they wouldn't register on his *Heat Vision*. Whatever they were, Jared wanted to steer clear until he had a better grasp on the situation.

Most of the areas he'd visited during his exploration bore evidence of nuclear attacks, bombs, craters, and often had an absence of any kind of plant life. This area not only had a massive amount of vegetation, there was also no evidence of the destruction prevalent in other parts of the continent. Surprisingly, the buildings he saw appeared abandoned.

Where are the survivors? Jared wondered. *This area looks very habitable, but I see no signs of human life.*

Warning bells went off in Jared's mind. There had to be a reason why no one lived here anymore. Perhaps it was simply an excess amount of radioactive waste in the air and people couldn't survive here prior to the nanites being released a decade ago. There weren't a whole lot of explorers. Most people preferred to reside safely within the boundaries of their colonies. Jared hoped it were that simple, but exercised caution by asking Scarlet to land safely away from the water, and the abundant life therein.

Scarlet circled a few more times.

"We should check out some of these buildings." Jared paused

and looked at the sun's position. "On second thought, let's find someplace that we can rest for the night."

THERE IS A LARGE BUILDING JUST TO THE WEST OF US.

Jared looked to his left and spotted the building she'd referenced. "All right, let's land over there. We can do some exploring tomorrow."

The building they landed in front of resembled a barn, but he'd never seen one made of metal. Jared started toward the building and switched to *Heat Sight*. The ability was becoming second nature to him.

"Scarlet, something's moving around in there, and it looks big. It shouldn't be a problem for us, but be ready just in case. Who knows, maybe we can roast it for dinner. I've not had a fresh meal in a long time. Though if it's another nasty creature like those dogs or worm, you can take it somewhere else to whet your appetite. I can still taste the bile from last time you made me retch." Jared smirked and glanced back at Scarlet.

"Ouch!" Jared's foot caught, and he fell to the ground, Scarlet's tail quickly vacating the scene of the crime. Chuckling, he stood up and brushed himself off.

"Well played, Scarlet. Well played," Jared said, feeling amusement flutter across their connection.

Jared and Scarlet meandered closer to the building. Whatever was inside must've heard them as it ambled toward the door. Jared stopped and waited for the creature to come to them. He pulled his revolver and prepared to kill whatever lurked inside.

The hinges on the door screeched as a large, furry head poked out, making Jared freeze in fear.

A bear.

Even though he had nothing to fear from this bear given his weapons and Scarlet standing next to him, he had an irrational fear after what happened to his dad. He couldn't move, couldn't think, and the bear just stared at them. Jared tried to move his body, but it betrayed him; his mind experiencing the situation in the third person. It was like a waking nightmare where he knew of his surroundings but couldn't do anything to assuage his fears.

The bear rushed him. Jared's memories flashed back to his father lying lifeless on the ground, and the dead bear next to him with a gaping bullet wound in its head.

Why was I working so close to the boundary? Why didn't I move faster?

"No!" Jared roared, pain and anguish ripping through him. His paralysis evaporated. He raised the Colt and squeezed the trigger again and again and again. Long after the chamber clicked empty, Jared continued pulling the trigger, delirious and in a state of catatonia from the pain and hate.

JARED. JARED! JARED!

He blinked and looked around. What remained of the bear was a bloodied, headless corpse. He'd obliterated its head in his vengeance-fueled rage. Jared dropped to his knees, scalding tears leaving tracks down his face.

In his state of emotional turmoil, the events of the past few years slammed into his mind in a kaleidoscope of memories.

His father's death haunted him; the bear's lifeless eyes staring at him gave him nightmares from time to time. The sight of his mother's frail body as it wasted away wracked him with grief. The last few days ran through his mind on repeat as he watched himself kill Jon, Rob, and Lee.

"What have I done?" Jared shuddered, his shoulders trembling from the uncontrollable sobs that shook his body.

He thought back to the event Scarlet observed when she rooted through his mind during their bonding. Himself as a boy standing next to Tiny, taking the assault stoically and refusing to stoop to the level of the juvenile thug by hitting back. Jared's parents were so proud of him for standing up to him, and his refusal to stoop to petty violence as a quick solution.

Now I've killed three people.

The adrenaline-fueled, emotionless state he'd been in the past couple days was utterly and completely gone. He felt only a deep sense of loss and conflict about taking their lives. One half of his mind refused to believe it necessary, and he couldn't reconcile with the other half that believed it warranted.

Jared felt Scarlet nuzzle him and absentmindedly reached up to touch her. The moment his hand made contact, images of the prior days flashed through his mind. Images and events that transpired after the worm knocked them from the sky.

Watching through Scarlet's eyes, he saw the worm smash into Scarlet's side and send him falling from her back.

Jared watched Scarlet dive for him, but he was too close to the cliff wall, and in the process of catching him, she smashed her wing into the wall. A great snapping noise reverberated through him and he knew how her wing broke.

"Scarlet, I—"

W ATCH.

Jared watched, his admiration for Scarlet growing. She tried to arrest her fall by pushing off the wall and gliding, but it caused her to spin in a circle and spiral to the ground in an uncontrollable arc. While Jared watched, he saw the other explorers within sight as they stood and watched the events play out.

Just before Scarlet impacted the earth, he witnessed Loch and Iliana sprinting toward them as the other three hung back pumping their fists, broad grins splitting their faces. The scene ended when Scarlet lost consciousness. When she woke a short time later, she'd reached out her senses and heard the other explorers talking.

"I think we should kill them," Jon had suggested. "That dragon is evil, putting things in our head like it did."

"I agree with Jon 'ere. We tell a story in my family about dragons an' how they used to terrorize the world. I thought it be a myth growin' up, but now I ain't so sure 'o that."

Iliana had come to their defense. "Even if that were true, Rob, that had to be thousands of years ago. Why do you think this dragon is bad? She hasn't even done anything to harm us."

"Plus, we need to find out how Jared found her. If we had a dragon on our side..." Loch let his voice trail off.

Another voice Jared hadn't heard yet joined the mix. The accent was hard to place, and it had a strange halting quality to it. Jared surmised that was Lee's voice, since he was the only one he hadn't heard speak.

"My people have stories in our family about giant beasts. Beasts able to breathe fire and fly. We held them as celebrated legends of mythology, but all the best legends have some truth to them. I've heard tales about these creatures destroying whole cities, and just as many about the creatures standing next to humans in a fight for their lives. Still, I agree with Jon. We should kill it rather than risk it growing bigger. The world already has enough problems without adding a dragon to the mix."

Once again Loch had interjected, his voice turned menacing, "We will *not* kill them. We need them; it could change everything!"

Immediately after, Jared heard his own voice shout with rage, "I will kill you! Every one of—"

The scene ended, and Jared realized he'd stopped sobbing. He no longer felt conflicted about the men he'd killed. He was also extremely relieved he'd left the other two alive.

Curious, Jared asked, "Scarlet, why did you want to kill Iliana and Loch? They wanted to keep us alive."

ALIVE FOR WHAT? THEY WOULD TAKE US TO THEIR CAMP AND EXTRACT INFORMATION FROM US NO MATTER THE COST. THEN, IF THEIR LEADERS BELIEVED AS JON AND THESE OTHER TWO, THEY WOULD KILL US ANYWAY. THREE OUT OF FIVE WANTED US DEAD. DO YOU THINK THE PEOPLE AT THEIR CAMP WOULD BE ANY DIFFERENT?

Jared bowed his head in acquiescence. "I see your point and although a part of me agrees with you, I don't think I could've lived with myself for hurting someone that meant no harm to us."

YOU...YOU ARE RIGHT. I WILL TRY TO SEE HUMANS THE WAY YOU DO. I SENSE THE TRUTH TO YOUR WORDS AND REALIZE NOW WHAT IT WOULD HAVE COST YOU TO KILL THEM, AND I AM SORRY FOR GOADING YOU.

"It's okay, Scarlet. I know you want what's best for us, and I promise to make better choices about people. I was much too trusting of them, and we nearly paid the penalty with our lives. For that, please forgive me."

Scarlet accepted his apology, and they put the incident behind them once and for all. They knew where each of them stood, and they no longer needed to worry about crossing a boundary either of them would regret.

Collecting his wits, Jared drew in a deep breath to expunge the negative emotions and murkiness lingering in his mind. He stood and glanced dispassionately at the destroyed lump of bear.

"Eat the rest if you're hungry," he called over his shoulder. "I'll finish checking out this building and make sure there are no other creatures inside."

Replacing his spent revolver, Jared pulled out a phase pistol and slipped through the door the bear had vacated. It was mostly one large room, but there appeared to be stalls off to the side. He quickly opened each one and found all but the last one empty. The last one had all kinds of debris, fur remnants, and bones scattered around. It was a curious place to find a bear. It was possible they'd just happened upon it by chance as it was out looking for food. Or it'd chosen this place for a den. It didn't matter now, since it was dead, and he'd claimed the place for him and Scarlet.

Jared kicked the stall door closed and searched the rest of the room. The only other area within the building was a small alcove, or loft, with a ladder leading up. Jared climbed to the top, made sure it was devoid of creatures, and called out an all clear to Scarlet.

Scarlet, the building is empty. Let me get these doors open so you can come inside.

Jared dropped to the ground and made his way to the doors. He had to excavate the ground around the door before he could swing it open enough for Scarlet to enter. The opening was at least two stories high, and Scarlet had no problem walking in with her head down.

Shutting the doors, Jared barred them from within using a heavy metal beam leaning against the wall. The building wasn't entirely untouched by decay, and portions of the ceiling had caved in, but it had four walls and, as far as Jared saw, only the one door to enter. Safe for the night, Jared climbed up to the loft once more and dropped his gear next to some discarded plastic crates.

Scarlet settled on her haunches, her head level with the loft.

"All right, Scarlet, let's figure out where to put these nanites!" While Jared looked at his status screen and abilities, he remembered Scarlet hadn't told him about their abilities from the worm.

"Hey, did you figure out how these new abilities work?" As Jared scanned the growing list of skills, he noted two additional entries called *Thermoregulation* and *Aestivation*.

"You couldn't make them any easier to understand? What the heck are they supposed to do?"

I ONLY RECEIVED THE AESTIVATION ABILITY WHILE YOU HAVE BOTH. THERMOREGULATION DOESN'T WORK WITH DRAGON PHYSIOLOGY SINCE I HAVE FIRE ROILING AROUND INSIDE. I CANNOT DECREASE THE TEMPERATURE OF MY BODY. WITH THE ABILITY, YOU CAN ALTER YOUR BODY TEMPERATURE, THOUGH IT IS NOT AN INSTANTANEOUS PROCESS. THE NANITES INCREASE OR DECREASE YOUR HEART RATE AND BLOOD FLOW TO REGULATE TEMPERATURE, SIMILAR TO THE ABILITY YOU HAD BEFORE OUR BONDING. ONLY NOW, YOU CAN CONTROL WHEN THAT HAPPENS.

Scarlet paused to make sure Jared understood before continuing. AESTIVATION IS THE ABILITY TO SLOW YOUR HEART RATE DOWN AND ENTER A STATE OF DORMANCY. THIS SLOWS METABOLIC PROCESSES TO A CRAWL. YOUR BRAIN WILL CONTINUE TO FUNCTION NORMALLY, BUT THE BODY WILL ENTER A STATE OF INACTIVITY.

"I think both will come in handy at some point," responded Jared, but he paused while trying to sift through the lines of information on his display. "Reading through this status screen is getting complicated. Can you, I don't know, rearrange them maybe?"

I COULD; IT IS SIMPLE ENOUGH TO MODIFY THE NANITE CODE THAT DISPLAYS IT, BUT I THINK YOU SHOULD INVEST YOUR NANITES INTO MIND FIRST. YOU HAVE MORE THAN ENOUGH NANITES TO UPGRADE YOUR MIND SUFFICIENTLY TO UNDERSTAND AND REARRANGE THEM YOURSELF. YOU MAY NOT

EVEN NEED IT ANYMORE ONCE YOU DO.

Jared went through all of his options and eventually decided to follow Scarlet's advice. He already had major physical enhancements, and with Scarlet around, she'd augment any deficiencies in that regard.

"Okay, I'll sink half of my nanites into *Intelligence Enhancement*, the rest I'll put into *Hyper-cognition*, *Memory Recall*, *Telepathy*, and *Natural Armor*. I was going to just go with all *Mind*, but I think adding in some defensive measures is a good idea. These rags I'm wearing won't stop a bullet, but maybe between *Skin Hardening* and *Natural Armor* I can build up enough defense to stop one." Jared's selections looked like the following:

JARED - NANITES AVAILABLE: 95%

MIND

Brain Augmentation

Intelligence Enhancement - 45%

Hyper-Cognition - 15%

Memory Recall - 15%

Telepathy - 15%

BODY

Physical Augmentation

Physical Defense

Natural Armor - 5%

EXCELLENT CHOICES. THE IMPROVEMENT TO YOUR INTELLIGENCE SHOULD SUFFICE FOR YOU TO UNDERSTAND THE NANITES AND HOW THEY WORK. HOPEFULLY, YOU WILL ALSO UNDERSTAND THE VARIOUS AREAS IN YOUR BODY YOU MAY IMPROVE.

"It'll be great to understand what is happening to my body and be able to interface directly with the nanites. I feel like there's so much I'm missing."

I'VE DONE AS MUCH AS I CAN TO FACILITATE THE PROCESS, BUT THE REST IS UP TO YOU.

"Do you think the addition to *Telepathy* will allow us to communicate better? You said eventually we'll be able to share thought spaces and instantaneous communication, right?"

IT MAY TAKE MANY YEARS UNTIL YOU CAN COMMUNICATE AS EFFECTIVELY AS A DRAGON. ALSO, YOU SHOULD KNOW YOU ARE NOT USING TELEPATHY IN THE SAME WAY. INSTEAD, YOU ARE USING THE NANITES TO MIMIC IT. WHEN YOU WANT TO PROJECT YOUR THOUGHTS AND SENSES, YOU ARE INSTRUCTING YOUR NANITES TO SEND THEM TO MINE.

Jared finished making his selections and turned to Scarlet. "What enhancements do you want to make?"

DEFENSES. SPECIFICALLY, PHYSICAL DEFENSE, PHYSICAL ATTACK, AND REGENERATION. BREAKING MY WING THE OTHER DAY SHOWED ME THE IMPORTANCE OF FAST HEALING. PLEASE MAKE THESE SELECTIONS:

SCARLET - NANITES AVAILABLE: 60%
BODY
> Physical Augmentation
>> Physical Defense/Attack
>> Skin Hardening - 10%
>> Scale Hardening - 10%
>> Bone Hardening - 10%
>> Fire Breathing - 15%
> Body Manipulation

Regeneration - 15%

Jared remembered his desire to ask Scarlet about the color of her fire when he pushed more nanite into the category. "I was curious—the color of your fire changed to blue. I'm assuming that means it's hotter?"

YES, IT WILL CONTINUE TO CHANGE COLOR AS IT INCREASES IN STRENGTH. THE HOTTEST FLAME IS BLACK. MY MOTHER IS THE ONLY DRAGON THAT EVER ACHIEVED IT. I ALSO BELIEVE ONLY A FIRE DRAGON IS CAPABLE OF THAT FEAT.

"Wow, black flame. I don't think I've ever seen anything like that."

BLACK FLAMES ARE BARELY VISIBLE TO THE NAKED EYE.

"That would be creepy. Flames barely visible yet utterly destroying everything in their path."

IT WILL BE QUITE SOME TIME BEFORE I REACH THAT LEVEL OF MASTERY, BUT WITH THE NANITES AND ABILITY TO INCREASE THE HEAT DIRECTLY, IT MAY HAPPEN MUCH FASTER.

"Have I said how much I love these nanites and enhancements?" Jared had a cheesy grin plastered on his face. He imagined the whirlwind of destruction he and Scarlet could become. As they both grew in strength, they wouldn't have to worry about people like the Daggers anymore. Sure, in large numbers they'd still be a problem, but a group of five wouldn't pose a threat. Especially, if they became impervious to conventional weapons.

Finishing their selections, Jared minimized the status screen, and said, "I don't think we need to set a watch tonight. Let's get some much-needed rest."

I SAW NO OTHER CREATURES NEARBY WHEN WE LANDED.

Jared smacked his forehead, annoyed. "I didn't even bother to check the area around the building. I was...a little distracted. When I saw the bear I kind of lost it."

WE ARE A TEAM. NO NEED FOR YOU TO APOLOGIZE.

Jared lay back, his head resting on his pack, and enjoying the safety of their shelter. It'd been a while since he felt so safe and it allowed him to let his mind wander to questions he'd put off.

"Hey Scarlet, why is there only one female dragon for each domain?"

I WISH I KNEW. IT HAS ALWAYS BEEN SO, BUT MY MOTHER BELIEVED US DESIGNED THAT WAY TO PREVENT OVER-POPULATION AND ASSERTING CONTROL ON THE WORLD. WE LIVED WITH HUMANS AND OTHER CREATURE'S SIDE-BY-SIDE, NOT TO RULE OVER THEM OR DOMINATE THE WORLD.

"Do you know how dragons came to exist?"

JARED, YOU ARE ASKING QUESTIONS I HAVE NO ANSWER FOR. WE EXIST, AND HAVE EXISTED FOR MILLENNIA, BUT HOW WE CAME TO BE AND WHY, WE DO NOT KNOW.

"What about the rest of your family? You know how to get to them, right?"

I KNOW THE GENERAL VICINITY FROM MY MOTHER'S MEMORIES. IT WAS THE MOST IMPORTANT MEMORY SHE PASSED ON, AND SHE MADE ME PROMISE TO SEEK THEM OUT WHEN I AM STRONG ENOUGH. IT IS A JOURNEY I MUST MAKE ON MY OWN; A HUMAN WOULD NOT SURVIVE SO FAR BENEATH THE EARTH'S SURFACE.

"Well, whatever you must do, I will support you in any way I can."

THANK YOU, JARED.

It took Jared a while to fall asleep, his mind reeling with all the possibilities before them.

Jared awoke several days later feeling refreshed. Blinking the sleep from his eyes he looked around. All was as it had been when he went to sleep, and Scarlet sat in the same place, her eyes closed.

"Scarlet, you awake?"

HELLO, JARED.

"How long was I out this time?"

YOU WERE ASLEEP FOR THREE DAYS.

"Wow, this days-on-end sleep thing will need to change. We can't afford to have me knocked out for so long. Especially if we're in a more dangerous position."

YOU HAD A LOT OF CHANGES HAPPENING.

"What about you?" Jared asked, puzzled. She didn't look any different, though it was dark in the room and his *Night Vision* provided little detail.

MY CHANGES ARE MUCH SUBTLER THIS TIME AROUND. AS ARE YOURS.

Jared turned his thoughts back to himself. Physically he didn't look any different, but somehow, he could sense the nanites in and around him. Eyes closed, Jared sent his mind inward, an entirely new world blossoming before him.

With little effort, he understood his body in ways he'd never thought possible.

"Scarlet, how do I—"

FOLLOW THE NANITES.

"How did you—"

YOU ARE PRACTICALLY ADVERTISING YOUR THOUGHTS FOR

ANYONE SENSITIVE ENOUGH TO HEAR. WHEN YOU ARE READY, I WILL SHOW YOU HOW TO ERECT MENTAL BARRIERS. AS FOR FOLLOWING THEM, JUST FOCUS ON WHERE YOU WANT TO GO.

Follow the nanites. All right, here goes nothing.

Jared focused on a particular set of nanites that felt distinctly responsible for his muscles. Jared didn't know how he knew that, but he knew it to be right. The moment he focused on the nanites, his perspective fractured and expanded to encompass all of the nanites responsible for the same function. He knew how they interacted with his body, tearing down and rebuilding muscles, ligaments, and pathways.

No wonder my body felt raw after I increased my muscle mass, the nanites tore apart my muscles to rebuild and improve them.

Their coding and structure felt alien, but at the same time he understood them, and he realized how versatile they were. Instinctively, he knew he couldn't control these nanites anymore; their coding was permanent, immutable.

Jared dove deeper. The complexity of the coding amazed him. While he explored his body, information about various muscle groups and organs flooded into him, easily recalling lessons he learned in school. The memories of his lessons flashed by with vivid clarity, but at a fraction of the time it had happened in reality.

This must be the memory recall working, thought Jared.

It wasn't eidetic memory, and he couldn't recall verbatim everything he'd learned, but it was so much clearer, and he didn't have to spend long periods thinking about it before he made the connections.

"Scarlet, this—this is amazing."

I HAD TEN YEARS TO EXPERIENCE THE SAME THING YOU ARE GOING THROUGH, AND I KNOW JUST HOW OVERWHELMING IT IS

AT FIRST. WHEN THE NANITES FIRST APPEARED, IT WAS SUCH A SMALL NUMBER, BUT THEY'RE DESIGNED TO REPLICATE AND CREATE A COPY FOR EVERY CELL IN YOUR BODY. ANY ADDITIONAL NANITES ARE FREE NANITES, THE ONES WE USE FOR ENHANCEMENTS.

"Now, if only they didn't come with the techno-virus side effects. What exactly does the virus do anyway? I wonder if..."

JARED, NO!

"What's wrong?"

DO NOT LOOK FOR OR TRY TO UNDERSTAND THE VIRUS PORTION OF THE NANITES. I FEAR YOUR MIND IS NOT STRONG ENOUGH, AND IF YOU DWELL ON IT TOO MUCH, IT COULD FURTHER CORRUPT YOU. ALL I CAN TELL YOU FOR SURE, IS THAT SOMETHING IN YOUR GENETIC MAKEUP CORRUPTS THE NANITE CODE. IF YOU DON'T INJECT NEW NANITES TO OVERWRITE, OR RESET, THE CODING, IT BREAKS DOWN TO THE POINT IT ON LONGER FUNCTIONS, AND YOUR BODY DIES OR MUTATES FROM THE RADIATION POISONING.

"Thanks, Scarlet, but if we can figure out a way to eliminate the virus, perhaps we can cultivate a cure for everyone."

Jared spent an entire day learning about his body and the nanites that flowed through it. He learned how to compartmentalize his mind, control his senses, and recall images or memories at will. It wasn't a perfect science, and he had a lot of room to improve, but the control he now possessed gave him hope for the future.

One area that intrigued him was *Natural Armor*. It wasn't just a field of nanites around his body as he'd originally suspected. It was actually a kind of shield that fed off of the energy produced in his own body. He could strengthen it, but ultimately it depended on his available energy.

Perhaps the most interesting aspect of the nanites were those assigned to *Body Manipulation*. He discovered any nanites in the category could be re-assigned to *Remodeling, Regeneration,* and *Density*. All three areas used only the nanites assigned to regenerate body parts, restructure portions of the anatomy, and increase density. He could move those nanites around at will.

If he received a serious injury, Jared could instruct all the nanites assigned to *Regeneration* and expedite his healing significantly.

The possibilities are endless, thought Jared, as he drifted off to sleep once more.

12 AN UNEASY FEELING

Jared woke the next day, refreshed and ready to take on the world. He'd barely slept, preferring to spend the time learning about and understanding the nanites in his body. The memory recall did wonders to help him remember lessons on anatomy from childhood. He'd always been a good student, but as he relived the lessons from school, he wished he'd studied even harder to better understand things today.

"Scarlet, you up yet?"

YES. YOU REALLY MUST LEARN TO CONTROL YOUR THOUGHTS. THEY ARE...LOUD.

Abashed, Jared apologized. "I'll work on it."

Before he passed out the night before Scarlet showed him how to compartmentalize his thoughts, trapping them inside a mental box of a sort. It would take some work before he could do this while sleeping. A few moments of concentration allowed Jared to re-erect the barriers on his mind.

BETTER, Scarlet thanked him.

"I think we've been cooped up for long enough. I want to get out and stretch my legs, but let's take the exploration slow at first. We'll search the buildings on the outskirts of the town and work our way toward the lake. There's something off about this area, and I don't want to stumble into anything blindly."

Strapping his pack and weapons on, Jared jumped down from the loft and removed the metal bar from the door. Looking around, he ensured nothing lurked in wait for them and heaved the doors open.

SHOULD WE FLY? asked Scarlet.

"You can, but I'd like to stretch my legs. I'm a bit stiff from lying there so long."

Scarlet leapt into the air and flew around the area while Jared made his way into a little house a short distance from the barn. He switched over to *Heat Sight* before entering to make sure he encountered no surprises. The exploration went quickly, and he found nothing of interest. The wooden house was falling apart and anything of value was already gone.

He left the house to examine a nearby silo. Once again, it was empty, and nothing of any value to him remained.

Even the bear incident was strange given the extreme absence of life anywhere outside the nearby water.

Headed to the next house Scarlet. You see anything from up there?

NO, THE AREA APPEARS UTTERLY ABANDONED. THE ONLY OTHER LIFE FORMS I CAN SEE ARE IN THE WATER.

I just made the same conclusion down here. See if you can fly a little further afield to find anything else, just don't go closer to the water. We've no idea what's waiting for us there.

Scarlet acknowledged his request and wheeled away. Walking to the next field over, Jared spotted a modest-sized house and several other decrepit buildings that fell victim to rot and age. One of them had a faded red color and was fairly large in size, but what remained was a four-foot high wall, the roof completely collapsed into the interior. By-passing the destroyed building, Jared walked around the house, peering inside broken windows.

The floorboards creaked as he walked through each of the rooms, looking for anything worth taking. Most of the cabinets and drawers were turned out and empty. Leather and cloth furniture lay in tatters, only the skeleton of their structure remaining. A thorough search brought no insight into the people that once lived here, nor did he find any reason to stay.

Frustrated, Jared walked around to the back of the house where stairs to a cellar descended beneath it. The doors rested flush with the ground, and a rusted chain looped through the handles on both doors. Tugging on the chain, it fell away in his hands, the links disintegrating from age. Jared paused with his *Heat Sight* on to make sure nothing would jump out at him if he opened the doors.

After ensuring it safe, he threw open the doors.

"Ugh!"

Jared coughed and sneezed, the smell and dust assaulting his senses. The air was so thick from the stuff, it felt tangible and carried with it the stink of decay.

"Holy crap, this place is disgusting."

Jared hesitated to enter the underground chamber, but so far, he'd struck out with the few buildings explored and hoped he'd find something—really anything at this point. He fished a scrap of cloth from his pack and wrapped it around his head before stepping down into the concrete room.

Shortly after entering the room, he realized the smell diminished significantly as did the particles in the air.

Must've been the pressure of the doors opening, thought Jared.

The room was much larger than he expected, and he guessed this underground room extended well beyond the house above.

There were a few rooms off to the side and he picked the first on the right to begin his search. The rooms were mostly free of decay and there really wasn't a lot of dirt, most of it having shot into his face when the door opened.

"Figures," muttered Jared.

The first room he looked into functioned as a storage area. Boxes lined the wall along with cans that no longer held labels. Unfortunately, everything was empty. Dumping the contents of the boxes, he found random supplies, but nothing that would be of use to him.

Disappointed, he moved on. The next room looked like a bedroom, complete with a metal bed frame and remnants of what looked like a mattress. Along one wall rested a closet and a small bathroom. Opening the closet, a pile of rags littered the bottom, the remnants of the clothing that once hung there.

Jared's shoulders slumped in frustration, but right before he turned away, he spotted a black container. It had looked like part of the wall in the low light. He opened the other door and found the front of the box.

It's a safe!

Jared's dad had kept a safe in their home growing up where he'd store his Colt and ammunition. Jared remembered his dad telling him about the safe and how it would protect things inside and keep dangerous things safely out of his reach. Unfortunately, Jared also remembered his dad used a combination to open it.

He checked the lever to see if it was open, but his luck didn't seem to be with him today. Removing the safe, which was heavy even with his increased strength, he brought it into the main room.

Scarlet, I found a safe that might have valuable stuff in it. It's sealed and locked, so we'll need to figure out how to open it without the combination.

A SAFE?

A small…portable vault? Basically, a metal and concrete box that's fireproof and used to store valuable items.

SOUNDS LIKE YOU HAVE HAD MORE SUCCESS THAN ME. I CANNOT UNDERSTAND WHY ANYONE WOULD ABANDON THIS PLACE. THE WATER CONTAINS SO MUCH LIFE, IT SEEMS STRANGE, AND THE WHOLE SCENARIO IS TROUBLING.

I agree. Let me finish up here, and we'll see if we can't get this thing opened. I'm guessing that most of these buildings are empty and we'll just find more useless crap, but if this safe has some weapons and ammo, it will have been worth it. Who knows, maybe we'll even find some boosters, but I'm not even sure there's been anyone here in the last decade since boosters existed.

I SEE THE ENTRANCE TO THE HOUSE YOU ARE IN NOW. I WILL LOOK FOR MORE LIKE IT.

Jared paused to think about his conversation with Scarlet.

Why are we scavenging this place? The thought startled him. The last two years of his existence had been aimless wandering, scavenging random things here and there, always on the lookout for boosters, weapons, and ammo. He had a pack full up weapons and ammo, and enough boosters to last many years.

What am I looking for? Will one more gun really help my current mission?

Shaking his head, Jared almost turned around and left the cellar, intent on having a chat with Scarlet on what they should be doing. Instead of leaving, he decided to finish exploring this space and then decide what to do.

Jared resumed his search and entered the final room, pausing at the threshold as a fetid odor puckered his nose. The source of the original smell emanated from this room, and now he knew why. A metal table and chairs stood in the center of the room, and off to the side two skeletons sat side by side, limbs intertwined.

What? How—why were the cellar doors locked from the outside? Maybe there's another entrance.

Partly to get away from the smell and sight, Jared went back to the main room and looked around. He saw nothing on the ceiling that would lead to the house above. *How did they get in here, then? Did someone lock them in? Did I miss something?*

Examining the walls, Jared went back through the rooms in reverse order and saw nothing out of the ordinary until he reached the room with all the boxes and empty cans. Behind a stack of boxes stood the outline of a door. He'd missed it before because it matched the interior of the room, and it wasn't easy to pick out small variations with his night vision. There were also no handles or mechanism to open from inside. He pushed, but the door felt solid and held fast.

Who would've locked these poor people down here to die?

Whoever locked them up was long gone, and there was nothing he could do about it. Maybe the safe held more answers, but that would have to wait.

Jared turned his attention back to the hidden door. After an exhaustive search, he realized there was no way to open it from this side without force. He backed up a step and stomped on the door, but it held fast. A half dozen more kicks saw the same result. Frustrated, Jared tried once more, but this time activated *Maximum Muscle*. Right before he launched his foot forward he flexed his muscles, hoping his foot wouldn't break on impact, but the extra force was all he needed, and the locked door smashed open.

An odor even more powerful than the room in the cellar exploded from the corridor. His nose burned, and eyes watered at the fetid scent. Jared knew more death and decay awaited him down this passage. Chills creeped down his spine, and he almost turned around, but a facility like this screamed treasure to him. Even if nothing more than a conspiracy theorist nut job creating his own bomb shelter, there was a high probability he'd find something of interest. There was also the mystery of two corpses locked into the cellar. He'd look for answers further down the tunnel.

Scarlet, I found an underground tunnel. It's...well, I'm not getting the best vibes from it, but I want to follow it and see where it leads.

PLEASE BE CAREFUL. YOU REMEMBER WHAT HAPPENED LAST TIME WE WERE UNDERGROUND. YOU ALMOST DIED, AND I HAD TO WATCH OVER YOU FOR FIVE DAYS UNTIL YOU HEALED.

I'll be careful. If I see any signs of trouble, I'll run away.

Jared walked through the tunnel and followed it for several hundred feet before it rounded a corner. Taking the turn, he paused. The tunnel ended into a large room—a dining hall, based on the number of tables and chairs, all arranged in neat rows. There were enough for at least a hundred people to sit comfortably. Several rooms sat off to the right side of the hall.

Based on the smell permeating the air, Jared expected to see bones or evidence of decaying bodies, but there was nothing in the room.

He walked around cautiously, expecting creatures to jump out at him at any moment, but *Heat Sight* and *Night Vision* revealed an entirely empty room.

Although there was no visible reason for concern, something niggled at the back of his mind. That niggling sensation created unease and made the shadows come alive at the corners of his vision. Yet no matter how thorough his examination of the room, he couldn't find the source of his discomfort.

The closer he moved to the other end of the room, the more his senses behaved erratically. He started to notice dark splotches on the ground, but it was impossible to tell what they were with just *Night Vision*. Crouching lower, the faint metallic scent of blood reached his nostrils.

Scarlet, it looks like there was a massive fight or struggle here. Blood spatters are all over the ground, but there are no bodies, or even skeletons. I don't know what happened down here, but it's seriously creeping me out.

I AM GETTING THE SAME FEELING. THE MORE I WATCH THE WATER, THE MORE MY INSTINCTS SCREAM TO RUN AWAY.

If we run up against anything we can't handle, we'll leave. It looks like this might've been a survivor colony at one point, but something terrible happened to the people, and I'd like to find out what.

PLEASE BE CAREFUL, pleaded Scarlet.

I will Scarlet, I promise!

Jared walked through all the rooms dotting the sides of the hall, but didn't see any further signs of struggle, or anything worth taking. On the other side of the room, he found another hallway, unsurprisingly in the same direction as the blood spatters.

Jared marked the passageways he travelled, in case he got turned around, but so far, he'd found it super easy to recall everything he'd looked at. If he thought about the areas he visited, a photographic-like image appeared in his mind.

I can't believe I've been missing this all my life.

He'd heard about people having photographic memories, and now having experienced it himself, he envied the gift they'd had their whole life. He'd make certain he never took any of these abilities for granted.

Thankfully, the physical enhancements remained no matter what happened, but if the nanites in his body were somehow destroyed, then the abilities would disappear. The thought gave him pause.

What would happen if I got struck by lightning? Or, some electro-

magnetic pulse destroyed all electrical devices? Would the nanites survive because they're a hybrid and live off my biological energy?

Obviously, Jared had no answer for any of the questions running amok in his brain, but he filed them away for later inspection. It was possible Scarlet knew the answer, but now wasn't the best time to discuss it.

Hesitating at the next hallway, Jared looked at the floor and walls. It was obvious that someone, or something, dragged the bodies of those massacred through this entry.

Jared's heart rate increased, and the urge to flee escalated so much that he backed up a step, intending to bolt in the other direction.

Scarlet, how are we looking up there? Everything still quiet?

IT IS THE SAME AS IT WAS BEFORE, BUT MY SENSES ARE—IT IS AS IF SOMETHING VIOLENT LURKS JUST OUT OF SIGHT.

You aren't the only one. There's this other corridor I'm standing in front of, and it looks horrific. The walls and floor—heck, even the ceiling—have blood stains everywhere. The only reason I'm even considering going further is that the stains are old, faded. The weirdest part is that there are no remnants of anything killed here. Not even a single scrap of clothing. I just don't understand it.

JARED.

Don't worry Scarlet, I'll be careful. I'll take it very slow and if I see anything suspicious, I'll retreat.

Taking a deep breath, Jared crossed into the hall, pistol held in front of him. He crept along the tunnel as quietly as possible, looking at every crevice for any signs of danger. The tunnel continued a few hundred feet and opened into another large room. Switching *Heat Sight* on, Jared paused a few feet away from the opening and crouched for several minutes, ensuring nothing waited beyond.

Night Vision re-engaged, he stole forward in a low crouch and entered the room. What he saw stopped him in his tracks, icy tendrils of fear snaking through his body.

What the heck happened here?

The room had three entrances and every single one of them bore bloody stains. In the room itself, bloody patches and spray patterns painted a gruesome spectacle, a miasma of death and destruction.

The scent of death and decay emanated most strongly in this place. The metallic coppery taste was palpable. Though the smell wasn't much better, Jared forced his mouth closed, preferring the smell of decay to the taste on his tongue.

Like the dining hall he'd just vacated, only the blood remained. No other evidence aside from drag marks, and the occasional furrow in the stone, marked the passage.

Where did they go?

Jared looked around the room at the walls and ceiling and found a bunch of holes in them. Unlike the worm's den, these holes were no bigger than the span of his hand and filled with bits of bone and cloth. Walking closer made it clear that the putrid smell permeating the room, and the entire underground facility, originated here. This was ground zero for the mayhem that happened many years earlier.

Scarlet, whatever happened to these people was unimaginable. It looks like something dismembered them and dragged parts of their bodies through holes no bigger than my hand.

WHAT COULD DO SOMETHING LIKE THAT?

I've no idea, but whatever, or whoever, did it appears long gone. There's no evidence this place has seen a living creature in decades.

ARE YOU COMING BACK OUT?

Not yet. There are more tunnels to explore, and I haven't seen anything to indicate there are predators down here. Don't get me wrong, it's freaking creepy, but I think it's safe at the moment. From the size of these rooms and tunnels, I bet this underground complex weaves under the entire town. My main concern is getting too close to the water, but I think I've got a good idea where I am relative to the surface.

There were two additional tunnels branching from the chamber he stood in, the third being the one he'd just come from. His mind a bit rattled from the discovery of this place, Jared had trouble determining which tunnel led toward the water, and which away from it.

I wonder.

Jared brought up the image of the city from his and Scarlet's flight a few days earlier. Next, he replayed the moments when he entered the cellar and every tunnel he'd traversed since. Using the photographic images, he merged both the aerial view with his progress through the tunnels and a three-dimensional map emerged.

"Awesome!" whooped Jared.

The mental map allowed him to orient himself with the lake and ensure he stayed clear of it for now. The tunnel directly in front of him paralleled the water line and was several hundred yards from its edge. The other tunnel led at a forty-degree angle away from the water and towards the outskirts of the small town.

Wanting to avoid the water, Jared chose the direction leading away from it. At the end of the corridor, he found another large room with dozens of cots scattered randomly around the floor. It looked like a sleeping area, or an infirmary, but he couldn't tell for sure since nothing remained but the furniture.

Contrary to the scene in the dining area, this area showed signs of a massive struggle. Cots lay on their sides, the canvas stretched across them ripped and the metal frames bent out of shape. Blood stained every surface. Jared hoped there were some boosters down here. If it was an infirmary, this would be where he'd store them, if there were any left.

Hey Scarlet, have you seen any evidence to suggest people lived here within the last ten years? I'm curious if they knew of this place, or if they had any boosters before this massacre took place.

I...IT IS HARD TO SAY, BUT THERE ARE SOME STRUCTURES THAT LOOK MODIFIED, AS IF SOMEONE REPAIRED THEM.

If they were here after the nanites became available, and were a recognized colony, then they might have a stockpile somewhere. I'm in what looks like an infirmary, but so far haven't found anything worth saving.

A tiny room at the back corner was the only place he hadn't searched. It turned out to be a small storage closet with floor to ceiling industrial grade glass cabinets. Surprisingly, this room was untouched by the horrors just a few steps away. Opening the containers and cabinets, Jared found a veritable treasure trove of medical supplies.

"Wow," breathed Jared. The cache of medical supplies was equal to the stash back at his home colony.

Scarlet! I found a ton of medical supplies!

BOOSTERS?

Nothing yet, but I haven't finished going through everything yet. I'll try to bring as much of this out with me as possible. We can return later for the rest of it.

Jared opened cabinet after cabinet, placing everything he could into an empty crate off to the side. He grabbed bandages, healing salves, sealed bottles of disinfectant, surgical tools, and a smattering of painkillers.

All that remained was a locked cabinet he hadn't opened yet. Grabbing a knife from his pack, he wedged it into the door and popped it open. It was hardly heavy duty and not designed to keep a determined person out.

Jared eyes widened, his mouth dropping open in shock.

Row after row of booster shots lined every shelf. He fell back on his butt and stared in muted wonder. There were enough boosters to sustain a colony for years.

Scarlet, I found the mother lode here. There's got to be at least a hundred boosters.

Jared emptied some bandages and tools from the crate he'd packed and stacked the boosters inside.

We need to find some way for you to help me carry all this stuff after we move away from here. No way I'm leaving any of this behind.

I CAN HOLD THEM WITH MY CLAWS.

Yeah, but I don't think that's a good idea. If we need to fight, it will just get in the way, and if you have to drop them...no, I think I should fashion a sling or something you can wear around your neck.

YOU WILL JUST NEED TO MAKE SURE IT DOESN'T INTERFERE WITH MY WINGS.

We'll figure something out before we leave the area.

After he finished loading the crate, Jared hiked back to the cellar and deposited the box in one of the empty rooms. If he had to make a quick escape from the tunnels, he didn't want to lose it.

The crate secured in the storage room, he returned to the chamber and took the tunnel running parallel to the water. After a time, the tunnel branched yet again. One led directly away from the water, the other headed towards it. Sticking with his previous plan, Jared took the tunnel leading away from the water.

The corridor ran for a short distance until he ran into a huge steel door. Thankfully, it wasn't closed, since he doubted he'd be able to break through it otherwise. Entering the room, Jared froze, his eyes nearly popping from their sockets.

"Holy mother of all that's—wow!"

Forgetting all about decorum and caution, Jared ran through the room, his eyes darting back and forth at row after row of weapons and ammunition. The room held cages secured by padlocks and in each cage rested dozens if not hundreds of weapons. He saw pistols, rifles, shotguns, machine guns, grenade launchers, and even explosives.

The back wall held barrels of raw ingredients for various explosives and ammunition. There were multiple presses for reloading his bullets.

Scarlet, you'll never believe—

JARED, YOU NEED TO GET OUT OF THERE NOW!

Jared didn't hesitate; he spun on his heel and raced through the tunnels at breakneck speed. He made it back to the house, and Scarlet thumped to the ground as he exited the cellar.

What's wrong?

GET ON!

As soon as Jared leapt unto Scarlet's back, she leapt into the air. When she was a safe distance from the ground, she banked and headed toward the waterline.

LOOK.

Jared looked out over the water and vegetation. "It's moving. Scarlet, what—"

KEEP WATCHING.

As he watched, the vegetation writhed like tentacles on the ground. Even more disconcerting, they moved in the direction Jared just left. Not the small house, but the underground execution chamber he'd discovered.

"How?"

LOOK AT THE WATER WITH YOUR HEAT SIGHT.

Jared followed her instructions and gasped in surprise. Where before the lake looked like a bunch of independent creature's swimming around, now it looked like one giant undulating creature. All the life forms, or life form, coalesced into a giant ball of energy.

The water above the area bubbled and thrashed from the activity and mass of the creature.

"What is that thing?"

I DO NOT THINK IT IS A SINGLE THING, BUT A BUNCH OF LIFE FORMS THAT MAKE UP ITS WHOLE. WHILE I WATCHED FROM THE AIR, ALL THE CREATURES SWIMMING IN THE WATER HAD THEIR OWN VOLITION, BUT AS SOON AS THE PLANTS MOVED, THEY STOPPED THEIR INDEPENDENT MOVEMENT AND LIKE A HIVE MIND MOVED TO THAT SPOT YOU SEE NOW.

"So, all of this vegetation is part of that...thing?"

I DO NOT KNOW FOR SURE, BUT IT CAN CONTROL PARTS OF IT.

The vines wriggled across the ground, and Jared got a sick feeling in the pit of his stomach.

"In that chamber I found below, there's a bunch of holes just big enough for vines like that." Jared projected an image of the chamber to Scarlet. "I bet this thing killed them and dragged their bodies off."

IT IS THE ONLY THEORY WE HAVE AT THE MOMENT, BUT IT SEEMS PLAUSIBLE. THOUGH HOW DID IT HERD EVERYONE INTO THAT CHAMBER?

"I don't know, but we've got to get rid of that thing. We need to get back into that room I just came from. There're enough weapons in there to build an army. They have explosives and any kind of gun you can think of aside from phase weapons. We have to get back in somehow."

We will watch and learn. It did not start moving until you passed the chamber you showed me.

"How did it know I was there?"

I do not know, and I have been unwilling to get closer to find out. Did you come into contact with any plants below?

"No. At least none that I'm aware of."

Clearly, we are missing something.

"Whatever we're missing, we need to figure it out. I'm not leaving this area until we get back into those tunnels. That cache of weapons is much too valuable to leave here. I'm just glad I brought the boosters back to the cellar. We should at least return and grab them in case the vines spread out that far. We'll hole up in the barn until we figure out what to do."

They flew back to the cellar opening, and Jared carried the crate and safe outside.

Jared secured the lid of the crate, so nothing fell out. Even losing one booster would be a travesty. They were like gold in the world and he wanted every possible advantage he could get. Scarlet gripped both of the boxes in her fore claws and used her hind legs to launch them into the air.

"Let's see if we can find some place to rest farther away for tonight. The barn is probably far enough away, but I don't want to risk it."

Scarlet flew west, away from the finger-like lakes and to safety. They needed to regroup and create a plan to deal with the plant-controlling ball of energy.

We will find a way.

13 MYSTERIOUS NOTES

S carlet flew for at least thirty minutes before Jared spotted a row of crumbling buildings with no signs of life around. He patted Scarlet's side and showed her the location to set down. One of the buildings was large enough for Scarlet to climb inside. It wasn't the most comfortable, but at least it'd shield them from sight.

Scarlet set down and squeezed into the building through the partially collapsed room, giving him space to bring the crate and safe inside.

He popped the lid open and picked up a booster. Composed of surgical grade plastic with a near infinite shelf-life, Jared turned it over in his hand. It seemed like just yesterday he wasn't sure if he'd survive another two months, and now he had enough for an entire colony to survive years.

"Scarlet, do you think this booster would give me a lot of free nanites? For enhancements? There are hundreds of them here."

I DO NOT BELIEVE THEY WOULD. THEIR PRIMARY PURPOSE IS TO RESET THE CODING TO PREVENT CORRUPTION.

Jared sent his mind inward, examining the nanites. Now that

he was able to sense and understand them, it didn't take him long to find the code responsible for adapting to his DNA sequence. It was simple really. After injecting the booster, the initialization sequence allowed the new nanites to compare their coding with the existing nanites, and if they are corrupt, it sent a reset instruction, with code parameters to fix them.

"I wonder what causes the corruption? What exactly is the techno-virus?"

I DO NOT KNOW FOR CERTAIN. THE ONLY NANITES CODED TO HUMAN DNA MY MOTHER AND I CAME INTO CONTACT WITH PRIOR TO YOU WAS THE OTHER EXPLORER, SCARLET. THE NANITES WENT DORMANT IMMEDIATELY AFTER SHE DIED, SO WE DID NOT HAVE LONG ENOUGH TO STUDY THEM. NOW THAT MINE ARE CODED TO YOUR DNA, I AM ABLE TO STUDY IT MORE, AND BELIEVE THERE ARE CELLS IN YOUR BODY THAT EAT AWAY AT THE CODE LITTLE BY LITTLE.

"Why would it hurt me to examine them in my mind? You stopped me from doing it before."

IT MAY NOT, BUT I DO NOT UNDERSTAND THE CORRUPTION SUFFICIENTLY. ONCE YOURS START TO DETERIORATE I SHOULD HAVE A BETTER UNDERSTANDING.

Scarlet's explanation aside, he almost injected himself with a booster to see exactly how many free nanites he'd get. He decided not to waste any and figured it'd be better to use them for recruiting others to their cause. He might not need so many of them, unless an entire colony agree to join up with him.

Turning his thoughts back to their current predicament, Jared asked Scarlet. "Do you have any idea what we're facing with that creature we ran from? Or, better yet, what it did to the people that used to live there? Did it eat them? Absorb their blood? That chamber down there..."

I HONESTLY DO NOT KNOW, BUT IT LOOKS LIKE THE CREATURE CONTROLS EVERY LIFE FORM IN THE WATER AND CAN USE THE PLANTS AS AN EXTENSION OF ITSELF.

"If it doesn't pull back from the armory, we've got to find a way to kill it. We may never find anything like this place again, and we can't afford to leave the equipment behind."

IT IS UNFORTUNATE YOU DID NOT GRAB EXPLOSIVES ON YOUR WAY OUT OF THE ARMORY. PERHAPS, THAT WOULD HAVE BEEN USEFUL TO KILL THIS THING?

"I know; there's a lot of stuff in there that'd be useful to kill it. Well, at least I think so. We don't know what *it* is yet." Jared recalled the images of the armory and placed his hand on Scarlet's side. Here's what the armory looks like."

I DO NOT KNOW WHAT MOST OF THESE ARE.

"Look at the shelf in the first cage. There is a row of plastic binders, and if they are like the one opened on that table, they're all laminated instruction manuals for all the weapons and equipment in there. I can learn how to use them, if we can get back in there."

Jared put the boosters back inside the crate and closed it up. He'd have to lug this crate around until he found a home base where he could confidently store them without fear of someone stealing them.

Pushing the crate out of the way, Jared dragged the safe closer and examined it from every angle. He saw no way to open it short of smashing it apart. His phase pistol might work, but he didn't know what was inside and the energy might just destroy anything of value.

"Scarlet, any idea how we can open this?"

In answer, Scarlet lifted a claw and brought it down on the

edge of the safe. Jared watched in shock as her claw sunk into the safe like a warm knife through butter. He blinked and looked at Scarlet, his mouth open.

"Holy crap, Scarlet. This safe is several inches of reinforced steel and concrete, and you opened it up like a scalpel parting flesh."

I USED BODY MANIPULATION TO ENHANCE MY CLAWS AND THE SPIKES ALONG MY BACK, THE POINT AND EDGES ARE IMPERCEPTIBLE TO THE NAKED EYE, ALTHOUGH YOU MIGHT BE ABLE TO SEE THEM IF YOU USE YOUR MAGNIFIED VISION.

"That's pretty sweet." For a moment, Jared though about doing something like that on his body, but quickly dismissed the idea. He had no need of claws or spikes.

Curious if he could see the edge of her claws, Jared crouched closer and activated *Magnified Vision*. His vision swam until he managed to regain focus. Sure enough, he saw the nanometer-thin edge effortlessly creating furrows in the concrete beneath Scarlet's feet.

"I almost feel bad for anything that tries to attack you," Jared said. "I think I need to find some other way for you to carry this stuff sooner rather than later. It wouldn't take much for you to accidentally slice into the crates and spill everything to the ground."

He moved back to the now open safe at sat down.

"Thanks for opening it. I bet your razor claws are much cooler than anything inside."

With the steel bolts that secured the door cut in two, the door opened effortlessly. Jared grew disappointed.

He found a small pistol with no ammunition, a couple handmade items that held zero interest for him, and a stack of papers with handwritten notes on it.

"Well that was a bust."

Scarlet snorted. When he looked at her, her eyes shifted to the crate behind him.

"Yeah, yeah, I know. It was a successful hunt today, but that doesn't mean I'm not disappointed. Someone went to such great lengths to protect and preserve this stuff, but it doesn't seem like a great find to me."

DO THE PAPERS HAVE ANYTHING USEFUL ON THEM?

Shrugging, Jared picked up the pieces of paper and read. They were a personal accounting or journal of someone in the colony. It outlined day-to-day life and seemed fairly mundane until he read the final entries.

"Scarlet, listen to this."

...it created a problem with living space, and we let people stay in the old military bunkers throughout the area. None of us know what this place used to be, but the entire area sits on top of a giant underground facility. We only discovered them in the last six months, but we have already uncovered a massive complex. We use the infirmary and dining hall regularly for meetings and caring for the sick.

Again, I digress, and my words continue to scrawl across this page unbidden. I suppose I should wrap it up now and get on with the day. I've got to go see the Blooms and make sure everything is okay.

Year of the Colony - 123yc, Day 116

I visited the Blooms yesterday, and something is definitely off about them. They are acting strangely, and Jeff snapped at me in anger! He's normally the nicest old man, and I've never once had an issue with him. He seemed feverish but insisted there was nothing wrong with him.

I've asked some of his neighbors to keep an eye on him.

After my visit, I made a tour of the area and talked to other families. My concern grew, as the Blooms weren't the only ones exhibiting this behavior. Apparently, there are half a dozen families in the area that were acting strange of late.

Today, I'm off to speak with these families.

I've got to get an early start today with all the families I need to see, but I'll write again tomorrow about any issues I find.

Year of the Colony - 123yc, Day 117

Something strange is afoot. I visited half a dozen families in my search for answers. They were all very terse and short with me, and I even got into a shouting match with one of Jeff's right-hand guys. I don't understand what I'm missing. The community is doing well, we are expanding, and there's no shortage of anything right now.

I'll expand my search and venture down to the water to see if there's something going on that has all these people stressed and jumping down other's throats.

Perhaps there is something wrong with the mineral harvesting for the cities and they don't want to talk about it lest the rest of the colony get upset with them? Whatever the case, I intend to understand it.

Year of the Colony - 123yc, Day 119

The farther I ranged, the less anyone knew about the

problems. Certain that the problem originated from Jeff and his crew, I went to the docks. I asked one of Bloom's men to take me out on a boat and show me the harvesting operation. Grudgingly, he agreed, but he definitely didn't want to.

Again, I saw nothing amiss, but when I got back to land, I felt sick. It must've been the boat ride. I've never been fond of the water, but whatever it was, I went home and slept for an entire day!

After a day of rest and the amazing meal from my wife, I felt much better and relaxed. I still had a headache, but it wasn't serious enough to keep me from seeing to my responsibilities. Today I plan to continue observing the operation down by the water to see if there's something I missed the other day.

Year of the Colony - 123yc, Day 120

I spent the entire day sitting down by the docks, watching the crew harvest materials and saw nothing out of the ordinary. Well, I didn't think it was out of the ordinary. I noticed they didn't really talk all that much.

I left just before dusk and when I got home, my headache intensified. I spent the rest of the night in bed trying to shake it off. I don't know what's going on with this headache, but I really hope it's nothing serious. Ever since we received the nanite injectors, we don't really need to worry about sickness, but something is definitely bothering me. I'll go see doc today and get pain medication, if she can spare any.

I think I'll stay away from the water today, the sun on the water, or being near the water is causing these headaches to intensify.

Year of the Colony - 123ys, Day 137

I've been going down to the water for several weeks now and I've befriended the crew. They don't talk a lot, but I feel a kinship to them and really admire their commitment to the work.

Jeff seems like the same old man I'd always known, and I don't know how he could've punched anyone; it wasn't like him.

The headache disappeared after a week, and the growing concern I had evaporated. Now I've observed the operation for a time, I think I might head back out on the boat to see how things run better. My wife questioned it, but I sternly told her I'm going, anyway. I even raised my voice but apologized after. I rarely get upset, but maybe it was just my nerves from the past few weeks.

Year of the Colony - 123yc, Day 140

I've been going out on the boat the last few days and even helped the crew gather materials. After we'd finished for the day I wanted to look at the material stockpile and went to the warehouse where I thought we unloaded the day's work, but I saw nothing there.

When I asked Jeff, he seemed edgy and stuttered out they'd moved it into long-term storage already. I didn't question him since I know we harvested materials during the day. Where else would they be? Aside from the fish to eat, we had no use for the minerals anyway. As long as we have enough when the cities come calling, we'll be fine.

My wife and I had another argument today, and she said

I was acting all grouchy since I started my investigation and asked me to stop going down to the water and hanging out with the crew. I yelled at her for being so obtuse and told her I'm working for the best interest of the colony.

Why can't she see I'm doing this for everyone? If there's a problem around here, then it's my job to lend a hand where needed. They need me out on the boats helping.

Year of the Colony - 123yc, Day 150

I don't know why I've taken so long to write in my journal. It's happened twice now in the last month. For the last ten years I've written daily notes, but now I've got two gaps of time. Sometime, I must go back and record my thoughts for those days.

I guess I've been busy helping the crew and forgot to write in the journal. The crew accepted me as part of the team, and we have a great time even though we don't really talk. Days fly by so fast, sometimes I don't even think about what I'm doing and before I know it, the day's done.

The days have been fun and peaceful, but my wife insists that I stop working with the crew. "It's not your job," she says, but I shrug and turn away. If she's got nothing nice to say or can't realize that I'm helping everyone, then why should I talk to her?

Year of the Colony - 123yc, Day 172

Dan stopped writing in his journals, and I fear that something happened to him while spending time with the "waterfolk" as people called them. They keep to themselves, and if anyone questions them they snap out in anger.

Poor Dan fell victim, and now he's part of the problem. I don't know what to do! Any time I ask about it, he gets mad and lashes out with angry words. He's like a totally different person and he's always walking around stuck in his own head. It's like he's on autopilot all the time.

I asked doc about it, but she said they don't seem to have any medical issues, and I don't know what to do anymore. Well, I've got a plan, but I know he won't like it.

Year of the Colony - 125yc, Day 12

It worked. I got my husband back, but I'm dying now.

I asked a friend to lock us in the cellar.
She was supposed to let us out in a week.

I only wanted to see if time away from the waterfolk would bring the Dan I know back.

Dan went crazy afterward and banged on the doors until he broke his hands.

He lost strength to keep going and acted irrational, banging his head against the walls. He tried using our furniture to get out. He tried for weeks, and each day he grew weaker until finally he snapped out of his stupor. By that point, his hands, head, and body were broken.

I tried to help get us out, but it was no use. The doors would not budge, and my friend never came.

This is the last piece of paper we have, but I wanted someone to know what happened.

After Dan snapped out of his stupor, he remembered nothing from the past weeks.

I don't think I'll survive another night.

Dan died several weeks ago.

The nanites seemed to stop healing, and he got so weak. He couldn't talk or move. I moved him to the sitting room, and he died right there in the chair.

I'll join him soon.

I haven't entered that room since he died, but I want to be next to my love when I go.

"Holy crap, Scarlet."

I FEEL THE SORROW AND LOSS IN HER FINAL WORDS.

"Whatever happened here started with that thing in the water. Did it infect them somehow? Can it affect us?"

I DO NOT BELIEVE IT CAN AFFECT ME, BUT BASED ON THIS JOURNAL IT MIGHT BE POSSIBLE IT COULD AFFECT YOU.

"Promise to get me out of here no matter what if you notice anything strange? She said Dan eventually snapped out of it, so we know it's not permanent. Still. I'll monitor myself for any changes, but if you notice anything, even trivial, please let me know. Clearly Dan didn't know what was happening to him. He was in denial the whole time."

I WILL, I PROMISE.

"I hate to say it, but even after reading all these notes, I think it's still worthwhile for us to get back into that bunker for the weapons. The brainwashing, or whatever infected these people, took time, and we shouldn't be here long enough for that to happen."

WHAT ABOUT THE CARNAGE YOU SAW BELOW? THAT DOES

NOT LOOK LIKE SOMETHING THAT TOOK TIME. THAT LOOKS LIKE A MASS EXECUTION CHAMBER.

"If you watch from the air, then you can warn me before anything could even get close."

THAT IS ONLY IF IT COMES OVER THE LAND. IF SOMETHING COMES FROM BELOW OR STILL LIVES IN THOSE TUNNELS...

"I know. I know, but we've got to try. If anything happens, grab me and force me to come with you."

Scarlet didn't respond, and he knew she didn't like the plan.

"If we ever hope to have a chance at our goals, we need that arsenal. I very much doubt we'd get any existing colony to work with us. They created a way of life, a life in subjugation to the cities. More likely, they're liable to report us if we even hinted at a rebellion."

I UNDERSTAND, BUT I DO NOT HAVE TO LIKE THE PLAN.

"You and me both, but I believe we must do this. I know that I'll be fine with you watching my back." Silence reigned for a time before Jared suggested, "Let's get a little sleep, and we'll fly back in the morning to see if there are any changes."

The next morning Jared woke to see Scarlet staring at him from the confines of the small space they occupied.

"Good morning. Ready?" Jared asked, rising from the floor to stretch his limbs.

I AM. Scarlet sounded resigned and loath to get on with their current agenda.

Jared reached out to caress her head. "We'll succeed. I just know it."

Clambering outside, Jared dragged the crate with him and

waited for Scarlet to exit the building. Once again, he positioned the crate so Scarlet could grab it in her claw and carry it with them. Jared leapt onto her back, and they ascended into the air.

"Let's head back to the cellar. It seems like the best place to launch this operation."

When they got closer, the first thing Jared noticed was the vegetation. It no longer wriggled, and it seemed as if nothing had occurred the day prior.

"It looks like it stopped growing after I left the area. I can get all the weapons out before it starts back up," said Jared enthusiastically. Scarlet said nothing, but Jared knew her well enough at this point to know she wasn't as optimistic as him.

Setting down near the cellar, Jared secured the crate inside and went back out to speak with Scarlet.

"I'll do this as fast as I can. My strength and speed should make this a quick endeavor. I'll carry a stack of the crates from the room here over to the armory and fill them up as much as possible. In the meantime, please fly around and keep an eye on everything."

PLEASE BE CAREFUL, Scarlet said before launching herself into the air.

Jared took a deep breath and walked back into the cellar.

14 THE HUNTER BECOMES THE HUNTED

Jared grabbed the crates from the storage room and raced into the tunnel. He moved as fast as humanly possible. When he hit bends in the tunnel, he planted his feet against the wall and shoved to propel himself down the tunnel in the new direction.

The rooms flew by, and he saw no changes—the underground facility was exactly as he'd left it the day before. Jared made great time as he neared the armory. On the way there, Jared had two warring thoughts. They could grab all the weapons and gear and fly away from this place. Or they could come up with a plan to kill the creature in the lake.

The thoughts swirling in his mind, it went into overdrive. He moved as if in slow motion, but his mind accelerated much faster than he'd ever experienced.

This must be Hyper-Cognition!

He'd briefly examined the nanites responsible for this area of his brain, but they were much more complex than the ones that handled physical changes, so he'd not spent a lot of time learning about them yet.

All he knew for sure was that the nanites meshed into his brain and created an electrical array of sorts that allowed his neural pathways to expand and speed up his thought process. Even the thoughts about how the *Hyper-Cognition* worked happened in the space of a nanosecond.

Wanting to take advantage of the increased mental capacity, Jared used the rapid-fire thoughts to analyze what he knew about the creature in the lake.

Based on the congregation of life forms when it became active, it couldn't move locations, or perhaps it had an underground cave it lived in. Recalling the images he'd observed from Scarlet's back, he peered intently at the undulating blob under the water, hundreds of singular bodies swirling around it.

How could we kill this thing? I know there's C-4 in the armory, and it should work underwater, but I've never used it before, and I've only read about explosives in books. As Jared sifted through his memories of explosives, he never recalled seeing them in his colony, nor observing them in use.

Pulling up the images of the armory, Jared scanned the books on the shelf, looking for anything that might give him information about explosives, how they worked, and their limitations. A book sat on a shelf near the bottom, titled *Explosives: Nitroglycerin, Thermite, C-4, Semtex, & Gunpowder*.

Perfect!

The next thing Jared looked for was anything he could use as an explosive beyond the C-4 he'd already seen, but the only other barrels he could see from his cursory scan earlier was gunpowder, and he knew that wouldn't work.

Throughout the entire *Hyper-Cognition* process, he'd only managed to take two steps down the hall, even though he'd been sprinting when it activated.

This is amazing!

Jared thought of all the ways he could use it in combat. He vowed to spend more time learning and using the ability in less dire circumstances. Turning the images of the armory over in his mind, Jared skimmed over all the various handguns, machine-guns, and even rifles. None of them provided the penetration he needed under the water to have an impact against the creature.

Quickly realizing that explosives were the only solution, or something that would ignite underwater at the very least; he ignored the rest of the arsenal.

Jared wracked his brain for anything he'd ever learned about fire and its ability to burn underwater. Although he recalled fire that could ignite underwater, he didn't remember any details, and *Memory Recall* wasn't helping.

All the possibilities he remembered exhausted, Jared focused on only the items he knew would work. He'd come back for the rest after the creature was dead.

Jared deactivated *Hyper-Cognition*.

"Ugh." Jared stumbled into the wall, his brain slowed to a crawl, and throbbing pain pulsed at his temples. His limbs seemed uncoordinated and he struggled to regain his balance.

Wow, that hurts. I won't be doing that again so soon. Jared grabbed his head in pain, putting pressure on his temples to stop the throbbing.

Gathering his wits, he hobbled the rest of the way to the armory and set the crates down. Before Jared gathered the explosives and books, he used his rifle to smash the locks on all the cages, running around all the pillars to make sure he captured all the contents of the room in his memory. A mental inventory of sorts.

The crate near overflowing with materials, he saved the

manual on explosives for last and flipped it open to the table of contents. It only took a few seconds of scanning to find a chapter on *Unquenchable Flames*, just after sections on *Magnesium* and *Blasting Caps*. This book could prove invaluable to him, especially if it detailed how to create different types of bombs and components for reloading ammunition.

Scarlet, how're we doing up there? Jared asked before he started reading through the entry on *Unquenchable Flames*.

So far, I see no movement on the surface, but the activity within the water sped up slightly.

I'm almost done. I've got the start of a plan to deal with this thing in the water, but I want to make sure I've gathered all the necessary materials.

Jared returned his attention to the book in front of him and read the title of the section *Thermite*, a type of fire that could burn underwater. The list of ingredients made this an unlikely avenue:

1. Iron oxide
2. Aluminum powder
3. Magnesium ribbon or thermite ignition mixture

For military grade thermite, use the following ingredients:
4. Barium Nitrate
5. Sulfur
6. Dextrin

Jared's eyes roved over the various containers and barrels in the room. He found oxidized iron, aluminum powder, and magnesium strips. However, he found none of the barium nitrate or sulfur. He scanned the list of ingredients and then jumped back to the index to see if it talked about each component individually. Sure enough, there were entries describing each component.

Jared, you need to go! The plants are moving again.

I'm moving! Jared said as he quickly threw the ingredients and a few more weapons into the crate. For good measure, he raced into one of the cages and ripped off the wooden lid to a crate of grenades. Quickly grabbing a couple handfuls, he put two in his pocket and dumped the rest into the crate, filling up the empty space.

I really hope these things can't detonate accidentally.

Hesitating for only a second, Jared shrugged. Either he got out of there now or risked dying at the hands of the carnivorous plants gunning for him. An accidental explosion was a much better way to go.

Every nook and cranny of the container filled, he high-tailed it out of the armory as fast as he could run carrying his burden. He made good time even with the added weight, until he reached the execution chamber.

Jared skidded to a stop, throwing himself backward. The crate landed on top of him, spilling some of its contents. The chamber was no longer empty. Writing vines covered in thorns slithered around the room. They reacted to his presence and stretched for him. *Night Vision* didn't allow him to see much detail, but the tips of the thorns were darker than the vines and shared the same faded color as the blood splatters throughout the room. Jared imagined them stained with the blood of the many victims whose flesh they'd ripped into.

Panicking, Jared righted the crate, unceremoniously stuffed the items back in, and backpedaled from the entrance. From a safe distance, he watched the vines moving around the room. They were much faster than they'd looked on the surface, and Jared wondered if what they'd seen above was just an echo of the activity occurring beneath the earth.

Scarlet, I'm in trouble here! The plants already infiltrated the bunker. You remember that execution chamber I showed you? Well, it's full of thorny vines.

As Jared looked closer, he saw a viscous fluid dripping from the thorns and knew he couldn't let them touch his flesh.

CAN YOU GET OUT ANOTHER WAY?

There is only one path leading from the chamber to the armory. Maybe there's a hidden tunnel somewhere, but I don't have time to look for it. Hold on, I've got an idea. This is a military grade complex, so it should be able to withstand some serious damage, right?

JARED. RECKLESSNESS IS NOT THE WAY TO GO.

I'll be fine. My hearing on the other hand... With that, Jared pulled the pin on a grenade from his pocket, tossed it into the room, and raced back up the tunnel, putting as much distance between the explosion and himself as possible. Just before he rounded the corner, he glanced over his shoulder and saw the nightmarish vines clawing toward him in the tunnel entrance.

Oh man. I wonder what's attracting it? Can it sense my heat, my blood, or the nanites? What if killing the thing in the water doesn't eliminate the threat? Can we even kill it? Whatever it is.

A violent explosion interrupted his thoughts and set his ears ringing. A wave of intense heat washed over him, and the concussive force of the explosion rocked him back on his heels. After the explosion, it was silent for a short moment, and then Jared heard a furious scraping and thrashing from the room. Peeking around the corner, he found the explosion had only made it angry.

It blew apart dozens of vines, but it didn't diminish the danger in the least as more vines entered the room.

That didn't work, Scarlet. I think I made it mad!

Jared feverishly cycled through his options, looking for any way to get out of the situation.

I could go back to the armory and shut the door, but how much time would that really buy me? How long would it take to burrow through the ground? How long before I ran out of oxygen?

No, that wouldn't work. He needed to get through the chamber in front of him, or he'd die down here.

Scarlet, can you see where these vines enter the ground?

I SEE SOME OF THEM WIGGLING AROUND, BUT IT'S HARD TO SAY. THERE ARE HUNDREDS OF STRANDS, AND THEY SPREAD OUT ALL OVER THE PLACE.

See if you can pinpoint where they enter the earth and breathe your fire on them. I want to see if there's any reaction to the ones in here. Be careful not to get too close. I don't want one of these accidentally grabbing you. It looks like it secretes some kind of fluid from the thorns.

OKAY, DIVING NOW.

Jared didn't have long to wait as half of the vines in the room thrashed about. They entangled others and weaved about the room with abandon.

It worked! Do it again, Scarlet, I think I can get through if you take out a few more.

GET READY!

Again, Scarlet breathed fire on the vines, and half a dozen more of the vines fell limp, creating a narrow path for Jared to run through. It was still a great risk, since there was no way to predict how the vines moved. It seemed completely random. If the creature was smart enough to block the entrance, he'd be trapped.

It's working Scarlet. Let's go for one more pass just to be safe.

READY?

Yes, go!

At the same time, Jared threw another grenade into the room and picked up the crate filled with his loot.

Squeezing his eyes shut, he waited until the grenade detonated and surged ahead. The concussive and heat waves slammed into him, shoving him back a step. He pushed through and sprinted for all he was worth, angling for the tunnel that'd take him out and into the clear.

The moment he entered the tunnel, his body slowed, and his mind raced ahead, *Hyper-Cognition* activating of its own volition. It's possible he'd activated it subconsciously, but it came as a surprise to him. Jared almost deactivated it the moment it started. It only heightened his sense of dread to see several dozen of the vines laying limp on the floor while dozens more emerged from the holes.

Jared observed the vines with a mix of horror and fascination. It wasn't until several of the newly emerged tendrils sped up noticeably, even in the *Hyper-Cognition* state, that his fascination gave way to outright terror.

Filtering out any other thoughts but survival, Jared deactivated his ability and strained his muscles to the brink, *Maximum Muscle* activating and propelling him through the entry.

A grin on his face, Jared rejoiced in his close call as his upper body cleared the threshold. A moment later, a wave of fiery agony exploded down his back, wiping the grin from his face. Searing pain arced down his spine in waves, the pain clouding his mind and vision as he struggled to make it out of the underground facility.

Scarlet, I'm...I'm coming.

Jared! Are you okay?

Jared didn't answer as he continued his mad, stumbling dash through the corridors. At last, the storage room came into view. By this point, the pulsating agony cascading across his back spread to other parts of his body, and his mind fogged over. His brain was trying to shut down to separate his consciousness from the massive amount of pain he'd endured in just a few short minutes.

Jared dropped the crate and crawled toward the cellar.

Almost...there...

He made it into the room and collapsed face down, oblivious to Scarlet's panicked cries as darkness enveloped him.

Scarlet's screamed, her rage washing over Jared as he faded in and out of awareness.

JARED? JARED? ANSWER ME!

Scarlet? I'm here. The words echoed in his mind, but try as he might, he couldn't project them to Scarlet. Involuntary grunts passed his lips as he struggled to no avail.

Slowly, as if in a fog, Jared struggled to his knees, not in control of his own body. He looked up at Scarlet, his eyes dull.

No! Jared screamed in rage, but he was powerless to stop whatever controlled him. He watched from the recesses of his own mind as Scarlet ripped into the floor. Her rage washed over him again and again. If she didn't get to him before his puppet-master forced him back down the tunnel, he was a dead man.

JARED, STOP! Scarlet shouted, forcing as much psionic pressure into his mind as she could. Jared hesitated only a moment and took two unsteady steps toward the corridor.

Before he took another, half of the roof collapsed in front of him, and he cheered Scarlet on.

Scarlet's claws closed around him. She did her best to avoid squishing him or cutting him on the razor's edge of her claws. However, whatever controlled him didn't know or care and thrashed his body around.

Psionic pressure repeatedly battered his mind as Scarlet tried to break the hold of the creature holding him hostage.

Scarlet flew to the same building they'd slept in the night

before and set Jared down inside. She settled in behind him, blocking all the exits from the room. It served to keep him confined since whatever controlled him was not smart. It didn't try for his weapons, running, or using any of his abilities like *Maximum Strength* to get away.

JARED, PLEASE WAKE UP.

The anguish in her voice pained him. If only he could get a single thought to her. To let her know that he was still inside his head.

Several hours later Jared watched as his body changed direction and started scaling the wall. He fell multiple times before Scarlet's voice whispered in his mind.

FORGIVE ME, JARED.

The next instant, Scarlet's tail launched him into the wall, knocking him unconscious.

Several days passed, each the same as the last. Exhausted and desperate, Jared didn't know if he'd survive much longer. His body was broken and bleeding.

After four days, Jared returned to consciousness lying on the ground, his body unmoving. Not even the being controlling him could overcome the fatigue.

Scarlet lifted her head to look at him. The sadness in her eyes devastated him.

JARED? CAN YOU HEAR ME? Her tone forlorn, Scarlet pressed at the boundaries of his mind. For a split second, Jared felt the presence in his mind give way.

Scarlet? A single word was all he managed before his mind was once again shrouded. With that one word, he pushed all the love and hope possible along the bond. Her eyes widened in surprise, joy and determination bubbling to the surface after so many days of despair.

JARED, ARE YOU OKAY? JARED? No!

The scream pierced his mind, the psionic pressure pushing him past his limits. He passed out, spent from the effort of sending that single word.

Two weeks passed, but Jared only managed to break through a few more times. Again and again, he repeated her name, letting her know that he was still fighting, still holding on to hope they'd make it through. His body was in a state of catatonia. It might've been one of his abilities triggering, or a side-effect of the massive trauma he'd endured. Whatever the reason, it prevented him from dying, but also meant he wasn't healing completely.

The next time Jared's consciousness surfaced, he lay on the floor a few paces from Scarlet, feeling in slightly more control. He sensed his nanites, the barrier that'd been there before weakened. Rather than using energy to reach out to Scarlet, Jared sent his senses within and opened himself up to the nanites. Their familiar presence greeted him, but he didn't make it far before he realized there was something abnormal about them. Something blocked him from delving further or sending commands to regenerate himself.

Stepping back in his mind, he found a foreign presence encapsulating the nanites. The code algorithm was altogether alien, and he couldn't make sense of it.

What is it? Surely, it can't have taken over all the nanites? thought Jared.

Now that he knew what to look for, Jared cast his mind out wider, specifically looking for nanites responsible for *Body Manipulation*. He found several clusters that showed no sign of the malicious code blocking his access. For each of these clusters, he converted them to *Regeneration* and forced them to heal and eradicate the foreign substance within his body.

After the mental exertion, darkness once again enveloped him.

The next time Jared woke, he knew something was different. He felt stronger, his body no longer throbbing with the constant fever. The aches and stinging wounds along his arms and legs looked healed. He was still too weak to move, but his consciousness was finally his own.

Hello? Scarlet? Are you there? Jared asked excitedly.

JARED? I'M HERE!

Relief exploded into his mind as Scarlet lifted her head to meet his gaze.

ARE YOU REALLY HERE THIS TIME?

I am, but I can't move yet. My body is too weak.

JUST REST. I CAN FINALLY SENSE YOUR MIND AGAIN. YOUR BODY NEEDS UNINTERRUPTED REST. NOW THAT YOU ARE FREE OF THE OTHER ENTITY, YOU CAN GET SOME MUCH-NEEDED SLEEP. IT HAS BEEN THREE WEEKS SINCE YOU—

Three weeks? Scarlet, I—

PLEASE, JUST REST. I AM HERE FOR YOU AND WILL PROTECT YOU FOR AS LONG AS YOU NEED.

Thank you.

The effort of the short conversation was taxing, and he felt himself begin to fade once more. Before losing consciousness, Jared sent all available nanites to *Regeneration*.

His task finished, he entered a blissful slumber.

Several days later, Jared opened his eyes and looked around. He lay in the same place, but Scarlet was nowhere in sight. Careful not to push himself too hard, Jared struggled to a seated position against the back wall. The effort made him cringe at how weak his body was.

Scarlet? Where are you?

Jared! I am two minutes away. I went to hunt food. You need to eat something. Your nanites stopped regenerating your body because you no longer possess enough energy. There is not enough radiation to sustain the massive amount of healing required.

Two minutes later, Scarlet landed with a flurry of dust. Jared was about to try hobbling outside when two charred hunks of meat landed beside him. He looked up to see Scarlet peering at him through the partially collapsed roof.

It is good to see you awake!

"Scarlet, I'm so sorry. I know what you endured these last weeks. I heard every word you spoke, and I know the anguish and despair caused you a great deal of pain. I tried calling out to you many times but couldn't get through the mental barrier in place. Eventually, I gained consciousness for a few moments and found nanites in *Body Manipulation* that weren't infected. I set them to eliminating the foreign presence before blacking out. I think it's the only thing that saved me. The presence that had a hold of my mind was so strong."

Eat, sleep, and rebuild your strength. I will remain by your side no matter the trials.

Thank you, my friend. I am truly blessed to have someone care for me like you do, said Jared. He really meant every word and tried to convey that appreciation across their bond.

Jared weakly picked up one of the pieces of meat Scarlet tossed to him and bit into it. The tender meat melted in his mouth, and he savored the taste. He didn't remember the last time he'd eaten anything other than a ration, and even that was so long ago. Whatever the creature this came from, it tasted amazing, albeit a little charred from Scarlet's flames. After consuming all of the meat, more than he'd eaten in the last year, Jared's eyes grew heavy.

"I'll rest now, Scarlet. Thank you...for everything."

You are welcome, Jared. Take as long as you need.

Jared's eyes fluttered shut, and his breathing deepened. Finally, after what seemed an eternity, he entered a normal sleep cycle, and the nanites feverishly went to work repairing his body.

Just before his consciousness left him, he heard Scarlet's whispered words.

That creature will pay for what it did to you. It will die.

15 GOING FISHING

Jared woke the next day feeling refreshed and whole. Scarlet lay next to him, eyes open, watching him. He stood up and stretched, laying a hand on her side.

"Thank you again for taking care of me, Scarlet. I'd have died many times over if not for you, and I'm extremely thankful to have you by my side in all this."

THE FEELING IS MUTUAL; OUR FATES ARE INTERTWINED. FOR BETTER OR WORSE, AS YOUR KIND SAY.

"Worse seems to be the trend of late. Let's hope that changes in the near future. I've had enough of these close calls. The last few weeks..." Jared shuddered. "It was a nightmare. If this thing took over the previous inhabitants in the area like it did with me, I can't imagine the anguish they went through. I was conscious but had no control over my body. I was trapped in my own mind. This thing— whatever it is—needs to die."

WE WILL KILL IT! The venom and ferocity in Scarlet's response startled him and he took a step back from her. THIS

THING ALMOST KILLED YOU, AND I WILL NOT STOP UNTIL WE DESTROY IT.

"You and I both, but first we need to retrieve the crate of supplies I left in the tunnel. Do you know how far I made it before I lost consciousness? Everything's a bit fuzzy and *Memory Recall* isn't painting a clearer picture."

YOU WANT TO GO BACK RIGHT NOW? BUT—

I know. It was a terrible experience, but the sooner this thing is wiped from the face of the earth, the better. No one should experience torture like that, and I want to be the one that exacts revenge for its invasion into my body. A fire lit behind Jared's eyes, his tone promising retribution.

THEN WE HUNT AND KILL IT. AS FOR THE CRATE, I ONLY KNOW YOU COLLAPSED AT THE MOUTH OF THE TUNNEL. I WAS SO FOCUSED ON GETTING YOU OUT, I DID NOT THINK TO LOOK FOR ANYTHING ELSE.

"Well, the only way we've a prayer's chance of taking that thing out is to get that crate. I've got lots of explosives and material in there we can use to create a bomb or some type of flame that will work underwater. There's C-4, gunpowder, grenades, and bomb components that we can use. Even then, I'm not sure it's enough to take it out. Let's head over to the cellar and see if I managed to make it out with the container."

Jared jumped on Scarlet's back, and they flew to the destroyed cellar. The house was in a pile of shredded rubble, most of the cellar exposed save for a small cave-in partially blocking the tunnel into the underground complex.

"Wow, you did all this?"

IT WAS THE ONLY WAY TO GET TO YOU IN TIME.

At first, he thought they'd need to excavate the collapsed roof, but there was enough room for him to scramble through.

Sliding through the gap, Jared found the materials just a few feet from the entrance.

It's here! Help me get it out. I'll push it through the gap. Just make sure it doesn't fall off. I've no idea if the explosives in here are unstable.

After he'd retrieved the materials, they walked back to the barn they'd used when first arriving in the small town. Once inside, Jared carefully emptied the crate and paged through the explosives manual to learn more about thermite and any other mixtures that suited his needs. After reading about the different thermite concoctions, including thermate, a military grade version, he realized there was no way he'd find all the required components.

There was no barium nitrate, one of the required ingredients, in the armory. To synthesize it, he'd need to find barium carbonate and nitric acid. Worse, there was no synthesized barium carbonate available, and the materials where it existed were very difficult to find in any volume that made it practical. Small amounts existed in bricks and ceramic material, but he didn't have the means to extract the powder. Further, even if he found barite, the base mineral, he'd need to break it down with a set temperature and add additional reactants just to get into any form he could use.

Muttering to himself, Jared flipped the pages looking at various chemicals and components for making thermate. "It looks like I'll make regular thermite."

Wʜᴀᴛ ɪs ᴛʜᴇʀᴍɪᴛᴇ?

Jared blinked and looked up. Absorbed in his research, he'd forgotten Scarlet and didn't realize he'd spoken aloud. "Thermite is a mixture of iron oxide and aluminum powder that, when ignited by magnesium, will burn underwater as long as there is material available. I was looking for ways to kill that creature and wanted more than just an explosion in case it didn't finish the job. However, I'm thinking it'd be better just to try the explosives."

How hot does it burn?

"According to this, about four thousand degrees."

Scarlet looked alarmed. That would destroy anything.

"Well, yeah. That's kind of the point." Jared tilted his head to the side, a sarcastic expression plastered on his face.

Everything. Nanites included.

"Oh. Crap. I didn't think about that."

I think a large explosion would work best. Besides, we have no idea what this creature is yet. Does it have a singular body? Is it a bunch of life forms together? Or a bunch of nanites that gained a level of awareness? We don't know enough to assume this thermite would even work. It might only burn a small portion of it or kill off a few of its...extensions.

"All right, I get it. Thermite is off the table."

Jared spent the next hour reading about various explosives and their effects underwater. He learned that an underwater explosion was much stronger than on the surface, something about air pockets and pressure.

"Boom!" Jared shouted, his eyes alight with glee at the prospect of bombing this creature. Scarlet whipped her head around, alarmed at the outburst.

"Sorry, Scarlet. I guess I could read some of this out loud. It says an explosion is exponentially more powerful and deadly underwater, and C-4 will work for it. Okay, I think we've got everything we need to make this happen. Though, I only grabbed one roll of detonation cord from the armory," Jared said while rummaging through the components until he found the spool.

"First thing we need to do is figure out how deep we need to drop the bomb. Also, I think we should include some live bait to make sure the bomb gets to its destination."

Jared rattled off the steps they needed to take. As soon as he'd made a list, he set to work. He still carried rope from when the other explorers had bound Scarlet but knew it wouldn't be enough.

While Jared scavenged more rope and wires to use as a measuring line, Scarlet flew off in search of some creature to use as bait. He also wanted her to check on the water monster to make sure it hadn't changed in the time they'd been away. It took Jared a few hours of searching the city outskirts to find all he needed.

Scarlet returned a short time later with a giant rat wriggling in her grasp.

"Ugh, I really hate these things!"

IT WAS ALL I COULD FIND CLOSE BY. Scarlet gave him a toothy grin, complete with blood and bits of flesh peeking out.

"Oh, come on, Scarlet, that's gross. Don't tell me you ate some of these? Even after our encounter in the subway?"

FOOD IS FOOD, Scarlet said, keeping her teeth bared at him.

The least you could do is blow some fire and get rid of the remnants in your teeth. It's nasty.

Shaking his head at her Jared said aloud, "You know if there's one of these, there's probably a whole den of them, right? Just make sure we steer clear of wherever you found this thing. I've no desire to take out anymore elephant-sized rodents."

Grimacing in disgust, Jared tied one end of the rope around the rat's neck, looped the coil of makeshift rope around his shoulder, and climbed on Scarlet's back.

"All right, let's do this."

They flew to the area they'd last seen the creature congregate, and Scarlet slowly dropped toward the lake. Twenty feet from the water, Jared observed the life-forms using his *Heat Sight*. Their mere proximity aroused the creature, as hundreds of heat signatures swam toward a point just below them. Jared dropped the rat into the water, and for a tiny instant, Jared felt bad for the creature. Then he remembered the tunnels beneath New York, and his demeanor flipped to righteous vindication as an evil smile curved from ear to ear.

The moment the rat touched the water, it ignited a frenzy of activity. Jared watched as creatures from every corner of the lake sped to the epicenter. Most of the life forms created a shell around something at its center. All the while, the rat bucked and writhed as it dropped deeper into the water. Jared uncoiled loop after loop of the rope, counting the tick marks he'd made every ten feet.

He felt resistance against the rope and pulled a knife from a sheath on his back. He didn't want to get pulled into the water, but he also didn't want to lose what little rope he had left. As the rat reached the ninety feet mark, a sharp jerk on the rope wrenched his arm down, and he quickly severed the line.

"Let's go, Scarlet!"

Flapping her wings to gain altitude, they soared over the lake for a few minutes.

Ninety feet. I can work with that, Jared thought. The spool of detonation cord contained exactly one hundred feet.

"We've only got one shot at this. Let's make it count. I need to rebuild another rope, and we need another victim as bait. Find something bigger this time. We need to make sure it survives long enough to reach this things lair."

It may take me some time.

"Hold up." Jared poked his head outside the barn and saw the sun descending. "Okay, let's hold off until morning for the bait. I've got to find enough material for a new rope and then get the C-4 prepped." Jared looked at the bricks of C-4—at least that's what the book called them. The bricks ignited using a shock wave, which is what the detonation cord and blasting caps were for. He'd insert the silver tubes into the bricks of explosives, and a small plunger on the other side delivered a charge to the blasting cap for ignition.

Jared spent the next few hours gathering materials for another rope while Scarlet provided overwatch, monitoring the water for evidence he'd been made. Thankfully, it didn't seem the creature could sense them this far out. After he'd prepped the rope and explosives, they turned in for the night, planning to get up with the sun and kick off their mission.

As soon as the sun was up, Jared sent Scarlet to fetch their bait. For good measure, he re-checked all of the knots in the rope, the measurements, and the C-4. When Scarlet came back, a massive antlered creature bucked wildly, trying to free itself. Several lacerations on the creature suggested it'd injured itself on her claws. The blood would make the bait more appealing.

"This thing looks like a m—" He'd been about to say it looked nothing like a moose but cocked his head and looked at various body parts. "I mean, I guess I can see the resemblance, but wow." Jared shook his head in revulsion. "I remember moose being mysterious and proud, elegant even. Not this grotesque mutation."

The creature stood eight feet tall on all four legs, its head was more rounded than oblong, and its teeth sported sharp canines instead of the squared teeth of an herbivore. The horns on its head boasted sharpened points stained reddish-brown, similar to the blood Jared found in the tunnels. Its body sported huge muscles, scars, and splotchy patches of fur. It was gross, and Jared had a hard time imagining its ancestors ever being something so majestic as the moose he envisioned.

"Can you carry both of us? That thing must weigh a thousand pounds, at least."

I CAN MANAGE IT FOR A SHORT TIME.

Taking a deep breath, Jared picked up the rope he'd cobbled together with the detonation cord winding around the rope. He secured the rope around the body of the wriggling moose. Picking up the explosives, he placed them in a sling he'd made from scraps of cloth. There were six bricks of C-4 in the sack, with two more he'd saved as backup.

"Are you ready?" asked Jared, a hint of fear in his voice.

I WAS READY THE DAY YOU GOT INFECTED BY THIS THING. LET US FINISH THIS!

Jared reminded himself never to get on her bad side. She was quick to righteous anger, and the vehemence she portrayed frightened him.

As soon as they reached the location of the creature, Jared carefully looped the makeshift patches over the moose's head, making sure the blasting caps remained in place.

"Bombs away, Scarlet!"

She needed no further prompting and dropped to within ten feet of the lake to drop off their payload. The moose sank a lot faster, and it was all Jared could do to keep up with the unraveling rope. As it sank, Jared counted off the tick marks.

"Ten, twenty, thirty…seventy…" At eighty feet, there was a tug on the rope, and their bait veered to the side. "Oh no." Jared couldn't make out the form of the mutated moose anymore, because there was so much activity in the area, but he knew from the position of the rope that it was slightly off target.

Jared held his breath; they only needed a few more feet. His arms were shaking from the effort of holding the moose in place. Whatever snagged their rope was strong and made Scarlet dip down slightly until with a jolt, the rope slackened, and he once again had control of its descent.

"Almost there. Ninety." There was no tug on the rope like

before, and the moose kept sinking.

Oh no.

Jared panicked as their only way to kill this thing slipped through his fingers. He was out of rope. He held the end of the rope in one hand, his other over the plunger to detonate as soon as the creature took the bait. Thinking the water monster had moved to a different location, Jared was about to begin the arduous process of pulling the moose back up, when the rope went taut. He nearly lost his grip on the rope, but quickly slammed the plunger home.

"Go!" Jared screamed.

In the same instant, he activated *Hyper-Cognition*, his mind racing a thousand miles a second. He wanted to have heightened awareness to warn Scarlet about any danger from the explosion or creatures below.

Scarlet thrust her wings as hard as she could, wanting to escape the concussive force when it rocketed from the water. Everything happened in slow motion for Jared as he sat atop Scarlet in relative safety and comfort. Curious if he could communicate with Scarlet normally while he had the ability activated, Jared reach out to her using *Telepathy*.

Faster, Scarlet! We've got to get away from here.

Thankfully, the mental communications moved just as fast as his thoughts and Scarlet had no trouble keeping up with the accelerated speech.

I CANNOT GO ANY FASTER.

Flicking his eyes to the water, Jared flipped to *Heat Sight* just as the bomb detonated. A brilliant flash of light blossomed in the depths of the lake and rapidly expanded outward. It engulfed the swarming mob of life forms, wreaking havoc to anything in its path. He watched as the force wave ripped through everything; the super-heated wave expanded outward at a frightening pace. The moment it touched a life form, their body exploded into tiny bits, residual heat from the creatures fading like afterimages. Each creature popped apart in a spray of body parts like tiny fireworks exploding in rapid succession, a grand finale. Every moment passed in slow-motion as his hyper-cognitive state allowed him to watch in exquisite detail.

Nothing will survive that. Then again, the creatures on the outside might survive if those closer absorb the explosion.

Enthralled as he was, Jared hadn't paid attention to the rapid progression of the concussive wave until he realized it was about to crest the surface of the water.

Hold on, Scarlet, this could get rocky!

As fast as Scarlet was, she couldn't outrun the pressure wave that exploded from the water. She was high enough it caused no serious harm, but it shoved her upward violently, her wings snapping taught as the updraft propelled her higher.

The pressure from the rapid ascent forced Jared into a hunched position atop Scarlet's back, and he fell to one side, scrambling for a handhold.

Scarlet, help!

JARED!

He lost his grip and plummeted to the water below. Scarlet could do nothing to help him as the pressure wave lifted her higher into the air.

Jared still had *Hyper-Cognition* activated, but it didn't allow him to move his body any faster. He had plenty of time to process everything, and there was nothing he could do but prepare for impact in the water.

Before hitting the surface, he turned off his ability, his mind screaming in agony, which quickly faded to a minor nuisance as his body smashed into the water. A fresh wave of fire rolled up his side from the impact, but the only thing on his mind was, *Did we kill it?*

The moment he resurfaced, he pinwheeled his arms and kicked his legs as fast and hard as he could. He made a beeline for the beach, which thankfully wasn't very far.

Scarlet, let me know if anything comes after me!

I THINK THESE CREATURES HAVE MUCH MORE IMPORTANT THINGS TO WORRY ABOUT AT THE MOMENT. THAT BOMB WAS IMPRESSIVE. ANYTHING NOT DESTROYED IN THE INITIAL BLAST IS SWIMMING AROUND ERRATICALLY.

Regardless of Scarlet's reassuring words, Jared pushed all of his will into strength and speed as he splashed his way to the shore. With fifty yards yet to go, Jared saw a glow in the water and felt the telltale sign of nanite infusion.

Oh no.

HURRY, JARED!

He pushed with all he had, causing *Maximum Strength* to trigger. He shot forward in the water, but not fast enough as the nanites swarmed into him, the torrent burning through his body. Just as the burn ramped to an unbearable level, his feet touched the bottom of the lake, and he launched himself from the water, leaving a glowing trail of nanites in his wake.

He fell onto the sand and lay there panting as his whole body burned from yet another massive influx of nanites. Scarlet landed beside him and nuzzled his side.

ARE YOU OKAY? asked Scarlet, concern thick in her voice.

"I'll—be—fine," Jared said, in between massive gulps of air. "Get some—of the nanites." He weakly pointed to the water.

Scarlet trundled forward to absorb them. He watched as the glow increased in brightness, and the rush of nanites shimmered over Scarlet's body. The entire lake took on a faint glow as the nanite activity increased.

JARED...

Scarlet? Jared asked, propping himself up on his elbow. *What is it?*

HELP! The pained cry made his exhaustion disappear, and he rushed to help. The torrent of nanites buffeted her body like a raging inferno, and her mouth opened in a silent rictus.

"No! Scarlet!"

Panic set in as Jared wracked his brain for a solution. Seeing no other way to help, he jumped in front of her, activated *Maximum Strength*, crouched, and drove his body into her, the impact throwing her back a few steps. He felt a sharp slicing pain lance up his right leg, and a pop resounded from his shoulder.

The pain threatened to overwhelm him, and the edges of his vision faded to black, but an overriding fear for Scarlet blasted past the pain.

Ignoring the agony, he limped forward and placed a hand on Scarlet's side where she'd collapsed to the ground, her body convulsing with waves of iridescent color pulsing over her. The last remnants of nanites pulsed over her body as they finished assimilating.

"Are you okay?" Jared looked over her body, searching for any other injuries and probing along their bond to make sure there wasn't anything else wrong.

I THINK SO. THAT HURT SO MUCH, AND I COULD NOT SHUT OUT THE PAIN LIKE USUAL, Scarlet said, her voice sounding labored.

Jared sympathized with her. The whole absorption process sucked, and his whole body felt raw. Add to that the injury to his shoulder and leg, not to mention the past few weeks, and he was in rough shape.

Jared examined his injuries to see just how bad they were. He'd dislocated his shoulder and torn some ligaments in his leg. Every slight shift felt like a knife jab. He couldn't do much for his leg aside from ensuring any spare nanites went into regenerating his injuries. His shoulder on the other hand, he could pop back into place and help expedite the healing. Removing his belt, Jared folded it and placed it into his mouth. Bracing his shoulder on the ground he yanked his arm forward.

Jared bellowed through clenched teeth, hearing an audible pop as the bone settled back in place, the pain subsiding. It still felt tender to the touch, and he knew it'd take time for his regeneration to heal it.

Next, he examined the torn ligament, and quickly realized it would take a while to heal from this injury. "Scarlet, I'm going to need help walking away from here. I think the combination of using *Maximum Muscle* to swim to shore and then to knock you out of the water was too much for my body. I tore some ligaments."

Jared lay on his side, stabilizing his leg, while looking around for anything he could use as a splint.

"Let me know when you can get moving. I don't have anything with me to stabilize this leg, and I'm not much use in this condition."

I AM READY, BUT...

Jared looked at Scarlet when she paused. "But? What?" Scarlet looked out over the water before she answered him.

THERE IS SOMETHING OFF ABOUT THESE NANITES. IT'S AS IF—I DON'T KNOW HOW TO EXPLAIN IT.

Once again, Jared sent his awareness inside and looked for the nanites they'd recently gained. He found them easily since they'd not fully integrated until after he assigned them. Focusing on a cluster of them, he studied the coding. At first, he felt nothing different, but the more he looked at them, the more he realized Scarlet was right. They were different, but he couldn't put a finger on it either.

"It's almost like they are alive, or almost like they have awareness."

All the other nanites he'd absorbed were just machines. They only reacted to his will and command, exactly as a machine should. These new nanites remained dormant, but he could feel as if they wanted something, or had a sense of belonging to them. It was impossible to describe exactly what he felt, but he agreed with Scarlet that they were different.

LOOK AT ONE OF THE NANITES YOU ALREADY HAD AND COMPARE TO A NEW ONE.

Jared did as he was told but couldn't see any differences. Part of that was he couldn't make much sense of his own genome. He could pick out a DNA molecule and even see its makeup, but he couldn't discern what everything meant, or compare that against bio-machine code that made up the nanites.

Scarlet lowered her head and touched Jared. An image blossomed in his mind of Scarlet's DNA and two nanites side by side. Looking at Scarlet's DNA, Jared marveled at how different it was from his own. He almost understood his own DNA, but Scarlet's was infinitely more complex, and it weaved a beautiful symmetric pattern around a quadruple helix that made up a DNA molecule.

LOOK AT THEM SIDE BY SIDE.

"How can I see what maps to machine code versus your DNA? I'm just not seeing it."

Mentally sighing, Scarlet said, THIS WILL BE MUCH EASIER AFTER YOU INCREASE YOUR TELEPATHY ABILITY. ONCE WE

SHARE A THOUGHT SPACE, YOU WILL UNDERSTAND EASIER. FOR NOW, IGNORE THE DNA AND JUST LOOK AT THESE SECTIONS OF THE NANITE CODE. THIS IS THE SECTION OF CODE THAT BONDS WITH OUR DNA.

Jared scrutinized them and recognized the differences in the code right away. There was another layer of code weaving throughout the nanites.

"I didn't think this was possible? You said we can't absorb nanites from other humans."

IT...IS NOT HUMAN. IT IS TOO SIMPLE. OR, RATHER, IT IS COMPLEX, BUT NOT IN THE SAME WAY AS THE HUMAN GENOME.

"Again, how is that possible? These things bind only to human DNA."

I DO NOT KNOW. WHAT IF, Scarlet began.

"Any theory is better than what we currently know." Jared motioned for her to continue the thought.

I SUPPOSE I DO NOT KNOW THESE NANITES AS WELL AS I THOUGHT. IT SHOULD NOT BE POSSIBLE FOR THIS TO HAPPEN UNLESS THERE IS A CREATURE THAT IS ALSO PARTLY HUMAN SUCH THAT IT CAN INTEGRATE AND CONTROL THE NANITES USING HUMAN DNA. IT WOULD NEED TO REMAIN IN CONTROL OF THE ASSIMILATION PROCESS AND PREVENT THE HUMANS FROM FULLY ABSORBING THEM, MUCH THE SAME WAY AS MY MOTHER DID WITH YOU.

"Wait, what? You're saying the creature controlling all this might be as strong and intelligent as your mother?"

Annoyed that he'd suggest anything was as strong, Scarlet responded, NO. AT LEAST, I DO NOT BELIEVE SO. IT USED HUMAN DNA, OR INFECTED HUMANS, TO MANIPULATE THE

NANITES. IT WAS SMART ENOUGH TO MANIPULATE THEM AND ENSLAVE MINDS, BUT FROM WHAT WE SAW FIRST-HAND, IT APPEARS RATHER PRIMITIVE. SIMPLE.

"Is this going to be dangerous for us? These new nanites, that is. I don't see how it could be, since we killed that thing."

NO, I BELIEVE THEY ARE SAFE FOR US, AND WHATEVER INFLUENCE EXERTED BY THE CREATURE IS GONE. THERE IS ONE OTHER THING I MUST CHECK. Scarlet stepped toward the water, claw outstretched.

"Scarlet? What are you doing?" An edge of panic laced Jared's words.

DO NOT FEAR. I WILL BE FINE. I WAS UNPREPARED BEFORE, BUT THAT IS NO LONGER THE CASE.

Jared watched as she placed a claw into the water, bowing her head as the nanites started streaming toward her again. She stepped back from the water's edge before it became anything more than a slight glow.

"What were you doing?" asked Jared.

I WAS CONFIRMING ANOTHER THEORY. THE LAKE IS A CONDUIT FOR THE NANITES.

"Conduit? Like a battery? So you're saying we have a massive source of nanites at our disposal to keep getting stronger? What about other creatures absorbing them?"

YES—AND I DO NOT THINK SO. THE CREATURES IN THE WATER WILL ABSORB SMALL AMOUNTS, BUT THE TINY PORTION OF MODIFIED DNA CODING WILL PREVENT ANOTHER CREATURE, A NON-BONDED CREATURE, FROM ABSORBING THEM.

"And other humans can't absorb them if they aren't bonded! Scarlet, this is amazing! We've got a huge military bunker, hundreds of weapons, medical supplies, boosters, and now a huge pool of nanites to absorb."

Jared couldn't believe his luck! They'd set out to hunt creatures and grow stronger but only stopped in this area on a whim. Of course, it wasn't all rainbows and sunshine, but now they had all they needed to build an army of bonded. It was almost enough to make him forget about his brush with death the past few weeks, or his plummet to the lake just a few moments ago. The possibilities they now had in front of them sent excitement coursing through him.

We've got everything we need! Well, everything except people.

16 THE WATERFOLK

J ared and Scarlet remained by the water for a time recovering, the pain in Jared's leg and shoulder aching. Somehow, he managed to pull himself to his perch atop Scarlet. His leg screamed in protest as he swung it over her back. Before doing anything else, Jared made sure all of his *Body Manipulation* nanites had instructions to regenerate. Thankfully, he'd not changed their instructions since his last injuries, and they'd already repaired some of it, the tear in his leg noticeably smaller. He couldn't afford to be hobbled long since there was no telling when they'd need to outrun the many predators in the world.

From his vantage on the dragon's back, Jared looked out at the water, deceptively peaceful until he flipped to *Heat Sight* and saw the mass of movement just below the surface, and an increasingly large number swimming toward the shore. They moved at random and didn't really have a sense of purpose other than to escape the water.

"Scarlet, I think we're about to have company."

Scarlet lifted her head and looked out over the water.

"Can you fly yet?"

YES, I CAN FLY. ARE YOU READY?

Jared ensured that he had all of his gear with him, which wasn't much, since he'd left most of it back in the barn.

"Yep, let's go."

Scarlet bunched her legs under her and vaulted into the air, her body jerking more than normal as she gained altitude and hovered over the lake.

Concerned, Jared asked, "You sure you're okay? That seemed like it was a bit difficult for you."

I AM STILL A BIT WINDED FROM THE INFLUX OF NANITES, BUT I AM FINE.

"All right just let me know if you need to set down and we'll head back. I'd like to observe these creatures for a bit if you are okay. Maybe we'll get some insight about what held them captive."

Jared watched as the creatures made their way toward land. Every type of creature imaginable tumbled out of the water onto the sand they'd just occupied.

"Scarlet, let's make a circuit around the lake, I want to see just how bad this is."

Scarlet circled the lake, and everywhere he looked, warm-bodied creatures pulled themselves from the murky water. Although he couldn't see a lot of details with *Heat Sight*, he saw humanoid bodies, bipedal creatures of all shapes and sizes, and even creatures that had no legs or arms swimming for shore. Jared switched back to normal vision to observe some of the creatures already on land and heading away from the lake.

"Scarlet, can you drop lower please? I want to get a good look at these things."

Scarlet descended, and Jared examined all the beasts that came out of the water.

"Holy crap. What—Scarlet, how is this—what is going on here?"

I...I DO NOT KNOW.

The first thing Jared saw were naked humans waddling out of the water on unsteady feet. Their skin was a sickly white blue color, and their bodies showed signs of mutation. They had webbed feet and hands and what looked like gills on their necks. Judging by their lack of coordination, it'd been a long time since they'd walked on dry land.

When Jared and Scarlet flew over, no one looked up. They plodded forward with no clear direction in mind. Some of them stopped on the sand and heaved, great hacking coughs wracking their bodies in spasms.

The hacking repeated itself like an echo all down the coastline as creatures struggled to breathe out of the water. It confused Jared, since most of the things exiting the water were land dwellers and should have no difficulty breathing. Aside from the coughing, no other sounds reached his ears. None of the creatures growled, yipped, or mewled. It was deathly silent, the occasional retching the only noise to slice through the silence.

The scene disturbed him deeply, raising his hackles. It seemed as though they were in a state of shock, stupefied, and didn't remember how to act anymore. Many of the animals emerging from the lake looked like genetically altered amalgamations of many species.

"It looks like most of these creatures went through some transformation that allowed them to survive down there," Jared said, his thoughts taking voice. "I wonder if they'd attack us?"

The silence ended abruptly as a commotion several hundred yards down the coastline drew his attention. When they reached the other side, Jared exhaled sharply.

"Whoa."

The sight made Jared crinkle his nose in disgust. Dozens of different species reverted to their natural predisposition, attacking anything in their path. The ghastly spectacle below stained the sand crimson, their blood creating ribbons of red streaming down the beach.

Immediately below him, a group of crocodiles twenty feet long with massive rows of sharp teeth squared off against several dozen creatures that resembled giant badgers. The badger-like creatures nimbly bounced around with massive tails ending in two sharp points. Fangs, protruding from their long snouts, sank into the crocodiles' thick hide.

"What the heck are those?" Jared wondered.

THEY LOOK LIKE BEAVERS OR BADGERS, BUT MODIFIED?

"They look like nightmares," Jared said, disgust obvious in his words.

"I don't think it's a natural mutation. I mean, look at those things. It's like someone spliced three different animals together to create them! They all look like science experi—" As he said it, a lightbulb went off in Jared's head. "Scarlet, maybe these are science experiments. We know there is a huge military bunker below. It stands to reason they might have a lab down there too."

IT IS POSSIBLE AND MAKES THE MOST SENSE LOOKING AT THESE THINGS. THEY DID NOT MUTATE NATURALLY.

"Let's make another circuit of the lake and check out some of those neighboring ones." Jared pointed in the distance. "I want to see if they're connected."

Battles raged up and down the entire coast as creatures vied for dominance. Their blood decorated the sands in a macabre display of red gore as it spurted violently from severed limbs and decapitated bodies.

"Scarlet, what did we unleash?" Jared shook his head, concern etched across his face. "Maybe whatever controlled these things was doing the world a favor?"

Jared sat on Scarlet's back watching the horrors emerge from the water and fear gripped his mind, suffocating rational though. They'd fought rats, lizards, rabbits, and a giant worm, but there were thousands, if not tens of thousands of mutated creatures crawling for the shoreline.

Nothing we have seen is deadlier than the worm we killed, and not a single group is larger than the rat horde to cause us concern. Together, they would pose a problem, but clearly, they have no love for each other.

Scarlet flew to a neighboring lake, but it was completely devoid of the mayhem just a few miles away. Thanking their good fortune, they returned to the battle royale.

"Head over toward the group of humans. I want to help them. If they want any help, that is."

The cluster of humans stuck together, whether from a conscious decision or a base instinct to congregate with their kind, Jared couldn't say. When he got closer, he noticed many of them were wounded. Some had blood streaming from their ears and nose. Several of them bore signs of burns, their skin a vibrant pink.

"Oh no, Scarlet! They must've been in the radius of the bomb blast."

Jared, there is no way we could have known.

No, I know, but we must find a way to help them.

While Jared contemplated a way to help the group of survivors, a group of rats charged across the beach. No one reacted until the rats came within a few dozen yards, and Jared wondered if they couldn't see very far. When the humans saw the rats, several stepped forward, picking up pieces of debris from the ground to use as weapons.

The rats didn't hesitate and surged into the group.

"Go, Scarlet! Drop me close by and take care of the rats furthest from the group. I don't want to scare them any more than they already are."

As soon as she landed, Jared gingerly dropped from her back and drew his phase pistol. Limping and taking care not to exert too much pressure on his injured leg, Jared sighted down the barrel at the attacking rats. One by one he picked them off, the rats' attention shifting to him. They didn't get within twenty feet as Jared expertly exterminated them, leaving a dozen smoking corpses.

Jared holstered his pistol and very slowly hobbled toward the group of humans. He held both of his hands in front of him and called out, "Hello? Can you understand me? Are you okay?"

No one responded, but he could see several people writhing on the ground in pain where the rats had scratched and bit. Silence greeted him as he neared the group. The forty or so humans stood in a compact circle, their bodies pressed so close they could barely move. When he got within ten feet, the two defenders left holding the makeshift weapons stepped in front of the group and brandished the crude weapons at him.

He backed up, keeping his hands out in front of him. "I don't want to hurt you—please lower your weapons. Can any of you speak? I can help with your injuries." Jared paused, waiting for someone to acknowledge him. Trying a different tactic, Jared fished some bandages from his bag and held them up for everyone to see.

"Heal?" Still nothing. Sighing in frustration, Jared said, "If you understand me, nod your head?"

A woman behind the line of defenders placed a hand on the shoulder of the two defenders and stepped forward. She nodded her head in exaggerated movements, showing she understood him.

She turned back to the group and met each of their eyes in a silent exchange they each seemed to accept.

Scarlet, this is creeping me out. Why aren't they talking? Are they mute?

I THINK THEY MIGHT BE USING TELEPATHY. I THOUGHT I HEARD SOMETHING WHEN SHE TURNED AROUND, BUT I WAS UNPREPARED. IT VAGUELY SOUNDED LIKE OUR LANGUAGE, BUT IT WAS HALTED. BROKEN.

The woman who stood facing him was beautiful, in an otherworldly sense. She stood at six feet tall, perfect figure, with long raven hair that glistened in the sun. He couldn't guess her age, or really any of them for that matter. Their skin was flawless, and they all had a look of agelessness to them. If Jared looked past the disfiguration, she was a very attractive woman.

AHEM. Startled, Jared looked over at Scarlet whose eyes bored into him. YOU LET YOUR THOUGHTS BLEED OUT THERE.

Jared's cheeks flushed red, and he dropped his gaze.

Sorry.

Clearing his thoughts, Jared focused and addressed the woman again.

"You understand the words I'm saying?"

She nodded.

Jared smiled and said, "My name is Jared, and this is Scarlet." He pointed behind him at Scarlet who lowered her head in greeting. The woman's eyes widened briefly, and she squinted in Scarlet's direction, then cocked her head again. When Jared really focused on her eyes and the eyes of the group, he noticed they were all a murky white.

"Can you see her?" Jared motioned to Scarlet again, and the woman shook her head.

"Scarlet is my friend and companion. She will not harm you, but I'll warn you now, she's intimidating," Jared cautioned. He motioned for Scarlet to come forward. As soon as she was within range of their sight, they all dropped into a crouch and hissed, bearing teeth sharpened to points. Their faces contorted into rage, and their eyes narrowed as they advanced on her with their crude weapons.

"Whoa, whoa, whoa." Jared interposed himself between Scarlet and the group of humans. "She is my friend! Back off!" To emphasize his point, Jared brandished his pistol and fired a round at their feet. "Back. Up," he repeated.

They stopped advancing but held their defensive positions.

Scarlet, take a few steps back please.

Scarlet did as Jared asked, and the posture of the group changed from outright hostility to looks of trepidation, since they could no longer see her.

"Look, I've asked her to give us some space, okay? Scarlet is my companion, that makes us a family. She won't harm any of you. In fact, none of you would be free right now if not for her. If anyone tries to harm her, I will kill you." Jared spoke in a deadly calm voice, clearly intimating the dire consequences should anyone not abide by his wishes. "You don't have to like it, but you will respect it. Do you understand?"

Most of the group nodded their heads, but a few refused to acknowledge him and let their disagreement show on their face.

Scarlet, keep an eye on the few who refused to agree. I don't like the way they are looking in your direction. He didn't want to risk another confrontation like the Daggers, but if these people refused to heed his warning, it was entirely their fault.

"Can you speak?" He motioned to his throat and mimed projecting sound from his mouth.

Cocking her head to one side, she opened her mouth, showcasing rows of needle-like teeth. It was an uncanny sight to behold, and definitely put a damper on her whole alien, exotic beauty vibe.

Forming her mouth into various shapes, the woman tried to push sound out. At least, Jared thought she tried, but it only resulted in a hacking noise and then a fit of coughing. The woman looked up at him and shook her head.

"It's okay. We will find another way. Look, I know you don't know me or trust me, but I can lead you all someplace safe. These creatures that came after you are smaller than most of the ones that left the lake. Whatever held you captive also held them captive, and now their predatory instincts are driving them to kill anything in their way. Either way, I'll stay and protect you, but I can't promise you'll all survive if we stay. It'd be easier if you come with me. I'll take you to a place where you can rest and recover."

She huddled together with the group and they exchanged silent words, nods, and other body language Jared couldn't decipher.

Scarlet, are you getting any of this?

I THINK THEY ARE DISCUSSING WHETHER TO GO WITH US, BUT THE WORDS THEY ARE USING ARE...DISJOINTED. IT IS REALLY HARD TO FOLLOW ALONG.

Jared waited for the group to finish conversing and turned his attention outward.

"We've got incoming. We need to go now!" The same badger-like creatures he'd seen face off against the crocodiles bounded down the beach toward them. They pounced on any poor creature in their wake, sinking their fangs into them and eviscerating them with their sharp two-pronged tails.

He pointed down the beach, but then realized that the group

couldn't see far enough.

"There's a bunch of creatures coming toward us, and they're killing everything in their path. From the looks of it, they already killed a group of massive crocodiles. I don't know about you, but I don't want to face off against anything that can do that. Especially not in such an exposed location."

A look of alarm passed their features, but just as many frowned in suspicion. Jared realized it'd be a convenient tale to get them to go with him, so he clarified.

"Look, I'm not lying to you. You don't have to trust me, but I promise if you stay, some of you will die. Either choice requires a bit of faith. If, after I lead you to safety, you want to strike out on your own, I won't stop you. You have my word, for whatever that's worth from a stranger."

Again, the group hesitated, clearly uncertain what to do in the situation.

"Choose now!" yelled Jared.

Quickly turning back to the group, the woman turned to face him once more and motioned for him to lead.

"As fast as you can, please follow me. I know you are still unfamiliar with walking again, but try to move as quickly as you can. Please help those that have injuries. I'm recovering from one myself, so I won't be much help there."

Jared hobbled away as fast as his injured leg allowed. Scarlet brought up the rear in case the creatures caught up to them.

"Keep going," Jared said, dropping back to help where he could. "Scarlet will guard the rear in case they catch up to us. It looks like we avoided that group of creatures, but we're still visible from the water, and to any creatures that already ventured out this way."

The pace quickened as the...*waterfolk* plodded forward. The word used in the journal he'd read weeks earlier made a lot more sense now. Granted, Jeff hadn't seen any of these mutations, but it fit even more after those changes.

Scarlet was the last to crest a small hill obscuring them from the strange creatures frolicking on the beach. She gave Jared the all clear, and he heaved a sigh of relief, a tension he'd not noticed lifting from between his shoulders.

"We can slow down now. They're unable to see us from the beach and there shouldn't be any more dangers between us and safety."

Jared heard exhales from the waterfolk.

Jared drew up short. He hadn't heard any of them breathe since they'd left the water. They hadn't cried out when attacked by the rats. Even now, they weren't panting from the fast clip they maintained.

Scrutinizing them, Jared realized no one had their mouths open. It's possible they were all really good at regulating their breathing through their nose, but Jared suspected that was not the case. They could barely stand, their muscles so atrophied from their time in the water.

To make vocal sounds, air needed to pass through the vocal cords creating a vibration and then the throat, tongue, and lips formed the approximation of speech. If they used their gills for oxygen, then it stood to reason they'd used their lungs little in the time they'd spent beneath the water.

Scarlet, I think these people need to learn how to speak again. I heard some of them exhaling after the exertion of the fast walk, and I only noticed it because it was the first time I'd heard it.

IF THAT STASH OF BOOSTERS APPROXIMATES UNUSED RESOURCES, IT IS POSSIBLE THEY HAVE BEEN UNDERWATER FOR ALMOST A DECADE, SHORTLY AFTER IGOR DISTRIBUTED THEM.

You would know better, given that you grew up in a colony. Is it normal to have that many boosters for a long-standing colony?

"No, it's not. We rationed them back home. Sometimes getting so close to the three years that people died. Like my mother."

I am sorry Jared. I did not mean to——

It's okay, Scarlet. Truly, it is. I've come to accept everything. The only feelings I get when I think of it is righteous anger at those responsible.

If these people really did spend a decade enslaved to that thing... My own experience pales next to what they went through. The torture and sheer helplessness these people endured boggles my mind.

It will take a lot of time for them to recover, if they ever do.

A few moments later, Scarlet spoke again. It is possible you found your army.

Let's not get ahead of ourselves. Jared held up a hand. If they kept any of the memories over the past who-knows-how-many years, they might unravel hearing the truth of the world. They'd go from one prison into another, where the expectation is slave labor to the rich and powerful. That's not a reality I'd want to force on anyone, let alone people that might've spent years as prisoners in their own minds.

The human mind is an impressive creation, and its resilience is astounding. I would not put it past any of them to want to make the next step in human evolution. Also, they can revert their bodies back to a more...human form.

I didn't think about that, I suppose you're right. I'd want to rid myself of any reminders from the experience. Heck, I'd want to avoid water for the rest of my life. What I don't get is how a non-human entity *controlled them. If this really is one giant science experiment, we need to figure out who is responsible for it.*

WE MAY NEVER KNOW, BUT I AGREE. WE SHOULD SPEND SOME TIME TRYING TO FIND OUT. CLEARLY WHATEVER CONTROLLED ALL THESE CREATURES IS DEAD, SO IT SHOULD BE SAFE TO RESUME EXPLORATION OF THE TUNNELS. YOU CAN TRY TO FIGURE OUT WHAT HAPPENED AND FIND OUT WHAT MANNER OF CREATURE CONTROLLED THEM.

Let's get everyone settled in the barn, and then we can talk about venturing out again. I'm still a bit leery about going back in the tunnels after what happened. What if some part of the creature lives on and those vines are still down there?

I UNDERSTAND. PART OF ME WANTS TO JUST LEAVE THE AREA, BUT I ALSO KNOW THE THINGS YOU FOUND ARE TOO VALUABLE TO LEAVE BEHIND.

A short time later, Jared brought the group to a halt and asked everyone to sit down and recover strength before they walked the rest of the way. While they waited, Jared had time to reflect on their situation, and as much as he wanted to give them the benefit of the doubt, he decided to exercise caution.

Hey, Scarlet. I feel really bad for these people, but at the same time, I don't want to rely on the goodwill of having saved them as a reason to trust them. We've had too many brushes with death and close calls lately, and if whatever kept them prisoner somehow transferred its consciousness, or retains some foothold in their minds, I don't want to risk anything with them.

AGREED. WE WILL BRING THEM TO THE BARN AND ASSESS EACH OF THEM THERE. I CAN HUNT AND BRING BACK FOOD TO HELP THEM RECOVER FASTER. WE WILL LEARN THEIR WHOLE

STORY IN TIME.

Sounds like a plan to me, Jared said, rising to his feet.

"All right, let's keep moving, everyone. We should be well-enough ahead of the creatures, but no sense taking risks."

Jared dropped back a few paces to walk beside the appointed representative of the waterfolk. He told her about their destination and plans to help them recover strength. She nodded in response but remained impassive.

The attitude almost offended him, but after what they'd been through, she had every right to distrust anyone but her own people. She had an allure about her that intrigued him. The gills, sharp teeth, and webbed hands and feet were strange, but it didn't diminish her beauty. Her very presence invoked a feeling of strength and determination. It was obvious why she led the people here.

Every time he glanced her way, a blush crept up his cheeks. It wasn't like he hadn't seen a naked woman before, but for some reason his pulse started racing when he looked at her.

Jared felt several pairs of suspicious eyes on him, several directing openly hostile looks his way. Sensing he'd overstepped their comfort level, Jared resumed his position at the head of the group. Jared cast furtive glance over his shoulder and found the woman staring at him, the corners of her lips curled into a smile.

She really is beautiful, thought Jared, quickly checking to make sure his mental barrier was in place, so Scarlet didn't tease him.

A few minutes later they crested a small hill, the barn looming in the distance.

Scarlet, can you please fly ahead and make sure the coast is clear?

A few minutes later, Scarlet reported the all clear, and Jared led the group to the building where he opened the giant doors and motioned for them to step inside.

"Please make yourself comfortable here, but please stay away from the loft," Jared said and pointed to the ladder. "I have some dangerous equipment up there and it's safer for everyone if you stay away."

The few waterfolk that clearly didn't trust him narrowed their eyes.

Shrugging, Jared climbed up and packed everything back into the crate he'd taken from the bunker. They didn't have to trust him if they didn't want to. He planned to help them regardless.

Aside from the two or three directing malevolent gazes in his direction, everyone else appeared at ease, clustered together in silence. Several people found empty stalls along the wall and collapsed in exhaustion.

The gear put away, Jared settled back to rest, but a light tapping on the ladder drew his attention and he peeked over the edge. The waterfolk leader stood at the base, trying to get his attention.

"Do you need something?"

The woman nodded her head and motioned for Jared to come closer.

Securing his pack in the crate, Jared slid down the ladder, careful not to land hard on his injured leg.

The move startled her, and she stumbled back.

Jared's quick reflexes kicked in and he reached out, catching her hand before she fell backward. The momentary brush of her fingers on his sent shivers up his spine. Her skin was smooth, silky, and cool to the touch. Another blush lit his cheeks on fire, and Jared looked down to hide his face.

"Sorry, I didn't mean to startle you," Jared apologized.

She didn't respond, but Jared heard her forcing air through her lungs as she tried to tell him something. Her brow furrowed in concentration as she struggled to articulate something to him.

"It's okay. Please don't push too hard. I don't want you to get hurt."

Jared's words sparked determination in her and she increased her efforts to make a sound. After an entire minute of forced breathing, a soft, feminine moan escaped her lips.

A triumphant grin lit up her face. Jared was equal parts enthralled and appalled. Her face morphed from a depressed frown carrying all the weight of the world into a happy, carefree spirit. If he overlooked the sharp needle teeth, she was even more beautiful when she smiled, but those teeth made her look evil. Creepy though it was, Jared smiled in return, happy she'd managed to make a sound. When most of her people were already passed out in exhaustion, she'd pushed herself, once again showing that strength of will Jared found alluring.

She tried again, but the most she could manage was a few vowel sounds.

A look of disappointment passed across her face, and Jared quickly said, "Please don't get upset! I really want to help you, but if you force your body to use a muscle that is too weak, it could cause more damage than if you wait for it to regain its strength."

Sighing, a look of disappointment passed her features, but she stopped trying and retreated to one of the stalls along the wall. Jared climbed back to the loft and sat against his pack. He glanced over to see Scarlet staring at him.

You should not get too attached to them just yet.

I understand, Scarlet. I'll not let my personal feelings come between us or our safety ever again. That lesson remains fresh in my mind. Still, I'm hoping that we can help them, and they can join our cause. I may not talk about it much, but I miss human companionship. It is nothing against you at all, it's just…

I TOO LONG FOR MY OWN KIND IN MUCH THE SAME WAY. IT IS NATURAL FOR US TO SEEK ACCEPTANCE AND BELONGING WITH OUR FELLOWS.

I'll be careful, promised Jared.

ALSO, KEEP IN MIND THE DISCOVERIES WE HAVE MADE SO FAR. IF THIS FACILITY FUNCTIONED AS A SCIENCE LAB, SOMEONE IN THIS GROUP MAY KNOW SOMETHING AND MAY NOT HAVE THE BEST INTENTIONS.

We know from Jeff's journals they knew about portions of the facility, but if they had a hand in scientific experiments, it seems odd he'd write about the problems in the colony like he did. I doubt they had anything to do with the experiments. Otherwise, how did they end up a slave to the very same experiments that they may have had a hand in?

YES, BUT ALSO RECALL THEY RECEIVED AN INFLUX OF NEW COLONISTS SHORTLY BEFORE THE WATERFOLK INCIDENTS OCCURRED. JEFF SAID IT HIMSELF; HE DID NOT KNOW EVERYONE WELL BY THE TIME EVERYTHING KICKED OFF.

Good point. I hadn't thought about it. I assumed that this complex predated the wars, but I suppose it could've functioned as a lab later.

MY POINT IS WE NEED TO MAKE SURE WE DO NOT GET TOO ATTACHED OR LET OUR EMOTIONS CLOUD GOOD JUDGMENT.

Duly noted. Thanks, Scarlet. That won't happen again. I promise.

Jared thought about the implications surrounding the military complex. There were so many unanswered questions swirling around in his mind. He wondered what horrors awaited him beneath the earth. A part of him relished the new discoveries and freedom to roam, but the more he learned of the cities and mankind in general, the more he longed for simpler times when he could walk for days and weeks with nothing to concern him but the occasional wild animal. Jared's world had flipped upside down in less than a month. The world was much harsher than he'd known, but he also had innumerable paths before him, needing only to choose which to travel.

17 A HARD TRUTH

Jared slept little that night, curious about the people he now presided over and cautious to the point he refused to let his guard down. He hadn't even explored his status screen after the massive influx of nanites the previous day. He used every spare moment he had to study these people and glean any insight that could lend him some information on what to do with them—and how to begin their rehabilitation.

Scarlet hadn't slept a wink either, and their senses remained on high alert. Not just for the people inside the building, but also in the event something came from without. The number of creatures that poured from the lake had to be in the tens of thousands, and they'd scattered like leaves in the wind.

Their escape into the wild was a two-edged sword. They posed a significant risk to him and those now under his care, but they also served as fodder to increase his and Scarlet's strength.

Jared lay in the loft, mentally flipping images in his head of all the creatures that emerged from the water. Every one of them represented a threat to those around him. Out of all the creatures that emerged from the lake, the mutated crocodiles—twice the size of any he'd ever seen in pictures—resembled their predecessors the most.

The terrifying badger-like creatures were clearly man-made abominations. He focused on an image of one and magnified it in his mind. Matted brown fur coated its body, and its tail looked like large, flat pieces of black rubber honed to points on either side. It looked like a large machete ending in twin points. Fangs jutted from the creature's upper lip, curving down over the bottom portion of the jaw. Its legs shared similarities with that of the rabbits Jared had killed a few weeks ago, and they allowed the creature to bound across the ground in great galloping strides. Oddly, he saw no sign they could breathe underwater and assumed they had to surface for air periodically.

It amazed him that he'd ever gotten along without *Memory Recall*. The ability worked amazingly, and he'd never need to worry about forgetting something again. If he did, a few seconds concentration allowed him to recall and reflect on a memory. He used the memories from the lake to categorize all of the creatures and put them into assumed threat levels. Obviously, the Frankenstein badgers were at the top after they'd not only survived an encounter with a trio of twenty-foot crocs and seemed no worse for wear. Dozens of other creatures went on his list, including sleek-bodied bears with webbed feet, giant frogs sporting shiny neon colors, huge sea serpents with clawed legs and horns on their heads, multiple types of worms, and rats.

Always with the rats, Jared sighed. *Thank God I've not seen any giant cockroaches yet!*

His body stiff from lying on the ground so long, Jared rolled to his feet and stretched. When he got to his feet, he felt a tug at the injury to his leg, but no stabbing pain. With slow, deliberate moves,

Jared tested his weight on the injured leg. It felt sore, but well on its way toward recovery. Still, he planned to take it easy until examining it further.

Jared descended the ladder and turned around.

"Ah!" cried Jared.

The leader of the waterfolk stood right behind him, flinching away from his outburst.

"Sorry, it's my fault. I didn't realize you were there and hadn't heard you walk up. Did you sleep well?"

The questioned earned him a nod. Then she placed her hand on her chest, right between...

No, stop it! Get your head straight! Jared chided himself. She didn't deserve his ogling or ill-begotten thoughts. No, they needed a protector, someone that wouldn't take advantage of their precarious state of mind.

Jerking his gaze to her eyes, she opened her mouth, and a soft voice whispered, "Nessa."

Jared's eyes opened wide, and he grinned like a fool to cover his obvious shame from ogling her naked body.

Relieved to move the conversation forward to cover his embarrassment and shame, Jared said, "Nessa? That's your name?"

Shaking her head, she too wore a grin and said, "Va...nessa."

"Vanessa?"

Nodding enthusiastically, she grinned, the predatory smile on full display.

"I honestly didn't think you'd be able to talk so soon. Can anyone else speak yet?"

Vanessa shook her head and frowned.

"Really, it's okay. I mean it. Scarlet and I thought it would take you a while to regain the ability and that you'd need to relearn how to speak."

She snatched his hand and pulled him along.

Jared felt like a little kid with his first crush as her touch sent butterflies through his stomach.

Check yourself, Jared. You don't know her. You don't know these people, or what they're going through. Why can't I get my thoughts under control? Am I that desperate for human companionship?

Jared closed his eyes, exhaling slowly and deliberately to expel the flighty emotions. Time was the healer of wounds, and they'd only just left behind a decade of torment. It could take years for them to recover. Vanessa didn't need the added complexity of emotional attachment as she reestablished herself and her psyche.

He allowed himself to be led over to a cluster of her people.

One by one, she introduced each of them. He lost track after a dozen names, the process taking a long time as Vanessa struggled to speak the words.

After twenty introductions, Jared suggested she rest and let her voice recover.

Nodding in agreement, she followed Jared to the ladder.

"I'd rather you not come up here right now, Vanessa. I've got a lot of very dangerous equipment up here, and it's safer if we keep everyone away."

Nodding, she tugged his sleeve and pointed to Scarlet.

Puzzled, Jared stepped back from the ladder and asked, "You want to talk to her?"

Again, she nodded.

"I thought she terrified you?"

Jared received another nod, which puzzled him more.

Her hand on his sleeve, she tugged again, imploring him to bring her over to Scarlet.

"Okay, I'll take you over and introduce you, but Scarlet only uses *Telepathy* to speak."

Her forehead crinkled in confusion and she looked at him askance.

"Mental communication? She—she speaks with her thoughts?"

Understanding dawned in her eyes which quickly morphed into fear.

"Hey, hey…it's okay!" Jared soothed her. "I speak with her like this all the time. We—well, my connection to Scarlet is unique, and we can speak without touching. If you'd like to speak with her, you need to place your hand on her. Like this."

Jared walked over to Scarlet and showed Vanessa.

Holding out his hand, he beckoned for her to grab it and come forward.

She eyed his hand like a coiled snake, clearly afraid of touching Scarlet. Finally, she relented and grabbed his hand. Jared did his best to ignore the flutters in his stomach and the shivers racing up his spine. Turning back to Scarlet, Jared paused before placing her hand on Scarlet's side.

I guess I should've asked you first, Scarlet. Are you okay with this?

I—YES. I WANT TO HELP THEM. I FEEL ONLY SYMPATHY FOR THEM. THEY WENT THROUGH SO MUCH.

Jared guided Vanessa's hand to Scarlet's side, and the moment she made contact, pandemonium ensued as Scarlet bellowed in rage, causing all the waterfolk to cower in fear.

Vanessa and Scarlet both yelled in outrage, violently jerking away from each other. Vanessa crumpled into a ball on the floor, while Scarlet launched to her feet.

No! IT CANNOT BE.

Scarlet? What's wrong?

Scarlet didn't respond and instead crashed through the door and leapt into the sky. Vanessa curled into a ball on the floor, great sobs ripping from her tiny form. Jared gestured to some other waterfolk to look after Vanessa and sprinted out the door after Scarlet.

Scarlet? Scarlet!?

JARED, I—WE—KILLED HIM.

Killed who?

THE CREATURE. THE ONE IN THE WATER CONTROLLING ALL OF THIS. IT WAS A DRAGON. WE KILLED HIM!

The anguish Jared felt through the bond rendered him speechless.

How could we have killed a dragon? I thought dragons were peaceful? Wait, that means humanity knew of their existence all along? The military complex, the likely experiments, and the mutated creatures.

It all clicked into place for Jared, and no doubt Scarlet had already connected the dots the instant she sensed the presence of the other dragon.

Scarlet, I'm so sorry. Please come back. Let's talk this through. We didn't know.

I NEED TIME TO THINK, TO PROCESS THIS. IT SHOULD NOT BE POSSIBLE.

Please be careful, Scarlet! I'm here for you if you need to talk.

I WILL. HOW COULD HE DO THIS? WHY WOULD HE ATTACK? Scarlet's thoughts trailed off as she broke off their connection.

The tension that left after they killed the creature returned tenfold; the heavy burden made his shoulders sag and he dropped to his knees.

Heartbroken at Scarlet's loss, Jared sat forlornly in the field for a time before going back inside. When he got back inside, Jared found the entire group huddled around one stall in the back corner, Vanessa whimpering within.

Jared didn't know how or why a dragon had done all of this, nor who had done it, but it was exactly the kind of despicable, immoral actions committed by the cities above for centuries. Frustration threatened to overwhelm him and an uncontrollable desire to eradicate the cities clouded his mind.

They'll get what's coming to them! he vowed.

Jared marched to the ladder and climbed up with jerking movements, betraying his anger and frustration. He lay against his pack, evil thoughts of destruction churning as he imagined the cities blown to smithereens.

We need to get stronger as soon as possible!

Jared almost made a trek down to the water right then and absorbed even more nanites, but he knew it'd be an idiotic move without Scarlet there to keep an eye on him. Still, he felt little rationality at the moment, and he almost threw caution to the wind and made the trek.

Scarlet, when you've had time to think things through, we need to get down to business. We've a base of operations. We have an armory replete with weapons and munitions. And, we now have a giant lake filled with nanites. It's time we lay out our plans and create a blueprint for how we plan to fight the cities. I suspect that these experiments on your brother stem from the source of most of the world's current problems.

I WILL RETURN SOON.

Thoughts of vengeance raced through his head. It wasn't until a gentle tapping on the ladder below drew his attention that he snapped out of his funk.

Vanessa, surrounded by her people, waved her hand at him to come down.

Jared centered himself before climbing down the ladder. He didn't know what she wanted, or if they'd be able to communicate effectively enough to find out, but he needed to try.

"Vanessa, I'm so sorry. We didn't know one of Scarlet's kind kept you prisoner. She's a dragon, if you didn't already know." Her eyes widened in realization and she gestured wildly, pantomiming fire shooting from her mouth.

Nodding, Jared said, "Yes, she can breathe fire."

Vanessa tried explaining something else, but the communication challenges were just too great to overcome, and Jared couldn't figure out what she wanted to tell him.

"I'm sorry, Vanessa, I don't understand."

Vanessa paused and tentatively reached her hand out for him. Her cool hand touched his arm, raising goosebumps along his skin.

A soft, gentle voice brushed against his mind.

Can you hear me?

Jared's eyes widened. *Yes! I can. For some reason I didn't think to try this even though Scarlet said you could speak this way.*

Jared, I saw you react, but you aren't saying anything. Can you hear me? Vanessa asked again.

"I can hear you, Vanessa. I tried to send a thought back, but I guess my *Telepathy* isn't strong enough yet. Scarlet says it will get there in time, but it's new for me."

But…you communicate with Scarlet?

"Yes, but…well, as I said before, Scarlet and I have a unique connection, a bond of sorts. I'm not ready to go into detail, but it's probably similar to the connection you had with the dragon that enslaved you," explained Jared.

When I touched Scarlet, I felt the same mental presence from the water devil.

"Water devil?"

It is what we called the — the dragon that controlled us.

"Can you tell me anything about this *water devil*?" Jared asked, testing the words and finding they fit surprisingly well after his experience. "How did it control all of you? We thought only a human had the capability to control nanites based on information from their creator, a professor named Igor Janovich. The nanites specifically code to human DNA, and only a human can command them. Or so we thought."

I... Vanessa started, but trailed off, pain evident in her tone. *I know nothing of the nanites, but I am not ready to speak of my—of our—time under the water yet.* Vanessa waved a hand around to encompass the group.

"I understand. Rest and recover, and we'll speak of it later. It's only been a day for you, and I don't expect you are ready to talk about it yet."

Thank you.

"So, all of you can use *Telepathy*?"

Vanessa nodded and motioned for her group to come closer, gesturing for everyone to introduce themselves using telepathy.

One by one, they each placed their hand into Jared's and spoke their name.

He remembered half their names from the original introductions and snickered at some names he'd *thought* he heard only to find out he'd been way off. After each introduction, Jared responded out loud, repeating their names.

He saw tears well up in many eyes and a few wept outright at hearing their own name after so long. He did his best to comfort them, but often it wasn't enough, and Vanessa spent a few moments in silent communication before they recovered.

The last to introduce themselves were the two skeptics that kept throwing scowls at him.

At first, they refused to touch him, but a gentle nudge from Vanessa and they reluctantly placed their hand in his to speak their name.

My name is Damien, and you —

Jared removed his hand before the person finished speaking, earning him another scowl. The hate in Damien's mental communication made it obvious he didn't like Jared, nor did he trust him. Rather than greet him like the rest of the people present, Jared simply uttered his name and nodded, moving over to the last person.

George.

A single, clipped word. There was no anger or vehemence, but the cold calculation in the other's eyes made Jared wary of him. Jared responded in kind, with a single utterance of his name. He filed both their names in the back of his mind and planned to keep a close eye on George. Damien was a loud, arrogant type and wouldn't pose an issue for him, but something about George set him on edge. Careful not to let his train of thought show, Jared turned back to Vanessa.

"Vanessa, how long were you all enslaved by this water devil?"

Vanessa grabbed his hand again and said, *We've been prisoners for almost nine years.*

"Wow," Jared replied in amazement. "I don't know how you did it. How you survived so long without going mad."

We didn't have a choice. Bitterness laced her words as she recalled the years as a prisoner.

Rather than dwell on an obviously painful topic, Jared changed the topic, and asked, "Are there more of you? Others that might've come out of the lake in another area?"

No, we always stayed together unless commanded otherwise. We've lost several hundred over the years to madness. A couple died recently, in the explosion that freed us.

The blood drained from Jared's face. He'd killed them. It was an accident, but he'd killed them.

Vanessa saw the look on his face and mirrored it with one of her own. *What's wrong, Jared?*

"I killed them."

Killed who?

"That explosion, that was my doing. We didn't know..." Jared's voice trailed off as he plopped to the ground, dejected.

I swore I'd never kill innocent people, he thought. *Now I've killed who knows how many. My negligence. Carelessness. I should've taken more time to understand the threat.*

Jared? Are you okay? What happened?

We can speak of it when you return.

Vanessa tightened her grip on his hand. *Jared. You freed us. You freed all of us, even those that died in the explosion. We were totally and completely under his control. We couldn't end our own lives if we wanted to. Most of the time we just huddled together in the dark, wishing for an escape. Our thoughts were our own, but we were powerless to act on them.*

Jared looked up at Vanessa, her eyes soft while she consoled him.

She sat next to him, holding his hand and continued. *The water devil took anyone away that tried to escape. Eventually, everyone stopped trying, and some of them went mad. He made them leave the group, and we never saw them again. Some said the water devil ate them, but no one knows for sure. My parents...*

It was Vanessa's turn to go silent, small shudders passing through her body.

Jared squeezed her hand to reassure her.

"I lost my parents too. My father died from wild bears, and my mother..." A sob caught in his throat, and Jared stopped speaking.

It was too much. Everything was just too much to take in, and he needed some space to collect his thoughts.

Jared stood to his feet and addressed everyone. "I'm going to go out and wait for Scarlet to return. I'd ask that all of you remain inside for your own safety, and, again, please stay away from the loft. Also, please rest, and I ask that you keep working on your voices and physical strength. The days ahead will be trying, especially with all the creatures that emerged from the water with you. Whether you decide to stay with me, or venture out on your own, everyone needs to regain their strength as soon as possible."

All the creatures left the water?

"All but the creatures that normally live in the water," Jared said, and Vanessa's grip tightened on his hand. Her fingernails dug into his palm hard enough to hurt.

"It's okay, Vanessa. Scarlet will be back after she's had time to process, and we'll make sure no harm comes to any of you. We've faced much worse than what came from the lake, and we will protect you."

A palpable tension fled the room, several people crying in happiness and relief they'd finally found some measure of safety after so long. Their relief and happiness weren't enough to overcome his current mood, but it helped he had an immediate objective to occupy his thoughts.

I HAVE RETURNED.

Jared let go of Vanessa's hand, the absence of her cool touch disappointing.

"Scarlet is back, and I must go speak with her. We'll be back soon," Jared said to the group.

He joined Scarlet outside and pressed his hand to her head.

Scarlet, I'm genuinely sorry for your loss. If we'd known...

NO, JARED. I TOOK THE TIME TO REFLECT ON IT, AND I KNOW HE WAS NOT HIMSELF. HE WAS A WATER DRAGON, AND I KNOW THERE IS NO WAY HE WOULD ENSLAVE HUMANKIND WILLINGLY. IT GOES AGAINST EVERYTHING WE BELIEVE. IT IS

ONE OF THE REASONS WE FLED THE EARTH WHEN WE COULD HAVE DOMINATED IT. WE DO NOT WISH TO RULE THE WORLD, ONLY TO LIVE PEACEABLY IN IT. WHATEVER MY BROTHER'S CAPTORS DID TO HIM, IT CHANGED HIM. CHANGED HIM IN SUCH A WAY IT DESTROYED WHO HE WAS.

We'll find out who did this and bring them to justice, promised Jared.

THANK YOU. I FEEL AN OVERWHELMING DESIRE TO HELP THESE PEOPLE RECOVER NOW THAT I KNOW WHO HELD THEM CAPTIVE. YOU REMEMBER THE DOMINANCE YOU FELT FROM MY MOTHER? MY BROTHERS, ALTHOUGH NOT AS STRONG, ALSO EXUDED THE SAME MENTAL PRESENCE. WHEN HE TOOK OVER THIS AREA, THERE WAS NOTHING THEY COULD DO TO STOP IT.

Jared thought back to when he'd met Alestrialia. The intensity of her psionic abilities rattled his brain so much that it felt like an elephant trampled on him. His head ached at the mere thought of experiencing it again.

THERE IS MUCH I DO NOT UNDERSTAND ABOUT THIS SITUATION. FOR INSTANCE, WHY DID HE NOT JUST LEAVE THE WATER? EVEN A YEAR IN CAPTIVITY IS ENOUGH TIME FOR A DRAGON TO GAIN STRENGTH, AND HE CONTROLLED EVERYTHING WITHIN A RADIUS OF SEVERAL MILES. WHY THEN DID HE REMAIN HERE? WHY ENSLAVE ANYTHING AT ALL? WHY KILL PEOPLE? IT DOES NOT MAKE SENSE. NONE OF IT DOES.

All good questions that we'll seek to answer in time. I have to wonder though: if he'd sensed your presence, or if a vine had touched you, would he have called for help?

SADLY, I DO NOT THINK HE HAD THE CAPACITY. WHEN YOU

WERE HIS PUPPET, YOU MINDLESSLY TRIED TO GET AWAY, AS IF ONLY INSTINCT REMAINED. No, I THINK SOMETHING HAPPENED TO HIM THAT DESTROYED HIS MIND, HIS ABILITY TO RATIONALIZE.

Maybe we'll find answers in the tunnels below. I purposefully avoided any tunnels that veered too close to the water, but now that we don't have to worry about him, I can explore them and seek answers.

Scarlet nodded her head, sorrow and hopefulness wrestling within her. They sat a while longer before Scarlet asked, WHAT HAPPENED AFTER I LEFT THE BARN?

Vanessa said— Jared paused. *We killed them. Some of the people in the lake.* It was his turn to exude sorrow across their bond. *There's no way we could've known, I know,* he quickly added. *Not even Vanessa blames us for killing them, saying we freed them from a prison. Still. I vowed never to harm innocent people, but…*

I AM TRULY SORRY, JARED. I AGREE WITH VANESSA ON THIS POINT. DEATH IS A MUCH KINDER FATE THAN WHAT THESE POOR PEOPLE ENDURED.

Nine years, Scarlet. That's how long they were slaves.

Shock and outrage shot through their bond.

I MUST HELP THEM. IT IS UNTHINKABLE.

We will help them, even the two that don't trust us. If they want to go their own way after they've recovered, so be it. At least our consciences will be satisfied that we did all we could.

They sat for a time, enjoying each other's company. The more time they spent with each other, the less they needed words to understand one another. Touching as they were allowed them to sense slight shifts in their psyches and understand once they'd both come to grips with their current reality.

Shall we head back inside? asked Jared, standing up.

Scarlet hesitated a moment longer and rose to follow him through the door.

Oh, by the way, all of them can use Telepathy.

The declaration made Scarlet pause again. ALL OF THEM?

Yep, Vanessa tried it out. Although I can't communicate back yet. I'm guessing my ability just isn't strong enough. All the more reason to keep upgrading my Mind abilities.

DID YOU TELL THEM HOW WE COMMUNICATE?

I did, but I didn't go into details other than to mention we share a special bond, and they didn't question it. I feel confident we'll be able to share the secret with them in time, but I'm not quite ready to divulge that information to anyone else.

I WOULD LIKE TO SPEAK WITH THEM.

Jared paused at the door and looked back at Scarlet. *Are you sure you're ready for that?*

I AM. THE WAY I LEFT THEM MUST HAVE SCARED THEM SENSELESS, AND I DO NOT WANT THEM AFRAID OF ME. I WANT THEM TO KNOW I AM HERE TO HELP.

Jared smiled and opened the doors for Scarlet. All of the waterfolk stood to their feet looking uncertain.

"It's okay, everyone. Scarlet and I spoke about the water devil, and she holds no ill will toward anyone here. We don't know where to lay blame for the atrocity that destroyed her brother, but we will seek answers and bring justice to those deserving. I know all of you can use *Telepathy* now, and Scarlet would like to speak with you. I want to warn you now, so you're not surprised as Vanessa was. Scarlet is nothing like the water devil, and she wants to help you all recover as much as I do, but she speaks only using *Telepathy*, and her presence in your mind may remind you of your time enslaved."

Jared motioned for Scarlet to proceed.

Hello, my name is Sildrainen Maildrel, but you may call me Scarlet. I promise all of you I will protect you to the best of my ability and help you overcome the grip my brother had on your minds. I believe I can help each of you recover faster, but it will take time, if you are willing. I feel it is my duty to right the wrong done to you by one of my own.

Jared looked out at the hopeful faces, and a smile tugged at the corner of his lips. He met Vanessa's eyes, and she smiled in return, warmth spreading through Jared as he imagined a future with these people, with Vanessa and Scarlet at his side. They weren't exactly an army, but they were a driven people, and the fact they'd survived over nine years with their bodies enslaved, spoke to their resolve and willpower. Physically, they didn't resemble more than spindly, pale skeletons, but with time they'd overcome that obstacle and once again thrive as a people.

Jared listened to Scarlet as she continued her introduction.

Although the water devil, as you know him, was a dragon, we are not of the same lineage. He was what my kind call a water dragon, while I am a fire dragon, the matriarch of my family. I can only assume that humanity imprisoned him and eroded his mind with experimentation, driving him to commit these evil acts against you. I never met him personally, but I know from my mother's memories, that his name was Razael. He was one of less than twenty water dragons left alive. It pains me to know I had a hand in his death, but I am relieved to know his suffering is over. I have no

IDEA HOW LONG HE WAS A PRISONER HERE, BUT DRAGONS LEFT THE AFFAIRS OF THE WORLD THOUSANDS OF YEARS AGO. IF SOMEONE MANAGED TO CAPTURE RAZAEL, IT IS POSSIBLE THAT EVEN FEWER WATER DRAGONS REMAIN, AS THEY ARE THE ONLY OF OUR KIND THAT DID NOT BURROW BENEATH THE EARTH BUT PREFERRED TO REMAIN IN THE OCEANS.

Scarlet held the group enthralled as she spoke of her history, and that of the once majestic Razael.

IF YOU WISH ME TO HELP WITH YOUR MIND, I AM HERE FOR YOU. I WILL WARN YOU THAT IT WILL NOT BE PLEASANT AND THAT YOU MUST PHYSICALLY TOUCH ME FOR THIS TO WORK.

Fear spread across their faces, several taking a few steps back. After the revelation Scarlet just shared, Jared didn't blame them for their hesitation and fear. No doubt he'd feel the same way in their situation. He stepped in to appease them before things got out of hand.

"Look, I know this is scary. I know some of you don't trust us. I get it. I understand it more than you know. If you want to wait, to get to know us better first, that is up to you. We can promise to protect you over and over, but ultimately it is your decision to make, and we won't force the issue."

If Jared didn't know better, he'd have said the message fell on deaf ears, but the reality was that a lot of them conversed among themselves, and he just couldn't hear the conversations. While they discussed what to do, Jared projected a question to Scarlet.

How are you going to help them? Rather than respond to him directly, she explained to the entire group.

MY BROTHER USED HIS WILL TO DOMINATE YOU. SOMEHOW, HE EXERTED HIS WILL AND INFLUENCE OVER THE

NANITES IN YOUR BODIES, CONTROLLING EVERYTHING YOU DID. ALTHOUGH HE IS DEAD, THE NANITES HE MODIFIED STILL COURSE THROUGH YOUR BODIES, AND I CAN HELP ERADICATE HIS INFLUENCE ENTIRELY.

Wait, how come you couldn't help me when I got infected? Jared asked, and again Scarlet spoke to the whole group instead.

I DO NOT KNOW IF JARED TOLD YOU, BUT HE BECAME INFECTED BY RAZAEL A FEW WEEKS AGO AND NEARLY DIED RECOVERING FROM THE ORDEAL.

Many of the waterfolk looked at him in surprise, new appreciation apparent behind their eyes. Vanessa showed the most concern, covering her mouth with her hand as a sharp exhalation of surprise escaping her lips. Jared reassured them he was fine before Scarlet continued.

I TRIED TO HELP HIM THEN BUT COULD DO NOTHING FOR HIM. I CAN ONLY SPECULATE THAT MY BROTHER CHANGED SO MUCH IN THE TIME HE REMAINED HERE THAT I NO LONGER SENSED HIS PRESENCE, OR HE HAD A WAY TO MASK IT. NOW THAT HE IS DEAD, THERE IS NOTHING PREVENTING ME FROM REMOVING HIS TAINT IF YOU WANT.

At first no one moved to accept Scarlet's help, and Jared suspected they were reluctant to approach her after what happened to Vanessa, so he stepped in to mediate the affair.

"Vanessa? I know you've no reason to trust me, or my words, but I promise she holds no ill will toward anyone here. She only wants to help in the best way she knows how." Jared held his hand out to her, and she tentatively walked forward to grab his hand.

PLEASE SIT NEXT TO ME. THIS PROCESS WILL TAX YOUR BODY AND MIND.

Vanessa followed her instructions and placed her hand against Scarlet for the second time. There was no outburst or exclamation this time, but he saw Vanessa's body stiffen. Occasionally, she jerked or her eyelids fluttered, but otherwise she remained outwardly calm while Scarlet worked on her.

IT IS AS I THOUGHT. I CAN FEEL MY BROTHER'S PRESENCE. IT WILL TAKE ME SIGNIFICANTLY LONGER THAN I EXPECTED, BUT IN TIME ALL OF YOU WILL RECOVER FULLY, YOUR MINDS ENTIRELY YOUR OWN.

With those words, she released her mental grip on Vanessa, and she slumped forward, eyes closed. It took her several moments of rhythmic breathing to steady herself enough to rise to her feet.

"Please," rasped Vanessa. She beckoned her people forward to undergo the same procedure. Hours passed as one by one, each of the waterfolk went through the same process, several collapsing right next to Scarlet in exhaustion.

There was a faction of people that backed away, making it obvious they didn't want to undergo the same treatment yet. Damien and George were at their center, gesturing wildly and turning their heads from person to person.

Scarlet, those two are going to cause us problems. Jared nodded his head to the cluster of people.

I WILL WATCH THEM CLOSELY, Scarlet said and went back to her task of cleansing each person.

The process continued throughout the night, and by the end of it Scarlet needed to rest and recover herself. Jared had done little throughout the process, except to carry sleeping people away. Looking around, he realized he was the only one still awake, the deep peaceful breathing of sleep whispered throughout the room. Smiling, Jared couldn't shake the thought he'd witnessed a true miracle here. How anyone could survive as long as these people in such conditions he didn't know, but not only did they survive, they seemed on a quick path to recovery.

Well, at least most of them, thought Jared. Maybe *it won't take so long to build an army after all.*

No immediate concerns to grab his attention, Jared clambered up to the loft and pulled up his status screen. It was time to look after himself and grow stronger.

JARED - NANITES AVAILABLE: 81%

"What!"

Jared's exclamation startled a couple people, but they remained asleep. Looking at it again, Jared couldn't believe it.

How do I have eighty-one percent to assign? Jared looked up, casting his gaze in the direction of the lake. *How many nanites does that lake hold?*

18 RAZAEL

Jared spent a long time studying his abilities and exploring the changes to his body. There was still a lot he wanted to do and many areas to improve, but he needed to play the long game here and focus on things that'd really make a lasting impact. Strength or the ability to run super-fast helped, but it was more of an immediate impact versus a long-term strategy.

After weighing the pros and cons, he assigned twenty-five percent of the nanites into *Telepathy*. Not only did his deficiency in the ability prevent him from communicating more effectively with Scarlet, it now hindered his communication with the waterfolk.

Next, he slid another twenty-five percent into *Body Manipulation*, because without the regenerative abilities, he'd already be dead many times over. That left Jared with thirty-one percent. There was still much he needed to learn from his previous changes, so he left the remainder of the free nanites unassigned.

Satisfied with his selections, Jared turned his thoughts toward exploration of the tunnels beneath the city. He had several priorities including retrieval of the weapons in the armory, collecting the rest of the medical supplies, finding clothing and equipment for the waterfolk, and investigating the facility for some evidence of what happened to Razael.

Jared praised himself for having the forethought to bring the medical supplies and boosters with him on his first trek underground. They'd patched everyone up from the explosion at the lake and subsequent rat attack. He'd even found some ointment to apply to the nasty burns on their bodies.

Once things settled down and they learned more about each other, Jared could dole out boosters to everyone.

Jared paused, his mind grinding to a halt.

Wait. Boosters. Why—

Scarlet! Jared shouted.

Scarlet snapped her eyes open, rising to her feet in a crouch, ready to defend him.

Oops. Jared grinned sheepishly. *Sorry! I'm fine. I didn't mean to alarm you, but I just had an epiphany. How were these people able to survive for nine years without boosters?*

Scarlet didn't respond, but Jared watched the wheels turn behind her intelligent gaze.

I cannot believe it. Ah, I see it now. Jared, do you know what this means?

I have an inkling of an idea, but I don't know how. Care to enlighten me?

Oh, right. Sorry. I figured out how he did it! Well, mostly. Razael created a virus he injected into the host's body. Scarlet paused to collect her thoughts.

Virus might not be the right word. It was like a virus, but instead of infecting or changing the nanites, it encapsulated them. In doing so, it created a shield

AROUND THEM, EFFECTIVELY ISOLATING THE CODING AND THEREBY PROTECTING THEM FROM CORRUPTION. FROM WHAT VANESSA TOLD US, THESE FOLKS BECAME RAZAEL'S PRISONERS RIGHT AFTER IGOR DISTRIBUTED THE NANITES AROUND THE WORLD. THE WORK I AM DOING WILL START THE TIMER AGAIN.

Okay, so you remove Razael's virus. Is there a way to recreate the effect of isolating the coding without exerting control like Razael? Wait. What about enhancements and augments? Won't the isolation prevent those changes?

HONESTLY, I AM UNSURE. I AM NOT EVEN SURE HOW RAZAEL CREATED HIS VIRUS IN THE FIRST PLACE, BUT HE DID IT AND SUCCESSFULLY NEUTRALIZED THE TECHNOVIRUS. IT GIVES ME HOPE I CAN FIND A SOLUTION. AT THIS POINT, THESE ARE ONLY THEORIES, AND I WILL NEED TIME TO WORK ON AN EFFECTIVE SOLUTION.

Definitely take your time to find a solution. We've got plenty of boosters for them when the time comes, and I'd rather you have a better grasp on it before we start human experimentation, which will happen with me first. I won't subject these people to any more mental invasions unless absolutely certain it'll work and that it won't have any negative side effects.

AFTER SPENDING SOME TIME WITH THESE PEOPLE, I CAN SAY WITH CONFIDENCE THAT I BELIEVE ALL THOSE I'VE WORKED WITH ARE SINCERE AND LOYAL TO A FAULT. BY THE TIME I FINISH THE PROCESS OF ELIMINATING RAZAEL'S INFLUENCE, I'LL KNOW THEM WELL, IF NOT BETTER THAN THEY KNOW THEMSELVES. YOU SHOULD ALSO KNOW THAT THEY HOLD VANESSA IN SUCH HIGH ESTEEM, THEY PRACTICALLY

WORSHIP HER. IT IS HER RESOLVE AND STRENGTH OF WILL
THAT CARRIED THEM THROUGH THE YEARS. I BELIEVE MADNESS
WOULD HAVE TAKEN HOLD LONG AGO IF NOT FOR HER
STABILIZING PRESENCE.

Thank you, Scarlet. If you find anything to doubt their loyalty, or any reasons you think I should withhold information from them, let me know. Also, please assess their mental capability to handle the truths we have to share. They've already been through so much, I fear driving them to insanity with what we need to tell them.

I WILL.

One more thing. If Damien and George let you work with them, I really want to know what's going on in their heads.

I THINK IF VANESSA PRESSURED THEM, THEY WOULD
LISTEN TO HER.

Scarlet went back to sleep while he kept watch throughout the night. Once she woke, Jared asked how she wanted to allocate her free nanites. Jared pulled up her screen.

Wow, you've got ninety percent available!

He shuddered, thinking about knocking her out of the water. He didn't want to know what would happen if he hadn't broken her contact. It was hard to believe that only ten percent were assigned. She already stood over twenty feet tall, and if she kept with her same enhancement path, she had a lot of mass to put on next time she grew.

I HAVE NOT PUT AS MUCH THOUGHT INTO IT AS I SHOULD.
CONTINUING MY CURRENT PROGRESSION PATH MAKES SENSE,
BUT I WANT TO WAIT A WHILE LONGER BEFORE DECIDING.

Let me know when you're ready, and we'll get it taken care of. In the meantime, please keep working with everyone here. I'm going to head out for the tunnels.

Jared looked across the room and found Vanessa staring at him. He waved and beckoned her over. Smiling, she rose to her feet and joined them. "Vanessa, I'm going out today to get some equipment, and maybe some clothing for everyone."

Fear flashed in her eyes and she grabbed his arm.

Please don't go out there, she pleaded.

"I'll be fine Vanessa," he reassured her. "There may be a lot of creatures roaming about, but I saw nothing I can't handle, and nothing I couldn't outrun should the need arise. We've fought much stronger creatures and in much larger numbers at once."

Vanessa didn't want to let go of his arm, but Scarlet nuzzled her side and spoke.

IT WILL BE OKAY, VANESSA. JARED AND I CAN SPEAK OVER LONG DISTANCES. WHEN HE EXPLORES, HE KEEPS IN CONSTANT COMMUNICATION WITH ME, AND IT WILL LET ME KNOW IF HE NEEDS HELP.

Vanessa relaxed her grip, but it was obvious she was still scared. Jared didn't know if she was scared for him or scared of being left with Scarlet.

"I'll be careful," Jared promised. "I've experienced far too many close calls to take unnecessary risks."

Scrambling up the ladder, Jared retrieved his pack and walked to the barn door.

Hey, Scarlet, I know we both want to trust these people, and they've done nothing to show us otherwise, but please watch this gear and don't let anyone come up. The munitions in this crate are much too volatile for them to be rummaging through it.

I WILL WATCH IT.

Jared exited the building and made his way toward the ruined cellar. When he reached the now exposed storage room, he spent time clearing debris from the entrance so he could get to the door of the tunnel. With all the extra creatures in the area, he wanted to close the door and make sure nothing creeped up on him.

Debris cleared, Jared entered the tunnel, his sight automatically switching to *Night Vision*. He walked through the tunnels, pistol drawn in the event something had already made its way down here, but thankfully saw no signs of life.

Jared spent a little time re-examining the places he'd already explored. If there was anything down here with him, he wanted to know, plus his priorities had changed. He wasn't just exploring for the sake of finding valuable items. Now, he needed to find a whole laundry list of items for everyone.

Retracing his steps from the weeks prior, his added scrutiny proved pointless. There was nothing he, or the waterfolk, needed through the portions of the facility he'd already explored.

He reached the execution chamber where dozens of dead vines littered the ground. Just in case they could still infect him, he stepped over them, giving the thorns a wide berth. Halfway through the room, Jared heard something shift and whipped his head around. The room was empty, but Jared swore he'd heard something. Maybe it was his imagination because of his experience here.

Cautiously, Jared stepped over some vines, gently nudging a few out of the way so he could move past. The moment he moved the vine, he heard the noise again, confirming it wasn't his imagination. Jared brought his pistol up, looking around the room for whatever was in there with him.

"Show yourself," Jared whispered under his breath.

Unable to pinpoint the source of the noise, Jared took another tentative step toward the rooms exit. The moment he did, a vine crashed down on his head, and a large, crimson-colored thorn pierced into his shoulder.

Jared screamed in pain.

"No!" He panicked, ripping the vine free and sprinting back the way he'd come. The vine tore away, igniting another wave of pain across his shoulder. All Jared could think about was the unending torture from the past few weeks. Tears streamed down his face.

He couldn't endure another experience like that. Nearly back to the cellar, Jared opened his mind about to reach out to Scarlet, but paused. He hadn't felt any dizziness. His mind was still his own, and he felt in absolute control of his body. Jared skidded to a halt, several paces from the cellar and assessed himself.

His shoulder hurt, and blood trickled down his arm, but other than the normal pain associated with getting stabbed, there was nothing else. The symptoms from Razael's influence was gone.

Slumping to the ground, head between his knees, Jared spent several minutes calming himself. His heart raced so fast, he feared it would explode from his chest. The pounding of his blood throbbed at his temples. He'd really thought it was all over for him. Though, now that the threat was gone, the rational part of his mind chided himself for not thinking things through.

Razael was dead. There was no reason to think the effects of his mind control lingered, but in that instant, he'd panicked, throwing all rationality to the wind.

Picking himself up off the floor, Jared found a bandage in his pack and wrapped the wound. The thorn had pierced deep enough to penetrate his muscle, but it didn't hinder his movement. Flexing, the wound pulled taut and he winced. He needed to be careful with the next few hours until his *Regeneration* kicked in and sealed off the injury.

Making his way back to the chamber, Jared carefully picked his way across the room yet again but remained vigilant of errant vines clinging to the ceiling. He'd likely disturbed them before causing one to fall haphazardly across his shoulders. The vines were all dead, lifeless.

Jared almost left the room but stooped to touch a vine. He wanted to make sure there were no nanites to absorb here before moving on. After a full minute, Jared moved on, realizing there was nothing left in them worth taking.

His first stop after the chamber was the armory. He spent a lot more time going through all of the equipment in the room, opening boxes, crates, cages, and cabinets. The contents of the room were now captured in his mind, and he could reference them at will to see what was available.

On his way out, he examined the door to figure out how it locked. Unfortunately, it was a combination lock and he didn't know the code, nor was it wasn't written anywhere within view. Curiously, a ring of keys next to the door seemed out of place. If the main door used a combination, why have a ring of keys?

Then he remembered smashing open all the locks on the cages the last time he was here and smacked his forehead.

Idiot.

If only he'd spent an extra minute looking for the keys, he'd have the ability to lock up all the gear. There was nothing he could do about it now and decided it was best if he left the door open. There was no telling if he'd ever find the combination to the door and didn't know if it was possible to reset it.

Retracing his steps, Jared took one of two paths he had yet to travel. Keeping his promise to be cautious, Jared kept his pistol at the ready. The tunnel sloped downward as it neared the water, and he found the walls slick with moisture. The tunnel leveled off and ran straight toward the water for over a mile.

Wow, this must go straight to the lake's edge, thought Jared. Just to confirm his suspicious, he pulled up his mental map and compared his location to the surface. Sure enough, it led directly to the shore. Coincidentally, right in line with where they'd set off the explosion and killed Razael.

Scarlet, I found a tunnel here that seems to go directly to the water's edge. The tunnel aligns with Razael's location.

BE CAREFUL. WE DO NOT KNOW IF ANY PART OF HIM SURVIVED.

Actually, about that, I can confirm he is definitely dead and his influence no longer present.

HOW DO YOU KNOW?

One of the vines in the execution chamber fell from the ceiling, and a thorn stabbed me.

JARED! WHY DIDN'T YOU TELL ME?

I didn't want you to panic and leave everyone there if it was nothing. It happened an hour ago, so there's really nothing to worry about. I put a bandage on it, and the bleeding already stopped.

JARED, PLEASE LET ME KNOW IF ANYTHING ELSE HAPPENS, pleaded Scarlet. EVEN IF HE IS COMPLETELY GONE, PLEASE BE CAREFUL. THERE IS NO TELLING WHAT YOU MAY RUN INTO IF THE PEOPLE THAT USED TO LIVE HERE WERE WILLING TO EXPERIMENT ON A DRAGON.

Trust me, you don't have to tell me. I feel like a halfling about to enter a dragon's den filled with treasure to steal from him.

HALFLING? TREASURE? WHAT ARE YOU TALKING ABOUT?

It's called humor. Clearly Scarlet needed some lessons in human entertainment from the past few thousand years. Shaking his head, Jared continued. *I'm just trying to add some levity. It's freaking creepy down here. Especially after finding out about all the experimentation on Razael. If I see anything that explains how they imprisoned him, I'll let you know.*

Thank you.

Jared walked forward and encountered a blank wall.

A dead end? This can't be a dead end. Why would they create a tunnel like this and just block it off?

Jared saw scrapes and furrows where someone had tried to dig through, but it was obvious they hadn't succeeded.

"There's no way this is a dead end," Jared said, frustrated at the impassable object.

It wasn't until his third pass thoroughly examining the tunnel he noticed a slight variation in the stone. Peering closer, he realized it was a small hole. It was obviously man-made, as the sides were symmetrical, forming an octagon. Jared tried shoving a rod from his weapons cleaning kit into the hole, but nothing happened.

"Maybe I need a key?" wondered Jared. "The armory! Was there a key that would fit this?"

Jared's mind went into overdrive, activating *Hyper-Cognition*. Starting with where he'd first entered via the cellar, Jared raced through the images in his head, making sure he hadn't come across another set of keys. Pulling up the image from the armory, Jared zoomed in to the keyring on the way. Amongst normal looking keys, a wrought iron key in the shape of an octagon sat on the key ring.

"Bingo!" Jared exclaimed, deactivating his ability.

Racing back the way he'd come, he rounded the corner of the armory, snatched the key off the wall, and sprinted back toward the dead end.

Crossing his fingers, Jared inserted the key, hearing a satisfying click as it settled into place. Although it clicked, nothing happened until he twisted it, causing a soft rumble to shake the floor. The barrier remained in place, and he thought it was a bust until he tried pushing it. The wall swung inward with little effort, softly scraping against the floor.

Just beyond the door, the tunnel rounded a corner into what he guessed was another large chamber. Creeping forward, he held his pistol in front of him.

Peeking around the bend, Jared found a massive room, the edges lost to shadow. Quickly flipping through *Heat Sight* and *Night Vision,* he determined it was empty and holstered his weapon.

Methodically, he examined everything in his immediate vicinity. It didn't take a genius to see he'd found the laboratory they'd speculated about. Tables in orderly rows held rusting implements used for dissection. He recognized some of them because the scientists back in his home colony used them on creatures they killed. He'd never watched a live dissection, but they'd had to learn about it growing up.

Banks of lights, long since dead, adorned the ceiling. Some lay in pieces on the floor. Cages and glass enclosures lined one wall; dozens of skeletal remains littered their bottoms. Even those in the sealed glass were nothing more than bones, which told Jared this place hadn't seen use in many years, long before the colony existed. The row of glass enclosures gave way to a row of cages, which ended at a massive floor to ceiling viewport into the lake beyond.

He saw no evidence of cracks on the glass and wondered what material it was to survive so many years. Walking closer, Jared's heart leapt in his throat at the sight before him.

"Holy—what the—"

Transfixed, he stared through the glass, looking at a huge cage. Thick bars enclosed a massive sea serpent. It wasn't like the water dragons he'd seen in Alestrialia's memories. No, this dragon resembled a great serpent, as it had no arms, legs, or wings. Small nubs covered in hardened skin marked where his limbs and wings had been attached. Outside the cage, equipment with sharp implements glinted from the sunlight above, and a bank of consoles sat in front of the viewport.

Jared's shoulders slumped, and he slammed his mental barriers in place to shield Scarlet from the emotions rampaging through his mind.

Scarlet, I'm so sorry. I can't show this to her. These people were barbarians! What did they do to you?

Jared placed his hand against the viewport, staring despondently at the dead form of Razael. They'd dissected him. Removed his body parts. His freedom. They poked and prodded him with machines.

Jared collapsed to the floor, his back to the console. A hollow pit formed in his stomach. This once-magnificent creature reduced to a spectacle. An experiment. A test subject.

"What did they do to you?" Jared's voice forlornly echoed across the vacant space.

His mind flipped back to the images Alestrialia showed him of the once-great water dragons and the sense of deep remorse and sadness as one by one they'd descended into the ocean, never to be seen again...until now.

How could they do this to you? How could anyone do this to a dragon?

With the close proximity of the massive underwater cage, Razael no doubt had spoken into the minds of those here. *Did he question their actions? Did he plead for mercy? Maybe he asked for death?* Jared's mind was a place of turmoil as he tried to come to grips with the horrific display next to him. No matter how he tried, he couldn't rationalize why anyone would do this. If they'd known what Razael would become, they should have killed him.

Did he know what he'd become? Did he feel his mind slipping into madness?

Tears came unbidden to Jared's eyes, his mind reeling. Scarlet's desire for vengeance and willingness to end human life now resonated with him. He understood her plight. He now knew how it felt for Alestrialia to lose her family to the evil whims of men. Fire raced through his belly when he thought of the humans in this room torturing the poor dragon. If anyone still remained in here, he'd kill them no questions asked because of the spectacle before him.

Mustering a shred of courage, Jared rose to his feet and scrutinized the being in the cage. Scarlet would want to have as many details as possible.

Half of Razael's head no longer remained, and it was clear where the explosion had ripped into the cage, killing him. A gaping hole occupied one corner.

Your freedom granted too late, Jared thought.

He said a silent prayer for Razael and hoped he was in a better place. Although he was dead, Jared saw no creatures swimming around the dragon, but it was likely they'd wanted nothing to do with him and fled the area as soon as they regained free will.

Jared wanted to give him a proper burial. No way would he let this be the final resting place for the mighty dragon. If Jared could get the electricity up and running, then he could release his body from the metal prison.

Drawing in a shaky breath, he tried to push thoughts of Razael to the back of his mind, but no matter how hard he tried to think about something else, the suspended body haunted his thoughts. Finally, Jared gave up and concluded that until they laid his body to rest, exploration could wait.

Scarlet, we've got to put Razael's body to rest.

You found him?

I did.

WHERE IS HE?

You might not want to see what they've done to him. I can barely stomach the sight myself, and I don't think I'll be able to explore any further until we put him to rest. Only I'm not sure how to unless we can get some electricity to power these machines. Can you please ask the waterfolk if there's a power source around here and how to turn it on?

JARED. WHAT HAPPENED TO HIM?

It's bad, Scarlet. If you really must see it, I'll show you, but I'd just as soon spare you the pain. Jared knew how Scarlet would react to the scene, but he also knew she was strong, and she had him to help her through it. When Scarlet responded, it wasn't about Razael.

VANESSA SAID HER DAD USED TO TAKE HER TO A SOLAR PANEL ARRAY.

Does she know how to work it, if it's still functional that is?

SHE SAID SHE WOULD TRY.

All right, I'm coming back. I'll stay with the rest of the waterfolk while you take her over to the panels.

JARED?

Yes?

I WANT TO SEE RAZAEL BEFORE WE DO THIS, EVEN IF JUST IN YOUR MIND.

Are you sure? I'm warning you, it's really, really bad. No doubt you can feel the rage and anger coursing through me. So much, in fact, that I want to throw myself at the city responsible for this and massacre anyone that played a role.

HE IS ALREADY DEAD, AND I HAVE ACCEPTED THE LOSS. ANYTHING FURTHER TO LAY AT THE FEET OF THOSE IN THE CITIES ONLY ADDS FUEL TO A FIRE OF VENGEANCE BURNING

WITHIN ME.

I'll be there soon.

Jared jogged back to the barn, in no hurry to get back and show Scarlet. He knew the scene would devastate her and wished for some way to bring him justice, right then and there. Instead, he added this injustice to a tally he kept in his head, longing for the day of reckoning when he held those responsible accountable for their actions.

When he reached the barn, Scarlet stood outside the door awaiting his arrival. Sighing, Jared walked up and looked her in the eyes.

"Scarlet," Jared began, and rested a hand on her side. "I'm serious, this might be worse than you've ever imagined."

Scarlet bowed her head and said, I HAVE TO SEE IT. I MUST KNOW WHAT BECAME OF MY BROTHER.

Jared tensed. With great reluctance, and as gently as was possible, he recalled the images of Razael in the cage.

Anguish.

Heartache.

Rage.

Loss.

Helplessness.

These emotions swept across their bond, and Jared dropped to his knees at the same time Scarlet fell to the ground, losing strength in her limbs. Sobs racked through both their bodies, and it felt as though a small piece of Scarlet's heart died forever. The torrent of emotional pain raged through him, rendering him incapacitated. Neither of them moved for what felt like an eternity, Scarlet's desire for vengeance magnified tenfold, and like him, she wanted to fly to the nearest city and rip it apart.

"I'm so sorry. I wish we could've helped him."

All Scarlet managed was a single word.

Wᴜʏ?

That one word echoed in Jared's mind and flooded him with such a deep sense of loss and pain, he wept. Wept for Razael and what he endured. For Scarlet and the relationship she'd never have. With every tear that trickled down his cheeks, his resolve hardened. Nothing would stand in his way. No one would escape justice. All those complicit would feel his wrath. Now, more than ever, they had a driver pushing them to get stronger as fast as possible. They needed the strength to withstand the combined might of an entire city, and Jared purposed in his heart to achieve it.

They sat next to each other, letting the emotions run their course, and Jared did his best to comfort her, remaining by her side for as long as she needed. While he cared for the people in the barn, the one person he cared for most needed his love and support. No matter what it took, he'd do anything she asked of him to help ease the burden.

Several hours later, Scarlet lifted her head and nudged Jared from his stupor.

Tʜᴀɴᴋ ʏᴏᴜ. I ᴄᴏᴜʟᴅ ɴᴏᴛ ᴅᴏ ᴛʜɪs ᴏɴ ᴍʏ ᴏᴡɴ. Iꜰ ɴᴏᴛ ꜰᴏʀ ʏᴏᴜ ʙᴇɪɴɢ ʜᴇʀᴇ ᴡɪᴛʜ ᴍᴇ, I ᴡᴏᴜʟᴅ ꜰᴏʟʟᴏᴡ ᴍʏ ᴀɴᴄᴇsᴛᴏʀs ᴀɴᴅ ʟᴇᴀᴠᴇ ᴛʜᴇ ᴀꜰꜰᴀɪʀs ᴏꜰ ᴛʜɪs ᴡᴏʀʟᴅ ʙᴇʜɪɴᴅ. I ᴅᴏ ɴᴏᴛ ᴜɴᴅᴇʀsᴛᴀɴᴅ ʜᴏᴡ ᴀɴʏᴏɴᴇ ᴄᴏᴜʟᴅ ᴅᴏ ᴛʜᴀᴛ.

"Some humans are...evil. Those we've sworn to bring justice to, those that left most of humanity to die in the aftermath of the wars, consider themselves elite. Better than everyone else. That includes anyone or anything not human. Even then, they seek to dominate other humans.

"I'm sure many of the people who did this to Razael thought they were advancing science. Although, I must believe a few people didn't like the work they performed, but it's possible they had no choice. This is a military complex, and when someone in the military gets ordered to do something, they must obey, or the consequences are dire and immediate. I wonder if they thought him dead, and that's why they abandoned him. They couldn't have known about the nanites from Igor. Scarlet, maybe that's why Razael killed all the colonists here? Maybe he though they were those that imprisoned and experimented on him. Maybe he though we were coming back to finish him off?"

BUT HE WOULD KNOW THEIR MINDS.

"You said it yourself; he likely went mad. Maybe all he knew by that point was an instinctual desire to survive and do all he could to right the wrongs done to him."

PERHAPS YOU ARE RIGHT, BUT I DO NOT UNDERSTAND WHY ANYONE WOULD WANT TO DO THIS.

It took her another hour to muster enough strength to rise to her feet. Once standing, Scarlet focused her will, locking down her emotions and calming her troubled mind. When Jared stood and turned around, he found all the waterfolk sitting behind them in a silent vigil. He hadn't heard any of them approach, but then he'd been lost in the pain and misery roiling off Scarlet.

Jared opened his mouth to speak, intending to ask them back into the barn, but he changed his mind and turned to Scarlet.

"Can you show them Razael? Show them what he looked like before? Then show them what they did to him?"

Scarlet nodded her head in agreement.

Turning to the group, he asked them to walk forward and place a hand on Scarlet. Following suit, Jared urged Scarlet to show them.

When Jared placed his hand on her side, a brilliant, blue landscape filled his vision, and a beautiful, blue-scaled dragon dove in and out of the water. His scales reflected the sunlight and seemed to absorb the light, drawing the eye in a mesmerizing display.

Although not as large as Scarlet's mother, he was huge, his wingspan easily a hundred yards across.

While Jared watched the huge being frolic happily, he felt immense joy from Scarlet. The memories were exactly what Scarlet needed to help heal. Just before Scarlet showed them scenes from the laboratory, he felt the joy from Scarlet diminish as her pain once again surfaced.

WHAT I AM ABOUT TO SHOW YOU IS WHAT THE HUMANS WHO USED TO LIVE HERE DID TO MY BROTHER. IT DROVE HIM MAD, AND THE CREATURE YOU KNOW AS WATER DEVIL WAS NO LONGER MY BROTHER. IT WAS A SHELL OF HIM, DRIVEN TO KILL AND DESTROY.

The scenery flipped to the chamber, homing in on the viewport. It showed Razael in every gruesome detail. As soon as the group caught site of the water devil, he heard outcries, sobbing, exclamations of fear, and several people fell to the ground in shock. A clamor of voices rang out in Jared's mind, voicing their disbelief and anger at what became of the majestic being. Jared even heard whispered vows from several to see justice delivered.

It was almost enough to share the rest of the truth with them, but after his previous naivety trusting others, he wanted to have zero doubts before revealing their secrets. It would take several more nights for Scarlet to finish eradicating Razael's presence, and then they'd make a joint decision to reveal the truth.

At first, Jared thought all the waterfolk felt the same way after viewing the scene. However, George stood off to the side, a stony expression on his face, his arms crossed. But even Damien appeared deeply affected by the scene and looked at Scarlet with a new appreciation.

Scarlet, were you able to feel the emotions and minds of those touching you just now?

No, I—

Don't worry about it. I was just curious. This George character is really giving me some bad vibes. He's the only one that showed no response to Razael's plight. Maybe he's just good at keeping his emotions in check, but I don't like it.

I WILL WATCH HIM CLOSELY.

Jared waited patiently for everyone to recover from the experience before he addressed them.

"As you can see, dragons are not monsters. Mankind...we are the monsters. At least, some of us. What they did to Razael is unthinkable. An unspeakable act of violence. All of you saw the irrefutable proof of that evil. I, for one, vowed to see whoever is responsible brought to justice, and I heard a few of you utter similar sentiments."

Looking around at the faces before him, he saw most of them nod and agree with his words.

"I've no right to ask any of you for help in this. The last nine years have been a living hell for you, and it was because of Razael. I'm asking a lot from you, but if we are to see any kind of justice for what happened to you and Razael, we need all of you working hard to recover and regain your strength."

Jared watched the conflicted emotions cross their faces. Like him, they'd all felt the heartache and loss through Scarlet. They'd seen Razael in a new light. Yet, it was impossible to erase almost a decade in mere days.

Vanessa stepped forward, laid a hand on Jared's arm, and said *I will help.*

Not everyone was willing to go along with Jared just yet, but he saw willingness in many of their eyes. It would take time. Now that Razael was gone, time was something they had in abundance and he wouldn't rush their healing process for selfish reasons.

Jared turned back to Vanessa. "Are you willing to go with Scarlet to these solar panels? I'd like to give Razael a proper burial at the bottom of the lake, but I need the power on, so I can open the cage he's in. I'll stay here with everyone while we wait."

Her hand still on Jared's arm, Vanessa agreed.

Jared stepped to the side and offered Vanessa his hand to climb aboard Scarlet. Though her hand was already on his arm, when her fingers brushed his, they sent tiny sparks of electricity through his hand. He looked into her eyes, seeing compassion and determination.

"Are you ready?" Jared asked gently, his voice coming out in a whisper. He didn't know why, but her presence made him nervous.

Yes. Thank you for sharing the experience with us. It is truly heartbreaking, but I am glad to know the truth and understand how we became enslaved.

"You're welcome. Hold on tight to Scarlet's neck. First time I tried to fly I fell off her back."

Scarlet snorted at Jared's words, and Jared playfully punched her side.

Vanessa climbed into the makeshift seat on Scarlet's back and wrapped her arms around her neck.

Nice and easy, Scarlet. She doesn't have all her strength yet, and you formed that seat for me, so she isn't very secure up there.

Scarlet acknowledged him and gingerly leapt into the air, heading toward the solar array.

19 DESTROYED

While Jared waited with everyone in the barn, a few people expressed their sympathy for Scarlet, and let him know they harbored no resentment for the dragons now that they understood what happened. The amount of support and genuine sympathy from these people amazed Jared. After so many years entombed in the bowels of the lake, they'd emerged with such strength and determination it was astounding. He felt certain he'd be able to share the truth with them and they would agree to help in their fight to come.

Scarlet, how are things going?

WE FOUND THE ARRAY, AND VANESSA IS DOING HER BEST TO REMEMBER EVERYTHING HER FATHER SHOWED HER, BUT SHE SAYS IT HAS BEEN AT LEAST FIFTEEN YEARS AND IS UNCERTAIN IF SHE CAN GET IT WORKING.

If she can't figure it out, we'll find some other way.

WAIT, SHE MIGHT HAVE IT. I CAN FEEL A SLIGHT THRUMMING BENEATH MY FEET, BUT THERE ARE NO LIGHTS,

AND SHE SAYS ALL THE DIALS ARE BROKEN.

"Woohoo!"

Jared's outburst startled a few of those near him.

"Sorry, Vanessa got the electricity working," he apologized. "I had my doubts, but this will make our efforts a lot easier."

A few minutes later, Jared heard Scarlet thump to the ground outside, and he went to help Vanessa down.

"Thank. You," said Vanessa, accepting his hand. "That amazing! Everything beautiful up there. Forget about worry. I...free."

Jared smiled at hearing Vanessa speak and encouraged her to keep working on it.

"Yes, I felt much the same way when I first flew. As did Scarlet. I haven't told anyone this yet, but Scarlet is only a month old. Well, she's several hundred years old, but she didn't enter the world until about a month ago. I hope to show you how it happened someday, but right now I must head back to the laboratory."

Vanessa's eyes widened, and she looked at Scarlet in shock. She clearly didn't know what was more impressive, the fact that Scarlet was hundreds of years old, or the idea that a twenty-foot-tall dragon was only a month old. Jared didn't blame her; it was truly amazing.

"Scarlet, please keep helping everyone with their recovery. The sooner we can get everyone back to peak mental health, the sooner we can work on physical strength and rebuilding everyone's lives. In the meantime, I'm going back to the laboratory to get Razael out of the cage."

THANK YOU.

You're welcome, Scarlet. Jared laid a hand on her, expressing his sympathy and love before he turned on his heel and jogged off toward the cellar once again.

Jared immediately noted the difference in the tunnels as several lights flickered in the dining hall. He saw a couple sparks shooting from a few of them and suspected they'd blown out when the power came back on. Still, the few lights were a welcome reprieve from the darkness, though it made the tunnels even more creepy as shadows flittered against the walls.

In the laboratory, he found the panels in front of the viewport. They hummed with electricity, and lights blinked across the display. He read through all the labels until he found one that read "Cage Release." Pressing the button, he held his breath as he heard a metallic click, but nothing happened.

Frowning, Jared pushed the button again, and again the clicking noise followed by a whole lot of nothing.

Why isn't it working?

Walking closer to the viewport, Jared tried to figure out why the door wouldn't open and saw the problem right away. The cage bent at an odd angle, and the release mechanism looked jammed. The only other equipment outside by the cage was a pair of mechanical arms sporting sharpened implements, no doubt what they'd used to slice into Razael.

Jared went back to the control console and found levers that controlled the mechanical arms. Thankfully, one of them still worked, and he maneuvered it beneath the cage. Carefully, he stuck the sharp implement through the slats on the cage and twisted, bringing the tool perpendicular to the cage bars.

Jared pushed the release button one more time and then pulled down on the lever. A rush of bubbles outside the viewport followed in the wake of the cage's bottom dropping out. Razael's body slowly sank toward the lake floor, and Jared made certain to watch until his body disappeared from view. He wanted to give Scarlet a measure of peace knowing he'd put his body to rest.

It's done, Scarlet.

THANK YOU, JARED. I FEEL BETTER KNOWING HIS BODY WILL REST IN FREEDOM.

I'll keep exploring now that we've done what we can for him.

Jared spent another thirty minutes in the laboratory but found nothing else worthy of his attention and moved on. There were two tunnels branching off out from the lab. One tunnel led to a storage room lined floor to ceiling with boxes, creates and various lab equipment. Finding nothing of interest to him or the waterfolk, he quickly moved on and started down the other tunnel.

After a mile, he found a large, round room lined by dozens of doors. Staged plastic furniture decorated the area, but everything was sparse, minimalistic with no evidence of the massacres from the previous rooms he encountered.

All the doors looked identical, so he picked the first door on his left and entered. It was a small room that held two beds, a metal chest of drawers, a metal bookcase on one wall, and an LED light fixture that worked when he flipped the switch on. Aside from the furniture, the room was empty. No pictures. No objects. No bedding.

His hopes at finding equipment and clothing for everyone plummeted until he opened one of the drawers.

"Jackpot!"

His inspection rewarded him with a row of vacuum sealed packages containing shoes, clothes, blankets, pillows, and various toiletries.

Scarlet, I found clothes, blankets, and a place for everyone to live. There's a living space down here just past the laboratory.

I WILL LET EVERYONE KNOW.

I still have more exploring to do, and there's another tunnel that leads out of this room, but I'll head back with the items shortly.

Jared resumed his exploration of the living areas and found each room had the exact same items. There were thirty rooms in total, each capable of housing two.

Before moving on to explore the other tunnel, Jared grabbed packages to examine the sizing and material. Thankfully, all of the clothes were adjustable and came in two main sizes, small and large. Shoes, on the other hand, were a bit harder to use universally. Curiously, he picked up a pair to see how they worked.

They were a flexible running shoe, with half a dozen straps on them. He could adjust the length of the shoes using latches on the sides, the width using a single latch on top, and a pair of Velcro straps secured them in place in lieu of laces. The soles would need cutting for smaller shoe sizes, but otherwise they looked functional and durable.

They really thought of everything here.

The sealed clothing, varying sizes, and adjustable shoes suggested they'd prepared for any scenario and wanted each of these rooms equipped to house any two people who needed them. The blankets and pillow were a rough spun material that felt scratchy. And while it might be durable, it wasn't designed for comfort. Regardless of the material, Jared thanked whoever created and abandoned this bunker for their foresight.

It's as if the universe wanted them to stage a coup of the powers in play. Sure, it hadn't been easy with his near-death experiences, but he couldn't ask for a better, more equipped place than where he now stood. He and Scarlet had gone through numerous trials, but in the end, it had all paid off.

Jared returned the new clothes to the package, placed them back in the drawer and left the room.

He followed the only corridor remaining and found a door identical to the armory.

No way.

Jared opened the door and froze, his jaw falling open in shock. The room beyond boasted military vehicles of all shapes and sizes. Cars, trucks, motorcycles. He'd never seen so many gathered in once place, since they didn't use many vehicles these days. Many of the older ones relied on gasoline to function, and it was a scarce commodity to find. If they had fuel stored here, this would be the single most valuable place in the entire country, excepting the cities of course.

Walking around the vehicles, he quickly realized that every one of them ran on electricity. Excited, he tried turning them on, but not even a click or spark of activity registered. They were all dead. Then again, the solar array hadn't been on, so they'd all just lost their charge. Now that the power was back on, he'd need to find a way to recharge them. It would make getting around a lot easier. It'd also protect them from many of the creatures that now roamed the area.

Scarlet, I found an entire garage filled to the brim with vehicles. They're all dead, but we might be able charge them using the solar array. Wait, actually... After closer inspection, it looked like they each had a plug connected to a charging outlet.

"They're plugged in already." mumbled Jared. "Maybe there's a switch to turn on the charging station?"

WHAT IS A VEHICLE? Scarlet asked, interrupted his thoughts.

You know what a wagon is, right?

O**F** COURSE.

These vehicles are electric powered wagons made of metal but enclosed on all sides.

It sounds intriguing, but I will stick with flying.

Jared chuckled at her response. He'd stick with flying too if the situation called for it, but these could be invaluable for transporting their gear, weapons, and people when the need arose.

Jared looked for a power switch but didn't see one in the immediate area. He was torn between his desire to tinker with the new toys and get the much-needed clothing to the waterfolk. In the end, he decided duty must come first, and the vehicles could wait until they had more time to fully inspect them and the area.

Hiking back to the dorm area, Jared ran from room to room and pulled a pair of clothes and shoes out for each person. They might feel perfectly normal walking about in their birthday suits, but it made him slightly uncomfortable, and he looked forward to getting them into more civil attire.

Jared looked at the pile of clothes and shoes he'd created and realized he'd need another crate to carry everything. Jogging back to the laboratory, he emptied one of the containers filled with old lab equipment and carried it back to the dorm. The clothing loaded, Jared picked up the crate and made his way back to the cellar.

Hey Scarlet, I'm on my way—

Jared cocked his head to the side as he heard a high-pitched humming noise that grew in volume. In an instant, he placed the noise.

Scarlet, make sure you're in the barn! Is anyone outside?

No, what's wrong? We're safe in the barn.

Stay there! I'll explain in a minute.

While Jared spoke with Scarlet, he activated *Thermoregulation* and decreased his body heat. He ducked back into the mouth of the tunnel just to make sure he wasn't visible. The moment he crossed the threshold, a drop ship passed overhead.

What are they doing here?

It wasn't just passing through either. It hovered directly over the town. He couldn't risk poking his head out to see what they were doing. *Wait, why am I acting like this? They aren't exactly hostile all the time. I mean, I know they lied to us, but they don't know I know.*

Jared contemplated going out to see if he could get their attention but decided against it.

They may not show hostility in survivor colonies, but this was also the place of a research facility, military complex, a huge number of weapons, and a dragon imprisoned beneath the water. If they knew he'd discovered the complex below there was a good chance they'd just kill him and bury the secret with him.

After a few minutes, he felt the ground rumble, and his curiosity almost got the better of him, but he'd promised Scarlet—and now Vanessa—to exercise extreme caution, and he wanted to abide by his promises.

Fifteen minutes later, Jared heard the aircraft hum increase in volume, and it passed overhead again. Cowering back into the tunnel a short distance, Jared waited until he no longer heard the ship before he moved out into the open. Jumping out of the cellar, Jared looked in the direction the ship visited, but saw nothing that showed its purpose.

It was in the same general direction as the garage full of vehicles he'd found, and Jared wondered if he'd somehow alerted them to his presence. There was nothing he could do about it now in any case, so he picked up the crate and took a step toward the barn.

Before his foot landed, the ground bucked beneath him, sending him stumbling off balance. The crate tipped on its side, and Jared landed hard on his back. The ground bucked again and again, throwing him several feet into the air, only this time a loud explosion accompanied the shifting earth. Whipping his head toward the sound, he watched the ground erupt in a cloud of debris. Buildings around the explosion blew outward, and Jared's eyes widened as he looked to the lake.

The laboratory!

JARED! WHAT WAS THAT? ARE YOU OKAY?

I'm fine Scarlet, just stay where you are! A drop ship flew over, and now there's some explosions going off. I don't know what's going on but stay there until I can figure it out.

The ground stopped vibrating for a second before a whole series of explosions ripped through the air. Jared watched, dumbfounded, as a web of explosions blew apart the ground in a crisscrossing pattern.

"No!" Jared shouted, the blood draining from his face and a cold pit opening in his stomach.

The explosion pattern mirrored the underground facility. He watched in horror as everything he'd just discovered vanished in an instant. Buildings all across the area crumbled to the ground, collapsing into the newly formed craters. Every time the chain reaction reached one of the large underground rooms, the explosion magnified tenfold as massive bombs shook the ground and geysers of debris shot into the air.

Jared dropped to his knees, sick to his stomach. Everything he'd endured. The discoveries he'd made...all for naught.

Jared screamed incoherently, shaking his fist at the sky and wishing he could call down justice to obliterate the cities.

The explosions continued to ripple out from the garage, spreading throughout the entire sub-structure. He watched in horror as the armory exploded in a massive detonation that threw him to the ground. Despair welled up within him. He lay there, unmoving, staring at a cloudless sky while the explosions raged on, slowly tapering off, the occasional secondary explosion making tiny popping noises under all the rubble.

JARED, WHAT HAPPENED?

Stay. Please. I'm okay.

YOU DO NOT SOUND OKAY, I'M COMING—

Stay!

Jared instantly felt guilty for yelling at her, his emotions getting the better of him.

Sorry, Scarlet. Please, just stay. I'll be back soon and explain everything. I just...I need a minute.

Scarlet didn't answer, no doubt getting the message that Jared didn't want to talk about it right now. After several minutes, Jared picked himself up off the ground and surveyed the area.

"It's gone. It's all gone," he said, a hitch in his voice as rage and sadness warred for control of his emotions. The armory, infirmary, dining hall, laboratory, barracks, garage...all gone.

How did they know?

He didn't know where the city that had dispatched the ship was, so he couldn't be certain how long it'd taken them to arrive, or when they got the alert, but Jared suspected it was when they turned on the electricity and subsequently released Razael. It made sense they'd want to monitor what happened there. Although he didn't know which city deployed the ship to destroy the facility, Jared no longer held any doubts about who experimented on Razael.

"It was the cities," breathed Jared. "Just like the wars, the technovirus, my mother's death, enslavement of humanity, Razael's death, and his imprisonment of the waterfolk."

All the recent and past atrocities lay squarely on their heads. Jared looked at the crate next to him and the clothes he'd salvaged before everything else turned into a pile of ash. At least he'd gotten enough clothing for everyone. He already had the crate of boosters, medical supplies, and a crate full of weapons manuals and explosives. Not everything was a loss, but losing all those weapons and vehicles, not to mention a perfectly sound barracks, made him furious.

On his way back to the barn, Jared turned over everything in his head. By the time he reached the barn, he'd decided on a course of action and knew what needed done. He stepped into the barn with a grim look on his face. Scarlet waited for him within but didn't speak when she saw him. They knew each other well enough at this point to know Jared would speak to her when he was ready.

"Everyone," Jared said raising his voice. "Please gather around."

He waited until everyone assembled and then he opened the crate and grabbed the first outfit. He called names of each person, choosing the sizes that fit best with each person. Thanks to his *Memory Recall* he'd grabbed sizes to fit everyone. Clothing and shoes doled out, Jared suggested all of them dress before he explained what happened. Once everyone was clothed, he spoke.

"As some of you no doubt remember, there is a military complex beneath the city here." Jared saw looks of surprise flit across some faces, but most present nodded their heads in recognition.

"What some of you may not know is that there was an armory containing hundreds of weapons and tons of ammunition. That is where I got the explosives to kill Razael and free all of you." Jared pointed to the crate up in the loft. "There was a section of the facility unexplored by those that used to live here. Those in the colony," he clarified.

Again, he saw people nodding their heads in agreement.

"Well, as you know, I found a way through the barrier blocking the entrance and discovered Razael imprisoned beneath the water."

Vanessa place a hand on his arm, sending a warmth through his body. Her touch comforted him and helped him get through his explanation.

"What I also found in that facility would've kept us safe,

housed everyone, and given us the means to thrive as a new colony. Obviously, I found all these clothes," Jared gestured to those around him. "But I also found a dormitory, some kind of laboratory, and a massive garage with all kinds of electric vehicles."

Jared paused for a moment, anger threatening to drive him over the edge.

Composing himself as best he could, he seethed, "It's all gone."

Whispered voices echoed around the room, but a single, overpowering voice thundered in his mind, and the mind of all those present.

How?

Jared turned to Scarlet. "I'm sorry, Scarlet. I didn't tell you because I knew you'd try to fly over and protect me. A drop ship landed somewhere by the garage I found and set off a series of bombs throughout the tunnels. From what I can tell, it destroyed everything. The latticework of bomb detonations followed the same path of the tunnels below."

Jared bent his head to Scarlet's and said, *I think we should tell them about the techno-virus and bonding. We may as well lay it all on the table and play the cards as they fall. My only hesitation right now is this George character. We don't know his story, but in light of this recent development we need to push ourselves to get stronger as fast as possible. There's only so much two of us can do. We need allies.*

I THINK IT IS A GOOD DECISION. THE SHORT TIME I SPENT WITH THEM ALLOWED ME TO KNOW WHERE THEIR LOYALTIES LIE. ASIDE FROM GEORGE, THEY WILL NOT BETRAY US. I THINK DAMIEN IS ALL BRAVADO AND WHEN PUSH COMES TO SHOVE, HE WILL FALL INTO LINE. I ALSO BELIEVE THEY ARE STRONG ENOUGH TO HEAR THE TRUTH.

After a few minutes, he turned back to the group and his voice changed. Anger raged just beneath the surface, but an undertone of hope turned a few heads in his direction.

"Not all is lost. You have the clothes on your back, we have a temporary shelter, and the boxes I have in the loft are more than just explosives. There are dozens of weapons manuals for everyone to read and study, medical supplies that should last us a while, and over one hundred nanite injectors."

Jared paused, expecting some sort of fanfare or applause, but they remained silent, as if the news were commonplace. Shaking his head in bewilderment, Jared hesitated, trying to find the best way to broach the topic.

I CAN SHOW THEM?

In a moment, I think I need to prepare them first.

Jared hesitated, trying to find the best way to bring it up. He didn't see a great way to rip the bandage free and just started at the beginning.

"We have something else the cities above know nothing about. Well, only one person, but for all we know he's long dead, or imprisoned. He shunned the regime in charge up in the cities and brought us the nanite technology that allows us to survive the radiation. This professor gave a gift to mankind, but perhaps no one, besides me and Scarlet, stumbled upon that gift."

A BIT ON THE DRAMATIC SIDE THERE?

Jared ignored her and plodded forward.

"If you've not guessed already, Scarlet and I have a unique relationship. We are bonded, and not just a close relationship, but physically bonded together through a fusing of our nanites. That bond unlocks access to the nanites, allowing us to improve our strength and acquire abilities."

Shocked expressions and looks of disbelief washed over their faces, and Jared didn't blame them for second-guessing him. If he'd been in their place, no doubt he'd have done the same.

"The price for this bond is to learn the truth. It's to learn that much of what you know is a lie."

He emphasized each word and let it sink into their hearts and minds. They needed to know the gravity of the situation and to walk into this without false expectations. Jared motioned for everyone to gather around Scarlet and place their hand on her.

While everyone found a place next to Scarlet, Jared addressed her directly. *Scarlet, please show them the message from Igor and gauge their feelings and mental fortitude. Once they've had time to digest it, let me speak with them before we show them how I found you and the bond.*

Every person lost their desire to stand after reading the message. Many sobbed openly, crying out with names of loved ones, or spewing venomous words to those responsible.

Scarlet, is everyone okay?

They...will be fine. The emotional strain these last few days has taken a toll on them.

Jared gave everyone some time to process what they'd seen, recalling how he'd felt after learning the truth. The righteous hate, the rage, and loss of his mother still haunted him, and even now tinted his thoughts red with vengeance. He let the emotions out with a strong breath of air.

A clear head and mind were what these people needed, and thoughts of vengeance could wait until later.

After everyone vented their frustrations, Jared returned to his explanations. "What you read at the end of Igor's message gives me hope that one day, we can right the wrongs done to humanity. I hope you will stand with me in our quest to bring justice to the world. Not only did the elite take advantage of the helpless survivors here on earth, but they oppressed the dragons as evidenced by Razael's imprisonment. I've taken a vow to bring justice to everyone, humans and dragon alike. Before I ask you to decide, I've asked Scarlet to show you our bond."

Everyone in the room looked spellbound by the opportunity, determination sparking a fire in their eyes. This was the start of a revolution, and all he needed to do was stoke the tiny flame into a raging inferno.

"If we show you how to bond and become stronger, then you must promise to aid us in our fight to bring justice to the world. That means fighting. Perhaps in a fight that leads to some of our deaths, but a fight that seeks to bring justice to those deserving."

Tension permeated the room. Silent nods and whispered thoughts passed between those gathered. The look in their eyes spoke of their desire to pick up the torch and join the fight.

"To put it into perspective, I've already murdered three people that wanted to harm or kill Scarlet, and it haunts me every single day. However, I also spared two that intended us no harm, though they were part of the same group. Could I justify killing all five of them? Perhaps, but I showed them mercy, and if we show you how to gain this power, I'll expect every one of you to do the same. I'll hold each of you accountable for your actions, and I will *not* tolerate radicalism, or people that unjustly take lives. If we could win this fight with no death, I'd take that path, but I don't think it's possible, and I need to know you are of the same mind."

One by one, each person stood to their feet. Vanessa, leading the way, walked up to him and laid a hand on his arm.

I am with you.

You can count on us.

One at a time, each member of their small survivor colony walked up to him and voiced their acceptance and agreement. With each person who added their voice, Jared's excitement grew.

Everyone but George. After everything he'd seen and heard,

still he held back.

Dark thoughts clouded Jared's mind as he looked at him across the room.

Scarlet, I don't like this guy.

Should I force my way into his thoughts?

Not yet. We'll keep an eye on him to make sure he doesn't run off anywhere.

If only one person caused them problems, he could deal with that. Forty-three others willing to abide his wishes and join him in his cause was a success. As long as they kept George close, there wasn't much he could do to harm the group at large.

Looking over the faces before him, Jared couldn't help feeling they'd reached a pivotal point in their journey. There was no turning back. He'd found the start of his small army, and he'd do everything in his power to protect them and see everyone grow stronger.

20 THE VOW

Hope was a powerful thing, and Jared witnessed its effects as everyone's countenance changed to excitement at the opportunity.

Amidst the jubilant spirit, a subdued attitude pervaded because of the responsibility and challenge they were about to put on their shoulders. Burden aside, they now had some semblance of hope. It was more than any of them had in the last nine years, and they clung to it like a lifeline. These people needed a reason to keep living, to keep struggling, and now they had it.

Jared thanked everyone for their support and asked Scarlet to proceed.

"Please show everyone how I found you, and the events leading up to our bonding. Spare nothing." Jared wanted everyone to know it wasn't all rainbows and sunshine.

Scarlet showed everyone the events leading up to the theft of her egg, meeting with Alestrialia, battle of the rats, their encounter with the Daggers, and their victory over the worm.

After Scarlet finished the retelling, they looked at Jared and

Scarlet with newfound awe, many trying to ask questions of Scarlet, but Jared stepped in to stop them.

"I'd like you all to watch the history of dragons before you ask any questions. I told each of you before that if you stand beside us, we'll fight to see justice brought not just to humanity, but also the dragons. For you to understand and comprehend the magnitude of injustice done to Scarlet's kin, you must see their history."

Jared motioned for Scarlet to proceed. After they'd finished, Scarlet spoke to him.

I TRUST THEM, JARED.

*I'd say I told you so, but…*Jared smirked.

I BELIEVED YOU THEN, THOUGH I DID NOT THINK WE WOULD FIND SUCH PEOPLE SO SOON.

I'm with you there. Things are moving a whole lot faster than I thought they would.

Jared busied himself making plans for their next endeavor while Scarlet answered the many questions asked of her. First, he needed to dig out the armory to see if anything survived the blasts. With so many people, they needed more defense than just the few weapons he had. Next, they needed to scavenge the city for anything worth saving and get out of the area. It was possible the cities would come back to level the rest of the area, and they needed to be long gone if that happened.

"Scarlet showed you the history of dragons. You know the persecution they endured, and you know the vow I've made to help her. Now, I ask that each of you also make a similar vow. If you do not, I will not help you, you will get no boosters, and I will not help you find a companion to bond. The information is too powerful to give away flippantly. I won't prevent you from leaving after you've gained the knowledge, but know that I won't help you either."

Jared looked straight at George as he said this. He was the only one isolated from the rest. Damien fell in line readily enough and stood with those asking questions of Scarlet.

Um, sorry Scarlet. I guess I should've asked first. You can do that? The binding thing like your mother did?

I CAN.

How does it work, exactly?

Jared waved everyone to take a seat. "Sorry, I'm conversing with Scarlet for just a moment. Please have a seat and I'll explain shortly."

IT USES TELEPATHY. WHEN SOMEONE UTTERS A VOW, THEY MAKE A MENTAL DECISION. SINCE DRAGONS HAVE MASTERED THE MIND, I CAN TAKE THOSE THOUGHTS AND SEAL THEM TO EACH PERSON BY INFUSING THE WORDS INTO THEIR OWN MIND. THE NANITES ALSO HELP TO ENFORCE THE BOND, AND IF THEY BREAK THAT VOW, IT WILL TEAR THEIR MINDS APART.

So, the threat from your mother...

YES, IT WAS VERY REAL. IF YOU GO AGAINST YOUR VOWS TO PROTECT ME AND HELP MY KIND, IT WILL DESTROY YOU.

Wait, isn't this similar to what Razael did with the nanites?

IT... Scarlet paused as she reflected on his question. YES! I THINK YOU ARE ON TO SOMETHING; IT IS SIMILAR, BUT I DID NOT UNDERSTAND THE CONNECTION BEFORE.

Scarlet went silent once more, and just as he was about to ask her to continue, she exclaimed, I KNOW HOW TO ISOLATE THEM! I NEED MORE TIME TO WORK THROUGH EVERYTHING, BUT I CAN DO IT, JARED. I CAN HALT THE ONSET OF THE VIRUS.

Jared jumped in excitement, startling those around him. At the moment, he didn't care if he looked odd.

Scarlet! If we don't need to worry about the virus—

The ramifications of this development tumbled around in his head. For the past two years, his entire life had been about finding boosters, and now they might be irrelevant to keeping them alive. That would allow him to use their entire stockpile for bonding human and creature together.

Excited about the new development, Jared turned around to face everyone seated to explain the vow.

"You all witnessed my vow to Alestrialia. If her threat wasn't sufficient, let me remind you that if you fail to abide your spoken word, it will rip your mind apart. Do not make light of this vow, and if you are unsure, wait until you are certain." Everyone grasped the serious nature of the moment, but it didn't appear anyone had objections. Anyone but George, who refused to join the group. When Jared looked at him, he turned his back and walked into a stall in the far corner of the barn. Jared shook his head and look back to those on the ground.

"We'll do this one at a time. Vanessa? Can you please go first?"

Vanessa nodded and approached Scarlet.

"Please place your hand on her side. This will not be pleasant, but I'm here if you need help."

In the next instant, Scarlet's voice thundered into the minds of everyone present. She'd chosen to make everyone's vow a public affair, but he didn't mind as it held everyone accountable.

I CHARGE YOU, VANESSA CARLISLE, TO GUARD, PROTECT, AND STRENGTHEN ALL DRAGONS. SEEK TO RIGHT THE WRONGS AGAINST DRAGON-KIND AND USHER IN A NEW AGE WHERE DRAGONS AND MAN THRIVE SIDE BY SIDE. I CHARGE YOU TO DO NO INTENTIONAL HARM TO HUMANKIND UNLESS IN DEFENSE OF YOURSELF, OTHER HUMANS, OR DRAGONS. AND TO ONLY INFLICT

HARM AS A LAST RESORT IN PURSUIT OF JUSTICE.

He watched as Vanessa's eyes flitted to something in front of her.

DRAGON'S VOW

Sildrainen Maildrel, queen of the fire dragons has asked you to become the guardian of dragon's and humankind. To right the wrongs committed by mankind. To bring justice to the world. To act nobly toward dragon's and mankind. Do you agree to never stray from this vow?

When Vanessa finished reading the message, she looked up at Scarlet and rasped, "Yes."

The entire room watched Vanessa's body go rigid and still. Her breath quickened, and face contorted into a grimace. It lasted for a full minute before the mental grip on her vanished. Vanessa doubled over, breathing heavily from the exertion.

Jared walked over and placed a hand on her shoulder. "Are you okay, Vanessa?"

I'm okay. It hurt. Need to. Rest…, she managed.

Jared nodded and beckoned the next person forward.

One by one, each person made their vow, many collapsing from the strain. It was painful, but the sight made him smile knowing that everyone wanted to follow through regardless of the pain and trials that would come their way. Their purposes now aligned, they could focus on making a home and finding companions for everyone. Jared looked around and found only he and Scarlet remained awake, the light outside already fading to dusk.

"Scarlet, I need sleep too, but first I want you to change my bond to include the extra bit about protecting humankind." Just as before, he placed his hand on Scarlet and uttered the vow. The process wasn't all that painful for him, but he had also experienced it before and his enhancements helped to nullify it.

"Thank you. Are you okay to keep a watch while I sleep? I've got several enhancement waiting for me when I wake, and I'm excited to increase my *Telepathy*."

Yᴇs. Tʜᴇʀᴇ ᴀʀᴇ ᴍᴀɴʏ ᴛʜɪɴɢs ғᴏʀ ᴍᴇ ᴛᴏ ᴛʜɪɴᴋ ᴏɴ, ᴀɴᴅ sʟᴇᴇᴘ ɪs ғᴀʀ ғʀᴏᴍ ᴍʏ ᴍɪɴᴅ ᴀᴛ ᴘʀᴇsᴇɴᴛ.

"Thanks, Scarlet."

He climbed up to the loft, set his pack down and fell asleep the moment his head touched down.

Jared woke to the clamor of voices in the room, and he wished they'd go away and let him sleep more.

Voices.

Why so many voices?

His sleep addled brain couldn't make sense of anything, or why—

Wait, what?

Jared bolted upright, the grogginess vanishing. Thinking it was a trick of his mind, Jared shook his head and looked at the people milling around the room. He heard them speaking clearly, but none of their mouths moved as they exchanged words of *Telepathy* back and forth. Jared didn't know how long he spent eavesdropping on conversations before he realized that Scarlet was staring at him.

I sᴇᴇ ᴛʜᴀᴛ ʏᴏᴜʀ Tᴇʟᴇᴘᴀᴛʜʏ ᴀʙɪʟɪᴛʏ ɪᴍᴘʀᴏᴠᴇᴅ.

You could say that. Jared smiled at her. *I can hear everyone! I wasn't sure I'd be able to, since they only speak through touch, but...*He gestured around the room. "I'd forgotten what it felt like to be in a colony, hearing the multitude of voices and noises."

IN TIME, THEY SHOULD BE ABLE TO COMMUNICATE
WITHOUT TOUCH AS WELL.

What about thought spaces? Can we try it?

WE COULD, BUT I THINK WE SHOULD WAIT UNTIL YOU
ACCLIMATE TO THE IMPROVED ABILITY. I THINK YOUR MIND
WILL EXPERIENCE DIFFICULTY PROCESSING THE SPEED AT
WHICH I THINK.

Eagerness didn't begin to describe how much he wanted to move to the next step, but he relented, realizing Scarlet was right.

Jared returned to eavesdropping on all the conversations below.

This is so awesome! It no longer feels like there's a bunch of zombies walking around the room. It's...normal. Well, mostly normal. I don't think anyone would say forty plus people walking around talking without using their mouths is normal, but I can hear them just as well.

Jared looked around the room for Vanessa. He found her on the other side of the room. Concentrating on only her, Jared called out.

Vanessa.

She whipped her head around, but by the confusion evident on her face, she didn't know who had spoken until he tried again.

Vanessa.

This time her eyes widened, and she zeroed in on his position in the loft.

I can speak using Telepathy now.

Her mouth dropped opened, and she excused herself from the conversation. Vanessa walked over to the ladder and gestured for him to come down, but Jared waved her up instead. He held his hand out to help her the rest of the way up. Her cool skin on his sent goosebumps up his arm. Like all of the waterfolk, she was frail, and if he wasn't careful, he could accidentally hurt her.

Upon reaching the top, Vanessa grabbed his hand and asked, *How can you speak now?*

"I'm pretty sure we told you about growing stronger and gaining abilities, right?"

Vanessa nodded her head. *Yes, but why now?*

"Ah…I haven't had time after collecting the nanites because it requires sleep for the changes to go into effect. Sometimes I'll sleep for days during changes, but this time there were no physical changes, so it was much faster."

Collect nanites? What are you talking about? How?

"Wait, I thought—" Jared turned to Scarlet. "Did you not show them how to absorb and assign nanites?"

Scarlet cocked her head to the side, thinking back through all of the memories she'd shared.

No, it looks like I never let the memories progress that far.

Shrugging, Jared said, "I guess we left a few things out when Scarlet showed you the bonding. Let's gather everyone together so I only need to explain it once."

Jared called everyone over using *Telepathy*, receiving more confused looks.

Please gather around. I have more information to tell you about the bonding and what comes after. I'm sure many of you are wondering how I can speak with you using Telepathy, when yesterday I could not…

Jared proceeded to explain the entire process of absorbing nanites, how they could expand their status screens, and how to assign the nanites collected. Everyone listened with rapt attention, George included. As the only person who hadn't agreed to their vow not to harm humanity and dragons, Jared really wasn't a fan of him hearing all this, but there wasn't much he could do about it short of kicking him out of the barn. However, he'd rather keep the man close to watch him than to send him on his way and spill their secrets.

Jared narrowed his eyes and spoke into George's mind.

Until you bind yourself to the vow like everyone else, I will not give you a booster to bond with anything.

George scoffed at him, made a rude gesture and retreated to the corner of the room.

Shaking his head, Jared explained some of the abilities, but it wasn't until he mentioned *Remodeling* and how they could use it to revert back to human that cries of joy echoed in his head. Even George perked up at the news, but it still wasn't enough to draw him in.

Jared hadn't realized how many people hated their appearance. He'd grown accustomed to it, accepting them as they were. Their appearance had even grown on him, but now he wondered what people would look like going back to their more human selves.

Everyone had a ton of questions. A few voiced their skepticism, so Jared demonstrated a few of his abilities, quelling any doubt.

Finally, everyone grew tired and silent. At this point, Jared was weary himself and thankful it was over. Everyone dispersed, leaving Vanessa and him to themselves in the loft. Jared had one more important topic he wanted to broach with her before heading out for the day.

"Vanessa, I don't want to lead this colony." Jared held up his hand to pacify her after seeing the hurt in her eyes. "I want you to lead your people. That also means Scarlet and I will follow your desires as they relate to your people. For anything related to our mission and hunting, mine or Scarlet's word remains sovereign. Does that work for you?"

Vanessa nodded.

"Look, everyone here adores you, and they would follow you to the ends of the earth. You've shown your leadership by bringing everyone here through the worst days of their lives, and I think you are the best suited to continue doing so. Scarlet and I have several objectives that may take us far afield for long periods of time, and your people need someone strong to govern them. Someone like you. My focus needs to be on protecting, strengthening, and building up our fighting ability."

I'll take care of my people as I've done for the past nine years, Vanessa said, mollified. *Thank you.*

"Perfect! Now that's settled, it's time Scarlet and I got down to business. We are going to scout the area and assess the damage done by the explosions."

Jared turned to Scarlet and asked, "You good to go, Scarlet?"

YES. I NEED TO STRETCH MY WINGS.

"Vanessa, can you please make sure everyone stays inside with the doors shut? There's a lot of dangerous creatures roaming the area and we won't be here to protect you. We shouldn't be long," Jared added when he saw Vanessa's brow furrow.

Jared reached around to the crate behind him and pulled out his rifle.

"Does anyone have experience using weapons?" Jared asked.

Vanessa nodded, and replied, *Johan knows about them. I think his parents used to be in charge of the armory before...well, you know.*

"Excellent, I'll make sure to leave this rifle with him." Jared motioned to the crate and asked, "Can you pass these weapons manuals around? I understand your sight isn't fully restored yet, but if anyone can read, these will help everyone learn about the different weapons and how to use them. Oh, and please keep everyone from the loft. There's some really volatile substances in there that could destroy this whole building." Jared hesitated. He didn't want to call too much attention to George yet, but felt he needed to bring up his concerns because both he and Scarlet would be gone. "Also, please pay special attention to George."

Vanessa's brow furrowed. *George?*

"I do not trust him, and he is the only one of you who hasn't vowed to protect dragons and humans. He's shown nothing but distrust and resentment toward me since we rescued you. I fear he may not have everyone's best interest at heart. I won't force him into anything, but until we know his motives, I want to be extra cautious."

Thank you, Jared. We'll be fine here. I'll make sure everyone, including George, stays away from the loft. I'll speak with him, and try to find out why he is behaving that way.

Seeing things well in hand, Jared and Scarlet exited the barn to assess the damage to the tunnels and hopefully scope out an area for their budding colony.

21 UNEXPECTED ALLY

ared jumped on Scarlet's back, and she leapt into the air.

"Let's head out over the lake first and see if we can find a place to settle. I'd like to get back to this area soon in case something tries to get into the barn—or someone, tries to get out."

Scarlet banked and headed toward the section of land between the two lakes. Jared quickly ruled out the area surrounding the lake because it was all flat, with very little in the way of natural barriers and defense.

"Follow the coastline. Maybe there's something further down."

Turning around, Scarlet headed south, following the west bank of the lake. At the very tip of the lake, a large, ruined city sprawled for several miles. A short distance from the city to the southwest, a gorge cut into the earth, surrounded by miles and miles of desiccated forest. They followed the dried creek bed until they reached a large basin with sheer rock walls on every side. A destroyed bridge lay crumbled to the side. Steps and platforms were cut into the rock on one side.

"Scarlet, is that clearing large enough for you to land?"

I BELIEVE SO, BUT ONLY ONE WAY TO FIND OUT FOR SURE.

Scarlet dove into the clearing, flaring her wings at the last minute to arrest her free fall. Her wings easily cleared the trees on either side, and Jared suspected even a dragon three times her size would need little effort to land here.

A cursory scan of any life forms indicated the area was empty. From his vantage inside the basin, Jared saw a number of structures cut into the cliff wall. They were old, some of them crumbling, but it seemed there were enough to accommodate their small group of people.

The rock walls surrounding the area would keep creatures above from attacking, and the only safe approach was up the creek itself. The walls of the basin also protected them from view, and hopefully from any drop ships that passed overhead.

"Let's fly around the area and look for any creatures that might live nearby."

Scarlet launched into the air once more. After three circuits around the small clearing, he saw no life forms, but there were also many caves in the area, including the rooms built into the cliff wall. A creature could easily hide within, and his *Heat Sight* wouldn't penetrate the rock.

"We might end up clearing these caves of creatures, but I think this is a perfect place to move the colony. Let's fly low on the way back to the barn so I can plot us a path here."

The ruins at the tip of the lake looked old. Old even for today's standards. Jared wracked his brain for any information about this town, but aside from knowing the body of water was Cayuga Lake, he couldn't recall the city's name.

Most of the structures lay in heaps, the buildings long since succumbing to the elements. There was a larger building in the center of town that still had a couple of walls and a partial roof left.

The city itself was a bit out of the way of the creek they explored, but it seemed mostly flat from the barn to the city and they might be able to do it in a day. If they rested in the ruined building for the night, they could take their time navigating the creek the following day.

"All right, Scarlet, I think we've got a new place to hole up. I'm not super great with distance, but this place is what, seven or eight miles from the ruined city?"

ACCORDING TO YOUR STANDARD MEASUREMENTS, IT IS APPROXIMATELY SIX POINT THREE MILES FROM THE CITY CENTER TO THIS LOCATION, THOUGH THAT IS A STRAIGHT LINE. THE HIKE BACK TO THE BARN IS ABOUT TWENTY MILES.

"It won't be easy, but I think we can do this in two days. The first day is mostly flat travel, and we'll stick to the road as much as possible."

Relieved they had a plan, Jared instructed Scarlet to fly back to the barn. They wouldn't return yet, but he wanted to check on them before assessing the damage done to the military facility.

"Looks like everything is secure. Let's head over to the armory first."

When they reached the site of the armory, Jared's heart plummeted. It was much worse than he'd thought.

"I'm not sure anything could've survived that."

IT IS UNLIKELY.

"It could be a waste of time, but I still want to see if we can recover anything."

YOU HAVE SOME WEAPONS. PERHAPS DOLE THEM OUT TO THOSE WITH EXPERIENCE.

"Yes, but where else are we going to get free weapons? The colonies won't just hand them out, and we're not likely to stumble on anything like this again. It sucks, but I think we need to try and find something worth salvaging."

WHAT IF WE RAIDED A CITY? OR WE CAN FIND A MERCENARY CAMP AND RAID THEIR STOCKPILE.

"I hope you're not referring to the mercenary camp I think you are."

WHY NOT? LOCH TOLD US THEY WERE COLLECTING WEAPONS, AMMO, AND INJECTIONS. THEY MIGHT HAVE A LARGE STOCKPILE.

Jared raised his brow. "Don't you think we've had enough dealings with them?"

I THINK IT BEARS CONSIDERATION. YOU AND I ARE ALMOST AT THE POINT THEY CAN NO LONGER HARM US. ONCE I UNDERGO MY NEXT SET OF ENHANCEMENTS, NORMAL WEAPONS WOULD BE USELESS AGAINST ME. IF LOCH TOLD THE TRUTH, THEY ONLY HAVE A FEW DOZEN PEOPLE AT THE CAMP AT ANY GIVEN TIME.

The idea did have merit and Jared turned it over in his mind, looking at it from different angles. Even with their massive advantage, he didn't like the risk involved.

"I'll think it over. For now, let's try to salvage something from this armory. If we can't find anything—well, even if we do find some weapons—I'll consider your proposal. Honestly, the more I think about it, the more I want to do it. Even if it is dangerous."

Scarlet chuckled as Jared jumped off her back and started tossing debris out of the crater. He needed Scarlet's help with the larger pieces of steel support beams. Every time they cleared an exceptionally large piece, tiny tremors vibrated through ground as explosions popped beneath them. Jared hoped it was just the ammo detonating and there were no bombs left over. The raw destruction here spoke to the strength of the bombs, and a single one of them would be enough to end his life.

It took them half the day to excavate enough of the rubble for Jared to jump down in a hole they'd opened up. When he entered the destroyed armory, he saw the tangled webs of cages poking out from caved-in walls. Melted weapons and weapon parts littered the ground.

Not wanting to excavate the entire area, which might prove futile, Jared worked on the areas less affected by the blast. Unfortunately, Scarlet couldn't aid him inside the room and some parts of the wall were just too heavy for him to move solo. After another hour, he finally extracted enough debris to reach one of the ruined metal cages. At first it looked like everything was gone, but on the other side of the ruined pillar a row of pistols sat untouched by the explosion.

"Woohoo! I got some Scarlet. There's…eighteen pistols and several ammo cans filled with rounds!"

His energy renewed, Jared enthusiastically dove back into his work. Using his mental map of the room, Jared focused his efforts in areas that might have gear they needed. Another hour passed, and he began to slow from exhaustion. Finally, a single steel plate blocked his view to the next row of weapons racks. Careful not to move it too quick, he levered the piece of metal away from the column and found a row of sub-machine guns.

"Yes! We're in business," Jared yelled up to Scarlet. "Is there any way you can reach in and hold this piece of metal? It's too heavy for me to move, and I can't pull the weapons out while holding it."

Using her tail, Scarlet reached in and stabilized the sheet of metal while he collected all the weapons and ammunition. Idly, Jared wondered how the sheets of metal blew inward. It didn't make any sense unless…

"Scarlet, I think the bombs that blew this apart were in the walls. Look at the blast patterns and all these heavy steel plates leaning against the columns. If the bomb blew up from the inside, it should've just knocked out all the pillars and collapsed everything straight down."

A SELF-DESTRUCT MECHANISM?

"I wouldn't put it past them." Shaking his head, Jared finished pulling all of the weapons and ammo out. He tossed everything out of the hole and climbed out covered head to toe in soot.

Looking at the large pile of weapons and ammo, Jared realized he needed a way to carry them.

"Hey, I need to find something to carry all of this stuff."

WHAT ABOUT THE CRATES IN THE CELLAR? I THINK A COUPLE OF THEM MIGHT WORK.

"Are any of them still functional after you brought down the ceiling?"

I THINK THERE ARE A FEW WOODEN ONES LEFT. THE PLASTIC ONES ARE ALL CRUSHED.

"All right. I'm going to run over and grab a couple of them. Can you go check on the solar array while I get them? I want to make sure they are okay, so we can bring them with us."

Scarlet leapt into the air, and Jared jogged over to the cellar to grab the crates. True to her word, there were two solid wood boxes that would work for his purposes and should be big enough to fit all the weapons.

A few moments later Jared heard Scarlet's report.

THE SOLAR PANELS LOOK INTACT. THERE ARE A FEW OF THEM LAYING AT ODD ANGLES, BUT NONE OF THEM APPEAR DAMAGED.

Awesome, thanks. It'll take a while to transport them, but it'll be worth it to have electricity.

Jared arrived a few moments after Scarlet and packed up the weapons and ammunition.

"Can you carry these without slicing into them?"

Yes, Scarlet said, picking them up.

"Let's head back and share the good news!"

On their way back to the barn, Jared heard a faint sound brush his mind and asked, "Did you say something, Scarlet?"

No, I heard it too.

As they neared the barn, the voice became clear.

Jared, help!

"They're in trouble!"

Scarlet picked up her pace, and they rocketed toward the barn. When they reached it, Jared almost laughed out loud when he saw a dozen rats trying vainly to get inside. The mental shouts coming from inside made it seem like a horde of bears were demolishing the building instead of a few rats scraping the outside of the barn.

Dang rats. We'll never get away from them, thought Jared, then to those inside he said, *Vanessa, we're here. It's just a few rats trying to get in. We'll take care of them.*

Oh Jared, thank goodness you're back! We didn't know what it was, but it sounds awful in here. All those claws scraping and the angry chittering noises.

Just calm everyone down. We'll have them taken care of soon.

"You hungry, Scarlet?" Jared said aloud, his lips curling into a smile.

The two of them demolished the rats, allowing none to escape and report their location to yet more of the demonic hellspawn. Scarlet gobbled a few with a sickening crunch, causing Jared to shudder with each snap of bones.

"Seriously, I don't know how you eat these things."

WELL, THEY DO NOT TASTE GOOD, BUT THEN ALMOST NOTHING I HAVE ENCOUNTERED IN THIS SCARRED WORLD TASTES GOOD. PERHAPS SOMEDAY I WILL BE ABLE TO EAT SOMETHING NOT MUTATED BY RADIATION.

"We'll get you a proper meal one of these days for sure. Heck, it's been over two years since I've had a decent meal too." Regardless of how it tasted, Scarlet ate half of the rats and roasted the rest for everyone else. It might be rat meat, but they needed to build up their strength.

Jared opened the door and found everyone crowded onto the loft, the platform shaking from the weight of so many. He quickly turned around to hide his smile, snickering at the site. Forcing a straight face, Jared said, "You can come down now. We brought gifts!"

Jared set the crates down and brought in the fried rat meat. Thankfully, all the skin and fur had burned away in Scarlet's fire.

They eyed the meat skeptically until Jared ripped off a chunk and bit into it. Scarlet was right, it didn't taste good.

Everyone climbed down the ladder and made their way to the floor. Vanessa lingered behind to make sure no one touched the crate of explosives.

Jared looked at her from the ground and spoke into her mind. *Thanks for keeping everyone away from the crate, even with all these creatures out there.*

"Gather round everyone. I encourage you to eat the rat meat, even if it tastes gross. It'll help you grow stronger for the trek we need to make to our new home."

Several people threw questioning glances his way, and Vanessa walked over to grab his hand. *You found a place?*

Although they didn't need physical contact to talk with each other anymore, Jared didn't say anything. Her enjoyed the sensation of her hand in his—cool to the touch, yet it spread a warmth through his body. Thankfully, his thoughts behaved and he just enjoyed the simplicity of the touch.

"We found a place not too far away that should only take us a couple days to hike. If your physical bodies were strong enough, we'd likely make the journey in a single day."

Is it another city?

"I'm assuming you all can't hear one another unless you're touching, so I'll repeat any questions you have. Someone just asked if it's another city. No, it's not, it is a secluded spot in a well-protected gorge to the southwest of the lake."

What about shelter?

"Okay, I can see you all have many questions, so let me just lay this out for you. The place I found has homes built into the mountain. It's virtually invisible from the air and the only way to get there is up a narrow ravine. No, it won't have modern furnishings, but I think we can make it work, and it's safe. It's a whole lot better than this dirty barn," Jared pointed out. "Will it need work? Yes, absolutely, but it'll be our home, and there's a ruined city not far we can scavenge from.

"When Scarlet and I flew out this way, we'd set out to strengthen ourselves, stockpile some weapons, and find like-minded people to help us in our mission. We expected this to take years, but we have all that and more in just a few weeks. Surely living on a mountain is better than dead or at the bottom of the lake still, right?" A few reluctant nods were all Jared received, and he frowned.

"Look, I know it's not ideal, but what other options do we have? Wait here with our fingers crossed, hoping that the city doesn't come to wipe us out? Go to another colony where all of you would be outcasts because of your mutations?"

Jared hadn't meant to inject sarcasm into his voice, and he felt a little guilty for playing the mutant card, but clearly some people weren't getting the picture, and it was wasting time.

"Whatever you decide, I won't stop you. If you want to go your own way, go, but you won't be taking any of the supplies or weapons, because we need every advantage we can get."

Dismissing any other dissenting voices, Jared moved on.

"Now, onto the next bit of good news." He motioned to the crates beside him. "Scarlet and I found weapons and ammunition from the armory. Not enough for everyone, but enough to equip most of you. We have eighteen handguns and nine submachine guns in here. We've also got two rifles, four of my own handguns, and my two phase pistols. Aside from my own weapons, but that leaves thirty-two I can hand out."

Several people stepped forward to receive a weapon right then, but Jared held up a hand to forestall them.

"Before anyone gets a weapon, I want to make sure everyone knows how to strip them apart, clean them, and handle them safely. Even if you used to handle weapons before, I'm certain everyone could use a refresher. I know some of you already started reading through the weapons manuals, but I'd like everyone to read through the ones for these weapons and then practice stripping and re-assembling them. If you don't want to handle a weapon, that's fine as well, but I'm placing my life and everyone else's in the hands of whoever holds one. Because of that, I'll only give them to those that educate themselves on their use.

"We'll start at first light tomorrow. Scarlet and I spent most of the day working to excavate these weapons, and I'm tired. Tomorrow, we'll split the group in two. Half will remain here with Scarlet. You can use the time to rest or learn about the weapons. The other half, or those willing, can accompany me into the city to raid houses for anything you wish to bring with us. This is going to be a grueling hike for many of you with your depleted strength, so don't go overboard with belongings. We can come back later to get more."

While the group decided who would go where, Jared climbed up to the loft and rummaged through the crate, pulling out manuals for the weapons he'd gathered. He also deposited all the ammunition in the crate, so no one decided to ignore his instructions and accidentally shoot themselves. With nothing further to do for the night, Jared said goodnight and sank into a restful sleep, the day's hard labor exhausting him.

Jared woke before the sun cracked over the horizon and started pulling on his gear. By the time he'd finished, those accompanying him were ready to go. Everyone was eager to go visit the city and their own homes. Stacking all the manuals near the ladder, Jared asked Scarlet to once again keep people away from the loft, and then they set out to explore.

Vanessa chose to go with the search party and walked next to Jared, holding his hand since she still preferred using *Telepathy*.

I'd like to go to my home and see if there's anything left.

Jared replied out loud for the benefit of the whole group. "Vanessa asked to see her old home, and I think it'd be a good idea for all of you to go to your old homes, provided they are within the area we'll be searching. While we are in the city, everyone needs to remain close and always travel in groups."

No matter how many times Jared tried to pick up the pace, it wasn't in the cards for these people. They shuffled forward at an agonizingly slow speed, and Jared dreaded their journey to the mountain. They didn't even have any equipment to burden them.

Shaking his head, Jared used the time to get to know Vanessa better. He found out that her parents had been in charge for many years while enslaved, but that finally they'd endured enough and cracked under the strain, never to be seen again. He also found out she had a little sister, but never knew what happened to her after their minds were taken from them. It was obvious she wasn't with the group, so Jared surmised that she was dead. The conversation reached a lull as Vanessa lapsed into silence, thinking about her sister. There was nothing Jared could say to ease the pain, but he stayed by her side, ready to support her in any way he could.

"I'm curious—what exactly did you do beneath the water? You mentioned your parents were the leaders, and then you, but..."

We did nothing. Sometimes Razael gave us freedom to roam the lake, but we could not leave. From time to time, he commanded that we congregate with other creatures, though we didn't know why. Leadership was nothing more than comforting and supporting everyone, doing my best to keep them from going mad.

Jared squeezed her hand, hearing the hitch in her voice. He knew this was a difficult topic for her but talking it out with someone would help her recovery.

Smiling, Jared said, "For what it's worth, I'm glad that you survived and that I met you."

For a brief moment their eyes met, and a surge of adrenaline coursed through his veins. The strength she exuded enthralled him. His mother was the only other woman he'd known that matched the strength and compassion portrayed in Vanessa.

The moment passed, and Jared looked away, his heart thudding in his chest. He felt Vanessa's pulse racing under his fingers as he squeezed her hand and knew she'd had a similar reaction. Smiling tenderly at her, Jared nodded his head in the direction they traveled.

"I think we're here."

Several of those in the group disappeared into houses along the road. Jared guessed it was their homes as there was no order, but random selection. Remaining in the street with Vanessa, Jared kept a watchful eye on the surroundings and houses to make sure they weren't surprised by anything. He expected they'd run into some animals that left the lake, but surprisingly there were none. It could be that everything was deathly afraid of Razael's influence returning and had permanently vacated the area. If not for the cities knowing about this area, it would be the perfect place to stay. Just thinking about the destruction of the tunnels set his blood boiling.

"Ow!" Vanessa cried.

Jared snapped out of his funk and looked at Vanessa. "What's wrong?"

"Your hand," she rasped.

He looked down and saw that he'd squeezed her hand, leaving imprints. Snatching it away, Jared apologized. "I'm so sorry, Vanessa! I didn't mean to hurt you. I was thinking about the cities and their constant meddling. This would be the perfect place to start the colony again now that Razael is no more. Instead, we find ourselves slinking off to some hidden ravine where we must start anew."

The compassion Jared witnessed moments earlier returned, and Vanessa gave him a re-assuring smile, grabbing his hand once more.

We will survive this and come out stronger than ever before. We have each other, and we have hope, thanks to the nanites.

They stood in the middle of the street watching the others ransack their own homes and pile goods into the middle of the street.

He used the lull in conversation to check in on Scarlet. *Hey Scarlet, how are things back there?*

IT LOOKS LIKE EVERYONE IS WORKING HARD AT

DISASSEMBLING AND ASSEMBLING THE WEAPONS AND EVERYONE READ THROUGH THE MANUALS. THERE ARE ALSO A COUPLE PEOPLE THAT SEEMED LIKE THEY REALLY KNEW HOW TO HANDLE THE WEAPONS ALREADY. I THINK ONE OF THEM WAS JOHAN, THE ONE VANESSA SAID USED TO WORK WITH HIS PARENTS IN THE ARMORY?

Yep, and if he's up for it, I might put him in charge of the weapons again.

HOW ARE THINGS GOING OUT THERE?

Slow. Everyone moves so slowly, I'm not sure how far we'll get today. I'm thinking we can spend another day here, but then we should get out. If we don't get to all the houses we need, we'll make some trips back here in the future.

I AGREE. WE DO NOT KNOW WHEN THAT SHIP WILL RETURN TO MAKE SURE IT COMPLETED ITS TASK.

I'll let you know when we head back.

Jared turned back to Vanessa and asked, " Johan is the person you told me used to work in the armory, right?"

Well, he was young, but yes he often went with his parents. Why?

"I think I'd like to put him in charge of our small weapons stock if he's up for it. I know you all need time to recover, but maybe if we keep everyone busy and give them things to own it will help everyone take back their lives."

Thank you. The years with no control over our own bodies, our free will stripped away, will take time to overcome, if some ever do. Vanessa gazed lovingly over those in the group.

Jared's demeanor softened. Her compassion for her people warmed his heart, and he resolved to be more considerate of their plight and experiences going forward. He had a mission, certainly, but if he pushed these people away, his objectives became impossible.

"I think it would be prudent for us to know of any skills your people possess. When we get to our new home, we'll be entirely on our own. When you lived here before, the cities recognized your colony and provided supplies. I don't expect that to happen again, and—"

Jared's voice trailed off as he looked into her eyes. The white, murky eyes that was just one of the mutations wrought to her body.

"I—Vanessa, I don't want the cities to see any of you. If they— If they saw your mutations, they might kill you. Or worse, they might capture you for testing and experiments like they did with Razael."

Vanessa blanched and gripped his arm tighter.

"Scarlet and I set out on a mission to see justice brought to the world. These people sitting up there in their posh homes, their clean air, and with complete immunity to radiation poisoning need a reality check. I bet most of them don't know what it's like down here. Hundreds of years of technological advancements up there and we're still living a primitive life sharpening sticks and stones. They don't care about us. They never have."

I never really thought them evil. They gave us the nanites and occasionally some other things to help us survive. Now we know the truth, but it's hard to reconcile in my head.

"I know. My mother died because of the technovirus. I could blame the professor for it because he created them, but he only wanted to give us the same advantage as those above. It was those in charge of the professor that shut his research down, and they're the ones that lied to the world. Heck, if you need any more proof about how evil they are, just remember Razael. It's obvious they're the ones that mutilated him and drove him to madness. Your entire colony ended up at the bottom of the lake because those in the city perverted and destroyed him."

When you put it that way...

"It's the truth, and one day they'll pay for it all."

Vanessa didn't ask any more questions. They lapsed into silence, each lost to their own machinations. Thoughts of vengeance ran rampant in Jared's mind.

Their little band of survivors combed the city for hours, slowly making their way through each and every house. The pile of items grew, quickly becoming a mountain of supplies. There was no way they'd be able to take everything with them in one trip.

A short time later, Vanessa paused in front of a small single-family house, a faraway look in her eyes.

"Is this your home?" asked Jared.

It was.

"Would you like me to come with you?"

Yes. Please, Vanessa added, her hand tightening around his. After they'd crossed the threshold, her grip squeezed harder, and sharpened fingernails stabbed into his hand.

Jared grabbed her other hand to reassure her.

"Relax. I know this is hard for you, but I'm here and will keep you safe. Take all the time you need." He released her hands, and panic flared briefly behind her eyes. Holding up a hand to forestall any argument, he said, "I'll stay right here, please do what you must."

It didn't take long for Vanessa to finish her search. She held a small bundle of clothing and a metal box.

"Find anything worth taking?" Jared asked gently.

I found some old clothes, though they need patching, and a few pictures kept in this box. I also have a sewing kit, but I don't even know if the thread is strong enough to use.

"I've got a kit too, but I've rarely used it. Normally, I'll just find a new change of clothes and toss the old ones. My pack is the only thing I keep repaired."

Looking around the room, Vanessa whispered, *I'm finished here.* Her voice shook as she barely controlled her tears.

Jared held her for a minute until she calmed down. Once the tension left her body, he released her, and they left her childhood home behind. Jared admired her poise as she exited the building, not so much as casting a second glance behind.

It took the group another few hours to search the remaining houses in a five-block perimeter of the city center. Sifting through the massive pile, Jared found a decent amount of clothing, small pieces of furniture, various small appliances, all manner of backpacks and duffels, and lot of practical items like lighters, axes, hatchets, saws, and various tools. Out of all the items, the electronics and furniture stood out as excessive. Sure, they'd bring the solar panels, but it'd take them a long time to get it up and running.

"You know we won't have electricity where we're going right away, right?"

One of the waterfolk, a man named Pete, walked over and placed a hand on Jared's arm.

They are wind-up devices.

Jared furrowed his brow at Pete, wondering what that meant. "What do you mean? What's a wind-up?"

Pete showed him by grabbing a small object that had speakers attached. He extracted a small plastic crank on the back and rotated it in a circle. The lights on the front of the object came to life, and Jared's mouth dropped open.

"What's it do?"

These are walkie talkies, Pete responded. *We can use them to communicate over distances. Well, at least when everyone gets their voices back.*

"Wow, that's a great find, though I'm surprised they still work."

I like to tinker and can fix many types of electronics. Pete shrugged and returned the walkie talkie to the pile.

"Excellent! Vanessa, make sure you keep track of everyone's skills and abilities. We can jot them down later. I guess we'll have an immediate use for those solar panels after all. Now, the more pressing question, how the heck are we going to transport all this? I don't have nearly enough crates, and there's no way you all are strong enough."

Jared. He turned at Vanessa's touch. *We used to have carts for those that worked on the outskirts of the city. Some of them might still be in decent condition, and they're big enough to transport the solar panels.* Jared thought back to which houses he'd visited before and realized he'd not seen too many of the houses bordering the small town.

"Okay, I've been to a few of them and didn't see carts, but there's at least three houses I didn't get to yet. It's quite a hike, so it'd be faster if I went by myself. In the meantime, why don't all of you wait inside one of these houses and lock the door? I'll move quickly, but I don't want you exposed out here by yourselves."

They all piled into the house, and Jared ran toward the closest neighboring home. Unfortunately, it wasn't until the third and final house that he found a cart sitting against a rotting wooden barn. The cart itself was under a small metal covering and looked in good repair. It had a couple longer handles in the front to pull it, but there were also small handholds along the sides for others to help.

"Perfect!" Jared exclaimed.

The wheels looked like car tires, and the back had a tailgate that dropped to allow easy admittance. Carrying it would be a chore for him, but his extra strength should get the job done, and as slow as everyone moved, he shouldn't have any issues keeping up.

Grabbing the handles in the front of the cart, Jared strained to pull it from where it'd sunk into the dirt after years of neglect.

Once he'd freed the thick rubber wheels of dirt and started pulling, a teeth-grinding sound grated on his nerves as the rusted axels protested. He had the oil from his weapons cleaning kit, but nowhere near enough to satisfy the wheels. Jared rummaged through the barn until he found an oil can at the bottom of a tool chest. No longer liquid, the oil was a thick greasy substance he smeared over the metal rods. Once he'd greased the wheels, the cart rolled with little effort. No sense in wasting a good set of tools, he added the box onto the cart and headed back into the city.

Jared made it to the main street when he caught sight of something disappearing around a corner. He blinked a few times, unsure of what he saw. Before his recent *Perception* enhancement, he wouldn't have seen anything, but ever since the upgrade, he'd grown used to seeing things in his periphery that previously went unnoticed.

Setting the cart down quietly, Jared stalked after whatever it was he'd seen, but when he rounded the corner the street was empty.

Maybe, it's just my imagination.

Shaking his head, he moved back toward the cart. The moment he rounded another corner, another almost imperceptible movement caught his attention.

Ha, I'm not imagining this.

Certain he'd seen something that looked like a small person, he looked at the street they'd just ducked down. The layout of the city streets formed a perfect grid.

Jared recalled an image of the surrounding buildings as he planned to confront whoever stalked him. Sprinting toward a cluster of buildings, he ran swiftly and silently to an adjacent street, trying to corner them.

Standing at the corner opposite where he'd seen the person enter, Jared crouched and jumped around the edge of a building.

"Gotcha!"

The street was empty.

What the heck?

Jared was certain he'd moved fast enough, and he'd not made a sound.

How?

He spent a few more minutes looking around but found no signs anyone passed by.

I can't lead them back to everyone else. What if there are more of them?

Scarlet?

Yes?

I may need your help. I think there's someone stalking me, but whoever they are, they're too fast and sneaky for me to get the drop on them. Can you make sure everyone's safe there and come give me a hand?

Yes, give me a moment.

Jared didn't stand there waiting, but instead picked up the cart and made a show of lugging it through the streets. He glimpsed the tiny form another time but decided not to pursue until Scarlet arrived.

I am above you.

Instead of looking, Jared responded, *Can you see them? I think they're just ahead and to the right, down a side street.*

I see nothing.

Okay, keep an eye out for anything that moves.

Jared walked farther and once again saw the person.

There, on the right, about two blocks in front of me.

I saw something, but...they vanished from my sight.

How can someone just vanish like that? How can we—

Jared almost smacked himself upside the head. It was the second time he'd been an idiot and forgotten one of his abilities. Not wasting any time, he activated *Heat Sight* and moved toward the side street where he'd last seen the person.

Scarlet, make sure they don't leave out the other end when I get close. Oh, and use Heat Sight.

Rounding the corner, Jared peered down the street. Again, he saw nothing, but as soon as he started down the street, he noticed a small, huddled mass against some debris next to a house. The lump of clothing stirred and gave off a faint heat signature.

Casually strolling up the street, Jared pretended to ignore the small figure. Curious, he cycled through his normal vision and back to *Heat Sight*. If not for the enhanced ability to see thermal signatures, he'd walk right past the person, never knowing any better.

It was like they were using some sort of cloaking ability.

Keep an eye on the area just inside the mouth of the street while I double back, instructed Jared.

Jared circled around the building and scaled the roof. He positioned himself above the person, still visible with his *Heat Sight* on, and jumped.

He landed right in front of the person, brandishing his phase pistol.

A tiny, high-pitched voice squeaked, their concealment disappearing to reveal a small child. Jared couldn't tell if they were a boy or girl from the baggy clothes and gaunt appearance. Whoever they were, they held makeshift shivs in white-knuckled grips, their body quivering in fear as tears came unbidden to their eyes.

"Hey, hey. It's okay. I'm not going to hurt you," Jared said, trying to soothe them. "You lower your weapons, and I'll put mine away too, okay?"

A firm head-shake from the person made Jared tighten his grip on the pistol. He didn't think he could bring himself to shoot a child, but he also wasn't about to get stabbed. He'd learned his lesson not to trust humans outright.

"Look, I won't hurt you so long as you try nothing to harm me."

Glancing at his pistol, fear danced in their eyes.

Everything okay down there?

Yes, thanks, Scarlet. I think I can handle it from here. It's just a small child. Can you do a quick survey around the area? Make sure no one else is lingering nearby?

I do not see any others.

Okay, thanks. Go ahead and head back; I'll handle everything here.

Realizing he'd get nowhere if he didn't lower his weapons, Jared held his arms out wide in a non-threatening manner.

"Okay, let's put our weapons away at the same time. Can we do that?"

Hesitating a moment, Jared received a shaky nod as acceptance.

Ever so slowly, Jared re-holstered his weapons, while the child slid their knives back into sheaths on their wrists.

Jared knelt down and introduced himself.

"My name is Jared."

"Elle," she responded briskly.

"Hi, Elle. What are you doing out here all alone?" Jared glanced around him to make his point.

"I explore. Not get caught." She pouted at that last phrase, clearly upset he'd found her.

"How were you able to hide from me?"

"I hide. You not see first time."

He wouldn't get a clear answer this way. It sounded like they barely knew how to talk.

"You're right—I didn't see you at first, but now I know you can hide like that, I will always see you."

She tilted her head and a moment later her eyes lit up in understanding. "Like I hide!"

Her response confused Jared. Her clear lack of communication skills made it hard to understand.

"Your ability to hide like that, is it special? Um…you learned how to do it?"

Nodding her head emphatically, she said, "Special. I hide when want."

I wonder what kind of ability allows her to hide in plain sight like that? What did she have to endure for that to evolve naturally?

"Elle, do you have a home?"

Shaking her head, she responded, "No more. I explore now."

"Elle, it's not safe out here. What happened to your home?" asked Jared.

"This is home." She gestured to the surrounding houses.

Puzzled, Jared didn't think she understood him, so he tried a different approach.

"A bunch of creatures just escaped into the area, and they are very dangerous. I don't think it's a good idea for you to roam around here by yourself right now."

Elle's eyes darted around the area looking confused.

"It looks like they left town, but I don't know how far they went or if they'll come back. Also, if you heard that big boom, it's because a lot of this area got destroyed. Why don't you come with me? We can protect you, and if you want to leave later, I won't stop you."

She appeared to think about the decision and cocked her head from side to side. She seemed so young and innocent, Jared wondered what made her set out to explore by herself. It was one thing for him to strike out on his own in his twenties, but he couldn't imagine being on his own at such a young age. She looked barely old enough to be a teenager.

After what seemed like a long internal debate, she replied, "I go with."

Standing to his feet, Jared offered a hand to help her up.

JARED, WATCH OUT!

Scarlet's mental shout reached his ears the same time a giant black cat shimmered into view a few feet away. Its poise suggested it'd been ready to pounce on him.

Jared yanked Elle to her feet and pushed her behind him while fumbling to retrieve his pistol. However, Elle reached out to grab his arm and re-positioned herself between him and the cat.

"Kitty. My friend." She gestured at the cat and then herself. She walked over and wrapped her arms around the massive cat in a hug.

Jared didn't know what to make of the strange revelation before him.

How is this? Why hasn't it killed her? Why didn't I see it with Heat Sight? What in the world is going on right now?

Jared thoughts were a jumbled mess as he tried reconciling the scene before him.

"Elle, how did you find...Kitty?"

Elle shook her head. "Kitty find me, I stick with needle. We friend forever."

Jared blinked furiously as he processed what he'd heard.

Can it be?

"Elle, do you know what *bond* means? Can you read?"

"Some. We bond," Elle said pointing back to her giant cat. "Kitty help me. Talk. She protect me."

JARED, IS EVERYTHING OKAY?

Scarlet, they...she's bonded!

22 REUNITED

Stunned, Jared's gaze switched back and forth from Elle to the giant cat and back again. He never expected to meet another bonded, but after thinking it through realized it was inevitable. There had to be other people in the world that'd experimented with the injectors, he'd just never expected it to be a child. He had so many questions.

How did she get an injector?

Why did she use it on the cat?

Where did the cat come from?

How had it grown into this massive beast?

He wanted to play twenty questions with her, but knew he needed to get back to Vanessa and the others. They were probably panicking by this point, wondering what happened to him.

"Elle, will your friend be okay around other people?" Jared cast a sidelong glance at the giant cat. It stared at him with slitted eyes that seemed to burn into his soul. The feline exuded deadly grace, and if it came down to a fight between them, he didn't know who'd come out on top.

"Yes. Kitty good girl. She not hurt people. Only hurt stuff try hurt me."

Relieved, but still cautious, Jared asked, "Elle, how long has Kitty been your friend? How long have you been here on your own?"

Elle thought about the questions, cocked her head and frowned. She turned back to Kitty, and they shared a look, no doubt communicating with each other.

"Kitty say this many." Elle held up nine fingers.

"You've been here for nine years? And you can talk to Kitty?"

Blinking at him like he'd said something stupid, she nodded her head vigorously.

"Elle, can I speak to Kitty?"

"You try. Kitty say okay."

Hello, Kitty.

The huge cat crouched low, bared its fangs at him and hissed. Jared held his hands up in apology.

I don't want to hurt you. I can speak with my thoughts, just like Elle only I don't need to touch you.

At this point he didn't know if the cat could process logical thought or if Elle understood its instinctual nature.

The cat eyed him warily for a moment longer and then lowered its head for Jared to touch it.

After he'd placed his hand on its giant head, a mewling, derisive voice said, YES, I UNDERSTAND.

Stepping back from the cat, Jared couldn't believe the turn of events. He marveled at Elle's resiliency and clear fearlessness for the world around her, and Kitty intrigued him.

Was she a normal house cat? A wild feline that'd already gone through some mutations?

"Elle, how old are you? Where are you from? Do you have parents here?"

Again, she consulted the cat and responded by flashing ten fingers once, then four fingers.

She's fourteen? Jared couldn't believe she was so old with the way she acted and spoke. It was more akin to a toddler's development.

"I from colony."

"I guessed that, but where? Where is your colony? Did you travel far to come here? Which direction did you come from?"

Elle scrunched her face together as she thought through the slew of questions.

"I from here." Elle pointed down at the ground. "I sleep that way." She pointed in a direction leading away from the city center.

Stunned, Jared asked, "This colony was your home?"

He spread his arms wide to encompass the city.

Elle nodded her head in agreement.

No. It can't be. Putting the timeline together, Jared realized that'd she'd bonded around the same time this colony became enslaved by Razael. She was only five years old when her world turned upside down.

How had she survived all these years? Why didn't she end up like the rest of the colonists?

"Elle, how did you learn to talk with Kitty? Do you have one of these?" Jared fished a booster out of his pack and showed it to Elle.

Her eyes lit up in understanding and she pulled several boosters from a pocket on her coat. A few of them were empty, but she still had two unused injectors.

"I stick needle in Kitty. Kitty need shot to stay alive too. Mama give me shot. I give Kitty. Mama leave. Only Kitty stay."

Understanding blossomed in his mind as the picture became

clear. The poor girl thought her cat needed saving the same way she did. She gave it a shot, accidentally creating the bond much like he did with Scarlet. It must've been around that same time the rest of the colony had become enslaved. Jared didn't even know the girl, but he felt a deep sympathy at her plight, and wondered if she was alive because the bond allowed her to remain free of Razael's influence.

"Elle, there are others from the colony who survived."

A hopeful look sprang up in the girl's eyes. "Mama? Papa?"

An emotional dam burst open in Jared, and he turned away to keep the girl from seeing tears well in his eyes. He didn't know what to her. She'd gone through so much as it was, he didn't want to give her false hope.

Haltingly, Jared explained the situation. "Elle, many of the people that lived here died a long time ago. There are some who survived, but there may be no one you know."

Elle's bottom lip trembled, and her eyes filled with glistening tears.

"They come back?" she choked out.

That pushed Jared over the edge, and tears flowed freely down his face. He'd experienced so much emotional turmoil the last few weeks, but in that moment, Elle's loss penetrated deep into his heart. This poor girl stayed in the area for so many years. Hoping. Believing everyone would come back. Like they'd simply forgotten her and would return at any moment.

I really hope she has family alive, thought Jared, wishing that fate would intervene and she'd find some measure of happiness after all these years.

It took Jared several minutes to compose himself and dry his eyes.

Only the setting sun forced him into action. They needed to

load up the supplies on the cart and get back to the barn before dark.

"We've got to get moving Elle," Jared said softly, but she just lay in a crumpled heap, weeping softly.

Kitty nuzzled his arm and said, *Put her on my back.*

Carefully, he placed Elle on Kitty's back, making sure she wouldn't fall off, but the graceful cat walked as if it floated over the ground, barely jostling its tiny cargo.

"I'll be right back. I just need to go get the cart I was hauling here. Also, Kitty, when we get to the others, please stay back until I explain the situation. These people went through so much trauma the last nine years. I fear they may react with violence if you appear out of nowhere."

The large cat dipped its head in acknowledgement, and Jared led them to where he'd abandoned the cart. After retrieving the cart, they made a beeline for the house where he'd left everyone.

Scarlet, are you back at the barn yet? Oh, and don't think I noticed you didn't listen when I asked you to head back. He tried to push amusement into the bond, but he didn't know if he'd succeeded with the way his emotions were at the moment. *Everything is fine. In fact, the girl I found is another survivor from this colony.*

I FELT THAT SOMETHING WAS OFF AND TOOK MY TIME RETURNING. HOW DID SHE SURVIVE? Scarlet asked, incredulity in her tone.

I'll explain when I get back. And thank you, for having my back.

When they were a few houses away, Jared motioned for Kitty and Elle to wait. He dropped the cart and strode toward the house. When he'd made it within a few paces, the door banged open and Vanessa burst out, nearly tackling him in her rush to reach him.

What happened? she asked. *It took so long. We feared you—*

"Whoa, whoa. I'm okay. I'm sorry if I scared everyone. I have much to tell you. My short journey was…eventful. Please gather around everyone," Jared said, raising his voice.

Because he'd asked Elle and Kitty to hang back, none of the others could see them with their poor eyesight. That worked to Jared's advantage while he explained the situation.

"First, I found a cart, and even with my increased strength, we won't fit all this stuff on it. We can take a lot, but we'll need to make several trips to avoid overloading the cart."

No one voiced any dissent and agreed to do what they must.

"Now, the reason I didn't return right away." He paused, unsure how to phrase his discovery. He opted for simplicity due to their need to get moving. "I found another survivor of your colony."

An excited murmur swept through the gathering. He heard hopeful whispers, names of people unaccounted for and wishes to see their loved ones again.

Jared turned back to Elle and Kitty. "Elle, can you come forward please?"

After he'd said Elle's name Vanessa's grip turned into a death lock on his arm, and he turned to see her face drained of color. Frowning, Jared reminded Kitty to hang back until he was ready for her.

Elle dropped from the back of the cat and shuffled forward. She'd shown no sign of recognizing anyone here, but then she'd only been four or five years old when they'd vanished. The mutations had also changed their appearance a lot.

A sudden shriek caught everyone unaware, and several others gasped in surprise. None more so than Jared when Vanessa tore herself free of his arm and rushed forward.

Jared and the large cat leapt into action, prepared to defend their charges, but then Vanessa shouted again.

"Elle!"

Jared and Kitty paused in mid-stride. It was clear these two knew each other.

"Nessa?" Elle whispered.

Her face lit up in recognition, and her demeanor transformed into jubilation. The smile she projected lit the world like a sun, and Jared felt his heart soar as Elle and Vanessa ran into each other's arms.

Jared watched the happy reunion, tears streaming down his face…again. Only this time, they were tears of happiness.

I can't believe they both survived.

Jared thought about what the others said of Vanessa and how her willpower carried them through the dark days they'd endured. These two sisters definitely had that in common. They'd both survived harsh environments with all the odds stacked against them. Jared wished he could've met the parents that raised these two amazing girls and was sad they hadn't survived their ordeal.

The girls remained wrapped in their embrace for a long time, everyone else giving them their moment of peace and happiness. While the girls enjoyed their reunion, Jared tasked the rest of the colony to begin loading the cart with the first pile of gear. Every now and then, he had to veto a particular item or piece of furniture, explaining that they'd come back and get more later.

It took over an hour to load both piles unto the cart, and they stashed anything else people wanted into one of the empty buildings. The sun had already disappeared over the horizon by the time they finished, and Jared pushed everyone to move quickly back to the barn.

Jared smiled as they made their way back. The atmosphere was much lighter than it'd been when they set out this morning. Vanessa and Elle's reunion infected everyone with hope of a brighter future.

After all the hardship fate brought their way, things were finally starting to turn around.

Oh, crap. Kitty, I'm so sorry—I forgot to introduce you!

Jared set the cart down and raised his voice. "In all the excitement I forgot to make an introduction. She might startle you, but Elle assures me she is harmless. Kitty?" Jared motioned for the great feline to come forward. Kitty strode forward with the grace of a dancer, head held up in a statuesque posture.

"Everyone, I'd like you to meet Kitty. Kitty is Elle's companion, much like Scarlet is mine."

The looks of surprise mirrored his own when he'd found out.

Before anyone could ask questions, Jared said, "Elle can answer your questions on the way to the barn, but we've got to get keep moving.

"Vanessa, please lead the way. I'll bring the cart along in the back. Kitty, can you please walk up front with them and keep an eye out for any hostile creatures?" The cat cocked his head at him like he was an idiot for even suggesting she'd let her charge walk without protection. Kitty sniffed, and padded over to Elle, taking up the point.

Shrugging, Jared grabbed the handles on the cart and resumed his march. Once they reached the barn, everyone piled in except for Kitty because Jared wanted to introduce her again. As soon as Elle entered the room, they heard her shout of surprise, and Kitty dropped into a crouch prepared to leap into the room. "Whoa, hold on please. I promise you she's safe. My companion is inside, and, well—it probably surprised her. She's...intimidating."

The huge cat eyed him warily, her sleek muscles poised to launch herself past him to rescue Elle.

"I'm going to introduce you quick, and then you can come in."

Jared saw the rest of the colony surrounding Vanessa and Elle.

Elle tried her best to greet the others, but he could tell she grew agitated by all the people, and she kept stealing glances in Scarlet's direction.

"Everyone," Jared said as he entered the room. "Please, listen up for a second. Let's give Elle some space. There will be plenty of time for you to talk with her, and there's one more introduction I'd like to make. I wanted to warn you now so that no one freaks out. This is Elle's companion."

The moment he'd finished speaking, Kitty walked into the room, not bothering to wait for his signal.

Murmurs and whispers of surprise carried throughout the room, but thankfully, no one reacted violently like they had with Scarlet. Then, the black cat was much smaller and much less intimidating than a dragon. The more curious display was Kitty and Scarlet sizing each other up.

Kitty stalked over to Scarlet and crouched in front of her, their eyes locked together in a contest of will.

Curious, Jared reached out with his mind, probing Scarlet for any stray thoughts and found none.

Everyone waited in tense silence as the protracted showdown ensued.

Finally, the cat lowered itself to the ground in front of Scarlet.

Releasing a sigh of relief, Jared walked over to Scarlet and caressed her side.

Hey girl, what was that all about?

THE CAT CHALLENGED MY DOMINANCE. IN THE END, SHE BOWED TO MY AUTHORITY SO LONG AS IT DOES NOT PUT HER CHARGE IN HARM'S WAY.

Wow, you got all that from a staring contest there?

IT IS DIFFICULT TO EXPLAIN. MAYBE NOW IS A GOOD TIME FOR US TO ATTEMPT A SHARED THOUGHT SPACE? YOU CAN

EXPERIENCE THE MOMENT FOR YOURSELF.

Looking around the room, everyone ignored the two of them as they crowded around Elle, listening to her accounting of the last nine years. While Jared wanted to hear that story himself, he could wait until everything died down.

"Yeah. Let's do it, but give me a moment first."

Jared walked over to the group that accompanied him into the city and asked them to study the weapons. That finished, he rejoined Scarlet and sat with his back to her.

Okay, Scarlet, let's do it.

ARE YOU READY? I WILL EASE YOU INTO THIS SO AS NOT TO OVERWHELM YOU.

I'm ready.

At first nothing happened, but slowly thoughts and emotions not his own started trickling into his mind. The emotional exchange was similar to how they already communicated, but gradually they increased intensity until they felt like his own. Before he knew what was happening, his mind raced as if he'd activated a slower version of *Hyper-Cognition.*

The activity in his mind became a whirlwind as thousands of thoughts cascaded through Scarlet's mind. It was too much for him to bear, but gradually the strain lessened as he found his place within the maelstrom that was Scarlet's mind.

Jared knew and understood everything. Every thought that flitted through like lightning made sense. It was altogether overwhelming and amazing.

Where Jared's mind often had a singleness of purpose, Scarlet's fractured into thousands of threads at once, and Jared found it very difficult to focus on any of those threads.

Conversations weren't really a back and forth exchange, but a very intimate synchronized understanding between the two of them. A conversation that would normally take hours happened in the space of a heartbeat. If he'd had anything to hide, that was no longer the case. This method of communicating was an inspection of each other's souls. It revealed the core of who they were.

Even though Scarlet knew what he wanted to say before he formed the words in his head, it felt natural to form them anyway in order to slow down, and really express his amazement.

Scarlet, this—how do you have so many thoughts occurring simultaneously? Is it always like this for you?

YES. THOUGH I CAN CONTROL IT AT WILL. YOUR MIND IS ALSO COMPLEX, THOUGHTS RUNNING RAMPANT AND UNCHECKED. OBSERVE.

One moment Jared was awash in the torrent of Scarlet's thoughts, and the next it was like an all-encompassing wall of fog slammed into place. While there were still hundreds, thousands of thoughts flickering in and out of his waking consciousness, it was nowhere near the volume as Scarlet's.

THIS IS YOUR MIND, AND ONE DAY YOU WILL LEARN TO LIVE IN THIS SPACE AS I DO MINE. NOW, LET US PROCEED WITH OUR ORIGINAL INTENT.

Again, Scarlet switched focus to her mind, and the fog disappeared.

WATCH.

The next thing Jared felt was a primal surge of emotion and overwhelming dominance. In his mind, he beheld Kitty poised in front of Scarlet. Only instead of seeing a large overgrown cat, Jared beheld a predator.

They stared at each other, locked in a silent battle of will and domination. Raw, primal instinct, so utterly foreign to Jared flared in his mind, the very presence of another apex predator exuding an aura of power.

Then, suddenly, Scarlet's dominance asserted itself, and a switch flipped off, Kitty succumbing to Scarlet's will.

Whoa. All that happened with just a look?

It was a contest of wills, and although my intellect is more advanced than any human, I am a predator by nature.

Jared disengaged from their shared thought space. Though his mind still raced from the experience, his thoughts moved as if in a vat of molasses.

Instantly, Jared wished to experience it again. The experience thrilled him, and he wished he never had to leave that space.

Now I see why you said I need to work on my Mind enhancements, and that's exactly what I'm going to do until I can do this on my own, Jared promised. *That was incredible.*

Coming down off the adrenaline rush, Jared saw Kitty staring at them from across the room. He motioned her over.

Kitty, I'd like for you to work with Scarlet and learn how you can protect Elle better. She will teach you how to work with Elle and assign nanites so that both of you grow and learn new abilities. Meanwhile, I'll work with Elle so that she knows how to help the both of you grow. No doubt she doesn't know how to assign anything, and in fact her ability can be used more effectively than it is now. I think she knows how to use it instinctually, but most likely she can activate it at will, and I'd like to show her how.

I will submit, replied Kitty, bowing to Scarlet.

After ensuring everyone was set, he climbed to his perch for some much-needed rest. While he lay there, Jared listened in on various conversations, all of which revolved around their new members.

Everyone spoke with such enthusiasm, more optimistic about

the future than ever.

Vanessa and Elle broke away from the cluster of people and found an empty stall in the corner of the barn to spend one on one time with each other. As much as Jared tried to push the limits of his telepathy, he couldn't hear what they were saying.

It seemed as though Scarlet planned on waiting to instruct Kitty, as the giant feline took up residence just outside the stall, ensuring the two sisters had as much personal time as they desired.

Scarlet lifted her head to look at Jared and said, I WOULD LIKE TO ASSIGN MY REMAINING NANITES. I WANT TO HAVE EVERY ADVANTAGE WHEN WE SET OUT TOMORROW.

Rather than answer, Jared pulled up Scarlet's status window and looked at her available allotments.

You have 90% to assign, what's the plan?

I PUT A LOT OF THOUGHT INTO THIS OVER THE PAST FEW DAYS, AND I WILL PUT EVERYTHING INTO PHYSICAL ATTRIBUTES ONCE AGAIN. FIRST, I WANT TO INCREASE MY MUSCLE MASS FIFTY PERCENT. BONE DENSITY, SCALE HARDENING, AND SKIN HARDENING TEN PERCENT EACH. LAST, I WANT TO ENHANCE MY SPEED TEN PERCENT.

Wow, fifty percent into Muscle Mass. You're going to grow a lot!

I REALLY DO NOT KNOW AT THIS POINT. MY GROWTH RATE HAS ALREADY PROGRESSED SO FAST, I NO LONGER HAVE A FRAME OF REFERENCE TO GAUGE IT. ALTHOUGH I MUST HUNT BEFORE I SLEEP TONIGHT TO COMPENSATE FOR THE RAPID GROWTH.

You're sure about these choices?

I AM.

Jared trusted Scarlet more than himself and slid the nanites into the categories she'd specified.

All right, you're all set.

Scarlet lumbered toward the door, and Jared jumped down to let her out before closing it behind her. When he turned around, he saw Vanessa had approached, holding Elle's hand. The gesture brought a smile to his face, which was all too rare these days.

"Where Scarlet go?" Vanessa said haltingly. Her voice sounded much better and rasped much less than it had just a couple days ago, but she still had much work to do before she spoke normally.

"Your voice is getting much stronger," Jared said. "Scarlet went to find food. She will undergo changes tonight, and she needs to eat and build up her energy reserves before she does."

"She get strong, like you learn talk in mind?"

"Yes, but Scarlet decided to increase her *Body* instead of her *Mind* like me. Dragons have naturally high intelligence and mental capacity at birth, so she doesn't really need to get stronger in that area. If you stay awake tonight, you'll see the changes as she goes through them. It is a beautiful thing to watch, and I think you'd enjoy it."

"I try."

"Me too," chimed in Elle.

"You may join me in the loft if you'd like. I plan to keep watch through the night while she sleeps. The amount of changes she's likely to experience might take longer than a night, but it's hard to say for sure because she has really great control over the changes."

Scarlet returned several hours later looking satisfied. She dropped some roasted carcasses in the middle of the room for everyone before she curled up to sleep.

"Thank you, Scarlet. I'll keep watch while you rest." With that Scarlet fell asleep, and the three of them settled in to watch the magic.

23 MOVING DAY

Jared, Vanessa, and Elle sat together, their backs against a crate on the loft. Jared used the time to practice splitting his thoughts. Although he failed every time, he kept trying to replicate what Scarlet showed him. No matter how many times he tried, he hit some sort of barrier and just couldn't get beyond no matter what he did.

Growing bored with the failed attempts, Jared listened for any stray conversations, starting closer and working his way out to the edges of his ability. Unfortunately for him, most of those awake whispered in hushed tones instead of using telepathy.

It was a start, but based on the short snippets he overheard, it'd take a long time before they recovered enough to speak normally. Even once they regained the ability, their sharp teeth gave them a slight lisp.

Jared shook his head. *Razael really did a number on them.*

Something tickled the back of his mind, like an itch between his shoulder blades. Looking around, Jared found Kitty feigning sleep while keeping a close watch on him and her companion.

She'd wanted to jump up to the loft, but Jared was scared the added weight could make it collapse. Granted, everyone had been up here earlier, but he didn't want to push his luck. If the loft collapsed, many people would get hurt, and there's no telling how stable the explosives were.

It only took a few minutes for sleep to claim Vanessa and her sister. Vanessa's head rested on his shoulder and Elle in turn leaned into her sister. The both looked peaceful, content. Small smiles tugged at the corners of their lips. In spite of the trauma they both experienced, their reunion helped them reconcile the hand fate dealt, and nothing could diminish their happiness in that moment.

His options to eavesdrop on conversations exhausted, he returned to his practice. By the time Jared gave up, he found that Scarlet's transformation was underway. He hesitated in waking the sisters but knew that they'd want to see what was about to happen. It might be a long time before they saw anything like it again.

He gently nudged Vanessa's shoulder until she woke, sleep clouding her mind. She blinked a few times, squinting at him.

Is everything okay?

Jared pointed to Scarlet and whispered, "Watch."

Sleep vanished in an instant, and she whipped her head around to look at Scarlet. Just as gently, she prodded Elle awake to watch the magic unfold.

Jared almost sent out a mental communication to the rest of the room, but he saw many—including Kitty—already watching the transformation.

Mesmerized, everyone watched while the shimmer of nanites pulsed over Scarlet's body. With each pulse, her mass increased in size, her muscles flexing. After several hours, many of those sitting around her had to back up as her body expanded. Jared couldn't imagine going through such radical physical changes.

Eventually, the pulsing and flexing stopped, the nanites switching to waves that washed over her from head to toe. Each pass modified her scales and skin, adding layers to both. The hardening process didn't take as long, and just a few moments later, the outward transformation finished. No doubt there was a lot of work internally as the nanites worked on bone hardening and restructuring her musculature to support the increase in mass.

Jared looked to Vanessa and Elle, who sat unblinking, completely entranced by what they'd seen. After several minutes with no further change, everyone returned to their activities or turned in for the evening. Vanessa and Elle climbed down from the loft and returned to the stall where Kitty waited, falling asleep against her side.

Once everyone turned in for the night, Jared settled in for a long night of monotonous mental exercises. He'd been at it for six hours when he finally held two threads of conscious thought at the same time. It was fleeting, only a few seconds, but now that he knew what it felt like, he could repeat the steps to get there.

He'd needed to clear his mind using meditation, but it wasn't something he had a whole lot of practice with, so it took a long time to figure it out. Normally, subconscious thoughts only surfaced one at a time, and only as he changed the thread into an active, or conscious, thought. He'd never stopped to think about it before, but his mind was often a roiling mess of incomprehensible thoughts flitting by with no clear rhyme or reason. When he used *Hyper-Cognition*, he didn't add any threads to process either, but rapidly moved between them like a master orchestrator.

In order for him to control two at a time, he needed to clear his mind completely, tune out all other random clutter, his surroundings, and even his internal voice as he worked through the solution. In his mind, he came to a large empty room with an infinite number of doors lining the sides. In the middle of the open space, he existed. This was the byway of his mind, and each of these portals represented a conscious thought. Yet more branching entrances and exits represented the subconscious. Behind these barriers lay possibilities to come, past events, and memories sealed away. This was why he couldn't progress before; they were impassable until he reached this centering of his mind.

If he didn't center himself before trying to split his focus, all that happened was the opening and closing of a single pathway within his mind. Although, there were always multiple paths opening and closing in rapid succession, sometimes much faster than he could comprehend, it was a singular thought no matter how hard he tried to convince himself otherwise.

The first few times he tried opening all the doors at once, he immediately lost focus and snapped out of his meditative trance. Trying to limit the number he opened proved futile because the first one closed the moment the second opened. It was very frustrating, but his mind simply wasn't wired to process things in tandem. With continued practice, he could do it, but the only way he managed to process multiple thoughts at once was when he obliterated all barriers.

Once he realized this method worked, he concentrated all his efforts and quickly learned to focus on two separate threads at once. It was as if he'd entered a state between conscious and subconscious. Any time he tried to direct a thought, he reverted to a singular thread. If something outside the thought exerted influence, such as a diverging pathway, it yanked his focus into one thread.

It was too easy for his mind to run amok and stray from the passive state he'd reached, but now that he knew the room existed in his mind, he could get back there, and believed it was the right step in training his mind. It needed conditioning so that he wasn't stuck in this one-dimensional space that funneled all his thoughts into a teeny tiny bottle-neck, an information highway pinched off like an hourglass.

HELLO, JARED.

Scarlet's voice startled him, interrupting his training. After he'd learned to split his focus, he'd lost all track of time, but guessing from the light streaming into the room, it was well into the morning, if not the afternoon already.

He blinked and stood to his feet. Stretching his stiff muscles, Jared asked, *How do you feel?*

SORE. THOUGH THE PAIN IS TOLERABLE.

You should be sore after all that. Scarlet, you massively increased your size. I think this change took longer than any others you went through.

YES, BUT ARGUABLY THE MOST DIFFICULT DUE TO MY SIZE.

I don't know if you're going to fit through the door now. You barely fit as it was, but now? I guess it doesn't matter since you can probably just walk straight through the wall.

WHAT WERE YOU DOING JUST NOW? BEFORE I INTERRUPTED?

I did it! I managed to hold two conscious thoughts at the same time. Well, only for a few seconds, but I worked on it through the night.

EXCELLENT, said Scarlet excitedly. IT WILL TAKE A LONG TIME BEFORE YOU MANAGE ANYTHING WORTHWHILE. YOU ARE TRAINING YOUR MIND TO FUNCTION LIKE A MACHINE, OR AS HUMANS CALL IT, A COMPUTER. COMPARTMENTALIZING YOUR THOUGHTS AND THEN SEPARATING THEM REQUIRES THAT YOUR BRAIN SPLIT INTO SEPARATE ENTITIES THAT SIMULTANEOUSLY PROCESSES THE DISTINCT THOUGHTS. THE HUMAN MIND WAS

NEVER MADE TO DUAL PROCESS LIKE THAT, AT LEAST NOT
NATURALLY.

Yeah, I gathered that, Jared replied sarcastically. *Any time a stray
thought intrudes, or I try to force a thought in a direction, I lose the state
needed to process them both and revert to a single thought.*

WE MUST SHARE A THOUGHT SPACE AS OFTEN AS IS
PRACTICAL. THE MORE YOU EXPERIENCE IT THROUGH ME, THE
EASIER IT WILL BECOME FOR YOU.

*For now, let's aim to do this at least once per day. I want to push my
current limits to the max before I assign my remaining thirty-one percent.
I feel there is much more I can do and don't want to use the nanites as a
crutch.*

YES, I BELIEVE YOU CAN PROGRESS MUCH AS YOU ARE NOW.

*All right we've got to get moving. We already burned enough
daylight, but I think we can still make it through the first leg of our trip
today.*

"Listen up, everyone," Jared shouted. "Please bring all the
weapons and manuals over here. Let's get things packed up and
ready to head out. I thought we'd spend another day raiding the
houses in town, but we already have more than is wise on the cart.
We'll need to come back later for more. Based on the light streaming
in here, we're getting a later start than I wanted. I encourage you to
stretch and prepare for a grueling hike today."

It only took a few minutes to gather everything together since
the bulk of the items were still on the cart outside the barn.
Meanwhile, Jared grabbed the crates in the loft, verified he had all
of his belongings loaded up, and dropped to the ground, landing
lightly to avoid jostling the contents. It took a few minutes to
rearrange the cart so that the explosives were in the center.

In hindsight, he should've had everyone look for ropes, or something else they could use to secure the container. For now, he'd make do with packing everything as closely as possible. Next, he loaded up the crates of weapons and medical supplies. Jared took one last look around the room, confirming they'd loaded everything up.

"Our first stop will be to disassemble the solar panels and load them up on the cart. I imagine that'll take the rest of the morning. Actually, Kitty?"

The large cat padded over and looked him in the eye. It would take him a while to get used to this creature. A house cat as tall as he was at six foot five was slightly intimidating.

"Can you take point and lead everyone south? You'll follow the lake to its tip. I'll take Pete and a couple others to help me get the solar panels loaded up, and Scarlet will fly cover for everyone to make sure nothing lies in wait."

I will lead, replied Kitty.

"Okay, Kitty is going to lead all of you south while I take a small number of you to go get the panels, and then we'll catch up. If we didn't have to worry about that drop ship coming back to destroy more of this area, I'd say we come back for the panels later, but I don't want to risk it."

"The walk south is mostly flat, level ground and shouldn't pose any issues for anyone. Tomorrow is another story and may take significantly more effort."

"Pete and Johan, you two come with me. Everyone else line up in a column, three people wide. I'm going to dole out the weapons we have to those on the outside of the column, and you'll be the groups' protection. Those that aren't super familiar with weapons, or who don't feel comfortable handling them, can move to the center."

After he'd finished giving instructions, Jared dug into the weapons crate and handed the pistols and sub-machine guns to the group, ensuring that the machine guns were set to single fire so as not to waste ammo.

"Let's move out!"

JARED, PLEASE HAVE EVERYONE STAND BACK.

"Oh, right. Everyone, please move away from the barn." Jared moved the cart and gestured for everyone to get behind him. After they'd moved far enough away, Scarlet walked right through the wall of the building as if ripping through a flimsy piece of paper. The building never stood a chance. Wood splintered, metal crumpled, and the doors shattered into fragments.

Scarlet emerged from the crumbling building and stretched out to her new height.

"Wow."

Jared craned his neck to look up at her. While not as big as her mother yet, she was fast approaching the same stature. When she stretched her neck out, she stood at least thirty, thirty-five feet tall, and her wingspan looked at least sixty or more. Her muscles rippled as she stretched and adjusted.

The deep red of her skin and scales still burned with vibrancy, but instead of her shiny scales reflecting the light, they drank it in and glowed with their own inner brightness. Her whole body was darker, the scales thicker and harder. The spikes along her back and claws were longer, deadlier than before.

Scarlet snapped her wings out, bunched her legs, and vaulted into the sky, the wind buffeting everyone.

Wow, Scarlet. You look incredible!

THANK YOU. I...UNDERESTIMATED THE CHANGES AND NOW I MUST HUNT AGAIN.

All right. Just don't stray too far, so you can keep an eye on everyone.

If I need you, I'll reach out, but your priority is the group heading south with Kitty.

Jared, Pete, and Johan headed over to the solar array, while everyone else followed Kitty. It took the three of them two hours to get all of the solar panels disassembled and ready for transport. The panels were too heavy for Pete and Johan to lift, so Jared sent them to collect wires and any rope they could use to tie the panels down. The last thing they needed was for them to fall off and shatter after all the effort they went through. Finished with their task, Johan and Pete sat on the back of the cart while Jared set out at a brisk walk. The streets of the city, though cluttered, made it very easy to pull and they made good time.

Scarlet, we're on our way. How is their progress?

Jared heard nothing in reply and suspected she was out of range. He'd expected as much, but it still created nervous butterflies in his stomach. Every few minutes, he tried to reach her again. After agonizing for over an hour, he finally managed to connect with Scarlet.

Jᴀʀᴇᴅ, I'ᴍ ʜᴇʀᴇ.

How is everyone doing? Did you find something to eat?

Tʜᴇʏ ᴀʀᴇ...ᴘʀᴏɢʀᴇssɪɴɢ. Yᴇs, I'ᴠᴇ ᴇᴀᴛᴇɴ ᴍʏ ꜰɪʟʟ.

Should I even ask?

Aʙᴏᴜᴛ? Scarlet asked, amusement coloring her words.

Shaking his head, Jared picked up his pace. He needed to catch up and push them to move faster if they hoped to reach shelter for the night. Jared felt a little bad for asking a fourteen-year-old to lead them into unknown territory, but she'd survived nine years on her own, and Kitty could handle anything they encountered. At least until Jared or Scarlet arrived to provide her some backup.

It took Jared another hour to catch up to the rear of the column, and he called out a greeting and asked everyone to stop for a minute. Walking toward Vanessa, Elle, and Kitty, Jared addressed everyone.

"I know that all of you are still regaining your strength, but we've got to move faster if we hope to reach shelter by nightfall. If we don't reach it, we'll need to camp in the open area, a lake on one side and flat open expanse all around. Definitely not an ideal situation with such a large group and god-only-knows-what creatures lurking out there, stalking us. We'll rest for just a few minutes and then we move."

JARED, THERE'S NO—

I'm trying to motivate them. They don't need to know we're in the clear.

OH, Scarlet said, enlightened. PROCEED.

"So, let's pick it up. If you absolutely cannot walk another step, we'll rest for a short time." Jared paused to make sure everyone understood. "All right, let's keep at it."

Kitty started forward once more, Jared picking up the rear.

In the back of the column, Jared could watch everyone and keep an eye for any danger approaching. He also wanted to stay in the back in case he lost his grip on the cart, or any explosive fell and detonated.

With Scarlet in the sky and the ability to cycle through normal and *Heat Sight*, they needn't really worry about any threats sneaking up on them. Occasionally, Kitty bounded forward, quickly disappearing from view as she searched among rocks and dead trees for threats. It was obvious the cat knew how to activate its camouflage ability at will as it occasionally disappeared from any of his visual abilities.

I wonder if there's a way to share or transfer abilities, thought Jared. *Scarlet, do you think we can learn or transfer abilities amongst ourselves?*

I SEE YOU ARE WATCHING KITTY AS WELL. THE WAY SHE

DISAPPEARS IS FASCINATING. I WOULD LOVE TO STUDY THE NANITES TO SEE HOW IT WORKS. MY FIRST GUESS IS THAT IT MIRRORS THE SURROUNDINGS, MAKING HER EFFECTIVELY INVISIBLE.

Yeah, after Regeneration, I think that's the best ability I've seen so far. Granted, you still have to move silently, but even so, it is pretty cool. I know we can't just transfer the ability because of the unique DNA sequencing, but perhaps there's a way we can learn how it works and modify some of our free nanites?

I AGREE. TRANSFERRING WOULD ENABLE MANY NEW POSSIBILITIES. IT IS TOO BAD THE PROFESSOR DID NOT FORESEE THIS EVENTUALITY. AS FOR LEARNING THE ABILITY, I DO THINK IT POSSIBLE, BUT IMPRACTICAL. COPYING THE CODING WOULD BE THE EASIEST STEP, BUT THEN YOU ARE LEFT WITH ONE, OR A SMALL HANDFUL OF NANITES CAPABLE OF SUCH AN ABILITY. YOU WOULD NEED TO ASSIGN A LOT OF FREE NANITES INTO THE ABILITY TO MAKE IT VIABLE. GIVEN YOUR NEED FOR MENTAL ACUITY, THAT IS NOT A WISE USE OF YOUR RESOURCES.

Difficulty aside, I think it's worth pursuing further when I've sufficiently enhanced my Mind. Take Heat Sight, for instance. That ability has saved my life many times. Sure, not all of them are useful, but a good number of them are for different situations. An example would be the ability to regulate body temperature. While not super useful for most people, if someone wanted to be a scout or hide from creatures with Heat Sight, then maybe that's an ability they'd find useful.

IT IS AN EXCELLENT IDEA, AND I AGREE THAT HOWEVER THIS CAMOUFLAGE WORKS, IT IS VERY POWERFUL. ALSO, KEEP IN MIND THAT YOU'RE THE ONLY ONE IN A POSITION TO LEARN AND REPLICATE ABILITIES. ONCE WE GET COMPANIONS FOR

THOSE HERE, THEY NEED TO VASTLY IMPROVE THEIR MINDS, BUT HOW MANY ARE LIABLE TO DUMP EVERYTHING INTO MIND FIRST? AFTER YOUR SPEECH THE OTHER DAY, MANY OF THEM WANT TO REVERT THEIR PHYSICAL ATTRIBUTES TO LOOK MORE HUMAN.

I considered that a possibility, but I hadn't realized it bothered some of them so much. I've grown accustomed to it and find it uniquely…them.

I KNOW MANY OF THEM STRUGGLE WITH THE CHANGES. NOW THAT THEY HAVE CONTROL OF THEIR BODIES, AND EVENTUALLY WILL HAVE THE ABILITY TO CHANGE THEIR PHYSICAL APPEARANCE, MANY OF THEM WANT TO RID THEMSELVES OF THE REMINDER.

Regardless of what they choose, it looks like the two of us are in for a lot of work and training.

YES. MORE SO IF THOSE HERE DO NOT BOND WITH A DRAGON. I DO NOT KNOW HOW KITTY LEARNED TO SPEAK AS SHE DOES, SINCE HER MIND KNEW ALMOST NOTHING OF HUMAN BEHAVIOR AND SPEECH PRIOR TO THEIR BONDING. IT IS TRULY REMARKABLE.

Several hours passed as Jared thought about training these people. If they somehow managed to get everyone to a level similar to he and Scarlet, they'd be a formidable force, and might just have a chance against a city.

Though how many ships and soldiers a city could muster was still an unknown factor. He also didn't know if the cities had any defensive measures.

Jared let the ideas simmer in his mind as they trekked along the lake. It would still be quite some time before they attempted anything of the sort, but it never hurt to start planning and thinking ahead.

It was fully dark by the time the ruins he'd observed from Scarlet's back came into view. Sighs of relief echoed up and down the column as they struggled to put one foot in front of the other. It was a large, sprawling area and the architecture of the place looked older than most cities he'd explored, a Victorian era.

History was one of his favorite subjects growing up, and he loved staring at the great architecture from different eras. The more modern buildings became, the less beauty showed through. Some of the modern landmarks and monuments in the twentieth century showed an elegance to them, but it was nothing like the Victorian era, or even the Greek and Roman empires with their magnificent coliseums and temples like the Parthenon. Jared smiled to himself; the ability to recall the pictures with perfect clarity continually amazed him. Cycling through images of the Greco-Roman empire made him wish he'd been born in a different place and time, before the world went to crap.

Returning to the present, Jared led the group through the city, looking for the large building he'd found earlier. Jared asked Scarlet to direct Kitty through the streets. Unlike the city they'd come from, this one wasn't laid out in a grid-like pattern, but rather wound back and forth with no rhyme or reason.

Once they reached the building, everyone but Kitty, Elle, and himself collapsed, totally exhausted. Surprisingly, only a few had fallen behind during the walk and it only slowed their progress a little. He suspected that wouldn't be the case tomorrow as they entered rough terrain. Jared really hoped the cart fit up the dried creek, or it was going to be a very long day for him.

Preparing for the night, Jared offered to take first watch even though he desperately wanted to sleep after keeping watch the previous evening and the workout of pulling the cart. Except for

Elle, Kitty, and Scarlet, everyone else was near exhaustion and needed rest before they could pull a watch rotation.

Scarlet, you okay to keep flying for a while?

Yes, I can do this for hours yet. You may rest if needed.

Thanks, but I'll take first watch. As tired as I am, these people need the rest much more than we do.

Jared walked over to Elle and Kitty. "Are you okay to help take the second watch tonight? We'll only have two rotations of guards. I'll take first, and I'd like to have you both on the second."

Elle and Kitty nodded their heads in agreement and quickly found a place to rest before their watch began. After everyone settled in, Jared addressed them even though half had already fallen asleep.

"Please get as much rest as you can, and we'll begin at first light tomorrow. The second leg of this trip is liable to be much harder, and we need an early start. Also, we will have guard shifts throughout the night so you've no need to be afraid."

A collective groan sounded through the room, and he watched as people massaged sore feet and backs. Jared didn't blame them, his own body groaning with aches and pains. Fortunately for him, *Regeneration* would kick in soon and wash those pains away.

Dropping his pack on the cart, Jared checked his weapons and started his patrol.

24 TRIAL BY BUNNY

Jared and Scarlet patrolled half the night before Scarlet landed in the middle of the ruined building, barely clearing the broken edges of the walls. She landed as lightly as possible, but it still made the ground tremble, startling a few people awake.

Jared whispered in their minds that all was well and to go back to sleep. In hindsight, that was a bad idea so recently after their ordeal with Razael, but they had no lights, and he'd instructed them to avoid a fire lest they attract unwanted attention. Thankfully, it didn't look like anyone panicked, and he quickly woke Elle and Kitty to take his place.

Jared fell asleep instantly, exhausted from the day's work, but an instant later someone gently prodded him awake. He'd been about to make a rude comment until he realized the sun was already cresting over the horizon. Groaning, Jared stood, his body aching, in spite of his *Regeneration* ability. He winced at the thought of trekking up a mountain with the cart.

By the time Jared was ready to continue the hike, everyone else was waiting on him, and all he had to do was equip his pack.

Having little of their own definitely allowed them to remain highly mobile and ready in a moment's notice.

Rolling his shoulders and neck, Jared flexed his hands and arms as he approached the cart. Selfishly, he wished that some of the others could help, but the only two strong enough were Kitty and Scarlet, and they were best suited to scouting the area for other threats.

"Okay, everyone, same formation as yesterday. Today's hike will be much harder, and I expect we'll need to stop more often. Please do your best to push through, and if you really need to rest, you may sit on the cart again. Once we get to our destination, there are rooms built into the mountainside that are easily defensible and will allow everyone to rest in comfort. We'll still keep a watch, but it's a more secure area, so you'll be able to take all the time you need to rest and recover."

After his pronouncement, everyone cheered, and he saw relief in their eyes. The activity of the last few days and their clear lack of physical strength made it difficult for any of them to maintain the constant pace. Jared suspected they'd curse him before the day was through, but at least his little speech spurred them forward.

They quickly left the tip of the lake behind and headed west toward their new home. For the first few hours everyone managed to keep up the pace, with only one person straggling behind. Jared was grateful he didn't need to pull anyone yet because his hands and back already ached, and they'd only made it a third of the way there.

JARED, YOU HAVE COMPANY INCOMING FROM THE EAST. THEY ARE TOO FAR FOR ME TO SEE CLEARLY. JUST A MOMENT.

Jared called everyone to a halt.

"Listen up, everyone. Scarlet says there are creatures closing on our position. Those with weapons, please move back here with me.

Remember what I said about the safety on your weapons, and never point your weapon at someone else."

IT IS A SMALL GROUP OF RABBITS HEADED YOUR WAY.

How many?

IT LOOKS LIKE EIGHTEEN, BUT THEY ARE JUMPING REALLY FAST, SO IT IS HARD TO SAY FOR CERTAIN.

"Scarlet says it's just a few rabbits," Jared said, downplaying the number so as not to freak them out. "Those of you with experience shooting weapons form a line back here. Everyone else, get behind us."

Everyone visibly relaxed at the news, and Jared smirked, recalling his first experience with a face full of the giant fur balls. The thought made him flinch and look up to the sky, just to be certain Scarlet wasn't up to any funny business.

"Some of you might think rabbits warm and cuddly, but I can assure you these rabbits can—and will—hurt you if they have the chance. They are quick, can leap very high, and have really long sharp teeth. Now, that's the bad news. The good news is that if you stay out of their way, they are relatively harmless."

They definitely didn't look convinced after his initial scare, but Jared thought that was a good thing, so they didn't get complacent. Jared wasn't very concerned about their inexperience in battle facing the rabbits. This might be their easiest fight in the days to come and it provided good experience for them.

"These rabbits showing up is actually fortuitous, since I'd just been thinking we need to go hunting for some pelts to use as blankets and pillows. However, if we want to use their pelts, they can't be filled with hundreds of bullet holes, so please conserve your shots and let those more experienced shoot first."

THEY ARE NEARLY UPON YOU.

"Get ready!"

Jared watched as those more experienced raised their pistols, flicking the safeties off. A few others raised their weapons but forgot to switch off the safety. He mentioned nothing to them, wanting to see how they reacted under pressure.

A few seconds later the rabbits bounded round a bend in the creek, and two people immediately fired their weapons.

"Hold! Wait until they get closer or you're just wasting ammunition. I know most of you can barely see anything other than blurry shapes at that distance."

Jared flashed a look of irritation when another shot rang out, but everyone else held their fire until the rabbits closed to within fifty feet. A flurry of pistols retorted, sending half a dozen rabbits to their grave and leaving a dozen more to contend with.

Jared darted behind the group with weapons to protect the unarmed colonists if any of the rabbits made it past the front ranks. Weapons fired in rapid succession, as those who'd forgotten their safeties switched them off to join in the assault. Only three of eighteen rabbits made it to the front lines, which was significantly fewer than he'd anticipated. The rabbits jumped over the line of defenders, right into Jared's reach, which he conveniently punted back over the line of defense where they were summarily cut down without mercy.

One of the defenders turned with his weapon and pointed it at a rabbit that jumped over the line. Moving on instinct, Jared kicked out at the hand holding the weapon, hearing an audible crack in the man's arm.

Wincing, Jared booted the rabbit back over the line and knelt next to the man he kicked.

Dang, I didn't mean to kick so hard.

"Are you okay, Joel? It's Joel, right?"

The man nodded weakly as Jared asked, "Let me look?"

Joel tried pulling back, but Jared grasped the arm firmly and kept the injury stable.

"Look, I'm sorry I had to do that, but you pointed a loaded gun at other people. If you'd fired a round, it would've torn right through the rabbit into the people behind it."

The blood drained from Joel's face as he stammered, "I-I-I...d-d-didn't—"

"I know you didn't mean to, but in the heat of a battle, we don't think through everything. Instead, we act on instinct, not considering our surroundings. Trust me, I've done more than enough stupid things myself. It will take time for everyone to adapt and learn. I'm just as new to this whole fighting in a group thing as you, but my father taught me the basics of firearm safety. I'll do my best to recall those lessons and instruct each of you that need the training."

Jared caught whispered phrases from several in the crowd, criticizing his actions, one voice in particular louder than any other.

Of course, George would use the opportunity to sow discord. This guy is really getting on my nerves.

Jared shrugged off the scoffers, chalking it up to naivety. They wouldn't have the same outlook had Joel unloaded the weapon behind him and hit someone.

"Let's get a bandage and splint to stabilize the bones."

Rummaging through the crate of medical supplies, Jared found a splint, but had no idea how to use it. He'd made splints for himself using sticks and strips of cloth. The contraption he held now, was much more complicated, containing dozens of straps and metal inserts.

"Do we have a doctor? Or medic?" Jared paused, waiting for a response. "Does anyone have even a tiny shred of medical training? I know some basic stuff, and I could probably make a more primitive splint, but I'm not sure how to use this."

Jared dangled the splint in front of him.

Finally, after he gave up and attempted to figure it out himself, someone walked forward and knelt next to him. Jared turned and searched his memory for the guy's name.

"It's Casey, right?"

Casey nodded his head and grabbed Jared's arm. *I've got a little training. My brother worked with the colony doctors and taught me a little of what he knew. I was only a teenager back then, but I think I can remember some of it.*

"I'm sure you'll do much better than me."

Relieved, Jared handed over the medical supplies to Casey, taking a step back so he could work. Although most looked on in concern, they didn't appear to harbor any resentment. There were a couple that still scowled openly, including George, and it was to those few he addressed with his next words.

"Let this be a lesson to you. Pay attention to your surroundings. Never put your brothers and sisters in danger. I regret to say I learned that lesson the hard way, and Scarlet and I flirted with death on more than one occasion because of my stupidity." Jared's tone of voice brooked no argument and wiped the scowls from their faces. "Always take the time to think through your decision. If in doubt, rely on those around you to help. I promise you, if I see anyone recklessly endangering another, I'll react in the exact same way. Every person here survived through perilous times, me and Scarlet included, it would be tragic to see someone injured or killed due to recklessness."

Although a few directed hateful glances his way, most of the group nodded their heads shakily, their eyes round with fear.

This was a new world for them, many never having left the colony prior to their enslavement. While Razael held them enthralled, they hadn't needed to worry about wild creatures, or defending their lives at every turn. Striking out on this new adventure was foreign territory for all but Jared and Elle, and it would take all of them time to get used to it.

"Now that's behind us, these rabbits you fought were one of the easiest creatures I've come across in the past two years. They can hurt you sure, but with our superior number and firepower it wasn't even a contest. However, had this been a group of those weird badger creatures we ran from on the beach a few days ago, it might've turned out different. I won't speculate on the outcome, but that would be a fight even I'd try to avoid."

Looking around the cart, Jared found Elle and Kitty toward the back and motioned them forward. "Elle, you and Kitty go around the dead rabbits and place your hand on them. Everyone else, watch as they go from body to body and see if you notice anything."

Elle and Kitty did as they were told and with each body they touched an almost imperceptible glow pulsed into them.

"What you observed is the nanites from the rabbits flowing into Elle and Kitty, the same way I explained the other day. These creatures have tiny amounts, but it'll add up over time, so never ignore a kill. I asked Elle and Kitty to absorb them, because you can only do so once you're bonded. The only other way to absorb them is if you consumed the flesh of the rabbit. There's also a good chance these nanites will give Elle the same *Maximum Muscle* ability I demonstrated for you."

Everyone looked deep in thought, and even the naysayers who didn't like what he'd done, seemed to forget all about the incident while they thought through the possibilities.

"We've got to keep moving, but first does anyone know how to gut an animal? If we don't gut them now, they'll spoil by the time we get back and we won't be able to eat them."

A couple folks raised their hands and Jared passed out a few knives they'd gathered from the old colony. With everyone working together, it didn't take long to rid the dead rabbits of their entrails.

"If you can lift one, load up the bodies on the cart. We can worry about skinning them later, and we'll have a decent meal once we reach our new home."

After loading up the rabbits, the group continued the trek. They needed to rest multiple times, Jared included. Pulling the cart through narrow passages and over rocky terrain depleted his stamina rapidly. His arms and legs burned from the effort, and his breath came in sharp gasps. It didn't help that no fewer than a dozen people had intermittently ridden on the cart for a time.

The short breaks helped him recover enough to keep going for an hour or two before he'd call another halt. Eventually, they reached some of the rock falls he'd seen when scouting the area, and the rest of the colonists didn't fare so well. Many seemed near collapse. Given the steep incline, he limited passengers on the cart to three at a time. Even that was almost more than he could handle, and he struggled for purchase on the loose rubble.

This leg of the journey took them eight hours from start to finish, and by the time they reached their destination, all of them had nothing left to give. Only Elle, Kitty, and Scarlet were no worse for wear after the journey. Jared rolled the cart to a flat area and lay right there on the ground, uncaring about anything else. Scarlet and Kitty could search the area and alert them to any dangers. So far, they'd seen nothing in this ravine to suggest any large creatures lived here so he wasn't concerned.

Please scout the area, Scarlet. Let me know if you see anything. You can send instructions to Kitty if you find something that needs a closer inspection, but I need to rest. Even Jared's thoughts came out labored, and he passed out immediately after sending instructions.

It took Jared less than two hours to recover, but it was already nearing full dark and he needed to make sure these rooms in the cliff were safe for everyone. When he stood up and looked around, half the people still slept where they'd dropped, and the other half sat in states of delirium.

Chuckling to himself and extremely grateful for his *Regeneration*, Jared left them to recover and explored their new home. The area he'd chosen cut into the earth, creating sheer cliffs on every side. It proved a great defensive position and concealed them from view. Even flying overhead, people would find it difficult to spot anything here unless they specifically looked for it like he and Scarlet had.

A dense forest of bleached white trees crowded the area, and Jared imagined a green canopy once covering the land. The trees stood as petrified wooden sculptures, absent any color as the sun mercilessly beat down on them. Although he hadn't noticed it before, the large clearings they landed in earlier likely served as a small pond or reservoir when water used to flow to the lake. The basin was smooth and deep enough to hold a decent amount of water.

Although it'd be nice to have water here, it worked to their advantage to have a place for Scarlet—and hopefully her family—to land. Though the area wouldn't be big enough for her whole family.

The rooms built into the rock wall were far enough below the ridge line that it'd be impossible to pick them out from a drop ship cruising overhead. This was just one of many ravines in the area, and as long as they kept a low profile, they should remain safe.

A short distance into the trees he found a staircase carved directly into the rock. The stairs, worn by time and smoothed around the corners, were mostly intact, but a few crumbled under his weight, making the ascent treacherous.

They'd need to repair them and add in something to prevent slipping if it ever rained. In the weeks he'd been there, he hadn't seen any yet. If it did, Jared wondered how much of the reservoir would fill up, and if the water would be safe to drink. So far, all of the rains he'd experienced brought a fifty-fifty chance of it being toxic.

Pushing these thoughts from his head, he picked his way carefully up the stairs. They carried him above many of the dead trees until he reached a wide platform on the southern cliff face. It had to be a solid forty feet wide, with rooms carved into the wall on one side. A few of these rooms had collapsed, and debris spilled out of the doors.

Jared walked over to one of the intact rooms and stood at the doorway. He peered around the doorjamb, but didn't go in. Normally he wasn't claustrophobic, but the thought of the entire cliff dropping on his head gave him pause. Jared took a breath and stepped into the room, his *Night Vision* activating.

The main space was open and included furniture carved from rock itself. There were stone benches and counters to one side and a series of shelving inset in the wall.

Two rooms branched off the main space, including what looked to be a bedroom with two raised stone platforms resembling beds. An open closet with shelves and small cubbies took up an entire wall.

Stone wouldn't be the most comfortable thing to sleep on, but they'd collect pelts of the animals they killed for mattresses and blankets.

Stepping out of the room, Jared tried the other end of the hall and realized it ended abruptly, a wall of dirt and rocks barring his path. He stepped back from the area and oriented himself to the room next door. Based on his current position, this tunnel might've previously led straight to the adjoining room.

Back outside, Jared walked down two doors, directly opposite the collapsed room and found three branches off the main room. One led to the collapsed portion of the tunnel, the other a bedroom identical to the one before, and the third leading to the next room over. Jared walked the tunnel past five other identical rooms before he reached yet another collapse.

From outside, he looked down the row of rooms and found four of twenty rooms collapsed. Each room would house two people, which meant they couldn't all fit on this level comfortably.

At the end of the first platform, another staircase—in even worse condition—led further up the cliff wall. Several steps no longer existed, and he ended up jumping several sections at a time to get to the upper area.

When he reached the top, he found another row of rooms, only these were much more elaborate than the ones below. There were fewer, but they were large and had arched doors and windows. There were also some low benches dotting the wide platform he stood on, all positioned to look out over the reservoir below. Glancing over the edge, Jared peered down at the group resting below and saw that not a single person had moved while he'd been gone.

Returning his focus to the rooms on this level, none of them looked collapsed, but then he didn't know how stable they were considering rooms just below them *had* collapsed. Warily, Jared entered the first room, careful to inspect the floor for any cracks, or signs of weakening.

Inside the room, he noted the architecture and furniture showed much more attention to detail. The carved furniture had seat backs, armrests, and intricate swirl patterns. The doorways and windows had arches instead of straight lines, giving the space a more elegant feel. It flowed much more seamlessly with the natural composition of the rock. Instead of one bedroom with two beds, there were two bedrooms with one bed apiece. The same stylized shelving and archways extended into the rooms.

Each of these rooms also held wash tubs, but without a water source they were little more than decorations. Continuing his exploration, Jared found each of these rooms isolated from the next.

Reaching the end of the rooms on the second level, Jared found yet another staircase leading up. The third, and final level had only two rooms, spaced far apart. Fire pits and low benches made it seem like a communal gathering place. He picked the room closest to the staircase and entered a large, vaulted space with several smaller rooms along the sides. The main room had a long stone table with benches flanking it. A hearth to one side looked ventilated, based on the small rays of light filtering through.

A single larger room off to the right held several rows of counter space and one large island in the middle of the room. Open stone cabinets completed the area and allowed for ample storage. Obviously, a dining area, and some place to prepare food.

Jared left the room and headed toward the last space.

It turned out to be a very large living space, complete with half a dozen chairs, couches, several rooms, multiple washrooms, a separate kitchen, and even a room with an open area overlooking the gorge.

Looking out over the sea of bone-white trees, Jared wondered if he'd ever see it returned to its former glory. For a fleeting moment, Jared through about bringing plants from the lake to start a garden, but he quickly dismissed the idea. Without a steady source of water, he didn't think they'd be able to grow anything of any significance. They could start a small farm down by the water's edge eventually and just make daily hikes out there to tend it.

Although Jared was excited about their new home, despondency always creeped in when he thought of how the world used to be, making him long for better days. Heading back down to the ground, he saw people were finally coming around from the strenuous hike. He saw no reason to restrict their movement and left everyone to roam about the area.

Scarlet, where are Elle and Kitty?

RIGHT BEHIND YOU.

Jared spun around and jumped. Standing right behind him, the pair stood not five feet away. He'd neither seen nor heard them approach.

"Dang, you two are sneaky. Did you find anything we should worry about?"

Elle shook her head, and her cat padded a few paces away to lie down.

Turning back to the group gathering around him, he addressed them. "I finished exploring the rooms up on those platforms." Jared pointed to the three ledges. "There are plenty of rooms for everyone, but I suggest everyone double up. Preferably, with someone comfortable handling a weapon. I want everyone to have each other's back, and it'll work best if there's at least one weapon in each room."

Jared outlined the housing situation and described the rooms he'd examined. Many wanted to take rooms on the first landing, preferring to be closer to the ground. Everyone suggested he take the top room with Vanessa, Elle, and Kitty since it was easier for them to climb up the stairs.

At first, he resisted and wanted to be the one closest to the staircase leading up, but everyone quickly overruled him, suggesting that Scarlet, who'd be on the ground anyway, was sufficient protection for them. He could also observe the surrounding area from the top.

Eventually, he agreed to their demands. If something were to climb the stairs, a couple leaps would carry him to the lowest platform, anyway. Jared let the group fend for themselves on sleeping arrangements, but asked they keep at least one person with weapons training in each room.

Meanwhile, he walked over to the cart and began unceremoniously tossing the dead rabbits to the ground. Hopefully, they had someone that could skin them and cure pelts. His first priority was securing the explosives and boosters away, then he could find someone to work with the animal pelts. Three trips allowed him to lug both crates and any remaining ammunition up to his new home. He stowed them in a closet furthest from the entrance. Somehow, he'd need to fashion a lock or a way to cordon off the area to keep everyone safe.

By the time he'd finished moving everything up, Vanessa, Elle, and Kitty had made their way up to the platform. They examined every room before choosing a single room to share.

Kitty found an empty spot in the large sitting room and claimed her territory. That left three rooms for Jared to choose from. He picked the one with the opening out to the ravine, feeling less confined with the open platform.

Electricity would've been a boon, but they had multiple hearths in the rock home and a plethora of dead trees to use for firewood. They definitely wouldn't lack for warmth and light once they cut down trees and lugged them up. Thoughts of hauling all that wood up here made him groan, but then an epiphany struck.

Oh, Scarlet, Jared thought, a mischievous grin spreading across his face.

25 A NEW HOME

I t didn't take long for everyone to settle into their new quarters, establish routines, and carve out a new life. Jared sat on the ledge outside his room, watching the colonists go about their new daily chores.

Several weeks had passed as everyone settled into various roles. During that time, he'd taken no fewer than five trips back to the vacated colony to gather materials. Every time he traveled back to the village, Jared paused at the edge of the lake. The nanites beckoned to him. It was all he could do to resist dipping his body into the water to absorb as much as he could. The only reason he didn't absorb them every day was that neither Scarlet nor Jared knew how many nanites there were, and they had an entire colony to strengthen.

He was already stronger than several humans combined. It would be selfish to take everything for himself, but at the same time he'd most likely be in the more dangerous situations. Jared could justify it but checked himself every time and refused to take the easy road at the expense of everyone else. The momentary pauses overlooking the lake helped him to reassess his priorities. His primary purpose for the many excursions was to scavenge enough materials and provisions that the waterfolk could survive for a time without him, but with every passing day, Jared grew more restless to move their missions forward.

For now, he spent the time helping acquire items to sustain the colony. On one such trip they'd gathered enough lighting and wiring to put lights into all the occupied rooms. It looked super tacky with all the wiring exposed, but now everyone had at least one functioning light in their homes.

When they'd first wired the lights into the homes, many of them no longer had a protective coating, and they'd had a few incidents with people getting zapped. It wasn't until it finally rained that they were able to use clay to cover the exposed sections of wiring. Although, the rain also fried half of the wiring and caused a few of the precious light bulbs to burst.

Jared put Pete in charge of all the solar panels, wiring, and electronics. The guy's skill with electronics bordered on magical as he breathed new life into ancient machines. His tinkering had come in handy several times over the past week, starting with the little wind-up walkie talkies he'd salvaged. The range on them was incredible, and they could stay in contact with any groups that went out hunting or to the lake to bathe. The scrawny, bean-pole of a man could fix anything, provided he had the parts.

His small room turned into their electronics shop, housing anything Jared could want or need. The man even found a working television and game console, bringing so many memories back of Jared's home colony.

Keeping up traditions from his childhood, Jared decided to have it brought out only on special occasions to preserve the little electricity they had. Pete wanted to reverse engineer one of the solar panels so he could build his own, but Jared just couldn't bring himself to allow that. Vanessa backed him up in the decision. They were just too valuable to risk losing any of them.

Casey, their only medic, set up shop in a spare room on the second level, and Jared handed all the medical supplies and boosters over for safe-keeping. Everyone in their little budding colony knew the stakes, and just how valuable the boosters were so he didn't have to worry about over-eager people making off with any of them. They planned to save them until bonding began.

A part of him worried that George would steal some of the equipment, but he'd seemed docile the past two weeks. Either he'd finally come to his senses, or he was biding his time to act. Either way, Jared couldn't spend every waking hour watching the man. Either he fell in line, or he stole a few supplies and went his own way. If he chose to go his own way, chances are he wouldn't survive long on his own. One man couldn't dictate Jared's actions. He needed to move on and let the consequences fall as they will.

In the weeks they'd been at their new home, Scarlet finished getting rid of Razael's influence, resetting the clock on everyone's time. She wasn't yet confident in her ability to isolate the code and keep it from turning into the techno-virus but was confident that she'd figure it out soon. Convinced of Scarlet's skills, Jared backed her and made sure everyone knew there was nothing to worry about.

As the days ticked by, Jared became increasingly agitated. Time was wasting away, and they needed to move forward with their plans to get everyone stronger and bonded. The need grew in urgency until it pressed in on his throughs and clouded his mind. He'd heard a few people talk about creatures to bond that they'd observed in the area, but it was like everyone was waiting for something to happen first.

They'd sufficiently settled into a new life here, but it felt stagnant. While it was a safe place to rest and recover, it wasn't an utopia. They weren't on the map and therefore received no supplies from the cities that helped sustain other colonies.

Instead, they were all on their own and they had nowhere near the expertise to cover all the needed professions. It wasn't all bad, and they'd identified people with skills that helped them a lot. The day they'd settled in to their homes here, a colonist named David offered to skin and clean the hides from the rabbits. He'd done a great job, and with the help of a few others, he'd fashioned drying racks for the skins. Now, everyone had blankets and pillows.

David also pointed out the need for a waste pit with all the dead rabbit carcasses. It wasn't something he'd ever really thought about. His colony back home had a partially working sewer system, but he'd never seen how it worked. On his own the past few years, he didn't need to worry about it either. The few times he needed to use the restroom, he'd just drop his pants wherever he was. In a colony setting, that wouldn't work. Thankfully, David had some ideas. He'd taken a group, along with Kitty for safety, and dug a trench several hundred yards away. Every few days, they burned the refuse to clean it out.

Another of their members, Maria, quickly volunteered to cook all the meat they collected. Even now, many of their latest kills hung from hooks in a room she'd fashioned into a meat locker. It was cold enough in the room that the meat lasted a few days before it spoiled, and for anything they didn't cook, Maria smoked and made into jerky for travel rations.

Many other colonists proved useful in scavenging and hunting, but they still lacked carpenters, tailors, blacksmiths, and farmers. There were a few who tried their hand at carving, but it was terrible work, and all the dishware and utensils they used came from the ruined city a few miles away. They'd found a large room in one building with a bunch of plastic tables, chairs, and thousands of plastic dish sets. The dishes were flimsy and rarely lasted longer than a few uses, but it was better than the crude wooden ones they'd made.

They didn't need to eat all the time, but it helped keep their strength up and brought the village together in one place. It was a good time for them to discuss plans, updates on how everyone was doing, and to talk about their future endeavors. For most, it was the only meal anyone ate daily, and Jared wanted to keep it going as a tradition for the group. It was partly sentimental for him to remember his mother's efforts to always bring the family together for supper.

Jared glanced behind him to see folks already making the climb up the stairs to the dining hall, many already gathered around the fire pits, chatting amiably. It'd taken weeks for everyone to get their voices back and just as long before their speech flowed naturally, but now they were able to, everyone preferred using their voices to telepathy unless they were trying to be silent. Which was a very useful skill to have for the hunter groups gathering pelts. It was much easier to sneak up on unsuspecting prey if you didn't need to talk aloud to coordinate an attack.

On the other hand, Jared requested everyone recover their voices, because they couldn't rely on physical touch to talk and coordinate if they happened to engage in a group fight. It was also inefficient to their daily chores and routines if they always had to stop what they were doing to touch someone.

Professions were well and good, but this was a temporary home. Eventually, they'd take the fight to the cities and need to leave all this behind for a time.

Rising to his feet, Jared watched everyone assemble on the

platform for a group dinner. He'd asked Elle to round everyone up for tonight's meal, even if they hadn't planned on it. It was time to set the next phase of their plans into motion, and he wanted everyone there to hear it.

"Hey, Elle, were you able to find everyone?"

"Yes, everyone is here."

"Thank you, Elle." He heard a low growl from Kitty and was quick to add, "And Kitty."

The corner of Jared's mouth twitched up as the cat sighed dramatically and sauntered off to lie near one of the fire pits. Chuckling to himself, Jared walked into the dining room to see everyone else waiting patiently for dinner.

Poking his head back outside, Jared said, "Can I get everyone to join me inside please?"

Once everyone seated themselves at the table, Vanessa and Maria brought flanks of meat out from the prep room. They also had some kind of seaweed from the lake below, and it was a welcome addition to their daily meals. After everyone received their food, Jared motioned for them to eat while he outlined his plans.

"We've been here for nearly a month without incident, and it's time we start pursuing our mission. You've all done a tremendous job to improve everyone's livelihood, and we lack little in the way of day to day needs. But—" Jared paused for dramatic effect as some people put their forks down to listen to him, "—we're merely delaying the inevitable here. We've not progressed forward with our vows to make this world a better place. We have yet to takes steps down a path to bring justice. I know," Jared said, forestalling the argument showing plainly on some faces. "We had to get everyone's strength up and make sure we could eke out a life here. We've done that and done it pretty dang well, if I do say so myself, but we need to get back on track."

Many nodded their heads in agreement.

"We need to find companions for all of you to bond. Scarlet and Kitty are fearsome predators, I've enhanced myself significantly, and Elle has incredible stealth. But there are only four of us. We need everyone to grow stronger, and not just exercising, but using nanites to drastically improve yourselves so that you can stand toe-to-toe with our adversaries. They'll have far superior weapons and numbers. Igor also perfected the original nanotechnology for them, so they may far surpass us in strength and abilities. Basically, we know almost nothing about them. We must rely on stealth, surprise, and quick action as our allies. Even then, it may not be enough."

Jared slowly ate a few bites of his meal while his words simmered in their hearts and minds.

"One thing we have they won't expect: the power of flight." Jared looked toward the door and found Scarlet's head resting a few paces from the doorway. Smiling at her, Jared waved a hand. Many of those around the table glanced over and waved.

"While we have advantages, we sorely lack in numbers. This brings me to my main point." He had everyone's attention now and every eye turned his way. "Scarlet and I will leave first thing tomorrow."

"No!"

Vanessa's cry pierced the rumble of voices echoing around the room. Jared locked eyes with her, but quickly looked away, fearing his own composure. His heart leapt into his throat, threatening to choke him. He hated seeing Vanessa distraught. They'd grown closer over the weeks, and he'd come to cherish her friendship and closeness. Leaving was hard, but a necessary decision, and he hadn't come to it lightly.

Holding up a hand to cut off any further arguments, Jared

explained, "I know you don't want us to go, but we must." Meeting Vanessa's eyes, Jared showed her just how difficult this was for him.

"Elle and Kitty will remain here to protect you should anything—or anyone—attack. Scarlet and I must go find her family. I've considered finding all of you companions around the area, and although there are possibilities, nothing compares to a dragon.

"Carla, I know you've eyed that bird we've seen flying around, but that is the only creature I've seen that can fly and looks intelligent enough to serve as a good companion. The other birds we've seen are small and would take much too long to grow into something worthwhile." The bird in question looked like an eagle of sorts but had the body of a cat. Some mythical sphinx or griffon. Who knew what creatures roamed the earth. Surely if dragons existed, then other creatures of legend must exist.

"Some of you expressed interest in the many bears or wolves we've seen, and they aren't out of the question, but we should exhaust the possibility of dragon companions first. If you can't fly, we'll never reach the cities, and if we can't reach them, then what are we doing here? We could survive here for years, the rest of our lives, but I cannot sit idly by while the rest of the world suffers and those above remain unchecked. So Scarlet and I will leave at first light to find her family.

"I know many of you expressed an interest in a dragon companion, and although we can't promise you they'll be receptive, we will try. First, we need to find them. Scarlet's mother showed her where to begin our search before she died, but we've got a big task ahead. We don't know how far underground they are, or if the passage is still intact. It's been over ten years since her mother surfaced, and in this chaotic world, that is a long time for things to radically change. As big and deadly as Scarlet looks, she's barely a fourth the size of her mother. It's possible we'll encounter stronger creatures along the way that wouldn't have been a challenge for her mother. In any scenario we've considered, it's much too dangerous to bring any of you with us."

Several people threw sympathetic looks his way, but others radiated concern over them leaving.

"I urge all of you to remain here. Elle and Kitty can hunt for any food you want, but please leave off on any forays into the ruins and old colony until I return."

Vanessa, who stood next to Jared squeezed his arm. "What if you don't come back?" She spoke with halting words, and he felt something drip onto his shoulder. Looking up, he saw tears leaking down her face, and fear shone behind her soft gaze.

Jared reached up and rested his hand on her cheek. He wanted desperately to bring her with, but knew it was much too dangerous. When he'd first found Scarlet, he'd felt his world coming together, but it wasn't until he grew closer to Vanessa that he truly felt complete. He longed for more than friendship with her, but he was scared about their future. If he committed to anything more and something happened to either of them, he didn't know if he could go through that heartbreak and come out the other side.

"I will be back. I promise," Jared said, his voice catching as he wiped the tears from her eyes.

The sober mood caused everyone to lapse into silence, their meals forgotten. Though some of them feared their safety in the colony, most seemed genuinely concerned about him and Scarlet and the challenges they'd face.

Jared felt his desire to protect them grow. He'd found amazing friendships with these people, and no matter what happened in his search for the dragons, he'd find his way back here and resume his goal of making the world a better place for everyone.

First, they needed to find the dragons.

The next morning dawned much too fast, and he soon found himself at the mouth of their little village, his pack loaded with weapons and ammunition. He'd needed to borrow another satchel to carry a few medical supplies and a change of clothes.

Scarlet rested a few paces away, just beyond the tree line, and the entire colony showed up to wish him luck and safe travels. Vanessa lingered a moment longer, and just as Jared was about to turn and walk to Scarlet, she rushed into his arms and gave him a fierce hug. Just as quickly, she planted a timid peck on his lips and dashed off to follow the others.

Stunned, Jared absentmindedly touched his fingers to his lips, feeling her lingering presence. Her cool skin left a prickle of electricity dancing across his lips, and he nearly ran after her to return the gesture. Barely restraining himself, Jared grinned like an idiot. Vanessa cast a furtive glance over her shoulder and blushed crimson. She blew him a kiss before darting around a tree and out of sight.

Now you have another reason to return quickly, teased Scarlet.

I like her, Scarlet. A lot. But I just—I'd very much like to be more than friends, but I just don't know. Does she like me because we rescued her? Is it some kind of Stockholm syndrome? Does she genuinely like me for me? And, what if something happens and one of us doesn't make it? Is it worth it?

You are asking questions that have been asked countless times through the ages, but until you make the leap of faith you will never know.

I know. Jared sighed. *I'm going to give it a lot of thought while we're gone and will hopefully make a decision when we return.*

Are you ready to find my family?

Absolutely, let's go!

With a powerful thrust, Scarlet launched herself into the air and glided out of the ravine.

We must head back to the city where you found me, so I can trace my mother's path. I could find it based on the angle and speed she travelled, but it will be easier if we retrace her journey.

Okay, let's try to stay airborne as long as possible. The sooner we find your family, the better.

Hang on!

Glad Scarlet warned him, Jared wrapped his arms around her neck just in time as she rocketed through the air. She moved so fast, he had to squint and duck his head just to see where they flew. It'd taken them five hours to lazily fly to the lakeside town, but it only took just over an hour to fly the two hundred miles back to New York City.

The entire flight back, Jared fiercely clung to her back. He didn't even think to speak with her, and he didn't dare ask to share a thought space. He focused only on not falling from her back to a gruesome end.

When the city came into focus, Scarlet slowed her pace, allowing Jared to relax his grip and sit up. The city looked unchanged from the last time he visited, but as they drew closer, Jared realized they weren't alone. A drop ship sat close to the home he'd made by the Statue of Liberty.

Go down, Scarlet!

Scarlet immediately dropped to the ground, and Jared crept to the top of a small hill. Activating *Magnified Vision*, he zoomed in on the drop ship. He didn't see any people wandering about, but a few weird mechanical spheres rolled around, lights blinking on their bodies.

All at once, every sphere jerked to a stop, rotated toward the drop ship, and moved in one accord back to its ramp. Then, it launched into the air and headed toward the city itself. The ship landed and disgorged more of the mechanical objects.

I think they're scanning for something. I wonder if they're looking for you and your mother? Unless they're monitoring things down on the ground, how would they know to look here?

THEY MIGHT HAVE SOME KIND OF SCANNER IN THE CITIES THAT ALERTED THEM? REMEMBER, MY MOTHER TOOK DOWN SEVERAL BUILDINGS, AND SHE WAS THE SIZE OF A SMALL SKYSCRAPER.

Right, but why would it take so long for them to realize what happened here? Something doesn't add up. They must be here for another reason.

I DO NOT KNOW.

They watched the drop ship for some time but again saw no people leave the ship. More of the strange balls disgorged from the ship heading into the city itself. He noticed that the scanners—at least that's what he decided to call them—traversed the same path he'd taken that led him to Scarlet.

I think they've got a way to track the path I took through the city. Those things are following my every footstep.

LET US HOPE THEY HAVE NO WAY OF TRACKING US THROUGH THE AIR. THEIR SEARCH WILL ONLY LEAD THEM TO THE PLACES WE WALKED.

Yeah, and a giant Godzilla worm that we managed to kill. If they make it that far, that doesn't bode well for us, and it'll put them on guard.

WE DID FLY PART OF THE WAY THERE.

Again, they'll know something is off when all of a sudden they can't follow us on the ground.

SHOULD WE ATTEMPT TO DESTROY IT?

I don't know. Let's observe it for a time and see what happens.

Lying on his belly, head barely visible over the rise in the land, they watched and waited. Jared hoped for a glimpse of the ship's pilot or whoever controlled it and its scanners. To Jared's knowledge, no one he knew, including himself, had seen someone from the cities in a very long time.

A moment later, they saw flashes of light and small echoing retorts from within the city. His eyes darted back and forth trying to find the source of the activity. They watched as half a dozen people emerged from the city, firing on the rolling spheres and the ship itself. The ship rotated in place, and a massive bolt from a phase canon pulverized a slab of concrete, the person hiding behind it disappearing in a flash of light. They didn't even have time to scream. It was a near instantaneous death.

Dang. Did you—

YES.

The barrage of rounds from the humans destroyed all the remaining spheres on the ground, but not before another beam of phase matter snuffed out two more people. A smaller group of three ran from cover toward the ships open ramp. Just before they started up the ramp, it closed and lifted from the ground. The three people, along with two others, roared in frustration as the ship took off. Just when Jared thought the ship was leaving the area, the phase canon swiveled once more and eradicated two more of the people firing upon it.

Scarlet, we need to help them.

IT IS PROBABLY THE DAGGERS AGAIN. MAYBE THEY CAME BACK TO FINISH THE JOB THEY STARTED.

Even if it is, I can't stand by and let them get decimated like that. I swore a vow to protect mankind. What if they're nothing like the Daggers and we're watching potential allies get massacred?

Jared bit his lip in thought. *Do you think you can take down the ship? You're at least twice its size.*

I CAN TAKE IT DOWN, BUT IT MAY REVEAL MY PRESENCE TO THE CITIES AND OUR ABILITY TO FLY.

Dang. We don't want that. Though, they already know dragons exist, and they are probably in this city because they detected your mother. So, would it really be revealing our presence? If we can take the ship down, gather more intelligence, and find out who these people are, it might be worth the risk.

I DO NOT DISAGREE WITH YOUR LOGIC. ADDITIONALLY, WE WILL DISAPPEAR SOON FOR MANY DAYS OR WEEKS TO FIND MY FAMILY AND IT WOULD ALLOW US TO EVADE FURTHER SCRUTINY.

Jared darted his gaze to the ship, looking for any cameras, view ports, or panels that might hide scanning abilities. While Jared worked on a plan of attack, a few more people came running from the city. Without warning, another phase round sizzled through the air, and an anguished cry echoed off the buildings.

Screw it. Let's go, Scarlet! Fly high into the air. We'll drop on this thing from directly above. I'm taking a gamble that they don't have any scanning abilities for directly above themselves. All the pictures I've seen of aircraft have the cameras mounted underneath. Even if they are in constant communication with their city, if they can't see what's attacking them, we can hopefully avoid them learning more information.

Scarlet jumped into the air and rapidly climbed into the sky. She flew high enough she'd merely appear as a speck to someone's naked eye. Once satisfied she was high enough, she nose-dived right on top of the ship. They landed with a jarring impact, and the ship immediately sank.

It fired its thrusters and sped away.

With her razor-sharp claws, Scarlet clamped down around the

ship and flared her wings, slowing the ship down.

Jared jumped from her back and landed with a metallic thump on top of the ship. He located a hatch and crawled over to it, clinging for dear life, as the ship bucked and tried to break free.

Scarlet's claws sunk into the metal, tearing large gashes and making her scramble to maintain her grip.

JARED, MY CLAWS ARE RIPPING RIGHT THROUGH THIS THING. WHATEVER YOU WANT TO DO, DO IT FAST.

Panicking, Jared grunted as he ripped open the hatch on top of the ship. A piercing shriek of rending metal punctuated the roar of the engines as the hatch peeled away. Saying a quick prayer, Jared dropped into the ship, pistol in hand.

He landed in a crouch and brought the phase pistol up, ready to defend himself against any assailants inside. Except nothing happened. Confused, nerves on edge, Jared was flabbergasted.

Scarlet, there's no one in here.

CAN YOU STOP THE ACCELERATION AT LEAST? THIS SHIP IS ABOUT TO BREAK FREE, AND I WILL NOT BE ABLE TO KEEP UP AT FULL SPEED.

Everything inside the ship was alien to him. It might as well have been from outer space. He saw translucent panels and screens all over the interior. Dozens of lights blinked around the space and images from below flitted across the forward display. In front of him, a humanoid machine sat in a chair adjusting dials and controls on a console.

It's driving the ship?

Jared creeped over to the machine, aligned the pistol to its head, and pulled the trigger. Just before he fired, its head swiveled in his direction, and he saw a glowing mechanical eye pulse before the head exploded in a shower of sparks.

The instant its head exploded the ship came to an abrupt halt, throwing Jared against the front viewing screen. One display cracked, and a stab of pain pierced his skull as his head rebounded against the metal bulkhead.

"Ugh, that hurt!" Reaching up to grab his head, it came away slick with blood as stars danced in his eyes.

Jared, are you okay?

Yes, I'm fine. The sudden stop threw me against the wall, but I'll manage.

The ship is hovering in place, just outside the city. I think we are far enough from the city and the people down there. They will not reach us before we can leave.

Good! I'll see if I can figure out how to land this thing.

Land? Why would you do that?

I want to give it to the people that tried to capture it.

What? Why?

You heard me. I want to give it to them. Well, not directly. We'll bring it down, and they can come out here to get it.

Jared, why would you give them technology like this?

I want to see if they even know how to use it, and if they are Daggers, then perhaps it will protect innocents if they still plan to hijack a ship at one of the colonies down south. As Jared spoke, more ideas came to mind. He voiced them, making them up as he went, but feeling more confident in his decision.

Also, I'd like to see what the response is from the cities and the Daggers. Will the city send out a rescue party? Will the Daggers attack the cities, or use it steal from more people?

Oh, that's—

I know, I know. It's not like me, but if these people are Daggers, then I won't be super disappointed if they don't survive the attempt. If they can test the defenses and response time of the cities, it'll give us valuable information to fight back. I've thought about scouting the cities a few times, and I don't think we're going to get a better opportunity than this.

I LIKE THAT PLAN.

Jared smiled at Scarlet's response, not revealing that he'd pulled some of those justifications out of thin air. Still, he was impressed with himself for improvising on the fly. Although, it did make him pause.

Is this because of my increased Intelligence perhaps?

Jared had no way to gauge small effects like that, but it was an intriguing prospect and one he'd keep in mind from now on. Setting his ego aside, he examined the ship.

It was a small area, with the one chair in front of the console where he'd killed the machine. Dozens of compartments and hatches decorated the walls, and Jared darted over to them, ripping them open and stripping out the contents.

He found boosters, a couple of phase pistols, several cases of phase ammunition, medical supplies, and a few changes of something that looked like a uniform. In several of the larger compartments he found minerals and metals similar to what they'd harvested back in his home colony. What the cities used the raw materials for, he didn't know, but judging by the full compartments, it appeared this ship had been out collecting them.

Stuffing all the items he could in his pack and satchel, including the uniforms, Jared had to leave the medical supplies. They had enough already, so it wasn't a huge loss, but he couldn't bring himself to leave any of the other items behind. After scavenging all he could, Jared crossed over to the console to bring the ship down. The humanoid robot sat in front of a console with hundreds of buttons and a half dozen levers, several of which had arrows next to them.

Easing the left lever forward, he felt a slight pressure that made him scoot backward a few inches.

Forward, check.

The lever next to it had arrows in the same direction and when pressing the stick forward, the ship dropped a few meters, and his stomach climbed into his chest.

Jared!

Yep, got it, Jared said wryly. Slower this time, he eased forward on the lever, and the ship descended to the ground. He could see the earth rise to meet them in the screen, and the ship thumped into the terrain. There was probably a button to extend some landing gear, but he didn't want to spend the time to find out.

Not wasting time, Jared spun on his heel and rocketed down the ramp. Scarlet was already waiting for him, and he jumped on her back before she launched into the sky. They gained altitude quickly and disappeared into the distance.

Let's put some distance between us and the ship. Stay close enough so we can watch with Magnified Vision, but far enough not to attract attention from them or any response from the cities.

It took a while for the people to reach the ship, and they cautiously approached, guns at the ready. When nothing happened, three of the five tentatively walked inside. Without warning, the ship suddenly launched straight up, and the ramp closed with a hiss. The two guys on the ground gestured manically, but the roar of the thrusters kicking in drowned them out. A moment later, a head popped out of the hatch he'd used, and they gestured to the men below.

Jared didn't know what they said, but it seemed like the ship had a mind of its own as it shot forward.

Suddenly, the ship dipped, and the man standing in the hatch popped out and fell into nothingness. He plummeted to the ground where he landed in a broken heap. Jared felt a pang of remorse for these people and wished they wouldn't have attacked the ship.

Scarlet.

I KNOW. EVEN I FEEL PITY FOR THEM. THEY HAD NO CHANCE AGAINST THAT THING.

Can you follow that ship? I know it's faster than us, but it doesn't appear to be at full speed.

I WILL TRY.

If it looks like any other ships are coming, let's make a beeline for the ground and find some cover. Once we've gathered some intelligence, we'll return here and go find your family. I think this chance to scout is too important to pass up.

AGREED. WE MAY LEARN CRITICAL INFORMATION ABOUT THE CITIES, HOW THEY RESPOND, AND HOW TO COMBAT THEM.

Scarlet answered him by shooting forward after the ship, which she managed to keep in sight. Jared was curious if the ship had some sort of autopilot, or if someone was controlling it remotely. Either way, he was thankful it wasn't going at full speed or they'd never keep up. Even now, they must be flying just shy of two hundred miles an hour.

They flew away from New York City out over the ocean. The sight no longer sent revulsion or fear through him like it used to. He knew there were creatures of all sorts in its depths, but he also knew deep beneath the surface rested some of the most majestic beings to roam the earth.

Someday, he hoped to meet Scarlet's extended family, the water dragons. First, they'd find her fire brothers and then look for the rest.

The ship flew for an hour before a dot in the sky announced its destination. The city grew larger, and towering spires came into focus.

Wow.

JARED, THIS—HOW CAN WE HOPE TO GO AGAINST THAT?

Because we must. Let's learn what we can and leave this place. We have much growing to do before we attempt a coup.

Sweeping arcs and terraces punctuated by massive towers that rose in a staccato of steel and glass throughout the city. It glimmered even from this distance.

Scarlet, fly higher. I don't want to take any chances of them seeing us. If they have scanners, no doubt they already know something's here, but hopefully they'll discount us as a harmless creature.

They kept pace with the ship, close enough Jared could watch with his enhanced vision, but far enough they'd show up as merely a spec in the sky. The closer they flew to the city; the more impressed Jared became. Not only were the buildings magnificent, the floating island looked like paradise. Trees, green grass, and flowers covered every open area.

Scarlet, it's—

BEAUTIFUL.

How could they do this to the rest of the world when they have all this?

Scarlet didn't answer, and he didn't expect one. Neither of them had any idea why they'd keep these advancements from the rest of the world. He saw no people, but that didn't surprise him with the massive scale of this floating metropolis.

The ship approached the floating city and swiveled around so the ramp pointed at the city. Lined up to greet the ship, a row of humanoid machines held phase rifles. They looked like the same thing he'd killed inside the ship, and once again, he saw no humans present. The ramp touched down and the two remaining people tumbled out of the ship, standing face to face with the robots.

They immediately dropped their weapons and held up their hands, but a split second later the robots opened fire with deadly precision. A few wisps of clothing and cloud of red mist was all that remained of the two stowaways.

Scarlet.

Yes.

They'd surrendered, but the lifeless machines didn't care. They dispassionately eradicated them. A pit opened in Jared's stomach, and his desire to bring these people to heel re-doubled. Blatant disregard for human life. It sickened him. Jared's thoughts were in disarray, and he couldn't believe what he'd just witnessed. Any ideals he held about keeping some of these people alive dissolved.

His desire to see justice served, pressed upon him an urgency to build their army as fast as they could, beginning with the dragons.

Let's get out of here and go find your family.

26 A DRAGON'S QUEST

After watching the people on board the hijacked ship become nothing more than a cloud of blood and bits of bone, Jared and Scarlet had a single-minded focus. They'd find Scarlet's family, help others become bonded, and increase their strength. These three tenets drove them forward in their quest to become harbingers of justice.

Harbingers. Maybe that's what we should call ourselves? Jared thought. *Too melodramatic.*

He bounced other ideas around like Justicar, Enforcer, or Avenger, but these words all sounded pompous when he formed the words in his head.

What are we trying to do here? What's our purpose?

The questions echoed in his mind. He wanted to bring justice to the masses that'd become nothing more than slaves. He wanted to bring justice to those that died because of false information, and the cities not lifting a finger to help. Those that lived in the cities deserved to experience what it was like to live on the surface. On the other hand, the second part of his vow was to bring about a new age of dragons, protecting and strengthening them.

Freedom?

Law and order?

Maybe Freedom Fighters? Agents of Freedom? Freedom Seekers? Protectors?

Protectors. The name struck chord in his heart and resonated with everything he wanted.

"Hey Scarlet, what do you think about the word *Protectors*?" Jared asked, emphasizing the word.

FOR WHAT?

"I've been thinking about what we should call ourselves. You know, like an official group name that represents our goals."

Scarlet didn't answer for a time. No doubt she was going through the same process. Only, she came back with a response much faster than him.

I LIKE IT. IT FITS WHAT WE ARE TRYING TO DO, BUT IT ALSO SIGNIFIES THAT WE WILL FIGHT TO ACHIEVE OUR GOALS.

"Protectors it is!" Jared whooped, liking the way it sounded.

The moment New York City came into view, Scarlet banked, heading away from it yet again.

Scarlet?

THIS IS CLOSE ENOUGH. NO NEED TO DRAW YET MORE ATTENTION TO OURSELVES.

Fair enough.

SECURE YOURSELF.

Once again, Jared found himself hanging on for dear life as they rocketed through the sky.

IT MAY TAKE US SEVERAL HOURS TO REACH THE PLACE MY MOTHER EMERGED FROM. ONCE WE FIND THE TUNNEL, IT IS A VERY LONG WAY INTO THE HEART OF THE EARTH TO REACH

THEM. YOU WILL NEED TO STAY BEHIND WHEN THE TEMPERATURES INCREASE.

I'll go as far as I can with you. I'd very much like to join you the whole way, but I understand.

Jared wasn't sure how hot the earth's core was, but he knew it would be much more than he could handle.

THE DEN WHERE MY BROTHERS LIVE IS AT LEAST FOUR THOUSAND DEGREES, AND THE TEMPERATURE INCREASES AT VARYING STAGES ALONG THE WAY.

Wow, okay. Yeah, that's not going to happen. I wonder how much I can withstand?

I DOUBT MORE THAN TWO HUNDRED DEGREES. YOUR NATURAL ARMOR SHOULD PROTECT YOU FROM A LOT, BUT YOU DO NOT WANT TO RISK YOUR NANITES FAILING, BECAUSE IF THEY RUN OUT OF ENERGY YOU WOULD BURN UP IN AN INSTANT.

If you can endure those temperatures, do you think you'd withstand a phase round? I mean, if you can handle the heat of the earth's core—

I KNOW NOTHING ABOUT THE TECHNOLOGY USED. NOR DO I KNOW HOW HOT THE PHASE MATTER BECOMES. IT MAY CONTAIN MORE THAN SUPERHEATED MATTER. I AM NOT ABOUT TO TEST THE THEORY, IF THAT IS YOUR DESIRE.

Don't worry, I won't shoot you. It was just an idle curiosity. If you didn't have to worry about phase weapons, we might take out a lot of the defense in the city before they realize you're impervious to their weapons. I'm sure they have ballistic weapons, but based on what we saw in the city, it looks like their primary weapons are phase types.

WE SHOULD TEST IT OUT, Scarlet said thoughtfully.

No, I meant it. I won't shoot you. If you're impervious to the weapons, great, but we'll operate under the assumption you're not. Also, they might have much more advanced weapons than phase rifles and cannons. I can't imagine the cities giving any current technology to those of us down here like they do with the phase pistols.

WE COULD TRY EXPERIMENTING SOME. I KNOW HOW HOT MY FIRE BREATH IS. WE CAN COMPARE ITS EFFECTS VERSUS THE PHASE ROUNDS. IT WILL GIVE US A BASELINE TO WORK WITH.

That could work. Definitely something for us to think about before we mount an assault. We already took quite a risk earlier today attacking that ship, and it's possible we tipped our hand, but I think it was worth the effort and risk getting the intel we did.

I AGREE, BUT THEY ALREADY KNOW WE EXIST BECAUSE OF RAZAEL. IT'S PLAUSIBLE THEY DO NOT REALIZE THERE ARE DIFFERENT DRAGONS OR THERE ARE MORE OF US. EITHER WAY, I THINK WE LEARNED VALUABLE INSIGHTS TODAY.

With nothing further to discuss on the topic, Jared turned his thoughts inward, exercising his mind. Already, over the past few weeks, he'd been able to improve his mental abilities a lot, frequently splitting his thoughts into multiple threads. He could eavesdrop on telepathic communications from several hundred feet, enter a meditative state at will, and split his thoughts into four threads simultaneously. Unfortunately, he couldn't maintain that level of thinking without entering the meditative state, but he was getting closer.

Scarlet, can you help me with my mental abilities while you fly? I'm assuming you can split your thoughts sufficiently for me to share a space with you?

I CAN, BUT MAKE SURE YOU HOLD TIGHT.

Jared's mind exploded into action. No matter how many times they did this, it amazed him. Scarlet's ability to split her thoughts in so many directions at once overwhelmed him. Several weeks of practice, and he still couldn't maintain this state for long. Each time they finished a session, his mind felt numb.

While Jared spent time in the shared space, he often had trouble separating Scarlet's thoughts from his own as they blurred together. It was extremely disorienting since some things Scarlet did completely instinctually.

If he followed her thought process for flying, it baffled him how she could do it with almost no effort. She had to balance her body's weight, her breathing, and maintain enough velocity to take advantage of thermal waves. Each beat of her wings required the perfect amount of exertion and balance.

It showcased the complex nature of her mind and the ability to effortlessly perform tasks that required his undivided attention. Thirty minutes later, Jared disengaged from their shared thought space, his mind spiraling with the information overload. He feared falling from Scarlet's back if he kept it up any longer.

A by-product of the constant training and sessions with Scarlet was that he could think much faster than before. It wasn't quite like *Hyper-Cognition*, but he could rapidly switch between different thoughts without activating the ability or entering a meditative state. It was a slow, but gradual process of building the *Mind*.

Throughout the flight, Jared managed three separate sessions with Scarlet in decreasing intervals. The last session lasted only five minutes. He'd hit his limit for now, every nerve in his head screaming in protest.

WE ARE HERE.

Jared looked down, confused.

"I don't see—oh, yeah, I think we found the right place."

Within the bottom of a dried-up reservoir, a large blackened patch of ground surrounded the tunnel leading into the earth. Jared looked around the area, trying to gauge where they were on a map.

When it clicked into place, he laughed out loud, startling Scarlet.

JARED?

"Scarlet, do you have any idea what this area is called?"

I DO NOT.

"This is Lake Eerie! Even to this day, the legend of Bessie persists. I loved dinosaurs growing up and was always fascinated by folklore about sightings of them. It's rumored that a giant serpent lives in Lake Eerie. A serpent that often looks like a dinosaur—or dragon, from the few who say they've seen it. Surely, this can't be a coincidence that your family burrowed just a couple miles from the lake."

I DO NOT KNOW, BUT WE DISAPPEARED FROM THE EARTH FOR THOUSANDS OF YEARS. HOW THEN COULD SIGHTINGS OCCUR?

"I've no idea. I'm just telling you the rumors I've heard. There're other such instances like Nessie, the Loch Ness Monster in Scotland. There were few sightings over the years, but enough that there's some truth to them. Even today, ninety-five percent of the oceans and lakes of the world remain unexplored, so there's a definite possibility for creatures of legend to exist."

I SUPPOSE IT IS POSSIBLE ONE OF THE WATER DRAGONS TOOK UP RESIDENCE IN THE LAKE. THE LAKE IS LARGE ENOUGH IT COULD STAY HIDDEN, AND THERE ARE SO MANY OTHERS NEARBY IT COULD HIDE IN AS WELL.

"I'm not saying it's factual, but now that I know dragons exist and still roam the oceans, I'm not so sure it's a myth anymore."

WE CAN FIND OUT LATER. IT IS ONLY TWO HUNDRED MILES FROM OUR MAKESHIFT HOME FROM HERE AND DOES NOT TAKE LONG TO FLY.

"Let's table that discussion for now and focus on finding your brothers," Jared said, looking back at the scarred, gaping hole in the ground. "How long did it take her to reach the surface? If she had to re-create the tunnels like we see here, I imagine it took a long time."

I— Scarlet said but cut herself off. A few moments later, she responded. She took several weeks to get out.

"Several weeks? How far is this journey? We told everyone we'd be gone a few weeks at most."

Our journey will progress much faster. She had a lot of clearing to do.

Looking into the massive tunnel, Jared began to sweat, his palms becoming clammy as claustrophobia surfaced. Weeks in a cave system didn't sound the least bit appealing. Nor did he want to encounter more hordes of creatures down there. They'd already faced a giant worm in a similar underground tunnel system, and if they encounter something like it here, then it would be a long and trying journey.

"Let's rest for the night, and I'll assign the rest of my nanites. Changes should finish by morning since we still have a solid part of the day left. I was thinking about where to put them on the flight over here, and I've decided Natural Armor is a good choice. I need more physical protection anyway, and if it helps me endure the heat better down there, then it'll be a good investment."

Investing that many nanites into the ability may allow you to shrug off gunfire and phase rounds. It might not completely protect you, and will not last indefinitely, but they at least would cause less damage.

"That would be pretty sweet. If I can shrug off a few hits, we can stand a better chance of attacking the cities, especially if they have any automated defenses in place."

His decision made, Jared pushed his remaining thirty-one percent into *Natural Armor*.

I WILL KEEP WATCH UNTIL YOUR CHANGES FINISH.

"Thanks, Scarlet."

Jared fell asleep against Scarlet's side, sleep claiming him immediately. The more he gained control over his mind, the easier it was for him to quiet it, resulting in near instantaneous sleep.

Jared woke a short time later and patted Scarlet on the side.

"Your turn, girl."

Scarlet blinked at him in confusion. ALREADY?

"How long was I out?"

THREE HOURS.

Jared mimicked Scarlet's confusion, but then remembered how *Natural Armor* worked.

"Wait, you assigned these names to the nanites? You should know how they work, then."

I... Scarlet started to protest, but then paused, her eyes widening. OH, I SEE. I SHOULD HAVE SPENT MORE TIME EXAMINING THE CODE. I UNDERSTOOD THEIR FUNCTION, BUT NOT HOW THEY WORKED, ASSUMING THEY INTEGRATED WITH YOUR SKIN TO PROJECT A TYPE OF NATURAL BARRIER. I DID NOT REALIZE THEY SIMPLY PROJECT A BARRIER OF NANITES. IT MAKES INTEGRATION UNNECESSARY. INTRIGUING.

"So, what you're actually saying is...you were wrong?" Jared smirked, earning him a playful shove from Scarlet. "I'll forgive you just this once, but next time—" Jared mimed giving her the smackdown with fist in palm. Smiling broadly at Scarlet's expense, he said, "I think you had the right idea about the ability from the start, and I've used it as such this whole time anyway. It still consumes my own energy when used by creating a barrier around my body."

I SUPPOSE IT DOES NOT MATTER AFTER ALL. YET I AM
DISAPPOINTED IN MYSELF FOR NOT SEEING IT SOONER.

"Don't sweat it. Do you need to rest before we head in?"

I DO NOT WANT TO, BUT I WILL SLEEP FOR A SHORT TIME.

"Good plan. Sleep well."

Scarlet's breathing immediately deepened, and Jared stood. Stretching, he walked about the area for a while to get his blood flowing. While he explored, he sent his focus inward to examine the changes wrought in his body. While nothing had changed physically, he felt an extra density surrounding him. It was a strange sensation. The increased number of nanites became a part of his outer layer of skin, but at the same time were separate. The added layers felt tangible. If he pressed down with a finger, he encountered an invisible barrier that rebounded at his touch.

Picking up a sharp rock from the ground, he tested the edge on his forearm. To his eye, the edge looked sharp enough to cut his skin if applied hard enough, but when he tested the rock, it was dull.

Curiosity got the better of him as he pulled out his knife. The last time he'd done this, Scarlet woke to find him about to shove a pipe through his arm. Quickly glancing back at Scarlet, he made sure she was sleeping so she couldn't make fun of him if his tests failed.

Again, he tested the edge of the knife, and although he could feel the sharpness and the metal edge, it didn't slice into his flesh when he ran his thumb along the edge. Pressing the point into the palm of his hand, he felt only the pressure of the point, but it failed to pierce his skin, nor did it hurt.

With slow, deliberate motions, he steadily increased the pressure until he needed to place his hand on the floor and put his weight into it. The pressure felt uncomfortable, but the point still failed to penetrate his skin.

"Wow," Jared murmured to himself. His *Skin Hardening* combined with the *Natural Armor* created a solid barrier to prevent damage to his body.

"Oh crap."

Jared thought about booster's and the need to inject the nanites and wondered how it would work if he couldn't stab into his skin. Opening his pack, Jared grabbed one of the boosters he'd stolen from the drop ship and plunged the needle down.

"Ow! Yep, that works still." Curious, Jared pulled the needle out of his arm and brought I closer to his skin. Before it made contact, Jared examined the area in his mind. It was as if the nanites in his *Natural Armor* sensed those in the booster. They parted ever so slightly to allow the needle to penetrate his flesh.

Jared sighed in relief. At least he was still able to use them in the event Scarlet didn't figure out how to isolate the code and prevent corruption. It was really the only needle he cared about since his nanites took care of any other infections or sickness.

I wonder if it has the same effect on ballistic pressure or something traveling at high velocity? wondered Jared.

A bullet created a spinning vortex that might rip through the protective barrier, and a phase round might burn through.

Okay, one more test.

Jared felt uneasy about this one, but he reasoned that he'd recover from it quickly should the barrier fail. Placing his hand against a rock, he raised the knife above his head, sucked in a breath, and plunged the knife down.

JARED!

The mental shout broke his concentration, and the knife clanged harmlessly off the rock, raising a shower of sparks.

WHAT ARE YOU DOING?

Alarm warred through Scarlet's words, and Jared looked at her sheepishly, a blush creeping up his cheeks.

"Well, you see, I was testing my new enhancement."

BY STABBING YOURSELF?

"No, I—It's not the *first* thing I did." The words died on his lips as he realized what he'd said.

Scarlet chortled with that annoying huffing sound as she stood.

"Um, shouldn't you rest more?"

AND LET YOU STAB YOURSELF AGAIN?

Jared looked away from her and sheathed his knife.

NO, I AM RESTED WELL ENOUGH AND EAGER TO START OUR JOURNEY.

Jumping on the opportunity to change the topic, Jared started for the tunnel's mouth. "I'll take point. It'll be difficult for you to move around in there."

I HAVE DRAGON'S BREATH.

"Okay, you win."

BESIDES, YOU MIGHT DECIDE TO IMPALE YOURSELF AGAIN, AND I DO NOT NEED TO SEE THAT.

Scarlet didn't give Jared even a moment to respond as she climbed into the hole followed by his sputtering excuses. Sighing, Jared knew he wouldn't live that one down for a while and climbed into the hole after her.

Heat Sight or Night Vision? While *Night Vision* made it easier to see his surroundings, it was a boring color, and it'd be much harder to use the further they went because there'd be no ambient lighting. He decided to start with *Night Vision* and move to *Heat Sight* at random intervals to scan his surroundings.

"I'll need help climbing back out of here," Jared said as he slid down the precarious slope. The texture was smooth as glass, and only the deep furrows made by Scarlet's claws allowed him to gain any purchase on it at all.

IT IS NOT ALL THIS STEEP OR SMOOTH. SOON IT LEVELS OUT AND BECOMES A MORE GRADUAL DESCENT.

Half sliding and scrambling down the tunnel, he stayed close by Scarlet to grab on if he lost his footing and careened down. Jared envied Scarlet and her ability to effortlessly navigate the tunnel. He almost jumped on to her back, but after Scarlet's comment about his misadventures, his pride required he attempt it on his own.

Thankfully, Scarlet was right, and the tunnel opened into a natural underground passage a few minutes later. In his mind, he'd thought the tunnel would be just large enough to accommodate her mother with her wings folded to her side, but this space could accommodate two of Scarlet's mother side by side.

"This is incredible. How far does this cavern go?"

IT CONTINUES FOR HUNDREDS OF MILES, BUT WINDS BACK AND FORTH IN A SERIES OF CONNECTED TUNNELS. THERE ARE ALSO SECTIONS WHERE THE ROOMS COLLAPSED AND ONLY A TUNNEL REMAINS WHERE MY MOTHER BURNED THROUGH IT.

"Do you have any idea how far beneath the surface we are?" They'd descended at a quick pace for an hour but given the slip and slide nature of the tunnel down he had no way to gauge how far they'd gone.

I BELIEVE IT IS AROUND THREE MILES FROM THIS POINT BASED ON THE ANGLE AND SPEED OF OUR DESCENT.

"This is pretty neat. We could almost use this as a bunker if the need arose."

I DO NOT THINK THAT A GREAT IDEA. SOME OF THE CREATURES MY MOTHER ENCOUNTERED ON HER JOURNEY OUT

WERE EXTREMELY DEADLY. IT WAS ONLY DUE TO HER SIZE AND PSIONIC ABILITIES THEY STAYED AWAY.

"Well, I hope we don't encounter any of them."

IF WE DO, I WILL TRY TO EXERT SOME OF MY OWN MENTAL PRESSURE. PERHAPS IF IT IS THE SAME CREATURES FROM A DECADE AGO, THEY WILL REMEMBER AND REMAIN AT A DISTANCE FOR FEAR IT IS MY MOTHER RETURNING.

"I really hope that works. A fight in these tunnels could get ugly."

The minutes blurred into hours and he lost all track of time. The awe he'd had for the underground system and natural caverns quickly fled as everything became monotonous, the scenery never changing. They'd come across two collapsed sections where smooth holes drilled straight through into the next section. So far, they hadn't encountered any creatures or collapsed areas.

"I hope you're keeping track of time down here, because I'm having a tough time with it. My internal clock is all over the place."

IT'S BEEN SIX HOURS SINCE WE ENTERED THE TUNNEL.

"How do you—" Jared's words cut off as he heard a clicking noise. "Did you hear that?"

YES, IT CAME FROM THE LEFT.

Switching to *Heat Sight*, Jared scanned the darkness, but saw nothing. Pulling out his phase pistol, he stalked toward the noise. A few steps later, a faint glow emanated from something hiding behind a stalagmite. Careful not to alert the creature to his approach, Jared skirted around the outside until he could approach from the side. Flipping to *Night Vision*, he saw the faint outline of a creature that resembled the lizards they'd fought before.

I think it's a lizard. But, I don't know why it isn't attacking. The ones in the other tunnel system were feral and attacked immediately.

MAYBE THESE ARE DIFFERENT?

Do you think they're intelligent?

Jared received the equivalent of a mental shrug from Scarlet, and said, *Only one way to find out.*

"Hey! Can you hear me?" The creature dropped to all fours and made a hissing noise.

Yeah, nope, not intelligent. Raising his phase pistol, Jared prepared to squeeze trigger, but Scarlet stopped him.

JARED, WAIT! IF YOU PULL THE TRIGGER ON THAT IN HERE, WE WILL GO BLIND FOR A TIME, AND THERE MIGHT BE MORE OF THESE THINGS WAITING JUST OUT OF SIGHT.

Good point. Jared almost grabbed his Colt but realized the retort would paint a Bullseye on their location for miles.

Unsheathing his knife, Jared readied himself for the lizard. It jumped in the air to pounce on him, and he easily sidestepped, his knife flashing inside the creature's outstretched arm. His enhanced speed let him deliver a precise cut into the lizard's neck as it soared past him. Its head lolled to one side, nearly severed from its body. The forward momentum of the lizard caused all the gore and blood spray to follow its lifeless body and splatter harmlessly against the stalagmites. Flicking the knife at the downed lizard, he cleared the remnants of blood with the edge of his shirt and re-sheathed the knife.

NICELY DONE.

Thanks. It's hard to believe that just a couple months ago, one of these things almost killed me. I was barely stronger, and definitely not faster. Now? That fight took almost no effort and it looked like it moved in slow motion because of my faster cognitive functions.

IF YOU STILL WANT TO REST, WE SHOULD DO SO QUICKLY AND MOVE ON. THE SCENT OF BLOOD MAY ATTRACT OTHERS OF

ITS KIND.

Let's keep going. One was easy, a horde of them—not so much, Jared said while walking around to the corpses absorbing their nanites.

Scarlet agreed, and they resumed their hike through the tunnels. It wasn't long before they heard more scraping and clicking noises behind them.

I think we're about to have company. Let's pick up the pace and see if they give up.

Scarlet moved faster, and Jared had to run to keep up with her, but the creatures clung to their trail.

Looks like they're not giving up.

Jared turned to face the oncoming lizards, counting thirteen in total.

Um, Scarlet. I'll need help on this one. Jared dropped his pack to the ground and fished around for a spare knife. He could deal out plenty of damage with one, but more was always better. This would also give him a chance to split his focus and concentration. Ever looking for ways to improve on his mental abilities, he relished this battle and the chance to test his mettle.

After the creatures closed within fifty feet, Jared darted to the right around an outcropping. It forced the creatures to split down the middle. One half rocketed for Scarlet, while the other half made a beeline for him.

Jared took a calming breath, then leapt forward into the midst of the lizards. They hadn't expected the move, and he caught two off guard. Standing in the middle of half a dozen lizards with sharp claws, teeth, and insane agility, Jared came alive. The thrill of the battle washed through him as he spun his right hand up to puncture the underside of a lizard in mid-leap. At the same time his left hand whipped across the legs of two others, severing them cleanly at the joints.

The next instant, the lizards were behind him, and he spun in place, planting both his daggers into the spine of his trailing assailant.

Three seconds passed, and three lizards lay dead or dying, and two others were missing the use of their legs, leaving only two more to contend with. Ignoring the two maimed lizards, he squared off against the uninjured ones.

The lizards hesitated, whipping their heads around in agitation. Their tongues flicked in and out as they tested the air. The lizard on his right peered at its downed comrades and took a half step back.

Clearly, these lizards showed some level of intelligence and appeared conflicted about attacking. A clicking noise from the creature on the left drew his attention. It looked like they were communicating with each other. In tandem, the two lizards split further apart and dropped into a crouch.

Another round of clicks and they leapt at him together.

Jared vaulted into the air using *Maximum Muscle.* He landed squarely on their backs, driving them into the rock beneath his feet. Dazed from the impact, the creatures gave half-hearted attempts to free themselves from beneath his body. Not wasting any time, Jared dropped the points of his daggers into both their skulls, the life instantly leaving their bodies.

Jared bounded to his feet and quickly located the hamstrung lizards. They were useless. Neither of them could walk, eliminating their only chance at survival or escape: their agility. In no rush, Jared walked over to them, and in two quick motions stabbed each of them through the eye.

Once he'd killed the final lizard, the cavern returned to its tomb-like state of quietness. Jared found Scarlet watching him with a predatory smile on her face and blood dripping from her maw.

Tasty.

She grinned, displaying her sharp canine-like teeth.

Grinning from ear to ear, Jared walked to each of the corpses and absorbed the nanites, careful not to walk through the growing pools of blood around their bodies.

"Now that was fun. Did you see my fight? I know it didn't last long, but I was awesome!"

I caught the tail end of the fight and saw your move where you landed on top. Impressive.

"If all our fights are like that, this could be a fun journey!"

Do not get too cocky. Remember, there are much more frightening things down here than lizards.

"All right, all right. I won't let it go to my head, but man that was a rush. Who knew dual-wielding a couple knives would be so much fun? Being able to think so fast with heightened reflexes, I barely had to expend any effort there."

Scarlet chuckled with her usual huffing noise. This time, it didn't bother him because she was laughing with him, rather than at him.

Absentmindedly, Jared said, "That made me hungry."

Frowning and thinking about what he'd just said, he froze mid-stride.

"Wait, why am I hungry? I've not been hungry in years!"

There is no radiation down here to fuel your nanites.

"Oh, that might be a problem."

27 PERILOUS FIGHT

The realization struck Jared like a hammer blow. If radiation didn't penetrate this far underground, he'd need to find water and food to keep his energy levels up. He eyed the lizards suspiciously, not really wanting to eat them, but it might be the only option for a while.

"Scarlet, can you please roast these for me?" Jared asked hesitantly. "I really don't want to eat them, but I don't want to burn through the limited food I brought with us either. We've no idea how long we'll be down here."

She plodded over, and a stream of fire scorched the flesh from the lizards.

The whoosh of her fire that accompanied the sound of sizzling flesh sent shivers down his spine as teeth, eyes, and claws sloughed off the lizard with a gurgling pop.

"I think I'm going to be sick..." Jared sucked in a breath and turned away from the spectacle before him. The lizards had a slick coat of skin and the fire caused it to shrivel away and flake off, disintegrating to ash.

While he stopped to catch his breath, the acrid scent of roasted lizard reached his nostrils and Jared retched. His stomach clenched and spasmed as his spine tried to claw its way out his opened mouth.

"Holy crap. There's no way I'm eating that!"

SUIT YOURSELF, Scarlet said and ate each lizard in one quick gulp.

The dry heaving resumed as stomach acid and bile foamed on his lips.

"Scarlet. No—no more—lizards." Jared wheezed out between large gulps of air while his stomach performed somersaults.

Without a backward glance, Jared quickly left the carnage behind, putting as much distance between him and the lizards as possible. The rations in his pack would need to last long enough for them to complete their mission unless he found something else to eat besides lizards. He already knew at some point Scarlet would need to continue the journey solo, and he'd be left alone. If he couldn't find some place to hole up in safety and regulate his metabolism, then he was going to run out of food and get very weak by the time Scarlet finished. The thoughts made him question his decision to accompany her along this path.

"Scarlet, maybe I should ride on your back. It'll help me conserve energy, and I can still keep watch behind us."

Scarlet lowered herself to the ground, and he vaulted up to the seat behind her neck.

Jared used the time to work on splitting his active thoughts without entering a meditative trance. He was too afraid of something sneaking up on them while he wasn't paying attention to meditate. However, Scarlet occasionally pulled him into their shared thought space when there were no branching tunnels ahead. It was the best they could manage while remaining alert for danger.

The more they walked, the more Jared felt lost. He couldn't tell where he was in relation to the surface. They had to be dozens of miles underground by this point.

"Scarlet, do you have any idea how long and how fast your mother travelled? I mean, is this even a good idea for us to attempt? How far can I go because of the heat?" Jared questioned, the darkness, and fading adrenaline allowing despair to creep in.

I HAVE VAGUE IMPRESSIONS, BUT IT IS HARD TO DETERMINE. MY MOTHER COULD MOVE MUCH FASTER THAN US, AND THE HEAT HAD NO EFFECT ON HER, BUT SHE ALSO HAD TO STOP FREQUENTLY TO BURN THROUGH THE COLLAPSED SECTIONS. AS FOR THE HEAT, I AM ALMOST CERTAIN YOU WILL NOT BE ABLE TO ENDURE IT PAST THE EARTH'S MANTLE. ONCE I REACH THE OUTER CORE, EVEN I WILL HAVE DIFFICULTY. MY FAMILY IS JUST PAST THE OUTER CORE...

Scarlet's voice trailed off, eliciting warning bells in Jared's head.

"Scarlet? What aren't you telling me? Are you saying this is a one-way trip if you can't find them?"

I WILL FIND THEM, she said with confidence.

"Whoa, hold on just a minute. You wanted to come here knowing you might not be ready, and it could be your end? Scarlet! Why didn't you say something sooner?"

I CAN DO THIS. I MUST DO THIS.

"I understand, but I wish you'd told me sooner. We could've gone on some hunting trips these past weeks to get stronger. Any advantage we can get will help in this."

I BELIEVE WITH THAT LAST SET OF CHANGES, I WILL MANAGE, THOUGH IT WILL BE A NEAR THING.

Jared knew there was no way he'd talk her out of this, so he changed the subject.

"All right, we need to pick up the pace if we want to get out of here and back home in three weeks' time. I don't want to leave the colonists any longer than that. I know they've got Kitty to help if they decide to leave home, but there's plenty of creatures that could make short work of her."

Scarlet immediately quickened her pace, and they moved at a steady gallop down the tunnel.

"Status update, Scarlet?"

I BELIEVE WE HAVE TRAVELED NEARLY ONE HUNDRED MILES. WE ARE TWENTY MILES BELOW THE SURFACE, AND TWENTY-EIGHT HOURS HAVE PASSED SINCE WE ENTERED THE TUNNELS.

"How far is this mantle where I'll need to wait?"

BASED ON MY MOTHER'S MEMORIES, THIS TUNNEL WILL SOON START DESCENDING FASTER, AND AT THAT POINT THE TEMPERATURE RISES PRECIPITOUSLY. EVEN NOW, IT IS AROUND ONE HUNDRED DEGREES.

"All right, let's slow the pace and walk a bit. I'm not in a hurry to be alone in here, let alone send you on a possible one-way trip."

Jared's voice broke at the end, his heart anguishing over the thought of sending her on alone. He could deal with being by himself for a time, but Scarlet's absence was another thing entirely.

JARED. Scarlet stopped to look back at him. I WILL SURVIVE AND BRING MY BROTHERS WITH ME. PLEASE TRUST ME AND HAVE A LITTLE FAITH.

"I do. It's just...I don't want to lose you, Scarlet," Jared managed, laying a hand on her side. "I've lost too much in this life. I couldn't bear to lose you."

I WILL RETURN, I PROMISE.

Scarlet's words did little to dissuade his fears, but at this point there was nothing he could do about it. He hopped off Scarlet's back and walked beside her. Fishing his pack off his back, he grabbed a ration, broke it in half and munched on the hard tack while they walked, trying to push his emotional turmoil away. It wasn't helping either of them to dwell in negativity.

Munching on his meager rations made him realize he'd need water too, but they hadn't seen any standing water in the one hundred miles travelled. However, all of the stalactites and stalagmites were slick to the touch. Curious, Jared walked over to them and tested the water with a finger. It tasted clean and looked pure enough. The stalagmite itself tasted like dirt, but the clean water on his tongue felt amazing. It'd been a while since he had anything that tasted so pure.

The water seeped into his mouth, cooling his parched lips and moistening his dry tongue. The last time he had anything that tasted so pure was before he left his home colony. They had the ability to purify water because of some technology granted to them by the cities. Jared suspected the cities only gave them the equipment because it was part of the mineral harvesting operations which allowed them to collect resources for the cities.

"Sorry, Scarlet. I didn't mean to stop so long. I only wanted to test it, but once I'd tasted the water, I forgot about anything else. I've not tasted anything like this in years."

YOU MUST KEEP UP YOUR STRENGTH. DRINK AS MUCH AS YOU NEED.

"I'm ready to go. I only wanted to see if it was a viable source of water. Otherwise, we'd need to find another soon."

They walked for several more hours before Jared called them to a halt. Although bearable, Jared could tell the heat was getting worse.

"Scarlet, what's the temperature?"

IT IS CLOSE TO ONE HUNDRED FIFTY DEGREES.

"I hate to say this, but it might be best if we part ways here. I may even walk back to the hundred degree area so that *Natural Armor* doesn't pull unnecessary energy from my body."

THAT MIGHT BE BEST. PLUS, I WILL MOVE MUCH FASTER WITHOUT YOU.

"Scarlet." Jared laid a hand on her side. "Promise me you'll be careful? Don't take unnecessary risks. If you can't make it all the way, come back and we will work to get you stronger before we attempt this again."

I CAN DO THIS, JARED. I MUST DO THIS. IT IS MY BIRTHRIGHT, AND I AM WILLING TO SUFFER SOME TO SEE MY FAMILY AGAIN.

The conviction in her voice was palpable, and her strengthened resolve carried through her voice. They held each other's gaze a moment longer before Jared looked away. He didn't want Scarlet to see the tears brimming in his eyes. This meant a lot to Scarlet, and he wanted to be strong for her, but he knew it'd be difficult, and he wished there was something he could do to aide her in the journey. This was truly a trial by fire, and it'd take every ounce of strength she possessed to make it.

Wiping his eyes, Jared set his pack down and pulled out all his rations. "Scarlet, please eat these. I'll enter a hibernation state while you continue onward and won't need to eat anything for a while. I can find a place to hide and barricade myself inside."

Quickly eating the rations, Scarlet turned around and rocketed down the tunnel, her steps fading into the distance. Jared stood for a moment longer, his emotions somersaulting as tears slid unbidden down his face.

Be careful, Scarlet.

I'LL RETURN JARED, I PROMISE!

Scarlet's voice echoed in his head as she disappeared from sight.

Jared gazed after Scarlet and the path she took for a long time before shaking off the feeling of dread and concern for her safety. His thoughts gravitated to despair and hopelessness, no doubt a by-product of his past experiences, but he forced himself to think positively. Scarlet was one of the strongest, if not the strongest, being in the world.

She'll be fine, Jared repeated to himself, cementing it in his mind. Now he needed to find some place to hole up for the coming days.

A few hours of searching revealed a formation of stalactites and stalagmites that formed a lattice of crisscrossing spikes suited to his purposes. Careful not to break anything, Jared slid his gear inside and wormed his way in after.

Secure, he found a comfortable spot and broke off sections of the formations with his knife. Choosing parts of the stalactites that didn't conceal him from view, he used the broken bits to stuff into the gap he'd used to access the hideaway.

Confident that he'd picked a good spot, Jared practiced his meditation and mental abilities. With nothing else to do, he spent the next several days working to split his consciousness. By the end of day three, he could hold six separate threads in his active consciousness. It was a huge accomplishment, but he was also sitting in a meditative trance and doubted he'd be able to do anything like that while engaged in a battle, or some other task that required a higher level of concentration.

Eight days after Scarlet departed, Jared felt the effects of no food, and while he had water dripping from the stalactites, it wasn't enough to sustain him. It was time for him to activate Aestivation to lower his body temperature, slow his heart rate, and conserve energy. While preparing himself to hibernate, he re-arranged himself into a half laying position, shifting bits of debris around himself.

He stopped moving, but the sound of small pieces of rubble shifting continued. Confused, Jared rotated his read, careful not to move his body and mask the sounds. The web of earthly spikes obscured most of his view, but after flipping to *Heat Sight* he saw several creatures milling about the cavern he'd staked as his own. Slowing his breathing, Jared did his best to remain inconspicuous, but it was too late. At least three creatures encircled his location, and Jared realized he'd need to take care of them.

Slowly, Jared removed piece after piece from his makeshift door and gripped the hilt of his knife. The gap cleared, he raised himself into a crouch and lunged though the opening, spinning into a somersault, so that he faced his stalkers. No obstructions in front of him, Jared realized it was a small group of lizards, only these ones were different than any he'd previously encountered.

Those he'd encountered thus far were silver with red heads and necks. These lizards were primarily green, with a smattering of yellow splotches across their body. These creatures also had five to six-foot-long tails with rows of short spikes along their length.

Jared spun into action, taking the closest lizard to him. These were much faster than their red metallic cousins and he narrowly avoided a swipe of its spiked tail. Jumping the tail swipe, Jared lashed out at the creature's lunging neck, severing it cleanly in two.

The fight only lasted an instant, but already the other two

lizards managed to circle him, closing from opposing sides. The lizards gave him no time to gain his footing. They lunged while he was still spinning from killing the previous attacker.

Jared threw himself backward, avoiding another tail swipe only for the third to slice into his calf.

Jared yelled in pain, performing a backward somersault to come up facing them. This fight didn't go as smooth as his past encounter, and it was everything he could do just to avoid their attacks. Jumping over the head of one, Jared landed between them, but his leg gave out, and he fell to one side.

The unexpected stumble was the only thing that saved him as the lizard he'd jumped over spun with its claws outstretched and slashed the air he'd just occupied. Using the opportunity of the lizard over-extending itself, Jared plunged his knives into its knee joints and rolled out of the way as another tail slash smashed into the ground.

One of the lizards temporarily out of the fight, Jared backpedaled to give him some room to face his remaining opponent. It raced after him, sensing the weakness in his leg. Jared pushed through the line of fire shooting up his leg and stepped into the attacking lizard. He knocked it off balance, catching its bite on one of his blades. Using his free hand, he slammed the knife into its chest three times, riding the creature to the ground. It lay unmoving, and Jared panted from the exertion.

Hobbling over to the handicapped lizard, Jared drove the daggers into its eyes to end the fight. He slumped against a cluster of stalagmites and rolled his pant leg up. An angry red cut showed where the lizard's tail had pierced his flesh. It was a very shallow cut, but it pulsed in tune with his racing heart and looked infected. His improved *Natural Armor* had prevented a more serious injury, but he didn't know why it hurt so badly.

Jared crawled to the dead lizards, using the opportunity to both absorb the nanites and inspect the tail. A thick orange fluid coated the lizard's body and spikes. The same color as the remnants around the cut on his leg.

Poison, thought Jared.

His nanites should take care of it, but in the meantime, it was painful, and he hoped his attackers didn't have more of their kind nearby.

Picking up his gear, Jared limped up the tunnel. The dead carcasses would draw attention from other creatures, and he didn't want to be around when that happened, especially with an injury that prevented mobility.

Another hour of searching, Jared found another natural formation he used as a barricade. This one wasn't fully enclosed, but he needed to rest and recover. As best he could, Jared broke sections of rock off to pile around him, going so far as to break off a few longer stalactites to lay over top of him, concealing him from above.

Going back to his previous plans, Jared activated *Aestivation*. When he activated the ability, nothing happened immediately, but his body became sluggish and his eyes heavy. Slowly, his body relaxed into the depression he'd settled into and his breathing slowed down.

Time passed incredibly quickly in this state, and several days passed in swift succession. If not for a scraping sound that increased in volume, he could've easily maintained that state until Scarlet returned.

Jared activated *Hyper-Cognition*, and his reality returned to normal, if not slightly slower.

The scraping sound that drew him from his hibernation grew ever closer. Jared listened for a time, trying to decide if he should cancel the ability and return his body to a waking state. If these creatures found his hiding place, he was completely and utterly defenseless.

Deciding it was much too risky to remain in hibernation, Jared canceled the ability. Slowly his body returned to normal, and he massaged his limbs to get his blood circulating. Shortly after his body returned to normal, he felt a hollow pang in his gut signaling the need to eat. His lips and tongue were parched, and he worked his jaw to return moisture to them.

Whatever it was that woke him sounded right on top of him. Jared didn't dare to breathe, or he'd give himself away.

He needn't have worried about the creature finding him since a moment later, a stalactite shattered as a cylindrical form penetrated the small space.

"What the—" Jared yelled.

He kicked away the debris piled on top of himself, grabbed his pack, and launched himself several yards away. He hit the ground in a roll and came up on his feet, running in the opposite direction. Glancing behind him, Jared saw half a dozen strange, wriggling cylinders covered in rocks.

Worms? Jared wondered.

He whipped his phase pistol out and fired a found at the creature. The energy beam hit the rock, fizzled, and died leaving nary a scorch mark on it.

"Crap."

Holstering the phase pistol, he brought out his trusted Colt and fired a round at the lead worm. A large chunk blew off, and the worm thrashed around, knocking a couple others out of the way. When it thrashed, Jared saw a round maw ringed by several rows of razor-sharp teeth. An image of the large Godzilla worm flashed in his mind as he evaded the living rocks.

Firing a second shot into its open mouth, the worm exploded outward in a spray of rock and chunks of white flesh. He dove behind an outcropping as the pieces of rock smacked into the boulder he hid behind. Stepping from cover, he fired two more rounds into the advancing worms and blew another one apart when it reared back.

Well, at least they're not smart.

Standing his ground, Jared fired two more rounds before his Colt ran out of ammo. Jared flipped open his pack, grabbed a box of ammo and then sprinted to the other side of the tunnel. He flicked his revolver to the side, ejecting the cylinder. With practiced hands he dropped the spent shells into his open palm, pocketed them, and rapidly reloaded the bullets.

Flicking his wrist in the opposite direction, the cylinder slid into place, and he spun it until the chamber locked into place. Feeling more confident about his situation and the ease with which he'd dispatched the first few worms, Jared rapidly destroyed the remaining rock worms with well-placed shots. The echoing explosions from his revolver functioned as a homing beacon for any creatures in the vicinity. Jared did not want to be around when they arrived. Quickly walking over to the destroyed worms, Jared absorbed the nanites, grabbed several chunks of the meat and sprinted up the tunnel.

Ten minutes later he slowed to a trot, then walk, and finally needed to sit down. The deficit of nutrients sapped his energy reserves, and his throat burned from lack of moisture.

Eyeing the chunks of white meat suspiciously, Jared cut a small piece from it and popped it into his mouth. It had a tough, sinewy consistency. The only saving grace of this experiment was the complete lack of smell. If it'd smelled anything like the massive worm they'd killed before, there's no way he'd even think of trying a raw piece of flesh.

But, here he was chewing through the membrane-textured flesh. Thankfully, it had no flavor or weird juices.

Jared chewed the piece thoughtfully. Hopefully there were no side effects from eating the meat raw, but at least now he wouldn't go hungry, and he'd recover enough strength to hold out for Scarlet.

He didn't know if entering hibernation again was the best course of action, especially considering these things zeroed in on him with no hesitation. He didn't know how they'd found him, but if they did, then it stood to reason that other denizens of the underground could too.

Turning the options over in his mind, Jared chose to stay awake. He had food, so there was no reason for him to conserve his strength. The only concern he had now being the possibility of attracting other creatures with the dead worms and the noise he'd made shooting his Colt.

Again, Jared found himself walking back up the tunnel looking for a place to wait for Scarlet. He settled into an alcove half a mile from the battle, pulled out his pistols, and settled in to wait. He planned to be ready for any further encounters.

He passed the time working on his mental abilities, but quickly grew bored after days on end with nothing to do, nothing to see, no one to talk to, and his food ran low.

Shortly after his battle with the worms, he'd heard noises down the tunnel and suspected creatures were eating his kills, though, they didn't travel in his direction. Part of him wished for another encounter just to pass the time, but when he though back to the poison that ate at his leg for an entire day, he checked those thoughts and went back to his mental exercises.

He was in the middle of splitting his fourth active thought when he heard a soft scraping noise up the tunnel. Admonishing himself for letting the distraction screw with him, he split the threads again and let one portion of his mind focus on what distracted at him. Assuming it was more worms, Jared would focus on maintaining the active threads while confronting them. He needed to practice, and these worms presented a great opportunity because they weren't all that fast or intelligent.

Jared decided to confront whatever was in the tunnel instead of letting them creep up and surprise him again. What he saw made his blood run cold. Jared turned into a statue, not daring to move a muscle. Not daring to breathe.

"Oh, Scarlet, please hurry," pleaded Jared.

A veritable army of lizards stalked toward him. They crowded the tunnel, climbed the walls, and clung to the ceiling.

Slowly, so as not to attract a lot of attention, Jared lowered his pack to the ground and fished out his second phase pistol. He double-checked that both batteries had near full capacity. He then reloaded his Colt and re-holstered it. Last, he pulled out a couple pistols he'd brought with him and checked their magazines, tucking them into his pants.

Jared reached an ultimatum. He could run the other way, back down the tunnel towards extreme heat and hope they gave up and he didn't run into yet more enemies. Or, he could take the offensive. If he could get past the horde, he'd have a clear shot for the surface.

Scarlet and her brothers would make short work of these lizards, but Jared either needed to find a way out, or survive long enough for Scarlet to return. It'd been two weeks since she left, but Jared knew she was fine. She had to be.

Running back down the tunnel was not an option. There was only one way to go. Up, through the sea of lizards.

Before they surrounded him, Jared centered his thoughts, splitting his conscious in two. Each half independently controlled one of his arms. He plotted the most direct path through the mass of bodies and charged.

Jared became a death personified as his split consciousness allowed him to fire with deadly precision. Every pull of the trigger sent a round of super-heated phase matter into the head or heart of encroaching enemies. Those nearest him didn't stand a chance. His dance with death stretched into seconds and then minutes as Jared waited for a break in the bodies to charge toward freedom.

No matter how many lizards he felled, there didn't seem an end. It was all he could do to keep them at bay. If he didn't find a way through the lizard-choked corridor, he wouldn't survive. His phase pistols would overheat, or he'd run out of charges. Either way, he needed a solution.

Risky though it was, Jared split his thoughts again. His left and right arms moved on auto-pilot while the bulk of his processing power worked on a way out.

Trying and failing to break through multiple times, the cuts and puncture wounds on his body took a toll, slowing him down. As fast as he was killing the lizards, new, fresh lizards took their place the moment the old ones died. Somehow, he needed to prevent that from happening.

Leaping backward, Jared sprinted away, giving himself time to stow his pistols and dual-wield his knives.

A plan formed in his mind that required the lizards to remain alive but injured. They would impede those around them and allow him to use his superior speed and agility to work his way through the crowd to the other side.

He contemplated doing this with the pistols but didn't think it'd be as effective. With pistols, he could only dish out damage in a singular point in front of the weapon. With his blades, he could weave a web of death through the creatures.

He cancelled the third thread to focus on his knives. He needed to cause mayhem and create a barrier of lizard flesh around him to minimize their reach and the number that could get to him at once.

Jared sprang into motion, jumping into a gap between two lizards. He dropped into a crouch and hamstrung both at the knees. They fell backward, tangling with the creatures on either side and behind.

In the same movement, he used the crouched position to launch himself in the air using *Maximum Muscle*. He was careful not to exert himself fully, so he didn't tear a muscle like the last time. As he launched into the sky, several of the creatures detached from the ceiling to drop on him. Before they could react to his move, he punched out with both knives into their skulls, instantly ending their lives.

Dropping back to the ground, Jared snap-kicked the legs from the lizards on either side, sending them cartwheeling back into their kin. Like bowling pins, it cleared a path to either side. Capitalizing on the moment of reprieve, he dove to the side and sprinted several feet before sidestepping a swiping claw and sliding to his knees to avoid a lizard springing at him.

As it passed over his head, he sank his dagger into its gut and disemboweled it as it collided with those he'd just sidestepped. A small bubble formed around him as every creature within reach was dead, maimed, or disoriented. Before any of them could recover, Jared activated *Hyper-Cognition*. The world ground to a halt. A slight pressure on his mind reminded him of the consequences for over-extending his mental abilities.

Collecting his thoughts, Jared realized he'd progressed far enough up the tunnel he could see over their heads to freedom. The crowd thinned further up the tunnel. He just needed to get past this last tight grouping and he'd have a clear path to run away.

Jared deactivated the ability, and reality slammed into focus once more. The mass of bodies pressed in around him. He danced away from their attacks, countering with jabs and slashes of his own. The trail of bodies he left in his wake kept any creatures from approaching his back, letting him focus on only those he could see. His body began to tire, and a few attacks slipped through his defensive maneuvering, igniting lines of fire across his arms and legs.

None of the injuries would cause any serious damage given his regenerative abilities, but if he took any more serious hits, it could be fatal.

One last thrust of his knives, and he punched through the last row of lizards into open tunnel. Digging in his heels Jared sprinted up the tunnel, almost running head first into three massive creatures that dropped from the ceiling to block his escape.

"What the—"

Giant lizards that blended in perfectly with the tunnel unfolded massive appendages with razor spikes trailing up their arms. Their heads held a crown of bony spikes. Fangs jutted from their mouths, and their bodies were covered in a thick looking shell. They resembled a praying mantis, and Jared hoped they weren't as fast, or this wouldn't end well.

The momentary halt in his forward progression cost him as he felt a sharp pain shoot up his back from a lizard that had caught up to him.

Concentrate, Jared!

Dreading the pain he was about to feel, Jared activated *Hyper-Cognition*. A sharp stab lanced through his head, and stars blossomed across his vision. It took several moments to collect his thoughts and focus on staying alive.

He'd only have a few seconds respite before the horde of

lizards he passed surged after him once again. His only hope would be to engage the giant lizards and hope the smaller ones would break off their pursuit. Not knowing if that would even work, he balked at putting his fate into the hands of mindless creatures. They'd shown little sanity or intelligence so far.

The only thing he could come up with was that these big guys controlled the hive-like behavior of the lizards and maybe they'd hold them at bay to avoid killing their own. It was risky, but he was out of options. For all he knew, these bigger creatures had special abilities that'd make short work of him. Whatever happened, he figured his best bet was to confront them and either take them out or get past them. Somehow, he doubted he'd be able to outrun them. They had powerful bodies and looked like they'd easily catch him.

When reality came back into focus, Jared lurched forward to avoid a second slash at his back. He rolled forward under a slash from one of the giant creatures and vaulted upward inside its reach. Jabbing a knife into one of its eyes, he planted his foot into the creature's shoulder and launched himself to the side. The creature elicited a menacing growl and staggered backward.

A second giant lizard tried to capitalize on the move and bat him from the air, but he pivoted mid-flight and spun horizontally around the arm. He didn't escape unscathed as the razor spikes on its arms shredded his shirt and ripped into the flesh beneath. It'd only caught a thin layer of skin, but it was enough to send a wave of fire up his arm. Blood trickled down to his fingers, making his palms slick. He had trouble maintaining his grip on the knife as he dodged and weaved among the giants. Dodging one appendage, Jared didn't see the second that smashed into his back. He lost one of his daggers and rolled across the ground.

He risked a glance behind him to see the horde of lizards held at bay several paces from their giant cousins.

Even if I kill these things, the rest will just rush me.

The situation looked hopeless, but he refused to give up.

Dropping his second knife into his other hand, he wiped the blood from his fingers and snatched the blade off the ground just as a clawed foot snapped out at him, catching him in the side and spinning him to the ground. The kick snapped something in his chest. His breath caught in his throat as a sharp, stabbing pain punctured his chest. Jared suspected he'd broken a rib, but he couldn't afford to stop, or it'd be the end.

Waiting for an opening in the onslaught of claws and feet, Jared found what he was looking for and darted at the giant lizard in the middle. Feeling like a Kung Fu artist, he ran up the creatures extended leg, sprang forward past a slashing claw, and jabbed both knives simultaneously into its eyes.

Jared dropped to the ground, losing one of his knives, his palm too slick with blood to hang on.

The blinded lizard thrashed about, laying into its kin on either side. Using the advantage, Jared dove to the side, through the legs of the giant lizard on the right. Hearing the movement, all the lizards turned toward him, but the middle lizard could no longer see its target and laid into its ally.

Retaliating, they both clawed and kicked at each other. In a desperate move to end the fight, the first lizard Jared had jabbed in the eye sunk its fangs into the other's throat. The blinded lizard cocked its arm back, and with a massive uppercut eviscerated the lizard through its stomach.

That just leaves one of you giant pests.

Looking up from the gruesome spectacle of the two dead enemies, Jared didn't see the last one. Frantically, he searched the ceiling.

Dang, where'd it go?

In answer to his question, a massive armored leg booted him down the tunnel, cracking several more ribs and his left arm.

Jared screamed in pain from the kick and again when he landed fifteen feet up the tunnel. His cracked ribs shifted inside and sent a fresh wave of agony through his body. The moment he hit the ground, a loud mental assault exploded in his head.

JARED!

She'd made it. Scarlet made it!

28 DRAGONS RETURN

J ared felt immense relief hearing Scarlet's voice. He lay on the ground in a mangled heap. His left arm hung limply by his side, and he used his right to cradle his ribs. Every slight movement sent shivers of pain pulsing through his body, punctuated by sharp stabs.

He'd never injured his ribs like this, but he knew from watching the doctors in his home colony it could cause severe damage to move around with cracked ribs. He could puncture a lung, cause internal bleeding, or the bone could perforate his skin. After the imminent threat on his life was over, he'd need to explore his injuries. He tried to re-task all available nanites to *Regeneration*, but no matter how many times he tried, he couldn't muster up the concentration needed. He was in too much pain, and the giant lizard poised over his body paralyzed him in fear. It hadn't recovered from Scarlet's mental assault yet, and he hoped it wouldn't until she got there, or he was dead.

These lizards were nothing for Scarlet, and she should be able to shred through them like paper. Jared was completely out of the fight with nothing to do but wait and pray she made it in time. A few heartbeats later half a dozen powerful roars cut through the commotion in the cave. Swaths of the lizards keeled over, their brains turned to mush, as his vision darkened.

The whooshing of multiple streams of dragon fire jolted Jared awake. He blinked his eyes against the intense, searing light filling the cavern. Superheated streams of fire in varying colors incinerated the lizards. It was like watching a person step on an ant. Completely outmatched, the lizards turned to run back up the tunnel, in Jared's direction. Before they'd taken a single step, Scarlet swooped over their heads and interposed herself between Jared, the mob, and the remaining mantis. Jared watched in awe as these massive beings of power plodded forward spewing a steady stream of super-heated fire ranging in colors from red to violet.

One dragon had a deep purple flame, and everything in its path ceased to exist. Coincidentally, he was also the biggest of the dragons. Scarlet included, there were thirteen dragons easily dispatching the hundreds of lizards.

Red dragons with crimson eyes.

Dark red dragons with obsidian claws and spikes.

Ancient.

Deadly.

They were as different from one another as one human to the next, but they all had similar traits that undoubtedly marked them as one family.

The shape of their heads, horns, and the spikes on their backs formed symmetry amongst them. Even Scarlet, who'd changed herself significantly, portrayed the same traits as her brothers. Their serpentine eyes held the same shape and inner fire he'd seen in Alestrialia and now Scarlet. They glowed with such intensity it was hard for him to hold any of their gaze.

His awe at seeing these magnificent creatures morphed to fear as the lizards, with nowhere else to go, raced up the tunnel toward him and Scarlet.

JARED, STAY DOWN.

The warning came just in time as Jared tried to lever himself to his feet and move out of the way.

He'd like to think the lizards a challenge for Scarlet, or that he'd done enough damage to make it easier, but Scarlet snuffed them out like tiny insects. Even the giant mantis didn't stand a chance, her single tail swipe impaling the creature through.

The onrushing horde staggered to a halt at the fearsome display from Scarlet. They hissed nervously as the dragons hemmed them in on all sides.

With a great roar, Scarlet unleashed a stream of brilliant violet flame into the remaining lizards. Jared watched in horror and awe as every lizard she scorched popped like a ripe melon and promptly disappeared into nothingness. One second, they were there, the next it was as if nothing existed. Small pieces of flesh and pools of liquified lizard the only evidence of what remained.

With no place to run and certain death on the agenda, the lizards went into a frenzy. Those on the front lines sprinted for freedom and died immediately as the dragons unleashed their rage. Those in the middle of the horde clawed each other to get away. Arcs of blood, limbs, and screeches filled the air. Scarlet and her brothers obliterated the lizards, but they wreaked as much havoc on themselves in their haste to get away. It didn't take long before they all lay in smoking pools of liquid and charred corpses.

"Thank you, Scarlet. I don't know how much longer I could've held out," Jared coughed, wincing in pain at his broken ribs.

USE TELEPATHY SO YOU DON'T HURT YOURSELF MORE. ALSO, I THINK YOU MANAGED JUST FINE ON YOUR OWN; YOU

KILLED A LOT OF THEM YOURSELF. YOU MUST SHOW ME HOW YOU MANAGED SUCH A FEAT WHEN YOU RECOVER. I CAN SENSE YOU HAVE GROWN YOUR ABILITIES.

Confirming all the lizards died in the onslaught, Scarlet turned to face Jared. When she turned around, Jared gasped in surprise.

Scarlet! You—you've changed.

I HAVE?

He watched her crane her neck to look at herself as if she didn't believe him.

How? Scarlet asked to no one in particular, but a deep, oppressive voice intruded into Jared's mind, straining his mental capacity.

The fires forged her anew.

The huge dragon Jared saw leading the group and spewing ultra-violet fire walked over to them and stared down at him.

I AM MALSOUR.

Ugh, Jared groaned, his head feeling like it was being crushed in a vice. *Nice to meet you, Malsour, but do you mind dialing back the mental pressure? I used several abilities that taxed my mind to the limit, and your voice is sending spikes of pain ripping through my head. I need time to recover before I can handle it.*

ABILITIES? HOW CAN YOU SPEAK IN MY MIND?

The voice still made him wince in pain, but he could endure it better than the overwhelming pressure he'd felt before.

Jared held up his hand toward Malsour, beckoning him to come closer.

Scarlet lowered her head, and said, IT IS OKAY, MALSOUR. HE ONLY WANTS TO SHOW YOU.

HE CAN MIND MELD? Malsour asked incredulously.

YES, BUT HE NEEDS PHYSICAL TOUCH TO SHARE A THOUGHT

SPACE. HIS IMPROVED TELEPATHY IS NEW TO HIM, AND HE IS LEARNING TO EXPAND HIS ABILITIES, BUT HE HAS A LONG WAY YET TO PROGRESS.

Malsour paused a moment longer before he lowered his head to Jared. Placing a hand on his giant muzzle, Jared sent thoughts, images, impressions, and feelings through the bond. He also showed the abilities he used and how his mind went into overdrive.

The communication felt odd to him and lacked the same level of intimacy he shared with Scarlet. He tried entering a shared thought space, but Malsour blocked his effort, preferring for Jared to show him without melding his thoughts together.

DO NOT PRESUME TO MERGE WITH MY MIND, growled Malsour.

BROTHER, admonished Scarlet.

Malsour didn't apologize, but bowed his head toward Scarlet and asked Jared to wait. He did not know Jared and didn't want to share such an intimate form of communication just yet.

Bending to Malsour's wishes, he sent the images and impressions like he used to with Scarlet. He also shared his gratitude for their arrival and willingness to aide him. They'd saved his life, and he wanted them to know how grateful he was.

As he shared the images, Jared smiled with extreme satisfaction as he watched himself bob and weave a deadly dance through the lizard horde. The moments he activated *Hyper-Cognition* were intense. Everything slowed, and it seemed like paths lit up in his mind as he worked out the best way forward, and when it ended, the deadly dance resumed. If he hadn't experienced it firsthand, Jared would've been in awe watching the intricate balance between finesse and power he'd exerted to survive the battle.

YOU DID ALL THAT? IN SECONDS? IMPRESSIVE. I HAVE

NEVER SEEN A HUMAN CAPABLE OF SUCH A FEAT. Turning to his brothers, Malsour said, COME, BROTHERS.

His brothers crowded around him and bent their heads together. In just a few seconds, Malsour relayed the scene to the other dragons. With one accord, they turned their gaze to him and all dipped their heads to him, acknowledging his skill.

Scarlet moved next to him and Jared placed a hand on her side. He felt her emotions through the bond and she positively beamed at the praise given him by her brothers.

Whispering to him alone, she said, MY BROTHERS GIVE PRAISE SPARINGLY. I HAVE THOUSANDS OF YEARS OF MY MOTHER'S MEMORIES; NOT ONCE HAVE I SEEN THEM REGARD A HUMAN WITH THE SAME RESPECT.

A blush crept onto his checks as he regarded the dragons.

Thank you! he said to them. This earned him several widened eyes as they looked to each other for confirmation they'd all heard him speak.

Another voice intruded into his thoughts, one not as powerful as Malsour's, but still more than his taxed mind could handle.

How CAN YOU SPEAK LIKE THIS?

Jared groaned and reached his uninjured hand up to clutch his head.

Yes, I can use Telepathy, but my abilities are technological advancements. I'm surprised it even works with you. It requires nanites, and I wasn't sure you'd have any this far beneath the surface. Also, can you please dial it down on the mental pressure please? As Malsour no doubt showed you, I pushed my mind to its limits, and your voices are much more powerful than I'm used to hearing.

Malsour took over the conversation again.

WE HAVE THESE NANITES, BUT IN TINY QUANTITIES. MANY

OF THE CREATURES WE FEED ON DOWN HERE HAVE NONE, BUT FROM TIME TO TIME THE CYCLES OF NATURE REACH OUR HUNTING GROUNDS. WE HAVE MUCH TO LEARN ABOUT THIS.

Scarlet is a great teacher. She taught me all about them, and she is the reason I can use Telepathy and some of my other abilities. If anyone can show you how they work and what you can do with them, it's her.

SILDRAINEN INFORMED US OF YOU, YOUR BOND, AND THE OTHER HUMANS THAT SEEK COMPANIONS. I CANNOT PROMISE WE WILL COMMIT TO THE BONDING, BUT I WOULD VERY MUCH LIKE TO MEET THESE OTHER HUMANS. IF YOU REPRESENT THEM AND THEY ESPOUSE THE SAME VALUES AND DRIVE, I MAY SUBMIT TO THE BONDING.

Thank you, Malsour. Scarlet delved into the mind of every human in our small settlement, save one, and found all of them pure of heart and purpose. I believe you'll find them acceptable. I'll warn you now, many of them still have fears because of Razael, but they all know he acted against his nature and will.

Malsour snorted and bowed his head in anguish.

Oh, I'm sorry. Scarlet, you told them about Razael right?

SHE SHARED WITH US THE IMAGES FROM YOUR MIND. THANK YOU FOR PUTTING HIS BODY TO REST.

It was Jared's turn to bow his head, which sent a fresh wave of pain through his body.

JARED, YOU NEED TO REST AND HEAL, stated Scarlet.

I will, but I need to examine my injuries first and make sure my ribs and arm heal correctly. The Natural Armor really helped me out here. I wouldn't have survived otherwise. The razor limbs on these things cut right through my defense, and I think only the armor kept me from losing an arm or my body being laid open. Even the arm and cracked ribs would've been much worse, but the nanites absorbed the impact when it kicked me.

Jared lay back on the ground.

Please absorb the nanites from those you...melted. It might be best for you to ask your brothers to eat any of the lizard corpses remaining, especially the larger ones. They need to absorb as many nanites as possible before they bond.

WE WILL TAKE CARE OF IT, PLEASE REST.

Thank you, Scarlet. I'm relieved to see you made it back safely. I want to hear all about it later.

Jared expanded his awareness, entering a trance similar to the one he reached when splitting his thoughts. Only this time, he wanted to probe his body and assess the damage. The lacerations and cuts on his limbs were the least of his injuries. In order of importance, he assigned all his available nanites into *Regeneration* to focus on the deep cut across his back, his broken arm, the cracked ribs, and lastly his mental exhaustion.

He had five cracked ribs, but thankfully didn't need to re-align any of them. Some bits of the ribs had broken off, but his nanites should remove the shards and repair the bone with little effort. His arm was a different story. He needed to re-align it to prevent it from healing wrong.

His humerus, radius, and ulna had all cracked in half and were misaligned. He needed to adjust them one at a time. If he pulled his arm straight, one of the jagged edges of the ulna would puncture his flesh and cause even more damage. No, he needed to press the humerus back together, then twist his lower arm to realign the bones.

Ouch.

Even thinking about what he needed to do sent a fresh wave of pain through his body. There's no way he'd be able to do this on his own.

Scarlet, I need your help. I need you to keep me conscious while I work on my arm. Otherwise the pain will make me pass out.

Jared also removed his belt and used it to bite down and keep from grinding his teeth together. Scarlet walked over and pressed her head to his side.

I AM READY.

If you can do anything to block out the pain like you did with the bonding, I'd appreciate it.

I WILL TRY.

Drawing in a few deep breaths, Jared reached over with his right hand, tenderly gripped his bicep and squeezed.

Blinding pain erupted along the length of his arm, causing him to scream. The bone scraped against its upper half, sending pulsing spikes of pain shooting up his arm. Pins and needles stabbed into his fingertips. A cold sweat broke out on his forehead and darkness invaded at the edge of his vision.

I AM SORRY, JARED. I CANNOT BLOCK IT ALL. IT IS ALL I CAN DO TO KEEP YOU AWAKE.

"It's okay," Jared said through gritted teeth. "I'll survive."

He grabbed a piece of cloth from his pack and used his uninjured arm and teeth to tie a makeshift bandage in place. He needed something much more stable, but it would immobilize the bones long enough for the nanites to work.

As much as that re-alignment hurt, he imagined the second break would hurt more.

Maintaining his slow, steady breathing helped calm his nerves and regulate the pain. After he'd reached a calmer state, Jared positioned his hand over the second break. One final breath, and he twisted.

A sickening crunch reached his ears as the blinding agony

enveloped him completely. White hot pain spread like fire up his arm and into the rest of his body.

He tried to hang on to consciousness and ensure he'd aligned the bones properly, but Scarlet whispered, **SLEEP,** and sweet, painless darkness wrapped him in a lover's embrace as he succumbed to oblivion.

Several hours later, Jared woke to a twinge in his arm. It throbbed and itched fiercely, but he felt no stabs of pain over the break. Sending his awareness inside, he found the nanites fast at work repairing the injuries. Already, the bones knitted back together, but they were thin near the break lines.

A dull ache in his chest was all that remained from his broken ribs. Granted, they'd only had hairline fractures so the nanites had healed them rapidly. His left arm was tender everywhere he touched, and the bruising extended from shoulder to wrist.

HOW DO YOU FEEL?

Turning to regard Scarlet, Jared answered. "Like I got hit by a truck and trampled by a herd of elephants. But I feel much better than I did. Thank you for helping me. I don't think I'd have finished if you hadn't helped me manage the pain and keep me awake."

I AM SORRY I WAS NOT HERE FOR YOU. I WORRIED THE ENTIRE JOURNEY TO MY FAMILY, AND I ALMOST DIDN'T MAKE IT TO MY BROTHERS. YOU WOULD HAVE DIED, JARED. The emotion behind Scarlet's voice pained him.

You didn't fail, Scarlet. You brought your family back, you grew in strength, and you made it back in time to rescue me. We are exactly where we set out to be.

Now that pain wasn't clouding his mind, Jared took the time to appreciate the changes Scarlet went through. Her scales were a blood-red obsidian, reflecting molten flame flicking behind Scarlet's eyes. Her claws, horns, and spikes sucked in the dancing light, their sharp edges invisible to his eyes.

If he'd met Scarlet like this the first time, he'd have crapped his pants. She looked fierce.

Deadly.

Sinister.

He knew better, but she gave him chills looking at her.

Scarlet, you look incredible. Your mother was intimidating, but I think you've surpassed her in every way except size. Your brothers might be bigger, but judging by your appearance and the color of your flames, I'd argue you're much stronger than them.

PHYSICALLY, I AM STRONGER, BUT I HAVE MUCH MORE GROWING TO DO. MALSOUR'S FIRE BREATHING IS SLIGHTLY STRONGER, AND ALL THEIR MENTAL ABILITIES SURPASS MINE.

I'm going to look like a vagabond sitting on your back, joked Jared.

YOU WILL NEVER LOOK BAD SITTING ATOP MY BACK. ANYONE WHO SEES A HUMAN RIDE A DRAGON SHOULD FEEL FEAR AND AWE.

Thanks. I suppose you're right. Also, I think your brothers are becoming impatient left out of our conversation. Jared looked beyond Scarlet at the twelve dragons arrayed behind her.

Are you going to introduce me to your family?

YOU HAVE ALREADY MET MY BROTHER MALSOUR. HE IS THE OLDEST OF THE REMAINING FIRE DRAGONS. THE SECOND OLDEST, ASHAZAD. THEN THERE'S KYNDERRI.

BRADDRA.

KIRGOR.

MYNDRIS.

NERSIN.

YRVERRO.

Ballog.

Kanundran.

Zavret.

Midri.

Scarlet rattled off each name. They each sent a greeting to him and a whispered thank you for taking care of their little sister. Scarlet being the matriarch, she carried the weight of her entire family on her shoulders with the need to produce an heir in time. Hopefully long after he died, because he couldn't bear the thought of losing her like Alestrialia.

Idly, Jared wondered how dragons reproduced. If there was only female, did that mean…

Does she even need a mate?

Jared shelved the topic for a more appropriate time. He didn't need a lesson on dragon anatomy while they stood dozens of miles below the earth's surface with an entire colony of people that depended on him awaiting his return.

After introductions, Jared addressed them all. "I told Scarlet and Alestrialia before, but while I live and breathe, I'll do everything in my power to see the dragons rightful place restored on the earth. No doubt you've already seen much from Scarlet's memories, but the world changed in your absence. In its place is a radioactive wasteland, swarming with mutated creatures, nanotechnology, and a subset of humankind that treats the rest of the world as slaves."

This is no different than it was when we last roamed the earth.

Jared turned to the speaker, intuitively knowing who'd spoken even though there were no outward indications.

"I think you're right in part, Kanundran. However, I believe there are many humans, like myself and those we care for, who'd love to live peaceably with dragons and mankind. But, the world is a hostile place and most of the creatures left alive are predators and often apex predators who've survived by eliminating the competition. Many creatures thrive in any situation like rabbits, rats, and worms, but even these mundane creatures became mutated over time and they multiply rapidly. The first challenge Scarlet and I faced involved a rat the size of a giant bear. We killed a worm hundreds of feet long. A rabbit as big as me that could jump forty feet into the air proved an interesting fight."

Ballog spoke next, his voice a gravelly rasp that grated in Jared's head.

WE WILL HUNT THEM ALL.

"I encourage you to hunt and eat the creatures you kill. The more you do, the more nanites you'll absorb. Not only are these beneficial for you to grow stronger naturally, they are very important in forming a bond with a human."

A few of Scarlet's brothers voiced dissent, but Jared quickly added. "Please don't make your choice now. Think on it. That's all I ask. If you choose not to bond later, that is your decision to make."

They agreed with him and resumed eating the lizards in the room. It looked like they'd made a solid dent in the cleanup effort while he was unconscious, but they had a few remaining.

Scarlet, did you absorb the nanites in the liquified lizards? I don't know if your brothers can do that, since they need to ingest the nanites to absorb them.

I ABSORBED ALL I COULD WHILE YOU SLEPT.

Awesome, as soon as they're done, we need to get out of here. We're nearing three weeks away, and I want to keep my word to everyone.

WE WILL MAKE IT.

Can your brothers fly?

I HOPE SO, BUT WE WILL SOON FIND OUT. MY MOTHER INJURED HER WINGS RETURNING TO THE SURFACE, WHICH IS WHY SHE COULD NOT FLY. IF MY BROTHERS CANNOT FLY NOW, THEY WILL WHEN STRENGTH RETURNS TO THEIR WINGS.

If they're unable to fly, make sure they know the way and we'll fly ahead to prepare everyone for their arrival.

It took a few more minutes for the last of the lizards to disappear into their mouths. All that remained was a mass of sticky fluid coating the floor where they'd died.

The memory of Scarlet's breath popping the lizards open would give him nightmares for years to come. Every time he pushed the thoughts away, the wet popping noise invaded his thoughts.

I've got to get out of here.

"Is everyone ready?"

He received affirmatives from all and carefully climbed aboard Scarlet. His left arm was still tender, but it was getting better, and he could move it around enough to hold on to her neck. It would take several days before it healed thoroughly, but at least the sharp pain was gone.

The journey out took a full day longer than their descent, but it allowed Jared to fully recover before they went home.

Throughout their trek to the surface, he and Scarlet enjoyed in each other's company, spending increasingly more time sharing a thought space. Now that they didn't have to worry about any dangers lurking in the shadows, they completely ignored their surroundings, choosing to focus on building their relationship and mental connection. Being separated for two weeks had not been fun, and neither of them ever wanted to repeat it.

Finally, the tunnel entrance came into sight, and Scarlet dashed forward into the open sky. Blessed sunlight shone down on Jared's face, rejuvenating him after weeks in perpetual darkness. Perhaps it was his nanites drinking in fuel from the radioactive waste. Whatever the case, he felt super-charged and ready to tackle the world.

Scarlet's brothers piled out of the tunnel and looked around, their faces turned toward the sun. They spread their wings wide to catch the rays on their magnificent bodies. Jared watched from a distance as their wings all snapped open. Each of them looked different, and patterns splayed across their wings gave them a uniqueness wholly their own.

A dozen dragons stood in the empty crater, relishing the freedom. Several of Scarlet's brothers flapped their wings. A few even gained altitude for a short period. However, each one of them eventually dropped back to the ground.

THEY CANNOT DO IT. Scarlet informed him. IT WILL TAKE TIME FOR THEM TO BUILD BACK THEIR STRENGTH. HOWEVER, NONE OF THEM SUFFER THE SAME PROBLEMS MY MOTHER DID. THEY WILL REGAIN THEIR FLIGHT IN TIME, BUT FOR NOW THEY MUST TRAVERSE THE GROUND TO OUR HOME.

"Can you get their attention for me? They seem a bit pre-occupied."

BROTHERS! PLEASE LISTEN.

"Scarlet and I must fly ahead to our home. Those waiting for us will be on the lookout for our return, and if we don't make it back in the prescribed time, I fear they'll venture out on their own. I don't think they're ready for that. Scarlet will show you the path to travel, and you can meet us there."

WE WILL COME.

Scarlet walked over to her brothers and entered a mind meld with them. Satisfied they memorized the location, and could find their way to them, Jared spoke again.

"Should you happen upon any creatures in your travel, please do what you can to eat them and absorb as many nanites as possible. We'll need it in the coming war. Along those lines, if you hear a high-pitched humming approach from the sky, hide yourself as best you can. If any of you regain your flight and cannot hide, do your best to destroy the metal ships quickly. I think the best approach is to descend on it from directly above and destroy it. They call these airborne vehicles drop ships, and they belong to the cities that enslaved mankind and your brother Razael."

Jared heard several snarls and whispered words of vengeance. He held up his hands to finish the thought. "Please do not follow the ships or try to attack the cities. If you thought the humans of your day vile and conniving, these humans are thousands of times smarter and possess technology I've only dreamed about. Come directly to our home, and we will work together to grow in strength and take the fight to them when we are ready, and only then."

BROTHERS... Scarlet met each of their eyes. HE SPEAKS WITH MY AUTHORITY AS QUEEN. ONLY STOP TO REST, HIDE, OR KILL ALONG YOUR PATH. ENGAGE NONE OF THE MACHINES IN THE SKY OR HUMANS ON THE GROUND UNLESS ABSOLUTELY NECESSARY.

As one, her brothers bowed their heads and uttered, AS YOU WISH, OUR QUEEN.

THANK YOU, BROTHERS. WE WILL SEE YOU IN A FEW DAYS.

Jared settled behind Scarlet's neck, and she vaulted into the air. Flaring her wings, they snapped taut as an updraft carried them into the sky. When Jared looked at her wings, his mouth dropped opened in disbelief.

"Scarlet, your wings!"

Craning her head around, her eyes widened in shock.

Midnight black skin stretched from wingtip to wingtip, and intricate patterns covered them, burning with a fiery light. The patterns swirled as if liquid fire burned through her veins. The effect mesmerized him, and the dancing patterns looked alive.

"Wow," breathed Jared. "Amazing!"

Scarlet had emerged from the fiery depths of the earth, reborn into an awesome, terrifying being. She'd embarked on this journey as a child and returned in her true form: *Sildrainen Maildrel, Queen of Fire Dragons.*

TO BE CONTINUED...

ACKNOWLEDGMENTS

I don't even know where to begin… There are so many people that aided me in getting this book written. Not just my editors, but all the fans on RoyalRoad, the various writer/author workshops and groups, the many conversations on Discord, and mostly importantly reading the excellent books from amazing authors.

First, I want to give a shout-out to Dawn Chapman for first inviting me to the Gamelit Society Writer's Workshop just two days after I started writing my first words of fiction.

Thank you to Blaise Corvin, Bonnie L. Price, Chris Johns, and the other amazing contributors and administrators of the Gamelit groups. I've learned so much from everyone, and I know for certain I wouldn't be publishing this book, at least not so soon, if not for the amazing folks there.

Thank you to Nick Kuhn, KT Hanna, Chris Mayer, Jeff Hays, Luke Chmilenko, Anneliese Rennie, Jami Nord and Alexis Keene for your friendship, advice, and help over the past year. Whether a discord chat, some awesome memes (thanks Luke), or thoughtful posts on Facebook, I ascribe many of my achievements to all of you.

Special thanks to KT Hanna, Alexis, Bonnie, Evan, Jami, Elias Dantas, Kaelan Rhywiol, and Caitlin Greer for help editing, typography, formatting, and generally helping to make my book look and sound infinitely better.

Huge thanks to Chimera Editing for their professionalism, expertise, and willingness to help a new author learn and improve my writing craft.

Dusan Markovic and Bonnie L. Price, thank you so much for making my cover absolutely stunning. It truly looks spectacular and the both of you helped bring my vision together so nicely.

CONNECT WITH ME!

If you'd like to keep in touch, follow progress on next book, or just chat with other readers use the following resources to join my Newsletter, Facebook Group, Discord server, Twitter, or Patreon. I will have some goodies available for newsletter subscribers in the near future. (HINT: It will include some awesome art from the talented Dusan Markovic)

Website: https://hummelbooks.com
Newsletter: http://evolve.radioactiveevolution.com/newsletter
Facebook Group:
https://www.facebook.com/groups/HummelBooks/
Facebook Page: https://www.facebook.com/hummelbooks/
Twitter: @RichardIHummel
Discord: https://discord.gg/M7MuaSR
Patreon: https://www.patreon.com/richardhummel

Looking for more LitRPG? Want to follow other authors and engage with readers?

Join the Gamelit Society's <u>Facebook Group</u> and <u>Discord server</u>

Join <u>LitRPG Books</u> for recommendations and reader engagement

Follow <u>LitRPG Podcasts</u> on <u>Facebook</u> and <u>YouTube</u> for reviews by Ramon Mejia

Curious about Russian LitRPG (frontrunners to the genre)? Follow <u>MagicDome Books</u>

To learn more about LitRPG, talk to authors including myself, and just have an awesome time, please join the LitRPG Group.

BOOK RECOMMENDATIONS

Did you enjoy Radioactive Evolution? Looking for more Gamelit/LitRPG to sate your appetite? Check out these other LitRPG's that take place in post-apocalyptic worlds:

All John wanted to do was get away for his life in Kluane National Park for a weekend. Hike, camp and chill. Instead, the world comes to an end in a series of blue boxes, animals start evolving and monsters start spawning. Now, he has to survive the apocalypse, get back to civilisation and not lose his mind.

"Life in the North is Book 1 of the System Apocalypse, a LitRPG Apocalypse book that combines modern day life, science fiction and fantasy elements along with game mechanics." - Tao Roung Wong

This is the first book in the Dark Elf series. It's a combination of my take on the zombiepocalypse and my favorite hobby (gaming) in a LitRPG/GameLit story. Which means besides the fantasy setting, the virtual world includes game mechanics like experience points, leveling, cool loot, and spells/skills the characters can develop. It's meant to help you feel like you're playing the game along with them as you read.

"I hope you enjoy reading this is much as I enjoyed writing it!" - Dave Willmarth

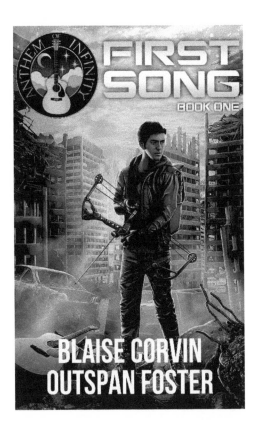

It has been two years since the Shift—when most technology stopped working, and the laws of physics changed. Humanity has been brought to its knees. Like other survivors, Noah Henson has heard rumors of the Aelves. Among other guesses, predatory aliens seem as good as any other theory for what caused the Shift.

- Blaise Corvin & Outspan Foster

Lightning Source UK Ltd.
Milton Keynes UK
UKHW041326271118
333021UK00001B/5/P